PRAISE FOR *EXECUTIVE*

"Excellent. Interesting, innovative, and unusual premise; not a common thriller."

"It's really well-written, technical when it needed to, and kept you on the edge of your seat."

"A white-knuckled thriller that drips with the juice of highly probable events"

"*Executive* is a seriously addictive thrill ride."

"The story moves quickly and maintains the level of suspense to the end."

"Intellectually stimulating and forward-thinking subject matter."

PRAISE FOR LESLIE WOLFE

"Let me just say that Leslie Wolfe has blown me away again."

"Leslie Wolfe seems to be one of the better storytellers of today with this trail blazing read of espionage and war."

"Praise goes to the author Leslie Wolfe for giving such a deep insight into corporate structure and business"

EXECUTIVE

BOOKS BY LESLIE WOLFE

TESS WINNETT SERIES

Dawn Girl
The Watson Girl
Glimpse of Death
Taker of Lives
Not Really Dead
Girl with A Rose
Mile High Death
The Girl They Took

DETECTIVE KAY SHARP SERIES

The Girl From Silent Lake
Beneath Blackwater River
The Angel Creek Girls

BAXTER & HOLT SERIES

Las Vegas Girl
Casino Girl
Las Vegas Crime

STANDALONE TITLES

Stories Untold
Love, Lies and Murder

ALEX HOFFMANN SERIES

Executive
Devil's Move
The Backup Asset
The Ghost Pattern
Operation Sunset

For the complete list of Leslie Wolfe's novels, visit: LeslieWolfe.com/books

EXECUTIVE

LESLIE WOLFE

ITALICS PUBLISHING

II **ITALICS**

Italics Publishing Inc.

Cover and interior design by Sam Roman

Editor: Joni Wilson

ISBN: 978-1-945302-00-8

For my husband, for everything he does.

"I checked her out, and everything is just as expected." Steve pushed a thin file over the large desk, toward his boss. The man took it and flipped carefully through the pages, mumbling his agreement to the various things he was reading.

"Is she available yet?"

"No, sir, waiting for your approval."

The man gave the file and the photo attached to it another thoughtful look.

"Do you think she's ready?"

"No, sir," Steve answered. "But she could be, with a little bit of time and effort."

"She's so young," the man said, "so young. I hope we're right about this."

"She's not any younger than I was when I met you," Steve replied.

"True."

The man stood up and paced the floor for a few minutes, looking out the windows of his office. The sun was climbing in the sky, inundating their world with the crisp morning light. Everything would turn out all right.

"OK, please proceed."

Steve could hear the smile in his voice.

"I can't do that. We're talking about one of the best tech support analysts I have ever had." George Auster's chubby face was sweating heavily, while trying to persuade his visitor.

His morning was turning into a nightmare that he could not begin to comprehend. The man standing in front of him was not willing to negotiate. This man had stepped through the door, put a picture on his desk, and looked him straight in the eye.

"She has to go. You have 48 hours. Or you lose everything."

He had no choice.

Your next opportunity awaits.

"I definitely hope so," Alex mumbled, waiting for a new search page to load, while staring at the promising slogan of yet another job board.

With little patience for what she was doing, and in desperate need of a job, Alex was browsing page after page of countless job postings, reading ads, and looking for possible fits. With rent due in just two weeks' time and no money left in the bank, she was considering a variety of jobs, spanning from boring-to-death customer service to marketing, but not ignoring any other available options. It was no longer the issue of making the right career choice; it was about survival and paying the bills.

At 29, she was living alone in a small two-bedroom apartment that looked like a war zone. Not preoccupied by the appearance of her home, she had furnished the apartment with a bizarre selection of items, all serving the purpose of functionality. She had focused on what she needed at particular stages in her life, with no consideration given to furniture styles or colors.

Her desk was huge, quite old, and made of solid wood. It had two sets of drawers, one on each side. Not one square inch of the desk's surface was visible, as it was covered with bills, handwritten notes, and office equipment. Her computer took most of the available space, together with a modem, two printers, a scanner, and a phone, all connected by numerous intertwined wires.

The past few days had been carbon copies of one another— search after search, application after application. She had no choice but to keep going.

...Chapter 4: Timing
...Friday, April 16, 8:40AM
...Corporate Park Building, Third Floor
...Irvine, California

"She's available and running out of money."
"Good. Place the ad in a couple of days. Let me know the minute she sees it."

Her chair looked as if it had been taken from a high-end, downtown office setting—black, massive, and all leather, in total contrast to the rest of the room. Leaning comfortably back in it, Alex was reviewing job posting after job posting, and applying to whatever would have had even the slightest chance of landing her an interview. Although she was quickly going through the ads, one caught her attention.

The Agency is looking for highly motivated, independent individual, possessing a variety of business skills and an adventurous spirit. Please email résumé.

"That's weird. The Agency? What kind of name is that?" Alex said out loud, breaking the silence. That had to be just another recruiter. The email address was a Yahoo account, and, without giving it much thought, she submitted her résumé and moved to the next ad.

Seconds later, a familiar sound let her know that she had new email. One look at the sender's name and she opened it right away.

From: The Agency
Subject: Received Application
Thank you for your application.
In order to perform an assessment of your skills, please click on the link below and complete the form. Please note that this process will take at least an hour of your time. Please give truthful answers to all questions, and indicate all the skills you possess. We will carefully review your online application. If selected to move forward in this recruiting process, we will be in contact with you.

"Oh, no, not another form," Alex cried. Most online recruiting forms had proven to be nothing but wasted time, without any benefit for her. Spending an average of 15 minutes on each online application form—creating profiles, usernames, and passwords for a variety of companies—was like shooting herself in the foot. She needed to spend less than one minute on each ad, because of the high volume of ads she had to browse every day. "And this has to be way worse, they say it takes at least a full hour," she complained, but there was no one there to hear her. "You have got to be kidding me . . ." Continuing to grumble, she clicked on the link indicated in the email. A browser page opened up.

Thank you for giving The Agency an hour of your time, the message read.

"Oh, we're not there yet, pal. I've only given you 15 seconds so far," Alex replied to the written text, as she continued reading.

Please grab a cup of coffee, and let's proceed.

"OK." Smiling at the thought of having a conversation with an online recruiting form, Alex rose and went into the kitchen. Seconds later, she came back to her black leather chair, carrying a large, steaming cup of coffee. "Got it, what else do you want from me?" She clicked *next*.

If you promise total honesty, I promise a recruiting process without any bullshit, the following page stated.

"Oh, that's fresh. That's totally new," Alex laughed. In an environment in which getting a job depended on how well you replied to some well-known questions by giving some well-known answers, the whole interviewing process seemed to her like a bad joke, told repeatedly. She was amazed at how most people refused to deal with intelligent, innovative people, preferring instead a standard, already-know-the-answer person, showing little initiative and absolutely no spark.

An old college buddy of hers was currently working as a human resources specialist for a big bank. She had taught Alex a few tricks and explained that recruiters look for specific indicators, such as no turnover of jobs without spending at least two years in the same company, no "empty time" between jobs, and no varied experience—the applicant should only reflect experience in the specific field of the job applied for. Therefore, if Alex wanted to apply for a customer-service position, she had a better chance to get that interview by listing only customer-service experience. Thanks to Leah, and to her own intuition, she was easily getting interview invitations.

With her curiosity at a peak level, she clicked *next* again.

Now that I have your full attention, let's start. Please select all options applicable to you.

The first page was the most bizarre selection ever put together. There was an endless list of skills and questions, grouped by categories. Next to each entry, there was a small check box, positioned next to an available option. By clicking in the box, a check mark would appear, indicating the respective statement was applicable or true. On the upper right corner of the Web page, a progress bar displayed that this was the first page out of 26.

"One hour? I might be fast, but I think you guys are trying to hire Superman." She took a long sip of coffee and started clicking.

...Chapter 6: Hooked
...Tuesday, April 20, 5:19PM
...Corporate Park Building, Third Floor
...Irvine, California

"She's online now, sir."
"I'll be right there."

The first category was listed under the title "About Yourself." Alex had options for everything that could describe her, such as height, build, hair color, and style. To her surprise, there were also boxes to check about age, gender, place of birth, race, and other questions considered illegal under current labor laws. She dutifully completed each one.

The form continued with a questionnaire meant to assess the IQ level of the candidate. Although dealing with the job market quite often, Alex had almost never run into intelligence testing. One thing was certain: this was no ordinary application form, and Alex had a growing desire to meet the people behind this original selection process. Suddenly, she found herself wondering what kind of job would require such a detailed and unique application.

"What?" The HR director could not understand. "Are you telling me I cannot hire this person? Why? Who are you?" She was getting frustrated, and her voice was showing it.

The man in front of her, without saying a word, slowly pulled a wallet from his pocket, opened it, and put it in front of the director's bewildered eyes. She recognized a Federal Bureau of Investigation badge. Her voice dropped to a whisper and her head slowly nodded in compliance.

"As you wish."

New category: *Language Skills.* This time, she had to type the words herself. *Please indicate the languages you speak fluently.*
English, Italian, German.
Please indicate the languages in which you can sustain a minimal conversation.
Spanish, French.
Please indicate the languages you can understand or speak a minimum of 15 words or short phrases.
Weird, Alex thought. She typed: Russian, Polish, Hindi, Punjabi, Arabic.
Please indicate the countries to which you have traveled.
"Are they recruiting for the CIA? Is that it? The Agency? Who are these people?" Her own voice, breaking the silence in her apartment, startled her.
Another page, a new category: *Computer Skills.* Another endless list of selectable options.

"Hey, Lenny, got a light, buddy?" Ryan's dirty hand, holding an unlit cigarette, appeared first, followed by the rest of his body, as he was coming around the front of the Nyala. The massive armored personnel carrier, rigged with multiple antennae and a remote weapons station, was releasing six dust-covered, sweaty Canadian armed forces.

"And you call yourself a smoker, eh?" Lenny said, extending his Zippo. "Fuck, man, you never have a light on you, like, never!" He lit Ryan's cigarette, then extracted one for himself, lit it, and took a deep breath of smoke mixed with the dry dust of the Afghan desert. "Ahhh . . . it feels good . . ." Lenny walked to the edge of the road, in the shade of the Nyala, stretching his legs. "What would ya' do without me, huh? Quit? What's it gonna take to get a stubborn Newfie like you to carry his own lighter, huh?"

"Gimme yours, and I'll carry it for ya', eh?"

"You better pray this baby doesn't just go AWOL on me one day," Lenny said, clutching his fingers around the engraved Zippo, "'cause it's you whose rotting corpse they'll end up finding in a ditch, got it?" Lenny's thumb was slowly going over the engraving on his lighter, feeling the words etched into the metal: *To Leonard, with all my love. From Dad.*

"Got a light, eh, Lenny?" A third soldier was extending an unlit cigarette, requesting service with a wicked smile on his face. Lenny obliged with a deep sigh.

"I don't get it, just don't. What the hell is wrong with y'all? What would y'all do without me, huh? Good thing I don't have to wipe your lame asses too." Lenny walked away from the road, toward a pile of boulders, not too far out. Farther away from the boulders, maybe half a klick or so, young herders were watching over sheep. They had all turned to look at the convoy. The wind was carrying the stinking smell of sheep, mixing it with the omnipresent, fine desert dust.

"Where you headin', man? You wouldn't be going to take a leak, would 'ya? Do you need my presence? Do you need help with that? Wanna show it to the natives?" Ryan asked, bombarding Lenny with his questions—each question raising more laughter from the rest of the men.

"Ah, fuck off, will ya'll? I can water this desert on my own, thank you very much." Lenny waved a dismissing hand right before stopping at boulders, his back toward the road.

Friendly advice kept pouring in, mixed with roars of laughter. "Don't forget to shake it. That's right. Good boy."

In response, Lenny's right fist rose above his head in a threatening motion. Then the fist continued its journey, raising the middle finger, combined with an upward motion. Unabated, the comments continued, "You're holding it with your left? That's not right—"

A shearing sound interrupted everyone and brought instant silence among the group. Lenny turned, half-zipped, crouching to the ground. "What the fuck?"

A fully armed unmanned combat aerial vehicle, UCAV, was approaching from the south. "Whose is it?" Lenny yelled.

"American. We're fine, there's no action scheduled here today."

"I hate these UCAVs; they scare the living shit out of me," Ryan said, serious now. "With a pilot, you can expect some judgment; but with a machine, you never know."

"Newfie chicken, who would have guessed? They're safe, man, safer than the planes. There are pilots flying them drones, just like they do real planes, only they fly them like toy cars, with remote controls." Jimmy, otherwise quiet, was the group's official geek, always ready to share his knowledge of anything to do with technology.

"Still hate the goddamn things, man," Ryan continued. "Objects were not meant to fly like that and blow things up. Jesus, what the hell?"

"But the robot we send into the mine field, you don't mind, do you? It's just like that, you idiot. It's just a flying robot, with a remote control, so pilots don't get killed or captured. You're too much of an idiot for me to keep explaining shit as simple as that." Jimmy waved away Ryan's ignorant concern.

However, no one really felt safe. The UCAV changed its heading and started descending, approaching them. The men were able to distinguish the onboard sensor array cameras, rotating in search for targets.

"Take cover!"

The yell could have come from anyone. A couple of men crawled under the Nyala, whose blast-resistant belly had the potential to provide some protection from air strikes. Lenny was still crouching by the boulders, weighing his chances to make it back to the vehicle.

From under the Nyala, they could hear the captain's voice. "Bravo One, Bravo One, this is Charlie Three, over. Bravo One, Bravo One, this is Charlie Three. Come in, damn it!"

The UCAV took a position and launched a Hellfire missile, aimed at the group of sheepherders. The explosion followed shortly, among the men's screams.

"Charlie Three, this is Bravo One, go ahead."

Lenny crouched tighter, getting closer to the ground. "Oh, God . . ."

"Bravo One, we're taking fire from an American drone, over."

The UCAV slowly circled the area, scanning for more movement and heat signatures. It found a target. Taking position on the new object, it launched another Hellfire.

Lenny's blood sprayed the Nyala's right front tire. His engraved lighter rolled into the ditch, reflecting the sunlight.

The UCAV was scanning again for new targets. It had two more missiles left.

Page 26 of the recruiting form was loading on the screen. This last page began with a paragraph of instructions.

Please read each question carefully, and reply truthfully. There are no wrong answers in this section.

The first question came as a shock.

Would you consider doing these things in order to reach your goal?

Alex replied out loud, "Well, depends on the damn goal, now, doesn't it?"

Lie?

She started typing—**Yes.**

Steal?

She thought, *Hmmm. Maybe*—**Yes.**

Kill?

"What?"—**No.**

Get someone physically intoxicated?

Alex laughed, "Buy them beers until they drop? Why not?"—**Yes.**

Use false identification?

Yes.

Blackmail?

"Am I going to get arrested, based on what I say on this damn form? Um"—**Yes.**

Cheat?

"I'd rather not cheat on Mr. Right when I find him."—**No.** "I'll try intoxication first, then blackmail, and if that doesn't cut it, then I'll reconsider this."

She chuckled, as she continued to fill out the form's numerous fields.

Finally, a field marked *Comments* concluded the form.

Alex looked at the digital clock on the wall. Four hours and 25 minutes had passed since she had started. It was already late, and she had just wasted more than four hours of her time on one single potential employer, instead of applying to at least 50 jobs during this time. She suddenly felt cheated, tired, and completely exposed. *Why did I go through with this insanity? What was I thinking?*

She typed a question in the *Comments* field.

Who are you people?

Then she clicked on the large button at the bottom of the page marked *Submit Questionnaire.*

A new page loaded on her screen.

Meet us for an interview tomorrow, at 10:00AM, and you'll find out. The address is 8 Corporate Park, Suite 300, Irvine, California 92606.

She suddenly felt she was not alone in the room anymore. Shivering, she copied the address on her notepad, turned off the computer, and poured herself a large Martini on top of the coffee leftovers in her mug.

Alex inhaled the aroma of her freshly brewed coffee.

"Thank God for caffeine," she sighed. She was tired after tossing and turning most of the night, thinking about the 10:00AM interview. She felt awkward at the thought of meeting a prospective employer to whom she had already admitted she was willing to steal, lie, and what not, and she had admitted it in writing too.

Getting behind the wheel of her car, her confidence started building. *What do I have to lose?* Her car was much like her apartment, with a variety of objects scattered on the seats and floor. It was a red convertible Suzuki Vitara, the only convertible SUV available for her budget. It suited her personality, and although the Vitara was a small-size SUV, the sporty feel of a four-by-four, manual-transmission convertible was able to bring her spirits up, every time she took it for a ride.

Taking I-5 north toward Los Angeles, she reached the address in just over an hour and a half. *It's not so close to home, but what a ride*, she thought, still enchanted by the spectacular views presented by the scenic drive along the Pacific coast. She pulled into a parking spot marked "Reserved—Visitors." Looking up, she saw a three-story building, appearing crisp, clean, and dignified in its white finish, sparkling in the morning sun. *Here we go. Good luck, young lady, you're gonna need it*, she encouraged herself, while stepping into the elevator.

The elevator stopped at the third floor and the doors silently glided open, allowing Alex to step directly into the reception area of The Agency. *So they have the whole floor. Or floors. Good.* She stepped up to the reception desk.

"Good morning. I have a 10:00AM appointment—" She abruptly stopped her introduction, realizing she didn't have the name of the person she was supposed to meet. *Damn.* The receptionist didn't seem to mind.

"Yes. Please take a seat; it will only be a few minutes."

She sat down on a comfortable leather sofa and began looking around. Written on the wall above the reception desk, in golden letters with a shadow effect, the company name, *The Agency*, made quite an impression, despite its upright, neutral font. The reception area was spacious, decorated with a lot of taste and a lot of money. On the left side was an incomplete wall made of glass bricks, masking what could have been the corridor leading toward offices. Discrete spotlights were placed here and there to emphasize the effect of the sunshine reflections on the glass bricks. On the right side, large windows allowed the sunshine to light up the room, while offering a spectacular view of a park.

The reception desk was a piece of furniture like no other Alex had ever seen. It appeared to be custom made, because it followed the shape and angles of the wall behind it. Three receptionists could sit at this monumental desk without even being able to touch one another. The entire visible surface had an impeccable dark oak, glossy finish.

Showcasing this remarkable desk, the entire office floor was covered in thick, beige carpet, but there was little furniture. Aside from the reception desk and the sofa she was sitting on, there were only two armchairs, with a small coffee table between them, and a cast-iron newspaper holder close to the elevator. *Strange.*

The elevator was still there, doors open. She looked closely at the elevator and noticed that no controls were visible next to the elevator doors. She turned her eyes to the receptionist. As if reading her mind, the receptionist turned her chair around and touched a button on a metallic panel, marked "Access" bolted to the wall behind her. The elevator doors closed without a sound.

"Good morning, Miss Hoffmann." A deep, powerful voice startled Alex. She stood up, ready to extend her arm for the usual handshake. In the black eyes of the handsome man standing in front of her, there was no willingness to shake hands.

She replied, cautiously, "Good morning. How are you?"

"Please, follow me." The man did not wait for her reply; he turned and walked around the glass brick wall into a dark corridor.

I was right, Alex thought. As the man entered the corridor, a light came on by itself. *Neat.* He stopped in front of an office, knocked once, and opened the door. He stepped aside, indicating that Alex should enter. Without any introduction, he quietly closed the door and walked down the hall.

"Welcome to The Agency, Miss Hoffmann." The man behind the desk was smiling widely and seemed friendly and open. "Allow me to introduce myself. My name is Tom Isaac, and I'm in charge of The Agency. Please, sit down."

She took her seat and looked around. It was an average office, with common office furniture—a desk, some chairs, two filing cabinets—and a window covered by Venetian blinds, partially blocking the sun. Nothing special about it.

She answered politely, smiling back, "Nice to meet you. Thank you for inviting me." She put down her briefcase next to the chair. *Ready as I'll ever be,* she thought, waiting for the interview to begin.

"So, please let me begin by asking, what kind of job are you looking for?"

Something to pay the bills and have some fun while at it, if possible, she thought. Instead she answered by the book, her training and experience in interviewing taking over.

"My ideal job is one that incorporates both my education and practical work skills to be the best I can be. Combining my education with a working knowledge of customer operations, my entrepreneurial abilities, computer skills, and administrative skills, I want to utilize my analytical expertise to help people meet their goals. This is exactly why I am convinced that I would be a valuable member of your team."

She had no idea what job she had applied for. She had no information allowing her to be more precise, and this was considered the best possible vague answer to this tricky question. *This is going to be tough*, she braced herself.

Mr. Isaac was watching her closely, slowly nodding as she spoke. He asked the second question. "How would you describe yourself in terms of your ability to work as a member of a team?"

Standard interview questions, what a disappointment; they promised me none of this dance. Alex almost sighed.

"I have had many opportunities in both academics and work experience to develop my skills as a team player. My experience as a market research team leader also helped me learn the role of team member. I viewed my position as that of group leader and individual contributor at the same time. I ensured that everyone in my group had an equal opportunity to contribute, maintained excellent communication among group members, and coordinated their energies toward reaching our team's goal."

Mr. Isaac looked down at the file in front of him and scribbled something on the print of her résumé. She continued to look directly at him, while smiling and waiting for the next question.

"Are you currently employed?"

"Yes," she lied, without any hesitation, knowing she had a better chance of getting a job if no one knew she was currently unemployed.

"Why would you like to leave your current employer? It is a nice company, from what I hear." Mr. Isaac leaned forward, curious to hear her answer. It came without delay or hesitation.

"I feel I am not challenged enough in my current position. I would like to move toward a more challenging, more rewarding position, which will allow me to fully utilize my skills and my abilities, and also offer me opportunity for self-improvement and professional growth."

"What a load of crap!" Mr. Isaac stood up abruptly, startling her.

She froze. *Oh, my God!*

Mr. Isaac continued, pacing angrily through his office.

"I promised you a straightforward recruiting process, if you were honest with your answers. Yesterday you were willing to discuss. Today you are giving me nothing but a nicely wrapped, well-rehearsed pile of bullshit. What happened?"

She started to speak, but her voice was gone. She made an effort, cleared her throat, took in a deep breath, and gave it her best shot.

"I am sorry, sir, but the habit of giving these standard answers took over. You did ask me some fairly standard HR questions. You are right, though, I am sorry for wasting your time with all this." She managed a faint smile.

"Are you willing to answer some questions without lying, leaving stuff out, or sugarcoating anything?"

"Yes, sir." She could feel sweat at the roots of her hair.

"Be careful, one more time with this kind of crap and we stop right there, understood?"

"Yes, sir." *Do I really want to work for this guy?*

"OK, again, what kind of job are you looking for?"

She realized she had been holding her breath. *Here's your truth, mister. Let's see if you can handle it.* She exhaled the air in her lungs and answered, looking straight into his eyes.

"I'm looking for a job that will comfortably pay my bills without boring me to death, have me living in fear, and slowly killing my spirit. I want to have some fun doing that job; I want some flexibility; and I want to work with smart, open-minded people who can teach me a thing or two." She stopped and held her breath again, waiting for his reaction.

"Was it painful?" he asked. His eyes were smiling, but his face was still serious.

Surprise. "Excuse me?"

"To tell the truth for a change." He sat up and walked around the desk toward her.

"No, it was actually quite relieving to hear myself say it." She smiled shyly, aware she was blushing. "I haven't done that in a while." She did not dare look him in the eye.

He was now standing in front of her. She stood up abruptly, ready to run. He reached out his hand and gave her a firm handshake.

"Then it's really a pleasure to meet you, Miss Hoffmann. Let's continue. Please sit down. Are you currently employed?"

"No," she sighed.

"What happened?"

"My boss used to be quite a nice guy. However, one day he went berserk. He started arguing with me without reason. He said I had the wrong attitude, and that a customer had complained that I was swearing while fixing her network."

"Were you?"

"Well, the strangest thing is that I was never with that customer. I was scheduled to go, but traded accounts with a colleague, because that specific customer was close to his home. I figured the boss just wanted me out, and I left. That was no life for me; I can't handle that kind of attitude. There was no fixing the situation; the more I tried to clarify the issue, the more aggravated he would get. His reaction came as a complete surprise. Until then, he had shown only appreciation toward my performance."

"Did he fire you?"

"No. After trying to talk to him, I realized I had no other options, and I quit. I couldn't just sit there, knowing he wanted me gone. I didn't want to wait for that shoe to drop, wondering when it was going to happen."

"Most people would have stayed put, while looking for something else. Pay a few more bills in the meantime," Mr. Isaac said, watching her reaction.

"I am not most people. In order to focus on damage control, I had to acknowledge the damage and discard all unnecessary weight, such as the dismissal waiting to happen pretending to be my job."

Mr. Isaac couldn't help but chuckle. "A good sense of humor is your best ally when times turn tough," he said, and resumed the interview questions. "I need to know how you see yourself as part of a team. No standard answer, please."

Alex took a deep breath. This was going to be one interview to remember.

"Well, it depends. A team is good to have around when you need someone's help, although I'm more comfortable on my own. I like to take full responsibility *and* full credit for my actions. The one thing I hate the most is office politics."

"Office politics?"

"Yes. For example, I'm minding my own business, while one coworker has nothing better to do and starts saying stuff about me. Before I know it, I end up asked to explain things I had nothing to do with. Or, here's another example, I am not given a promotion, because I am the only one who was too busy with work to be aware that the boss bought a new car, so I never had a chance to congratulate him on his excellent choice."

Alex looked up and smiled. *It will be a miracle if I get this job*, she said to herself.

"I totally agree, but this is not a perfect world we are living in. So, how do you manage to fit in the average corporate environment?" Mr. Isaac continued, undisturbed.

"I didn't say I can't do it; I just said I hated it," Alex replied.

"Oh. True. Let's move on. Where do you see yourself in five years?" Mr. Isaac gave an encouraging smile, as if to warn her to be honest.

"I really don't know; there are too many things to consider. If I win the lottery, then we might discuss what I *really* want to do in five years. If my luck continues to work the way it did so far, in five years I will be, most likely, interviewing for yet another job, and giving some recruiter exactly the answers he wants to hear. It's hard to say," she said, then shrugged and waited for another question.

"Do you have any questions for me?" Mr. Isaac offered.

Alex sighed thoughtfully.

"How many steps are in this interviewing process?"

"Just this. Based on this one interview, I will make my decision and let you know."

OK, now I know for sure I screwed up. He won't hire me, Alex thought. She was surprised to realize how saddened she was by this thought. She couldn't help feeling that the man in front of her was quite remarkable, and she would have liked him to appreciate her. She continued, out of curiosity.

"Thank you. I asked on my online form, 'Who are you?' And I'd also like to know what job did I apply for?"

Mr. Isaac leaned forward and smiled.

"I created The Agency 17 years ago, when a friend of mine, a business owner, got into some trouble. He had grown suspicious that someone was stealing his customer files and selling the info to his competition. In order to find out who that was, he hired me, not as an investigator, but as a payroll clerk. No one pays attention to the accounting clerks," he said with a chuckle and paused, letting the story and all its implications sink in.

As it did, surprise showed on her face. She saw the ramifications, the possibilities, and grew excited about the idea. *Yes. Obviously, this idea worked. I'd love to do that for a living, yes I would,* she thought, thinking fast. *Not a moment of boredom, no office politics, actually use my brain, my dream come true. Plus they have to be paying really well. However,* her enthusiasm abruptly cooled, *why the hell is he telling me this stuff if he's not even going to call me for a second interview?* She did not realize how well the man could read her thoughts, just by looking at her transparent features and bright, expressive eyes.

"Starting from that case," he continued, "I realized there was growing potential on the market for this kind of service. We are currently a small team of four people, and we need a fifth person. I'm looking specifically for someone with a little more computer knowledge than we currently have among us, to be able to work as an IT executive and assist with email and data-related fraud concerns."

She almost had tears in her eyes. *I can't believe they won't hire me—no other job will ever compare,* she thought. Mr. Isaac was now standing up, most likely preparing to show her out. Somehow, she found the courage and asked.

"Mr. Isaac, will you please tell me where I screwed up?"

"Who said you did? Let's go meet the guys. And please, call me Tom."

Her exhilarated scream was loud enough to make the receptionist wonder what the hell was going on back there.

Alex was born in Mt. Angel, Oregon, a charming city just forty miles south of Portland. The City of Bells is deeply German in tradition and heritage, with its population almost entirely of European descent.

Both Alex's parents were engineers, a profession quite compatible with their never-forgotten German origins. The young couple brought Alex into the world on a sunny June afternoon, in a whirl of joy, laughter, and happiness. Alex remembered her early childhood as a serene land of fairytales, with her happy parents holding her hands, while she discovered the miracles of the quaint world surrounding her. She started talking early, and soon she had lengthy conversations with her father. He loved challenging her young mind with all kinds of questions and problems. He bought her toy building sets and mechanical sets, carefully grading the difficulty levels of the tasks, so she would be able to succeed, yet stay challenged and learn new things every day.

Her mother was the one who opened her mind to the wonders of faraway places, and worlds she had seen on her numerous travels. She showed Alex pictures of distant cities and told her stories about strange places and people, filling her mind with images and people from all over the world. By the time Alex turned six, she knew the names of most of the countries in the world and their capitals. For her, they were not just simple names in some atlas, but they were amazing places she had heard awesome stories about. As Alex grew older, she started to read, and her mother suggested books about travel and adventure, starting her off with the inspiring works of Jules Verne, Alexandre Dumas, and Jack London.

Alex easily remembered those heartwarming days, as she kept their memories in a safe place in her heart. What she could neither remember nor explain was where and when it all had gone away. Slowly, creeping among her family, came misery, sorrow, and pain, uninvited guests whose appearance she had never been able to pinpoint in time. It was as if, over time, everything had turned bad.

The first sad memory she had about her childhood kept coming back to her, as an early clue for things to come. It was Christmas morning, and she had rushed from her bed directly to the living room to check under the tree and open her presents, but there were no presents for her to open. Her father sat quietly at the dining room table. Her heart sinking, she turned to him and said, "Daddy, where are my presents?"

He stared into emptiness for a few seconds, and then pulled a fifty-dollar bill out of his pocket, and said, "Here, why don't you go out and buy yourself something nice, all right?" She remembered crying herself to sleep that Christmas day. She remembered crying herself to sleep many days after that.

As things changed for the worse, her parents constantly argued, uttering unspeakable cruelty to each other, their voices filled with hate and contempt. Just a few years later, when Alex was thirteen, they took it to the next level. Her father told her one day that she was the only reason he was not divorcing her mother, blaming Alex for all the abuse he was enduring. From helpless and scared, she now became guilty of everything.

Soon her mother also blamed her for siding with her father. They would drag her into their arguments, and, on occasion, join their forces against her. Nothing she would do or say would make any difference. Nothing would buy her some peace. She soon gave up and put all her strength in trying to survive, to stay sane. To do that, she turned to her books and learned how to cope with hardship from her favorite authors. She dragged herself through school; nothing took her mind off her family issues anymore.

One day, it was over. She turned eighteen and had two more weeks to finish high school. As her parents briefly halted their daily disputes to wish her a joyless, happy birthday, she broke the news to them.

"I am out of here," she said, with a cold determination in her voice. "I already have a job and a place to stay, and my bags are packed. As of today, as I am sure you already know, I have become of age, and this is my first decision as an adult."

After the initial shock, both her parents attempted to turn her decision. Her father said, "We had dreams for you. You were going to college. This is what you wanted, right?" He looked confused and suddenly older by ten years.

She explained in a softer voice, "I can't do that while living here, Dad, I really can't. Maybe I will be able to go to college later, after settling in on my own."

Then her mother's intervention came as a painful shock. "Well, if that's your decision, then learn to live with it. You may not take anything with you on your way out. You haven't paid a dime for any of the items you call yours. Therefore, you will leave here with nothing. I expect the clothes you are wearing to be returned by tomorrow. You have one minute to leave this house. Oh, and don't you *ever* come back."

Alex was speechless, as she opened the front door. She closed it behind her, and, as she was walking away, she heard her father yell at her mother, "How could you do that to your own child?"

Her mother opened the door and called Alex back. She was stupidly hoping for an apology, or kind words, or good-luck wishes. Her mother said, "You forgot to leave your keys!"

###

Time had started its healing process.

At first, she lived in a small, one-bedroom basement apartment in Mt. Angel, constantly afraid she'd run into her parents on the street or at the mall. She feared that her landlady would one day judge her for leaving home or talk to her parents about her. She worked as a customer-service representative, barely making enough to cover her rent and expenses. She graduated from high school and forged her mother's signature on a change-of-address notice to the school, allowing her to receive all documents and transcripts at her new address, without having to ask her parents for them.

Neither of them showed up at her graduation ceremony. She kept looking for them in the crowd, but they weren't there. Naturally, she would have liked to show her parents she could still go on.

She had saved some money before leaving home—money she had earned in secret while tutoring young children in math and science. That money turned out to be useful in helping her get the bare necessities for her new life.

She hadn't found any logical reason to comply with her mother's demand to personally return her clothing by the next day. She couriered them instead, underwear included, saving herself from more pain and aggravation.

Then she started the systematic rebuilding of her life. She filed for a copy of her birth certificate, changed the address on her driver's license, and then started looking for a way to move to the big city. There were more job opportunities in Portland. She could make more money and meet more people—people who didn't know her family. Her only friend cynically argued that she wanted to put more distance between her and her parents to decrease the risk of running into them.

Of all the things she left at her parents' house, she missed her computer the most. She was able to find an older computer that she could afford and bought it. Later, she upgraded it herself. Once she had that problem solved, she started looking for a job and a new apartment in Portland.

When she moved away from Mt. Angel, all her possessions fit loosely in a rental sedan. Two years later, she was halfway though her college degree, and a beat-up blue Chevy was making her life a lot easier. She was gaining confidence in her abilities, and she was drawing strength from her achievements. She was ready for her next move: San Diego.

On occasion, she received phone calls from her father, who wanted to know how she was. She could barely endure the conversations; there was nothing left to say. She had never again spoken to her mother, and her last memory of the woman was of that moment when she had handed her the house keys.

She was healing slowly. For a long time, she had felt a sort of suffocating anger, waking her in the middle of the night, making her want to pick up the phone and ask her parents how they could have done that to her. She resisted that impulse. After a while, it disappeared, replaced with feelings of deep loneliness. She fought those feelings by reading, working, studying, and then one day she realized she had become comfortable on her own. She rarely cried anymore. Her only tears appeared on the rare times when she watched a movie in which a happy family was gathered around a Christmas meal.

Steve Mercer had been with The Agency for more than ten years. He enjoyed the practical applications of his extensive knowledge of human psychology. He could function equally well in customer service or human resources leadership. With bright, almost translucent blue eyes and a tall, proud posture, he instantly captured the attention of everyone in the room. His voice was melodious, while assertive and strong. He was persuasive and liked to hear himself speak, carefully constructing the messages he conveyed, in both content and feeling. He was Alex's assigned trainer for the day, and he was enjoying every minute of it.

"Companies can be like countries. You can find every possible political struggle tearing up the guts of a company. Fights over power, coups and counter-coups, opposition and dissidence, political imprisonment, espionage, sabotage, or even commando-type actions can take place, with the sole purpose of shifting power toward one or another of the players."

Alex was all ears, listening with an interest she never thought she would have for a training session. Usually, training had been boring and too slow for her fast and analytical mind. Her expectations were high, from both the course material and the training facilitator. With an IQ of 164, her patience was highly volatile, and her tolerance for mediocre materials was limited. This training session was different. All the information was new to her, concentrated and free of all unnecessary detail, and served by Steve as fast as she could absorb it.

He was continuing the fast-paced presentation, supported by images projected from a Dell laptop to a white screen on the wall.

"In such companies, you will find the darkest traits of modern society: corruption, theft, deceit, blackmail, fear, and worse. Sometimes, the reasons for these actions are downright unbelievable. In these specific environments, you have to be prepared for anything, no matter how absurd. You have to learn to see things through the eyes of different people. Expect things that are not worth doing, based on your system of values, to be well worth it for someone else. For instance, if you wouldn't consider stealing two dollars from someone else's unguarded desk, don't imagine that everyone else thinks the same."

Steve was slowly pacing the floor, but Alex wasn't letting him out of her sight.

"Your success in this line of work will depend on the accuracy of your diagnosis. In most cases, there is also a time factor. Your best ally is modern psychology. You will learn to read people, to assess their states of mind in just seconds, and then to decide if they have a role in your play, if they are simply ignorant bystanders, or innocent victims caught in a game they don't even comprehend. You will learn to find the real motives behind actions. You will learn to hide not only who you are, but also what you think and how you feel. And I have to say, there is a lot of work to be done in that respect," Steve continued with a smile. "Your face is like an open book, Alex."

She felt the blood rush to her cheeks.

Steve clicked the small remote control he was holding. A new slide came up, its title reading, "Surviving the Jungle of Corporate America."

"Do you want to stop for a break?" he asked. She signaled no without a word, eyes on the intriguing title.

"You have to remember, most of the people we are exposing have a lot to lose. Few of them are small-timers, who are only risking their jobs. Most of them are risking serious financial losses and jail time and will not go down without a fierce fight. Please take this job as seriously as you would take police work. It comes with all the risks, but unfortunately without the Kevlar vest, gun, or badge. And there is usually no way of knowing, before we actually take a position inside the client company and start the investigation, if we're dealing with a small time, non-dangerous case, or if there's a serious felony being committed. I have to repeat: your best ally in the field is psychology."

The following slide was a list of book titles with comments.

With a cynical smile, Steve continued. "Weekend is coming." He tapped on the pile of books on the table beside him. "You'll be busy."

Another slide.

"Always think Means—Motive—Opportunity. This is the base for any human action, criminal or not. The first book on the list will explain some unusual motives you might encounter."

The following slide was projecting a book's cover, *People of the Lie.*

"Written by a psychiatrist, who is also a man of the cloth, the book addresses issues of parental abuse. You might think, what's that got to do with anything? Well, two things actually. One is that I find this book to give the best descriptions of human evil I ever came across."

Alex blinked in surprise.

"Sometimes all we have to do to fix a company's problem is to identify and remove the evil person who is doing harm, without any material or professional gain whatsoever. This book will help you grasp the concept of evil and will give you some examples of evil people posing successfully as nice, pleasant people. The second reason for my selection is that the way we act and react is forever marked by our experiences as growing children. Parental abuse is unfortunately common in our society, and those abused children grow up and get jobs, so keep an open mind when you are assessing motivations in the corporate world."

The following slide was another book title, *The Truth about Burnout: How Organizations Cause Personal Stress and What to Do about It.*

"In other cases, corporations are to blame for causing the harm. The executives become too focused on profits and cost reduction, while neglecting the realities and limitations of their staff. Therefore, their actions are harmful in the long run. Read it, and let me know what you think. On the same topic, I have added another two titles."

The book list was quite long, a comprehensive selection of titles varying from Freud's *Totem and Taboo* and *Civilization and Its Discontents* to *Organizational Behavior*, including books dedicated to emotions, stress management, and crisis management.

"Wow," she whispered.

"For all these books, I made notes on the sections you should absolutely go through. That is because we are in a bit of a hurry. However, feel free to hold onto the books, and read the ones you like from cover to cover, when you have a bit of time. On Monday, we will proceed based on this homework. Oh, you have to finish all the books by Monday."

"But . . ." She stopped protesting, when he smiled encouragingly.

"Didn't Tom tell you? We're never bored at The Agency." He leaned forward and powered down his laptop. "Now, could I ask you to have lunch with me? It's been a long time since I had the privilege of sharing a meal with a beautiful, smart woman."

Alex was walking on a cloud.

When people looked at Brian Woods, they all thought he had to be rich and extremely powerful. He radiated power in a manner that most people found intimidating. When he walked into a room, everyone felt the urge to stand up and greet him with respect, despite the fact he was only in his mid-forties. If he were to be seen driving an average, full-size sedan, everyone would agree that it must be a rental, because he just *had* to own a Mercedes S 600 customized by Brabus, or at least a Bentley.

Tall and slim, with deep black eyes and beautiful, yet masculine, features, Brian was turning heads ever since he could remember, but without becoming arrogant about it. A combination of class and charisma was making him successful in his work with The Agency. When Brian joined an organization as a vice president or CEO, one look and no one doubted that he belonged in a top executive role.

With his tie loosened and sleeves rolled up, he sat casually at his desk.

"We met briefly last week. I walked you to Tom's office for your interview, but we haven't had the chance to talk. Welcome aboard, Alex; it's a pleasure."

Alex took the hand he extended and gave it a confident shake, trying not to show how intimidated she felt. She couldn't help wondering why these remarkable people had chosen her to be a part of their team. She didn't feel all that special. Now, after one look at Brian, she felt like the ugly duckling.

"The pleasure is all mine," she said, and sat down.

"I will be training you on systems, communications, procedures, and emergency protocols. I will leave all the psyche-and-soul-related topics to Steve. Tom will come toward the end of your training to tell you a few things about observing things, clues and other stuff like that. Any questions so far?"

"None whatsoever." *I didn't think men like these existed in reality. I thought you only saw them in movies.*

"Then let's proceed." Brian turned toward the wall and projected the image of a small electronic device, photographed in the palm of someone's hand. "This is a communications device. It's usually in your car, therefore, you have to make sure the spot where you're parking isn't too deep underground, or it won't work.

"It comes disguised in the climate control panel of your car. The reading for the temperature doubles as a reading showing the strength of the signal at a point in time and place. Let's say, for instance, you have the bad guy in the car, and he's getting talkative. All you have to do is start the heating or AC in your car; press and hold the fan button for two seconds; and we're receiving, monitoring live, and recording at the same time.

"Meanwhile, the car's heating or AC will also be working. If the temperature reading shows two dashes instead of digits, your coverage is zero, and you need to get out of that spot in order for the system to work. If the temperature is blinking, you barely have any coverage; so you'll need to drive around until those degrees stop blinking."

"So, if my AC is off, the device does not communicate with you and does not record."

"It does not communicate with us," Brian said, "but it will record any noise it senses in the car. At the end of each day, you have the option to decide if those recordings are to be saved or discarded. If you have an emergency, and you need to get our attention to the communication in the car, turn on the air recycling after turning on the AC and holding the fan button for two seconds. That will ping our pagers with an emergency code. Any other questions?"

"Only one small detail," Alex said, feeling a little embarrassed, "my car has no climate control."

Brian gave her an all-knowing smile. "Oh, yes, it does."

"How do our clients find us?" Tom Isaac actually expected an answer. He leaned forward, making inviting gestures with his right hand.

"Through advertising, maybe?" Alex volunteered.

"You aren't thinking. What would happen if we advertised? We would be shooting ourselves in the foot with everyone in the American corporate workplace knowing we existed. We'd have increasing difficulties getting the job done. Any other ideas?"

"Referrals?"

"Yes. Mainly, yes. Business owners tend to stick together and interact with one another at a level that is most times inaccessible to their staff, no matter how high ranking." Tom paused for a second and smiled. With a complete change in the tone of his voice, he swiftly became Alex's concerned friend. "How's it going? Are you comfortable with this pace? You know, we didn't get the chance to sit down and discuss what we plan to achieve and the best way to get there."

Surprised, Alex replied without thinking. "Yes, everything is fine, no problem."

"See? You're doing it again," Tom said, with the tone of a parent grounding a four year old. "Relax a bit; you got the job. Now you can afford to really talk to me. You see, experience has repeatedly taught me that in order to function in our line of work, we need to know each other, trust each other, depend on each other, and help each other. I know I should have started with this instead of our client acquisition procedures, but please allow me to make up for it. So, let's start over. If you could ask three questions in the utmost confidentiality, what would those be?"

"Well, I am wondering how come I was so lucky to come across your ad. It seems to me that finding someone for this job isn't exactly easy for you. On the other hand, you don't seem to be recruiting that often." Seeing Tom's expression, Alex felt the blood rush to her cheeks. "I don't want to sound arrogant or anything, but how did I get so lucky?"

"You were not lucky, you were selected."

"But—" she started and stopped, with a thousand more questions to ask.

"Remember, three questions for today, one is already answered," Tom warned her, with amusement in his voice.

She took a deep breath. "OK, then. Brian told me, during yesterday's training, that my car has climate control and it doesn't. Was a climate control device installed in my car?"

"Um . . . no. There goes question number two. Such a shame to see questions go to waste like that. You need to learn to trust. What's number three?"

She blushed, looked down, but somehow found the courage. "Is Brian married?"

"No. Again, such a waste of a good question."

Intrigued, she asked, "Why?"

"You are analytical to the roof and back, but only when you want to be. My question to you is, 'Why don't you use what you have?' You had the answers to all these questions before asking. For instance, you are smart enough not to believe in coincidences, and this is as far as I'll go explaining the first question. The rest you'll figure out on your own someday. You could have avoided question number two, if you'd only asked yourself what reason Brian would have to lie to you, or to make an unsubstantiated statement. As for number three, even if he's not married today, he could have been yesterday or could be tomorrow. What's the value of the answer you got?"

"I deserved it. I sure did, all of it."

"Don't be so hard on yourself. The training process can be exhausting and can cause, well, questions to be wasted," Tom concluded, laughing.

"And stupidity to manifest itself." Alex joined him in laughter, thinking what had just happened to make her feel she belonged.

It was her fifth day of training. While waiting in the training room for the day to start, she wondered what the day's subject would be and who would be her trainer. Probably they would continue to discuss the pile of books she had read.

Steve walked in and greeted her in a cheerful voice. "Good morning."

"Good morning." She stood up and shook Steve's hand. She was inexplicably happy to see him. After all, he had condemned her to a weekend of reading and no sleep, followed by more homework assignments since Monday.

He started the projector and the laptop and asked, without any other introduction, "Would you ever let that thing touch you? Crawl on your skin?"

She turned and saw on the screen a horrible close-up image of the black, shiny mandibles of a huge bug.

"Is that thing real?" she asked, shuddering in disgust.

"Very real, I can assure you."

"Alive?"

"Alive and well, thank you," he confirmed mischievously. "So, would you?"

"I don't think I would be able to let that happen, regardless of how much money I'd stand to make. Is this for a movie?"

"How about this one? Do you like this one better?" he asked, ignoring her question and changing the slide.

She looked in horror at another close-up image of insect mouths, just as terrifying as the first one.

"No way," she answered.

"Are you sure?" he insisted.

"Yes. Very sure. I'd never let any of those bugs crawl on me. They are equally ugly, and I hate all bugs."

"All right, I believe you. In reality, they are not that big, you know." He clicked his remote and the image started to zoom out. "This is the actual size of this bug, scientific classification: insect, from the order of coleopterans. Its scientific name is *Onitis pecuarius*, or the dung beetle. Do you like it better now?"

"Absolutely not."

"So you still believe you would not let any bug like this crawl freely on your skin."

"I am positive. If I had a choice, I would not consider it," she said, without hesitation, wondering where all this was going.

"Think again." As he spoke, Steve went back to the first image, and said. "This one, also a coleopteran and a close relative of the one before, is no other than *Coccinella septempunctata*, by its scientific classification." Zooming out the image on the screen repeatedly, he continued. "I am sure you are willing to reconsider for our little friend, the ladybug."

"Oh," Alex said, completely taken by surprise. On the screen, the terrifying image had zoomed out to show a tiny ladybug in the palm of a little girl's hand, as she was laughing in the sun.

"Our theme for today is the power of preconception," Steve said. "Somehow, someone decided a long time ago that ladybugs are OK, while the other bugs are not. Maybe because ladybugs are not harmful to the crops, but neither are the other bugs, and we wouldn't let them crawl on our skin, would we?"

Alex nodded, captivated by the idea.

"Because we are taught since early childhood not to fear these particular bugs, we accept them. We never think that these bugs are quite similar to others, which we fear in disgust. We never stop to wonder how these preconceptions came to be. We just accept them, and, most important, we act on them. When it comes to deeply set preconceptions, we don't have an open mind, and we never ask why." He turned off the projector and continued. "Alex, can you think of some commonly encountered preconceived ideas?"

"Yes, sure. All Germans like beer; women are worse drivers than men, that kind of thing?"

"Exactly. Those are broad examples, and they affect our judgment on a daily basis. For instance, if I had a German delegate visiting my manufacturing plant, I could assume that he likes beer, and would not ask him what he likes to drink. I could become tempted to act on my biased notion and make a decision for him, therefore offending him. Or I could be the sales manager of a company, in charge of assigning company vehicles to my sales reps. My preconceived idea of women's driving skills might influence my decision, and I might end up assigning the oldest, less-valuable vehicles to women sales reps. What do you think the consequences would be, in this case?"

"Well, the women sales reps would notice, would become demotivated, would feel the discrimination, and this would result in lost revenue for the company. Lower morale in the sales team could potentially lead to attrition, fractures in the team, revolt, and vindictive behaviors. Lawsuits for discrimination are also possible," Alex replied, without hesitation. Steve was nodding his approval for each item she listed as possible consequences. She asked, "Am I missing anything?"

"No, that's mostly it. How would *you* assign the company cars to the sales reps?

"Ideally, all the cars would be of equal value and in equally good shape. If that is not an option, there are two ways to fairly assign them. Based on previous sales results or based on a draw, with all the sales reps present. I think both ways would work."

"Perfect," Steven said, "and, by the way, statistics prove that women are, in fact, better drivers than men. Did you know that?"

She smiled. "Yes, I did. However, most people are still biased against women drivers."

"That is so true. You need to keep your biases in mind at all times. You have to ask yourself, every time you reach a conclusion, "Who reached that conclusion? Was it your freethinking, analytical mind? Or was it some pre-existing judgment you were not even aware of? Equally, when you see someone else's actions, decisions, or conclusions, you have to assume there could have been some preconceived notion influencing them." Steve leaned back in his chair, his body language saying he was done for the day. "Any questions?"

"Just one. Does superstition qualify as preconception, or should it even be considered a factor in analyzing human motivations?" Alex asked.

"What is superstition? It's a belief. Although irrational, it's widespread in its variety of forms, and it's influencing the human decision-making process, even for decisions of minor importance, such as refusing to pay a bill on a Monday or not walking under a ladder. Superstition is the preconceived belief that doom will follow certain actions. Therefore, it qualifies with flying colors."

"Thank you." Alex stood up, ready to go. She was hoping for another lunch invitation, but that never came.

An uncomfortable silence settled for a few seconds, ended by Tom's appearance. He entered the small office and pulled up a chair, so Alex sat back down.

"I will need just a couple of minutes with you, Alex."

Steve waved goodbye and left, closing the door behind him.

"One thing we haven't yet discussed about this job is compensation. I was actually surprised you took the job without the faintest clue about compensation."

Alex chuckled. "I am sure it's going to be a little better than what I previously earned."

"Correct. You will be making $145,000 per year, plus a significant bonus, conditional on your successful client-case resolutions." Tom paused, waiting for a reaction.

"Wow," Alex said in a soft voice, "that *is* a little better than before." It was almost three times higher, but instead of being thrilled, she suddenly felt afraid.

"This compensation will be deposited biweekly in an account of your choosing I'd recommend that you refrain from using your regular bank account. Setting up a special account, at a different bank, would be better."

Alex frowned, intrigued.

"In addition," Tom continued, "you will be compensated by each client, for the role you officially hold while working with the respective client. Those amounts should be deposited in your regular bank account. In case someone investigates your financial records, they will find nothing out of the ordinary with the deposits. I trust the compensation package is satisfactory?"

Alex nodded with enthusiasm. "And then some!"

Tom walked out the door, and Alex followed him.

"If you're done for the day, I'd like to walk you to your car," Tom said.

Brigadier General Seth Nichols went through a heap of paperwork, turning page after page from a massive dossier. He wasn't finding what he was looking for, and he was losing his patience. He picked up the phone.

"Jim?"

"Yes, sir," his adjutant on the other end of the line responded promptly.

"Get me the Kandahar Airfield commander, Colonel Sheridan. What time is it there?"

"They're eight and a half hours ahead of us, so that would make it 2:15AM, sir."

"Get him anyway."

"Yes, sir."

A minute later, the phone rang.

"I have Colonel Sheridan for you, sir," Jim advised, then put the call through.

"This is Sheridan, sir, good morning." The colonel's voice was almost covered by the background noise of roaring jet engines.

"Good morning, Sheridan. I got your report on the friendly fire mess on the 20th. I've read the reports you sent me, but I see no conclusions were drawn yet. What's the delay? Do you know what happened out there?"

"Not yet, sir. We're still working on it. The reports I've sent are covering everything we know so far, but there are still questions to be answered."

"Well, how hard can it be? Did we fire on the Canadians or not?"

"That's exactly it, sir. Our ground systems do not show any record of a missile launch. But, as far as we know, we were the only ones flying drones in the area, and the Hellfire signatures have been confirmed—they were ours."

"I've seen you debriefed the pilots. What are they saying?"

"They are not saying much. They maintained their original statements, that it was an uneventful drone deployment, which was completed without anything out of the ordinary to report."

"Sheridan?"

"Sir?"

"You need to get to the bottom of this and fast, do you read me? We have to issue a full report as soon as possible. We can't delay this any further. The media is already on this, as you would expect."

"Yes, sir, we're on it."

"Keep me posted," Nichols said, and then hung up. "What a mess," he said to himself, closing the thick file that held no answers.

Tom and Alex exited the elegant, white building, walking side by side. Alex started turning left, heading for her car.

"This way, please," Tom said, "follow me."

Intrigued, Alex followed, without asking anything. *They must have worked on my car,* she thought, *that would explain a few things.* Tom stopped between two rows of parked cars and handed her a set of car keys, attached to a simple, triangular keychain without any markings.

"Here you go. Come on, open it up," he said.

Alex was still trying to locate her car, but it was nowhere in sight. She pressed the remote button and a silver Toyota 4Runner flashed all four hazard lights. Confused, she looked at Tom.

"Go on, get in. This is your car from now on, at least for a while. I hope you like it."

Alex was speechless. *Wow.* Moving like in a dream, she opened the door and sat inside, taking in the exquisite, unmistakable new car smell.

"The only downside," Tom said, "is that you can't use your old car for a while. That one will remain parked here, or somewhere else at your discretion. Or we could sell it for you." Tom smiled. "This is the new you. Enjoy. You'll find this car has all the accessories you might expect: navigation, CD player, satellite radio, and, of course, air conditioning. I am sure you remember Brian and his words about air conditioning," he said, continuing to smile.

"Where were we?" Tom pulled out a chair and sat down. "Ah, yes, client acquisition procedures." He opened a drawer and pulled out a few business cards. The business cards were simple, black, raised ink on white stock, reflecting his name and phone number—nothing else. "Well, yesterday you reached the conclusion that our clients find us mainly through referrals, and you were right about that.

"Usually, after the completion of a project, we hand out a few of these business cards to our clients, and ask them to give the cards to other business owners in need of our services, but to use discretion before handing them out. We aren't letting ourselves be involved in turf wars within companies; therefore, the owner of the business, or the majority of the shareholders (confirmed by a secret vote in our presence), can sign us up. No one else can use our services. Any questions so far?"

"In case of a vote, how can you be sure of the results? I mean, what if the result is not in favor of using The Agency's services? How do you make sure information regarding our existence does not leave that boardroom?" Alex stated her question in a trembling, unsure voice, but, as the words started coming out of her mouth, her confidence built, and she finished the question sure of herself. After all, her question made sense.

"That's a good question. Part of our client acquisition procedure for larger corporations, for those with more than one shareholder, is to have them sign an NDA, just like this one. If there is only one shareholder, we use a different NDA, a more straightforward one."

"NDA?" Alex interrupted.

"Nondisclosure agreement." Tom reached in another drawer and pulled out a few printed pages, stapled together, on The Agency's letterhead. "Homework. Read the NDAs thoroughly and understand them in detail. Clients have to sign these agreements before they even learn our names. If you have questions, we will discuss them tomorrow. You will find this document to be quite comprehensive." Tom looked at his Breitling watch. "Moving forward, what would be our second source of business? Any ideas?"

"Repeat business?" Alex asked, again not sure of herself. She wanted so much to make a good impression; but felt uneasy every time she spoke. She was usually assertive and sure of herself, but in the presence of these people, she felt she needed to brush up to live up to their expectations. This was new to her.

"Yes, repeat business," Tom confirmed. "Currently it amounts to almost 40 percent of our revenue. Our former clients find it easier to call us at the first sign of trouble, than to hope the issue will get fixed on its own. And they find us to be the lower cost out of trouble, anyway."

"Lower cost? How come?" Alex was knowledgeable enough about the business world to be sure that The Agency's services could not come cheap.

"A company eaten alive from within can lose money at an unimaginable rate. These losses can happen overnight. Our former clients have become knowledgeable about how to recognize the early signs of trouble in their companies, and they call us right away. For us, it's obviously much easier to reacquire a client, than to acquire a new one."

"What are these early signs?"

"The main sign is unprovoked, inexplicable change." Tom paused, waiting for Alex to ask for more details. She did not wait long before asking.

"Change? What kind of change?"

"Have you ever heard the phrase: 'Numbers are a businessman's best friend'? I'm sure you have."

Alex nodded her agreement.

"So, unprovoked, inexplicable changes in numbers, in sales numbers, in staff attrition numbers, in sick days per employee numbers, and so on. Depends, case by case, on the type of business and the problems it is having. Makes a lot of sense when you think about it, right? For instance, let's say you have a customer support team whose members suddenly start being sick all the time, especially on Mondays. What would that lead you to believe?"

"Bad working conditions, maybe bad management, something like that," Alex said.

"Yes, but which? How can you know for sure?"

"Well, if they recently hired a new team manager and people started calling in sick, then—"

"That's not unprovoked change, my dear, in this case it becomes obvious why the change in numbers occurred," Tom interrupted.

"Oops," Alex said softly, looking down.

"You can do better than that, I'm sure of it," Tom said, smiling encouragingly.

She found the courage to try again. "Well, let's assume then that the existing manager is having a rough time at home and started taking it out on the staff, not caring any more, not making sure the staff members have support, leadership, and procedures. That builds up over time into a noticeable change in sick-day patterns."

"I told you," Tom said, stretching his arms and legs with a satisfied grin, "you can do it. Perfect scenario, plausible, and quite often encountered in one form or another. Now think some more, and give me one or two other possible scenarios."

"OK, how about this? An existing product supplier has slowly, but constantly, dropped the quality of the product, leading to an unprecedented increase in angry customer calls, therefore causing an unusual rate of burnout in the support team."

Tom nodded slowly, lifting his right hand in a fist with his thumb up. "That's another perfect example. Sometimes, the change in numbers is caused by some other change, like a procedure change, a system or equipment change, a staff change, something that wasn't even noticed initially, or wasn't considered as a possible cause; an initially planned change that led to some bad consequences. You have to look for this initial change. However, we're veering off track. We were discussing client acquisition, or at least we were supposed to be, weren't we?"

"Yes."

"Maybe this will help us stay focused." Tom turned on the multimedia projector and projected on the screen a bulleted list under the title "New Client Acquisition Steps." He started reading them aloud, one by one. "Step one, the call. We receive a call from the future client. Step two, if there is more than one shareholder, the extended NDA. They sign that, they vote, they sign a contract, they are onboard as clients. From this point forward, we refer to the business owner or to the group of business owners as *the client*—not the CEO, not the president, but *the client*. Step three, training on expectations for both sides. We explain what they should expect, how long it could take, what it could mean, possible outcomes, and so on. We also explain what we expect from them. What kind of support we should receive from the inception of our work. Step four, we listen to their grievances in detail. We ask questions, we try to fully understand the core of their problems. This is the first step involving anyone else but me. At this point, I would have already decided which one of my team would join our client's company. The respective would be present at that time. All clear so far?"

"Yes."

"Step five, is the hiring process. From this point forward, your fieldwork starts. The hiring has to happen as naturally as possible. The new position has to be created discreetly, and the human resources department has to select your résumé out of a pile of other résumés. They have to call you for an interview on their own, without pressure from the client."

"What if it doesn't work? What if they simply don't see my résumé?"

"Well, they will. It will be the best résumé ever written, with the exact experience they'll be looking for. Worst-case scenario, the client can push a bit, but it would be better if he or she doesn't have to. From there forward, you will pass two or three interviews: one with human resources, maybe another one that is more technical, and the final one with the client. You will have to pass those interviews, so you will be prepared. The interviews are the least of my concerns; I have seen you in action."

"Thank you." Alex smiled gratefully.

"Welcome, and well deserved. Step six, starts with your first day at work. Getting to know the company, the people, the atmosphere, looking at everything, while keeping in mind the client's concern, and asking yourself what caused it. Not disregarding any possibility; not discarding any theory, no matter how far-fetched; looking for causes and their effects; and analyzing what you see, hear, and learn. Step seven, is the diagnosis. You found it; you first bring it to the team at The Agency. You cannot discuss this with the client without running it by us beforehand. The clients will be instructed not to ask you, but some of them will still try. Once you have a diagnosis, we all sit together and brainstorm about the best way to fix the problem. Sometimes the fix is an obvious, simple answer. Other times, it's more complicated, or we have to get the authorities involved. Once we have a solution, we'll all present it together to the client. Finally, step eight is the fix. You apply the fix, or assist the client in applying it, and then leave the company. Case closed."

"Wow," Alex said, "this is amazing. This is impressive. It's a whole new world, I had no idea existed."

"Most people don't. Do you still want to be a part of it?" Tom asked. He sat up, shut down the projector and the laptop, getting ready to leave the room.

Alex answered promptly and enthusiastically. "Absolutely."

"Great. Then let's discuss this some more over dinner, at my place, 7:00PM tonight." He handed her a Post-it note with an address in Laguna Beach.

"Yeah. Sure, I'll be there," Alex said. Not many people would have sensed the hesitation in her voice, but Tom did.

"What the hell should I wear?"

Pacing the room in her underwear and stepping on scattered clothes discarded on the floor, Alex had trouble reaching a decision. She also had trouble keeping calm. She stopped her pacing in front of the mirrored closet door and admired herself, slowly turning around. The dark lingerie, making her sun-tanned skin appear luminescent, complemented her tall, slim figure. Her lean muscles, maintained by daily exercise and swimming, were not showing any visible sign of her sedentary activity in front of a computer screen. She was working hard to compensate for all the hours spent sitting at her desk, and she would have normally felt quite happy with the image reflected in the mirror, but today that image was causing her unrest. She went back to the closet, ready to attempt another search for the perfect outfit.

"Too sexy, too short, too colorful, too cheap." One by one, she pushed the disqualified clothes hangers to the left, focusing on the next in line, with her patience running short, and her voice rising in anger. *Damn it to hell. And back.* A hanger supporting the fine shoulder straps of a generously revealing black dress hit the floor. She sat down on the bed, head in her hands, thinking.

The dinner invitation at her boss's home had thrown her off, making her not sure what to believe. Was this a test? If so, what kind of test? She was afraid Tom would make a pass at her, to test her most likely, because he did not seem to be the type to romance his employees. He was too courteous, too reserved and professional at all times. Still, an invitation to his home could prove to be a tricky situation to handle.

She wanted her attire to make a statement of self-assurance, of casual confidence, but also to discourage any possible advances. She did not want to wear her designer business suit because she feared it would seem like she was desperate to make a good impression. She *was* desperate to make a good impression, but she was trying to hide it just as desperately.

Furthermore, the dinner invitation sounded casual, not formal, and she wanted her attire to demonstrate that she was able to dress appropriately for such an occasion. Well, she did have another reason for not wearing her formal business suit. That was because she only had that one, and she had worn it at her job interview. Tom would obviously remember. *Damn.*

With a resigned sigh, she picked out a pair of worn-out jeans, a gray T-shirt, and a charcoal turtleneck sweater. The sweater was at least three sizes too large for her. *Too damn hot for sweaters, but* I will *be able to endure.* She looked up at the clock on the wall. *I will also be late.* She picked up her keys and wallet, and stormed out the door. Twenty seconds later, she stormed back in, picked up the bottle of wine she had bought for Tom, and ran out again, slamming the door behind her.

She drove up Cliff Drive looking at the house numbers. Tom lived in a huge ranch-style home, with large windows and a neatly landscaped lawn, overlooking the breathtaking Pacific coast. She pulled into the driveway, in front of the double-car garage. Keeping her foot on the brake pedal, she quickly tied up her hair in a ponytail. She was postponing the moment she had to turn the engine off, which would cut the lifesaving flow of freezing conditioned air.

She tried to see if Tom was watching from behind the white tulle curtains hanging at the immense windows overseeing the driveway. It was impossible to see anything behind those curtains. *Damn. Of course, he likes his privacy . . .*

She got out of her car and walked straight to the door. She rang the bell and heard Tom's footsteps approaching. He opened the door with a welcoming smile and showed her in. "Welcome, come on in. Make yourself comfortable, take your pick."

His living room was huge, tastefully decorated with sparse furniture. There was a lot of open space, gleaming hardwood floors, with area rugs in harmonious, warm colors. In the center of the room were a sectional leather sofa, designed in a classy, contemporary style; a coffee table; and three matching armchairs; arranged in a quarter-circle in front of the sofa. A Siamese cat, sleeping serenely, undisturbed by her arrival, occupied one of the armchairs.

She started toward an armchair, relieved he did not invite her to sit on the sofa. She stopped midway, then turned and offered him the gift-wrapped bottle of wine.

Tom accepted it with a smile. "Thank you. You know, for a moment there I was worried you were not going to give that to me after all."

"I am sorry, I almost forgot." One look at Tom's expression and she started laughing. She sat down, feeling more relaxed, but really hot. *How many degrees is it in here? Damn sweater.*

Tom sat on the sofa and said nothing.

Alex felt compelled to say something, to break the awkward silence. "So, what's her name?" she asked, pointing at the cat.

"Tom. *His* name is Tom. He is a tomcat, so it makes sense." Tom chuckled.

"Oh," she said, biting her lip. *I am so not going to ask any more questions tonight. That's it.*

"Dinner is almost ready. You will find that we are used to having late meals because of the specifics of our business."

The sound of dishes clattering came from the kitchen. Alex relaxed a little hearing those sounds. Tom smiled, turning his face away, so his smile could go unnoticed.

A middle-aged woman entered the living room, carrying a vase of flowers.

"Alex, please meet my wife, Claire." Tom took the vase from his wife and set it on the coffee table.

"It's a pleasure to meet you, Claire." Alex shook the warm and friendly hand extended by Claire and relaxed another notch. She looked at Claire and wondered why her face seemed so familiar.

"Alex, I think you have briefly met Claire. She sometimes helps us at The Agency," Tom said.

"The receptionist," Claire said, seeing how confused Alex looked.

"Yes, now I remember," Alex said.

"Tom, dear, please go uncork that bottle of wine in the kitchen. Alex and I have something to discuss in private." Claire gave Alex a friendly wink. "Just some girl talk."

Tom started for the kitchen, taking the gift-wrapped bottle of wine with him. He was only 10 feet away, when the cat suddenly woke up, got off the armchair, and silently followed Tom, without paying attention to anything else.

"They are inseparable. Little Tom follows Tom everywhere, wouldn't leave him out of his sight for a minute," Claire said. "He even goes with him into the bathroom, waiting for him to take his shower. If Tom is taking too much time in the shower, and the cat wants to go to sleep, he meows so loud that Tom simply has to come out."

"I was wondering how you tell them apart when you need to call them," Alex said with a quiet chuckle, "so, it's Little Tom and Big Tom?"

"No, it's Little Tom and Tom, or just Tom for both of them, but they both know whom I am calling, by the inflexions in my voice. They never read it wrong, either of them."

A bit nervous, Alex asked, "So, what did you want to discuss in private, Claire? Tom won't take forever to uncork a bottle."

"Well, I wanted to ask you a personal question," Claire said, dropping her voice to a whisper.

"Go ahead," Alex encouraged her, also whispering.

"Aren't you feeling a bit warm in that heavy sweater?" Claire's smile was sincere and encouraging. In her eyes, Alex saw she completely understood her doubts and fears with respect to this dinner invitation. "You know, you could take that off and I could give you a T-shirt of mine," Claire continued.

"That won't be necessary, Claire," Alex said, taking a step back. She pulled the sweater over her head with one move, revealing the gray T-shirt she was wearing underneath. "I have my own." Alex hung the sweater on the back of her armchair and leaned back, letting out a long sigh of relief. "Thank you."

"Now you can come back, Tom," Claire called.

Tom entered the room, holding the bottle and three wine glasses. He sat on the sofa and started pouring the wine. "So, now tell me a little bit about yourself, off the record and completely casual," he said, handing Alex a glass of wine.

"Well, to start with, I am praying I chose a good wine," Alex said. "I am clueless on the topic of wines."

"So, how did you select this one?" Tom asked. "Did you ask a store clerk for help?"

"Initially, yes. However, he didn't seem to know what he was talking about. So I selected the wine based on pricing and the label."

"OK," Tom said, raising his glass. "Let's see how much wine for the buck." He took a sip, and then asked. "Alex, what do you normally like to drink?"

"Martini. And a beer sometimes."

"Then why not bring a bottle of Martini, or a six pack of your favorite beer?"

"Well, I didn't think of what *I* would like to drink; I thought more in terms of what's appropriate for such an occasion," Alex explained, blushing slightly.

Tom started toward the kitchen, followed closely by his cat. He turned and asked, "How do you take your Martini?"

"Half a glass on three or four ice cubes, slice of lemon, just the vermouth, nothing else. My Martinis have actual Martini vermouth in them, not vodka."

After a few moments, Tom returned and handed Alex a glass filled with Martini Rosso on ice, with half a slice of lemon on the side. He handed Claire a tall glass, filled with a clear drink, some herbs, and lots of small ice cubes.

"Was my wine that bad?" Alex asked in a sad voice.

"Oh, yes," Tom said decisively, and they all started laughing.

A rapid tap on the front door and Steve came in, followed closely by Brian and a third man.

"You're late," Tom said.

"Traffic. Only traffic could ever come between me and your steaks, you know that," Brian said, with a serious face. He gave Claire a hug, then headed straight for the table.

The third man approached the armchair where the Siamese cat was sleeping, grabbed him and put him on the back of his neck, like a scarf. The cat started to purr and stretch his legs, with his eyes half-closed.

"Alex, meet Richard Ferguson, our colleague," Tom said. Alex shook the hand he extended. The carefully manicured hand belonged to a handsome man in his late thirties, with a pleasant demeanor and an impeccable taste in clothing.

"Richard is currently working on assignment with a client, that's why you two haven't met until now," Tom explained.

"I am actually surprised that you allow the team members to stay in touch with The Agency while we're on assignment," Alex said. "Aren't we at risk of, um . . . blowing our cover?"

"Minimally," Tom said. "If anyone should run a background check on me and Claire, they will only find that we are semi-retired, living off our personal wealth, and occasionally engaged in brokering real estate deals. The Agency is listed in many places as a real estate agency, so whenever you come to visit, you won't raise any red flags . . . You're just searching for your new house and meeting with your Realtor."

"Interesting," she smiled. "How about them?" Alex said, waving toward Richard and Steve.

"Friends of the family, and relatives, such as Steve. We've sort of adopted Steve," Tom said. "Richard, on the other hand, since he's so busy with his client these days, he can only take you shopping tomorrow."

"Shopping?" Alex asked in surprise.

"Yes. You need to pick up a few things, clothing and accessories mostly, to complement your appearance on the job," Tom said.

"Meet me at the airport tomorrow morning," Richard said. "It will be my pleasure to assist you with your quest for the perfect wardrobe."

"Why the airport?" She didn't even try to disguise her surprise.

"We're going shopping in Minnesota. Have you ever visited the largest mall in the country?"

"No, never," she answered.

"It's in Minneapolis; well, in Bloomington to be exact.. It's called the Mall of America. It's near the airport, but I would still pack an overnight bag, just to make sure we have all the time we need to finish our shopping," Richard said casually. "After all, we're not needed back until Sunday night."

She swallowed with difficulty. "What time would you like me to be at the airport?"

"Whenever you'd like. How's 10:00AM?"

"Perfect," she confirmed. "How do I get my ticket?"

"We won't be flying commercial," Richard clarified with a wink. "Don't worry about anything; just be there at 10:00AM tomorrow."

Alex suddenly remembered how little money she had left. None of that amazing compensation package had hit her accounts yet. *This guy looks like he has an expensive taste in clothing. We're going to have yet another interesting day. Crap.* She frowned slightly.

"You'll be using this," Tom said, handing her a Gold MasterCard with her name on it. "We each carry one of these, and we use them for all expenses." He smiled paternally, encouraging her. "Have fun. I doubt you'll ever reach the spending limit."

"Thank you," she said, suppressing her sigh of relief. "I will follow your advice and Richard's guidance." *It's Christmas time again.*

The footage had been taken on an amateur camera, or maybe even a cell phone. Hospital images were dancing on the screen, as the videographer walked through doors and hallways, transmitting vibrations to his handheld video device.

Stephanie Wainwright's voice overlapped the image, saying, "Eleven days have passed since tragedy struck the Canadian Combat Logistics Patrol, while on a mission in Kandahar, Afghanistan. Eleven days that have brought no answers, but took yet another life. Sergeant Ross Stevenson, critically injured in the drone attack, had been fighting for his life at the US military hospital at the Kandahar Airfield. Today he lost that fight, bringing the death toll of this tragedy to four. Two Canadians are still hospitalized, due to severe injuries, and are scheduled to return to their homeland next week. Six families are waiting to hear why this senseless tragedy happened. So far, no one is willing to answer."

Stephanie paused for a second, giving her words time to sink into the hearts of the audience.

"Live from our studio, this is Stephanie Wainwright, with *News of the Hour*."

...Chapter 23: Morning Woes
...Monday, May 3, 9:02AM
...Ridgeview Apartments
...San Diego, California

Alex was not a morning person. Even more so, waking up was more difficult after the late-night flight home, following the mega shopping spree with Richard. She had planned for a day of sleep indulgence, but she found herself driving toward the office soon after nine. The change of plans had been caused by an enigmatic early morning phone call from Steve.

"No time to lick your wounds, Alex. Client meeting today, new client, 10:00AM," Steve said and then hung up.

She was barely going to make it on time.

The client, in his mid-sixties, a tall, distinguished man, slowly paced the floor of the conference room. Tom, Brian, and Steve, seated at the dark, glossy conference room table, were going over paperwork. Alex walked in at precisely 10:00AM, but she still felt late.

"Now we are all here, Dr. Barnaby, and we are listening," Tom said, after making the formal introductions.

"I don't even know where to start," the man said. "The entire situation is confusing to me. Bear with me; I will try to explain everything the best that I can." He had stopped pacing the floor, but he was still standing. "I founded NanoLance in 1986, in the heart of Silicon Valley. I hold several patents for programmable logic devices, encoding systems, architecture for multiple processor devices, and other such things. We have developed a number of successful technologies, some of which I am sure you must be familiar with, such as guidance chips for satellite navigation and positioning systems, guidance software, dynamic automation systems, terrain contour or elevation matching software, also known as landmark and landscape recognition software, pre-programmed flight plans, and so on.

"As I am sure you are suspecting by now, early in our company's existence we became a contractor for the United States military. It has been our number one client for all our newly developed technologies and applications. We collaborate with the US military for most of our research-and-development initiatives. NanoLance has grown nicely throughout the years and has made me, its founder, really proud." Dr. Anthony Barnaby smiled for a second, before letting worry regain control over his charismatic features. He looked at everyone sitting around the table, one by one, to ensure they were following his story and understanding every detail.

"When you are referring to the US military, who exactly are you talking about?" Steve's clarification question interrupted the brief silence.

"Everyone, including agencies, departments, and organizations partaking in the defense of our country. The Army, Navy, Air Force, Customs and Border Protection, even the CIA."

"Thank you, Dr. Barnaby, please continue," Tom said.

"Where were we . . .? Ah, yes. We are headquartered in downtown San Diego to be closer to our manufacturing facilities near Alpine. You see," he paused a little, catching his breath, "we also manufacture most of our components and subassemblies, and we have a complete assembly line for consumer GPS devices, both handheld and in-dash mount. Some of you might be familiar with our brand of navigation devices, the NanoGuide."

Dr. Barnaby screened his audience again, looking for signs of familiarity with his brand. Satisfied, he continued. "We've just recently launched the consumer navigation devices on the market; I am confident that, within two years, we could reach 2.4 billion dollars in sales with the help of our new brand. Last year, our revenue was a little over 2.2 billion dollars. We're publicly traded; listed on NASDAQ since 1998."

Another pause. Dr. Barnaby reached out for the glass of water in front of him and took a sip, without sitting down. "I should be happy," he continued. "Instead, I am increasingly worried that something is wrong. Here's why." He finally pulled out his chair and sat down.

Alex followed closely every move he made, the expressions on his face and the inflexions in his voice, looking to get as much insight as possible. She was taking notes, and so was everyone else on the team. She found herself wondering why no one was taking notes on a computer. She started to reach for her laptop, but stopped before completing her gesture; it might make her seem out of place with the rest of the team. She decided to continue taking notes in the old-fashioned, ineffective way, emulating the behavior displayed by her experienced colleagues.

Dr. Barnaby threw her attention back into high gear by resuming his address.

"After returning from the company's Christmas party this past December, I found this note in my coat pocket." He put a small, crumpled piece of paper on the table. Without a word, Brian picked up the paper and place it on the scanner situated on a nearby table. A screen descended from the ceiling, making a whirring noise. The projected image on the screen showed the enlarged note, revealing a few words scribbled in a hurried, broken handwriting.

As the words on the screen were becoming apparent, Dr. Barnaby's voice was following along.

"*Please stop this insanity, or more people will die.*" He gave a long, troubled sigh. "You have no idea how many nights I tossed in bed, trying to figure out what the note is referring to. What insanity? Who died? Is this a threat? Or a warning?"

"Dr. Barnaby," Tom said, "we will elucidate these mysteries for you, I am positive about that. Have you done any fingerprint analysis on the note?"

"I hesitated to take this to the authorities. Call it instinct, if you wish," he responded to the surprised glance Alex had thrown his way. "What if this was a warning, and, by involving the authorities, I would put my whistleblower in danger somehow? I am more inclined to believe this was a warning rather than a threat, because more than four months have passed since the day I found this, and I have received no other messages. Anyway, this is not all. The second reason for my presence today is of a different nature. It has to do with our stock price."

Alex was silently praying this would not get technical. Her limited knowledge of how the stock market worked could seriously hinder her ability to work this case. She made a mental note to ask Steve for a stock market 101 training session.

"Let me give you the basics," Dr. Barnaby continued. "Currently, our stock price is about $145, and I am still the majority stock holder of the company. This is not your typical situation for a publicly traded organization, but we have always had a strong cash flow position, plus we were quite small when we had our initial public offering, so I was able to retain control over the company, while raising the capital needed to launch our consumer products. I am leading the company with the assistance of a board of directors, which I also chair. All seems fine, but I have noticed a strange couple of coincidences in the past few months." He paused a little, allowing everyone to process the information he had presented. "Before proceeding, any questions so far?"

A quick look around the table reassured him everyone was following closely. A few seconds of silence encouraged him to continue.

"This time I have no evidence to show you, this is just my observation, so it might appear subjective. I've been trying to sell a significant part of my stock to be able to retire. My retirement plan requires that I raise quite a bit of free-flowing cash from the sale of a significant portion of my stock, which would cause me to lose the control position I hold now. I would also like to hold on to a bit of stock, to have a stable source of income in my retirement. Without boring you with too much detail, I need to sell roughly half the stock I own, to free up the cash I need for my retirement investment, and keep the rest for income.

"Well, in the past year or so, whenever I tried to make a move and sell my stock, it seems that something happens out there, and the stock price drops significantly. I can't keep my intentions secret; company control changing hands is an issue that requires all the executives to be informed, takes significant planning, and requires me to abide by the laws governing insider trading. This means that I can only sell or buy shares during specific periods of time, called insider trading windows, when all the company performance information becomes public on the market."

"What do you mean by 'something happens out there'? Could you give us an example?" Tom asked.

"Absolutely. One time it was a news article that appeared just before the trading window opened, stating that the company risked losing business from the US military due to pending investigations. It wasn't true. Our lawyers got in the mix, the paper issued a note stating the article had been published in error, but the damage was already done. The stock price lost almost 40 percent in a week's worth of trading. It took months for us to recover.

"Another example comes to mind: rumors of a potential US Securities and Exchange Commission investigation were leaked, just days before the trading window would open. The leak was anonymous, unfounded, but it led to an almost 20 percent drop in stock price and to another quarter in which I couldn't sell my stock. These trading windows only open after the quarterly results are made public. If I miss one, I have to wait another quarter."

Dr. Barnaby quickly looked around the table and added, "I know these examples sound like coincidences, and I know you might find me overly preoccupied with the cash value of the stock, but this is my company, this business has been my entire life. Whenever something bad happens to the company, I feel physical pain, which has nothing to do with money." He cleared his throat quietly, then resumed. "We do have, my wife and I, quite an ambitious retirement plan in mind, and considering the number of lonely nights I've put her through because of my demanding job, I have every intention of making it happen."

"Can you share with us what that plan is?" Steve asked.

"We've had our hearts and minds set on this island in the Bahamas. It's large enough to build a small resort and small enough to call private. Governments sell many things these days, trying to make ends meet in their economic struggles, and this is our opportunity. It's called Twilight Cay. Twelve hundred acres of undeveloped land in the Atlantic Ocean. My wife thinks I cannot retire without something to do, but she is adamant about spending her golden years by the water."

"Who else knows about your plans?" Steve's question was met with a nod of silent approval from Tom.

"I don't think many people do. Both my wife and I are quite careful. We wouldn't want our daydreaming to be misconstrued as boasting about our money, or whatever other negative image the words 'private island' could bring to people's minds."

"How about your intentions to sell significant portions of your stock? Who knows about that?" Alex ventured her first question in a timid voice.

"Quite a few people, I'm afraid. The board of directors, all the executive leadership team, and all support functions involved in drafting related paperwork, such as the legal department, and admin assistants."

Alex nodded a silent thank you.

"Please continue, Dr. Barnaby," Tom suggested.

Dr. Barnaby stood and began pacing the room again, slowly, as to gather his troubled thoughts. He briefly touched the perfect knot of his necktie, to ensure it was still in place.

"This might be unrelated, but I've decided to mention it anyway. We've conducted an employee engagement survey. We've surveyed all 900 employees, both corporate and manufacturing, on a number of key engagement factors: their satisfaction with their work, compensation, pride to be working for NanoLance, whether they are looking to change jobs, all standard engagement questions, all anonymous, of course. We have allowed for open-ended questions, so they can freely input whatever it is they see as dissatisfactory with their place of employment. The results were quite worrisome. Not only did we score well below the industry average, but also no one trusted me—us, the leadership team—with no reasons mentioned about why.

"Most open comment fields were left empty. What really triggered my suspicions was that the survey results kept being postponed; I had to insistently keep asking for them." He suddenly looked tired. "I am afraid of looking my own people in the eye. They are unhappy, and they don't even trust me to fix it anymore. They must think I am the most clueless dinosaur of all the technology CEOs in history . . . and they might be right!" His escalated tone of voice was a surprise. It revealed the storm brewing beneath the apparently calm surface of his contained demeanor.

"It might not be too late to convince them to the contrary, Dr. Barnaby," Tom said in a comforting voice. "Some of your people are still willing to provide you with the information needed to make changes and correct things," he continued, pointing at the handwritten note still displayed on the wall screen. "That's why we're here, to do something about all this."

"I'm sorry, you're right. I apologize for my outburst; this is an emotional issue for me. Let's continue," he said, sitting down again and taking a newspaper clipping out of his briefcase. Brian took it promptly to the scanner. The wall screen displayed a news article talking about a drone involved in a friendly fire incident, killing civilians and allied forces in Afghanistan.

"No one knows why this drone opened fire on our friends and allies. Yet. What we do know is that NanoLance makes the navigation and positioning chips for many US drones currently in service." Dr. Barnaby's voice was down to a whisper. "We make the guidance chips, guidance software, and target recognition and acquisition software for almost all drone manufacturers in this country, and also for some abroad. We have an assembly line for a few new drone models, as the most recent addition to our military product offering."

The silence in the room was deafening, as the implications of Dr. Barnaby's words were sinking in.

Dr. Barnaby stood slowly. He looked pale and exhausted, about to fall apart. He leaned against the massive conference room table with a wrinkled, trembling hand, trying to maintain his balance. "This company has been my life. It's supposed to be my legacy, and my retirement income. All my life I have held my head high, and I have been proud of my work, but now I don't know anymore. If we can't sort out and fix this mess, I am finished."

Alex could hear her heart rhythm escalating to a deafening beat, while her panicked thoughts were racing. *This is my first case? Oh, God . . . Where do I even start?*

A pile of blue file folders were scattered on the conference room table. A large binder caught Alex's eye, the one that had "NANOLANCE" written in black, bold marker across the front cover. It contained a brief history of the company, key dates, milestones and events in its recent history, financial results going back ten years, staff and client lists, and other various data that Dr. Barnaby had deemed useful for their initial review.

Alex picked that single binder and set it aside. She already knew most of the numbers in there, at the end of a sleepless night, powered by multiple trips to the coffee machine.

She pulled the rest of the file folders in front of her and opened the first one.

Angela Prescott, Vice President, Human Resources. Graduated with honors from San Francisco State University and held a master's degree in organizational development. The woman in the picture looked sure of herself, somewhat proud, smiling with confidence. A beautiful face with harmonious features, dark brown eyes, and wavy brown hair combed back, showing a large forehead with almost no wrinkles on it. *Nice to meet you,* Alex thought, while continuing to read. Her file indicated she was 47 years old and had been with the company for almost 15 years. Handwritten notes described a top performing human resources practitioner and an excellent leader and praised management initiatives she had implemented and organizational development initiatives she had led. Alex gave the photo one more look and moved to the next folder.

Dustin Sheppard, Chief Technology Officer. Graduated with honors from California Institute of Technology (Caltech) in 1992; majored in science. He had significant course work and achievements in software development, and was published in science journals. The man in the photo was still attractive, yet cold and somewhat unfriendly. Completely bald and clean-shaven, he had a sharp appearance enhanced by a black shirt and self-assured attitude, radiating strength of a dangerous kind. He had the "all business" demeanor; he seemed efficient, focused, and procedural. *The man who never smiles,* Alex thought, moving to the next file.

Benjamin Walker, Chief Operating Officer. Master of business administration (MBA), here was another executive dressed all in black, at least when the photos attached to his file were taken, another man who didn't ever seem to smile.

Relatively handsome, but with ice-cold eyes and a reserved, yet vigilant mien, his appearance was that of a feline predator hiding in the shadows. *Interesting specimen*, Alex thought, closing Walker's folder.

Chandler Griffiths, Chief Sales Officer. Another MBA, this degree was built on top of a bachelor's degree in marketing. He was the youngest executive so far— pure breed Ivy League, pale, with a fine moustache, and determined eyes. There was not a hair on his head either, most likely shaven clean to hide a receding hairline. *Hair doesn't seem to last long around here*, Alex thought. Chandler seemed all business, but in a different manner from Sheppard. He was less threatening. Alex could easily picture him selling to government agencies, discussing new technologies and research grants. His entire being radiated determination to succeed, a great attribute for a sales leader.

Alex opened the last folder in the pile.

Audrey Kramer, Chief Financial Officer. MBA and Certified Management Accountant. Here was the oldest executive on the team. She had a smiling face with tired eyes, and shoulder-length hair, bleached blond to cover the gray. Her roots were showing slightly, just enough to tell the story. Her picture revealed pale skin, somewhat wrinkled, which made sense for her age, well into her fifties. She seemed to have the coolness and mental power to lead the finances of such a complex operation through all kinds of hard times. Dressed in black. *What else is new?*

Alex sighed and closed the last folder. She picked up the pile of folders and headed toward Tom's office, where the others were waiting for her to finish her review. This morning they were meeting for a brainstorming session. They wanted to take a look at the initial facts, then analyze and speculate on the causes and effects stemming from these. With a little bit of luck, she hoped to leave the session armed with some ideas and directions to help her get started on the right path.

Tom's office door was wide open. He was comfortably leaning back in his leather chair, engulfed in the refined smoke of a cigar. Steve was standing by the open window, his features lit by the warm, spring sun. He was playing with the sunrays, casting shadows with the tip of his shoe on the various areas of the carpet pattern, deeply emerged in his activity.

"I'm done," Alex said, "want me to close the door?"

Tom nodded yes. "Any conclusions?" he asked.

"No, nothing so far."

"Alex, give us a summary, please," Steve said, moving away from the sunlit carpet near the window, in favor of a chair, closer to Tom's desk.

"All right. So, this is what we know," Alex started, pulling up her notes. "There are five senior executives on Dr. Barnaby's team. There are hundreds of employees, 932 to be exact. I've reviewed in detail the files on the senior leadership team. There is nothing obvious in the personnel files to account for any of the complaints."

"How about your gut? What does your gut tell you?" Tom asked.

She searched his eyes, a bit hesitant.

"Always look at things from all perspectives. While reviewing those personnel records, who did you like and who did you not like? That is how your gut speaks to you. Which one of those people would you invite into your home? With whom would you leave your kid?"

"Definitely I like Dr. Barnaby, I would have to say, although I know he is not the subject of this," Alex replied without thinking.

"Yes, but you might also be correct. Your gut gave you a piece of information right there: probably none of these executives measure up to Dr. Barnaby. Who's your next favorite?"

"That would be Chandler Griffiths, sales," Alex said, flipping though her files.

"And next?"

"I am hesitant between Kramer and Prescott, finance and human resources respectively."

"So you did not like any of the two front-runners? That is interesting. Could you tell us why?"

"I'm not exactly sure," Alex said. "They're both highly commended, have a lot of experience, and have exceptional credentials, so there are no valid rational reasons for this preference. I guess it's just my gut."

"What else do you have?"

"Not much. Not a conclusion, anyway. I do have a potential action plan."

Steve pulled his chair closer to the desk, clapping his hands with excitement. "Great, let's hear it!"

Alex started scribbling on the whiteboard. "We have four major issues that Dr. Barnaby brought to our attention: the handwritten note, fluctuating stock price, employee engagement, and potential issues with the products." As she was speaking, she was drawing on the whiteboard a table with four columns, each column titled by one of the issues. "Let's call these four issues the four key complaints, and number them one through four," she continued, picking up a red marker and numbering the columns. "Now let's talk about each one and see how, if at all, it correlates with the other key complaints." She picked the handwritten note from the table and quickly examined it up close. "Number one. We know it was sneaked into Dr. Barnaby's pocket, so we can assume the author was afraid to speak directly to Dr. Barnaby."

"Or be seen speaking with him," Steve added.

"Or be seen—that's a somewhat different story," Alex continued undeterred, "but we're still talking about fear." She wrote *fear* in the first column, right under the title. "Moving on to the note's content, we have a reference to people dying, which, to Dr. Barnaby's point, does not play like a threat. It sounds more like . . ." she turned and underlined the word she had just written on the board, "fear. Fear is also reflected by the note's content."

Both Steve and Tom were listening, and both seemed to agree with her thinking. Tom was taking quick one-word notes, making Alex curious. Was she missing something? Was she wrong in her deductions? There was going to be a time to find that out later, after she was finished.

"The note speaks of people dying," she continued, "so I would think it might be worth looking into past deaths involving, well, anyone connected to NanoLance. Employees, military personnel, civilians overseas, anything that could be related to NanoLance. My logic is that if a random employee was able to link people's deaths to the company, so could we."

"What if the employee was not random? What if it's someone whose position with the company provides access to information, allowing him or her to link the events?" Tom asked, with his usual encouraging smile.

"True," she conceded, blushing slightly, "I jumped to conclusions. I am sorry."

Tom dismissed the apology with a wave of his hand.

"We should still look into this," she said, turning to the whiteboard and writing the word *death(s)* right under *fear*. "Could be more than one dead," she said, justifying the potential plural of the word.

"Yes, we should definitely explore this avenue," Tom agreed, jotting one more note on his pad.

"We know Dr. Barnaby did not report the note incident, and we have no way to get fingerprints now, after the note has been through so many hands." She picked up the note from Tom's desk and continued. *"Please stop this insanity or more people will die,"* she said, reading the note again, to refresh everyone's memory. "I noticed the polite addressing, leading me to believe the author doesn't consider Dr. Barnaby directly responsible for these deaths, but rather someone who has the power to change things for the better, if he is willing to learn what's wrong in the first place."

"Interesting conclusion," Steve said. "What made you think that's the case?"

"There's no negative feeling in the note toward Dr. Barnaby. There's no venom, no contempt. If the note's author thought that Dr. Barnaby is directly responsible for these deaths, I think the note would read more along the lines of 'stop this insanity, you irresponsible maniac,' or 'killer,' or whatever. At the very least, it wouldn't include the word please."

"I think you're right," Steve said. "If there were a direct link between Barnaby and these deaths, the author's opinion would be directly accusatory toward him."

"And more venomous. Let's not forget the note's author is risking something to try to stop the bad stuff from happening, so he, or she, is a good guy. Such a good guy would feel strongly against someone who's directly responsible for one or more deaths." She paused to look at the note again. "We can assume, by the fact that the note was handwritten in a hurry and crumpled, rather than folded, that the author was pressed for time. This spells out that the author saw an opportunity and quickly took advantage of it. He did not expect to come so close to Dr. Barnaby. Then it's safe to assume he doesn't usually come into contact with him; they do not roam the same corridors, nor do they casually meet by the coffee machine."

She turned to the whiteboard again, writing and underlining at the bottom of the first column the word *author*, and under it the phrases *good guy, not usual entourage, rare encounters, remote?*

"This could mean they only came in contact in passing, didn't even speak at the party." She turned away from the whiteboard and continued. "Do we have any possibility to do a handwriting analysis on this note? Can we use a lab or something? I'm not expecting much, but it might be worth it."

"I'll see that it gets done," Steve said, taking a quick note on his pad.

"Number two, the stock price issue, has me stupefied. The only things I can think of doing don't seem promising in terms of results. I could investigate each leak, and find out where the information came from, but without authority, it's highly unlikely anyone will reveal anything to me. I could look at old emails and communications dating back around those events, but I think that whoever did this was no idiot. Chances are they covered their tracks well. So, on this one I am stumped," she sighed, shrugging and looking down.

"Chin up, Alex, if this was an easy job, anyone could do it," Tom said. "You did great on number one, on number two you need to change the approach."

"How?" she asked.

"Once you're going to be working for NanoLance, you'll have the time to observe. You'll be looking for motive and opportunity, and you will figure out who stands to gain the most from this maneuver. Then you'll piece the puzzle together."

"I see," Alex said, without looking convinced.

"When you presented the leadership team to us, you didn't like any of the front-runners, remember?"

"Yes, that's true. But why do you consider Sheppard and Walker to be front-runners?"

"Because they are the leaders in the succession race, the most likely choices for the CEO role, after Dr. Barnaby retires."

"I see. Well, to some extent. I can understand why Benjamin Walker is a front-runner. As chief operating officer he is second in command, and it makes sense for him to be the successor. However, why would you consider Dustin Sheppard as a front-runner? He's chief of technology, and these executives rarely climb higher in the ranks, to the CEO role."

"Questions are yet again wasted, Alex." Tom paused, allowing himself a long drag from his cigar, and then, slowly exhaling the smoke, he watched it twirl in the sunrays.

"Ugh . . ." Alex's reaction brought a smile on Steve's face.

"Again, you're not thinking. While it might be generally true that technology leaders seldom rise to the top level in corporations, the only exception to this rule happens in—"

"Technology corporations. Duh!" Alex finished the phrase, with a frustrated smile. "I wasn't thinking. OK, so they're both front-runners. That means some fight over power could most likely exist; we need to consider that."

"Or an alliance," Steve offered.

"An alliance? How could that be serving both their interests?" Alex asked.

"See how you're showing your true nature, Alex?" Steve said. "You wouldn't consider forming an alliance, then turning against your ally at the right moment and stabbing him in the back. However, any of these executives might consider doing just that."

"What would keep both of them in an alliance? Wouldn't it be obvious for at least one of them that he's at risk of being screwed?"

"Not necessarily. They might not think that far, or, most likely, if both of them believe they're smarter than the other, then they both think they stand a better chance of screwing their adversary first. They both could be thinking they're leading this game."

"Nice attitude," Alex said, rolling her eyes.

"Alex, why don't you continue your initial approach," Tom said, "let's move to the third issue on the list."

"Right," Alex said, turning toward the whiteboard. "Employee engagement. What I have seen is that, on most categories, employee engagement is lower than the local and industry averages, just like Dr. Barnaby stated. I'm also encountering, in the comments, few usable entries. Some caught my interest, though. One stated—" she shuffled her notes and found the one she was looking for, "OK, here it is: 'Do you think I don't know we've got static IPs?'" She looked at Tom and Steve and saw the need to explain further.

"An employee's so-called *confidential entry* in such a survey can be less than confidential in two situations. One is when he or she is alone or almost alone in a distinguishable category of the analyzed group. Let's say, for instance, that the manufacturing group gets the survey stats analyzed as a separate group, because they are large enough—they have hundreds of employees, so the assumption of confidentiality is realistic, due to the large number of entries.

However, this survey is also geared to analyze data separately, within the group, by job level. Therefore, if the executive level, for example, has only three roles, let's say two directors and one vice president, their specific entries can be easily separated from the rest of the group, thus their confidentiality is compromised. Especially in the case of leaders, expressing less-than-stellar engagement is risky, and they know it. However, not all of them know their entries are not as confidential as the company is stating. This is one mode in which the promised confidentiality in such surveys is breached."

She reached for her coffee cup and found it empty. She put it back on the desk, with a quick sigh. "The second one, the static IP this worker is referencing, is a bit more technical. All networked computers can obtain their IP dynamically, as in getting a new IP on each startup, or statically, where the machine has a well-defined IP that will remain associated with the specific machine and its user, even after the computer restarts. If the survey interface is set to capture IP addresses associated with individual entries, the confidentiality of the entries is compromised to the individual level, regardless of group and group size."

"What's an IP?" Tom ventured.

"Stands for Internet protocol, the rules under which a computer can function in a network. This set of rules contains an address that precisely identifies each networked computer."

"Why would a confidential survey platform capture IPs?" Steve asked.

"Generally there is some benefit from slicing and dicing the survey data by geographical area, therefore the functionality has been built in. There is also some expectation of ethics on behalf of the employer companies, so the survey service providers are not assuming their clients will abuse the confidentiality promise they make to their employees. If it happens . . . it's pathetic. But it does happen."

She instinctively reached for the coffee cup again, then she stopped midway, remembering it was empty, just as empty as it had been a few minutes before. "Going back to this employee's comment, his statement reveals, again, fear." She stopped to write the word under the third column of her table, on the whiteboard. "Because of the lower than average scores, we can assume that employees are dissatisfied with their work environments, while some might even be disgruntled." She wrote *dissatisfaction* under the same column, and then continued. "Another entry states 'Are you serious???' The comment ended with three question marks, showing an emotional response."

"What was the question?" Steve asked.

"The question? What do you mean?"

"What was the question these comments were answering?"

"Oh. Yes. The question was 'Please give us your feedback on any concerns you have with your work environment. Your confidentiality is guaranteed.' So the emotional response may be toward the confidentiality guarantee."

"Or toward the perception of futility of such efforts, or both," Steve said.

"How do you mean?"

"If the employee perceives that the feedback he is willing to give will fall on deaf ears, or be in the hands of a decision maker who is not interested in righting any wrongs, he would feel his efforts are futile, and he can decide to voice his disappointment. If, on top of that, the employee also perceives his willingness to give open and honest feedback as a potential career risk, he is even more frustrated. He can even feel insulted—insulted by the company's claim of confidentiality—which he knows is false—and the appearance of pursuing the employees' best interest—which he knows is hypocritical and deceitful. Hence, the emotional response. What do you think?" Steve asked, looking toward Tom.

"Very possible. I can't think of any other scenario for now, but more ideas might come to mind as time passes and we review more information. Alex, do you have any other notable comments from the survey?"

"One more. This one states, cryptically, 'I will not repeat myself for the third time over,' indicating he or she has provided feedback twice before and has seen no improvement. This comment is helpful; it indicates the problem is not new— it has been around for a while."

"So, what's your action plan for the survey?" Tom asked.

"I thought of spending some time further analyzing this data, looking at differences among groups, and trying to pinpoint which are the most troubled areas. But in my experience, employees are unhappy as a consequence, not as a cause. I'd like to pursue the causes, rather than analyze the consequences. My guess is that if we figure out and fix what's wrong in the other three problem areas, this one will fall into place on its own. What do you think?

"I agree," Tom said, "let's consider this a secondary issue."

Steve nodded thoughtfully.

"Proceeding to number four and the most troublesome one, the drone safety concerns. This one, well, is extremely risky to dig into."

"Why?" Steve asked.

"I can't go around and measure the reliability and safety parameters of the products. I can't even assess the quality of the software products they install, well, that maybe I could, but the physical quality of the products is out of my reach. I can't go around asking questions either." Her voice reached a higher pitch, reflecting her anguish.

"Take it easy," Tom said, in his calming voice, "don't think what you cannot do. Don't think impossible, make shopping lists. Don't think obstacles, think needs."

"Needs?"

"If I were to ask you to dig a sixty-feet long, three feet deep, two feet wide ditch in front of this building, before end of business today, what would you say? Can it be done?"

"Um . . . sure, but I need workers, shovels, excavators, power tools—"

"Yes, these are the needs. The resources needed to complete the task. Think resources; don't think it can't be done. If you take the complex task you have on hand and break it down into simpler, smaller tasks, then get resources for each task, you're home free. So, what do you need?"

Alex thought about it for a little while, her gaze out the window, at the perfectly blue sky. It felt good to construct the list, the feeling of frustrating powerlessness fading away, giving place to her relentless initiative and courage.

"I'd need to be in a job that has access to their servers. A technology assignment would work great. I'd need access to all their facilities, maybe tour the plant at least once or twice. Maybe launch a technology initiative that involves the plant, especially the metrics they use to measure the business, including quality outputs." She smiled mischievously.

"I'd need some freedom of movement, from corporate to plant and back. I'd need exposure to what Dr. Barnaby tells his executives, so I guess this translates as access to leadership meetings, even if it's on tape, after the fact. I'd need the use of a lab, outside of the office, that can run quick tests for me, both physical and software." She paused to catch her breath, saw the empty cup in front of her, and continued. "Oh, and I need a cup of coffee, real bad."

"Thought you'd never ask," Steve said, standing up with his empty cup in his hand, grabbing hers, and turning toward Tom. "Anything for you?"

"No, I'm fine, thank you." Tom opened a folder and examined an organizational chart with several spots circled in red marker. Steve came back, carrying two steaming cups of fresh coffee.

"There happens to be a suitable opening at NanoLance," Tom said, pushing the organizational chart in front of Alex and Steve, "one that would fulfill most of Alex's needs. It's the director of infrastructure and support."

Alex struggled to contain a smile. *Wow,* she thought, *my first executive role.*

"There are several advantages to this position," Tom continued, undisturbed, "mainly the fact that the role is already open, and Dr. Barnaby doesn't have to interject and create it. This role reports into the chief technology officer, Dustin Sheppard, one of your least favorites, Alex."

"I'll manage," Alex said, smile gone, replaced by a sense of doom.

"The role doesn't bring the freedom of movement between corporate and plant that you require, but this is where Dr. Barnaby can help. We will ask him to become more involved in the hiring and termination of executives and, as part of their onboarding process, to allow all new executives to spend time in all critical areas of the business, plant included. This can be easily done." Tom looked at Steve and asked, "Anything else you'd like to add?"

"Yes," Steve said. "Alex, we'd have to get you prepared to interview and get the offer for this role, ideally without any intervention from Dr. Barnaby. I'd like the two of us, and maybe Brian if he can find the time, to train you some more, offer some insights into leadership in companies as large as this one, and give you some more books to read. We have a couple of weeks, but not more. You do realize how pressed for time we are on this case. However, before anything else I'd like to know how you feel, Alex. Are you ready for this?"

"I am. I'd be lying if I said I wasn't scared a little bit, but I'm also excited to go in and find out what's going on. I love a good mystery, love the challenge."

Tom nodded, with an encouraging smile. "I was counting on your enthusiasm," he said, "and I am sure you will get to the bottom of this faster than any of us could. Tomorrow you'll be working with one of the best résumé writers I have encountered—my wife, Claire. She will write a résumé guaranteed to get you an interview for this job. The rest will be up to you, and you'll do just fine, I'm sure of it. But, before we proceed with this client, do keep one thing in mind, at all times."

Tom's voice turned grave, as he continued. "The issues you will be investigating are serious. One is a potential major fraud, the other one has a potential connection to the recent drone incident that led to the loss of innocent lives. The person or persons responsible will have a lot to lose if they are exposed. Be very careful."

Starting a new job usually brought Alex a mixture of excitement and energy, fueled by her hopes that the new opportunity would propel her career, while she would be recognized and appreciated for her hard work. Starting fresh, with her innate optimism, was a sure recipe for exhilaration, not shadowed by any self-doubt, or fear of the unknown.

This time was different though. The excitement of entering a new organization, dimmed by a cautious, rational alertness, was barely surfacing. Alex had to make a conscious effort to show the full-blast enthusiasm of any new hire—especially a younger one. Focused on the image she was presenting to those around her, she had barely noticed the imposing building that housed NanoLance headquarters.

She approached the high-rise office building in a state of growing vigilance, not paying much attention to the sun's reflections off the turquoise glass of the upper floors. The reception area, wide open, was flooded in sunlight reflected by shiny blue-gray tiles. The gleaming tiles forced Alex to focus on keeping her balance, while walking on the slippery floor.

Oh, yes, she thought, *the ultimate form of discrimination in the workplace . . . expect women to wear high heels, then shine these darn floors until we can't move anymore.* She approached the reception desk and gave a quick sigh before stating her name. The massive piece of furniture provided some relief in her efforts to maintain her balance on the gleaming floors. She gladly leaned against the desk.

"Miss Hoffmann?" a voice from behind her asked.

She turned to find a young, neatly dressed woman holding a clipboard and a file folder, with her hand extended in her direction. "Yes," she replied, shaking the hand offered to her, "I am Alex Hoffmann, nice to meet you."

"I am Kathleen Bentley from human resources, nice to meet you too. Please follow me."

Kathleen led the way down a wide corridor to a conference room. Alex followed closely, noticing the flooring was different. *Carpeting. Yes, I like carpeting*, she thought, straightening her posture, regaining her confidence.

She sat down at a conference table, across from Kathleen, whose smile seemed to be permanent, without variation, the typical professional smile that people-facing employees develop as a second nature and wear without any effort.

"Alex, please let me start by welcoming you to NanoLance. We are excited to have you here. A professional of your caliber will bring significant strength to our technology team, and we have all been looking forward to your start date."

"Thank you, I am excited to be here," Alex said. "I was happy to hear that you wanted me to come to work a day earlier."

"Yes, indeed," Kathleen explained, "we like to get the human resources paperwork and orientation out of the way, so on Monday you can hit the ground running, in a manner of speaking."

"OK, this is great!" She refrained from commenting on how unusual this practice was.

"Good, then let's start by filling out these forms," Kathleen said, pushing in front of her an open folder with paperwork in both pockets. "On the right side, you have tax forms, non-disclosure, non-compete, and emergency contact forms. On the left, you have benefits enrollment forms. All these need to be filled out and signed before we can proceed. I'll give you a few minutes," she said, promptly leaving the room and closing the door behind her.

Twenty minutes later, as Alex was just putting her pen down, Kathleen entered the conference room, wearing the same unaltered smile. "Are we ready? Great! Let's go for a tour," she said, showing Alex the way toward the slippery lobby, where the elevators were taking turns at loading and unloading hurried people.

They entered a luxurious elevator, complete with a flat screen TV showing the news and the stock-market ticker. On the back wall of the elevator, a mirror reflected Alex's image. She was dressed sharply in a Jones New York charcoal business suit, white satin shirt, completed by Gucci shoes and a briefcase. She smiled back at her reflection, proud of the image she presented, and reassured she looked her part.

"We're going to start at the top and work our way down," Kathleen said, pressing the top button, number 35. "At the very top, we have the executive floor, where Dr. Barnaby, our CEO, has his office. Also on 35, we have the boardroom and the offices of all the senior executives. Moira, Dr. Barnaby's executive assistant, also has her office here." The elevator stopped, and the doors slid open to reveal a quiet, lushly decorated floor, with thick carpets and massive furniture. The floor seemed deserted.

"Not a whole lot of activity here," Alex said. "Where is everyone? I was hoping to meet them."

"Oh, Dr. Barnaby is at the plant in Alpine today, and the senior leaders usually prefer to work from their secondary offices on the respective floors they manage, so this is quiet here most of the time. However, I think that you'll be able to meet most of the leaders today. I know Mr. Sheppard, your new boss, is in his downstairs office, waiting to meet with you."

After briefly touring the semi-dark floor, they headed for the elevators. One by one, Alex toured the human resources department, followed by finance, accounting, payroll, administration, purchasing, vendor management, manufacturing, marketing, and sales. Everywhere they went, Kathleen introduced her to countless, smiling people who shook her hand, welcomed her, and then resumed their activities.

No senior executives, in any of the business areas, were available to meet her. All departments seemed to operate quietly and effectively, without visible leadership, in a low-key hum of orchestrated activity. Alex was trying her best to remember as many of the faces, names, and job titles as she could. After a while though, they started to blend in her overloaded memory. *How will I remember everyone?*

"And, finally, this is your home," Kathleen said, leading her to the third floor. "This is where information technology resides." She paused for a second, took a quick breath, and then said in a quick whisper, "Good luck."

Kathleen led the way to an impressive office of glass walls. Facing away from them and looking out the window, a tall, bald man, dressed in black from head to toe, was talking on his cell phone. Kathleen opened the office door, alerting him to their presence. He turned, mumbled something in his cell phone, and then put it on his desk.

"Finally," he said, "you've made it, only twenty minutes late." His voice was a quiet, hissing whisper, conveying the paralyzing coldness of a snake.

Alex started explaining. "Sir, I was here—"

"Of course, you would have some excuse, no doubt," the man continued unabated, "of which I do not wish to learn. Sit," he said, pointing at the chair in front of his massive desk. He turned his attention toward Kathleen, who remained frozen in the doorway. "Anything I can do for *you*?"

Stammering an inaudible apology, Kathleen left hurriedly, closing the door behind her.

The man refocused his attention on Alex. "I am supposed to wish you welcome on a day like this." He paused, studying her.

Alex felt the sweat breaking at the roots of her hair. She remembered Dustin Sheppard from her interview—the interview she thought she had failed. She remembered how she got her courage up, after getting the job offer, thinking he couldn't possibly be that bad on a daily basis. She had been wrong.

"We'll have to see about that welcome," Sheppard continued. "Directors come and go, proving they are nothing but a waste of my time," he said, pausing slightly between words, as to emphasize them without raising his voice from that low hiss of a deadly snake. "I do not welcome any waste of my time. How will you be any different?"

She took a deep breath, remembering what she had to do.

"I am positive I can make a big difference and bring consistent value to the business. I have—"

"Don't waste my time," Sheppard interrupted again, "*please* tell me specifics." The venom in his voice removed all the politeness of the words he spoke.

"I am planning to start by evaluating current resources, capabilities, and infrastructure, and assess whether they are suited for the objectives that we have, for our short- and long-term future. Then I'll prepare recommendations for you to review." She paused, waiting for Sheppard's response, which did not come. Sheppard sat in his massive leather chair, eyes half closed, with an impenetrable expression on his face. His features, although elegant and harmonious, seemed carved in stone—cold and immobile.

She continued, repressing a shudder. "I would like to meet my team as soon as possible. I am planning to assess their skill levels and capabilities and prepare action items regarding staffing, again, for your review."

"If I would have had *any* interest to hire an assistant to prepare things for my review, I would have hired *that* person instead of you. From you, I am expecting results."

"Yes, sir, I understand."

"That's it for today."

Alex stood up abruptly. "It was a pleasure seeing you again," she said, extending her hand.

Sheppard did not move. "I doubt that. You are dismissed."

Alex did not recall how she got to her car, still under the influence of the intimidating Dustin Sheppard, her new boss. She sat behind the wheel, in the refreshing streams of conditioned air, trying to focus on her busy agenda for the weekend—moving into a new home, her first house. A long-time dream was coming true—getting out of apartment living and into the delights of suburban living. But somehow, she failed to feel the excitement.

Her prevailing thoughts were lingering around the strangeness of NanoLance's corporate culture. She had spent less than three hours in that building, enough though to notice a few troublesome signs of dysfunction. The notable absence of key executives was one example. The climate of fear fostered by Sheppard, without any apparent consequence or corrective measure, was another. The peculiarity of having new employees come to finalize paperwork on the Friday before their start date was unheard of. The overall weirdness of the building's atmosphere, regardless of department, was, by far, the most annoying and intriguing.

Leaning back in her car seat, Alex pictured Tom asking her, "Weird how, exactly?" She began a mental conversation with Tom, organizing her thoughts and drawing some conclusions, while her memories of the NanoLance tour were still fresh. Well, the absence of laughter, of relaxed human interaction was one aspect of it, especially considering that the key executives were absent and it was Friday, casual chatter should have been present here and there.

The overall feel was one of silent efficiency, which, at first glance, might seem ideal for a business environment, but it's not. In the realities of human psychology, such environments are not naturally occurring; there has to be a stressor of sorts to yield this kind of silent efficiency. She pictured Dr. Barnaby being the stressor . . . *Nah* . . . She rejected the thought as not plausible. She saw Dr. Barnaby more likely to engage in casual conversations with his employees, than obliterating the normal hallway interactions.

One look at the time and she started the engine, knowing she was going to be late for the appointment with her new landlord. Preoccupied with solving the mysteries of this odd corporate culture, she pulled out of the parking lot and into the solid traffic heading for I-5, oblivious to her surroundings. A few seconds later, a gray Ford sedan pulled out of the same parking lot, following her from a safe distance.

The anchor's voice was bubbly with excitement, moving at an incredible pace from one stock price to the next.

"NanoLance Incorporated, ticker symbol NNLC, lost almost 8 percent in trading today, bringing the stock price to $134 per share. This decline is attributed greatly to the findings released in the friendly fire incident in Kandahar. NanoLance has been confirmed as the manufacturer of record for the Kandahar drone. The market was quick to react, instilling relatively high volume sell-offs that brought NanoLance's stock price down significantly for a single day of trading.

"All UAV manufacturers shed blood on the markets today, but NanoLance took the biggest loss, declining from yesterday's closing by 7.69 percent. Further declines in this stock's performance are to be expected, but not as severe. Analysts still call NanoLance a definite "buy and hold" investment, and, after all, the full results of the Kandahar inquiry are yet to be revealed.

"From *Money Markets Review*, this is Vincent Moran, wishing you a fortunate day."

A multi-tone electronic chime startled Alex, unfamiliar with her new home's doorbell.

"Oh, crap," she muttered softly, then continued in a louder voice, "Just a minute!"

She wasn't expecting anyone. The frantic day of moving had left her tired and excited, ready to step into the shower and then call it a day. Her new three-bedroom rental house was clean, functional, friendly, and accommodating, despite the fact that the property owner wasn't all that bright. The movers had come and gone, having little trouble relocating her few belongings. These seemed even fewer now, because of the larger space. They were scattered here and there, without a clear concept, in an attempt to furnish all rooms, no matter how minimally.

Grabbing her bathrobe, she headed for the door and looked through the peephole. No one was there, but she could hear the sound of a small truck pulling away. She cautiously opened the door and looked around; there was no one there. As she was about to close the door, her eyes caught the large flower basket on her doormat. She picked it up, took it inside, and set it on her kitchen table. Under the lush flower arrangement, made of at least three dozen roses, lay a bottle of Martini Dry Vermouth, and a simple, white card with the words "Congratulations on your new home" on one side, and "Tom and the gang" on the other. With a sigh of relief and a smile reflecting the warmth she felt in her heart, she grabbed the bottle and put it in the fridge.

For the flowers, the solution was not so simple. Alex didn't have a vase. With a quick glance at the recently hung electronic clock on the wall, she decided to go out and get a vase that was suitable for the nicest flowers she had ever been given.

Almost an hour later, in line at one of the check-out registers of the Mira Mesa Target store, she was pushing a flat-bed shopping cart, filled with so much more than the vase she had come for.

A new 53 inch LCD TV that happened to be on sale, catching her eye. A wireless 5.1 surround system to go with it, a Blu-Ray player, and a TV stand to accommodate all that. A couple Blu-Ray movies she loved. A set of tall, cocktail glasses made of Bohemian crystal, and a vase, of course.

Chatting casually with the cashier, she noticed a skinny, bony man with intense eyes, two registers down, checking out with a mega-size pack of Charmin toilet paper. He was looking at her, but when their eyes met, he looked away.

"Sorry, ma'am, it's declined," the cashier woke her up to reality, returning her Visa card. "Do you have another card you can use?"

"Oh." Alex smiled uncomfortably, unzipping her wallet. "Let's see." Many cards were in her wallet, most of them still maxed out. None of them had room for the splurge. With a bit of hesitation, she pulled The Agency's Gold MasterCard, with the still unknown spending limit. She'd have to explain the expense to Tom and pay him back on her payday. He'd understand.

"This one worked just fine, ma'am, here you go," the smiling cashier invited her to sign the receipt. "Will you need help loading all that in your car?"

"Yes, much appreciated," Alex said. Seconds later, she was on her way toward the parking lot, with a store associate in tow.

The man who had caught her attention was nowhere in sight. *Oh, well,* Alex thought, *with so much toilet paper on his shopping list, I bet he's run home to his fifteen kids. Then, if that's the case, why was he checking me out?*

The man Alex had seen in the store was behind the wheel of a gray Ford sedan, no toilet paper anywhere. He flipped open a cell phone, speed-dialed a number, and then said: "She checks out." A pause. "Yes, sir." Another pause. "She was even declined on her credit card, sir." A silent frown. "Yes, sir, I will stay on it."

Stephanie Wainwright's perfectly arranged hair filled the TV screen.

"April 20th marked a day of tragedy for our allied forces, as friendly fire from a drone took the lives of four Canadian Combat Logistics Patrol servicemen and wounded two more. Official findings are yet to be released on this case, but, despite the dust of time settling, there are many Canadian and American families who are still waiting for answers to their questions."

The image zoomed out, making room for a view that showed an elderly man, seated on an armchair in his living room.

"With us today, we have Salvatore Romero, the father of Leonard Romero, who was killed on April 20 in Kandahar. Good morning, Mr. Romero, and thank you for speaking with us today."

"Good morning." The man's voice was frail and faint.

"We are sorry for your loss; please accept our heartfelt sympathies," Stephanie said warmly.

"Thank you," the man answered.

"Could you please tell us how you feel about this tragedy?"

"Umm . . . how can I feel? I feel dead inside . . . I'm finished. A man should never live to bury his child. That should never happen. And why? Because of some . . . some flying machine!" His eyes were filling with tears of anger and pain. "A machine! We don't even have people to fly the damn things anymore! A pilot might have seen the Canadian flag on their transport, might have thought about it . . . before firing, before firing . . ."

"Have you been told what happened? Has anyone brought forth an explanation for this tragedy to you?"

"No, nobody spoke to us. Not to me, not to any of the other . . ." His voice was drowned in tears. He made an effort to continue, "the other parents, and wives, and children. Maybe they'll never tell us anything. Maybe there's nothing to tell, just a machine, a damn robot, a flying piece of junk that made a mistake. Is that what took my Lennie away? How am I supposed to go on living with that? Who knows if they're ever gonna tell us anything?"

"We will press for answers, that I personally promise you," Stephanie said dramatically. "We will relentlessly pursue the answers to this tragedy, so that we can foster the hope that such senseless loss never happens again."

She turned to face the camera. "This is Stephanie Wainwright, with *News of the Hour*."

Travel coffee mug in one hand and briefcase in the other, Alex was mingling with other morning-rush NanoLance employees as they were making their way to one of the elevators in the large lobby. On her first day, she already had her day planned to the finest detail. See her office, get set up—30 minutes. Meet her new team—one hour. Meet with a series of directors and vice presidents from all areas of the company—the rest of the day. No time had been set aside for her to spend with her new boss; atypical, yet she felt grateful for that.

The elevator doors slid open on the third floor. She stepped out, trying to find her new office. Just steps away, in the opposite corner of the floor from Sheppard's office, was her workplace, with her name printed neatly on the glass wall and the door open. She stepped in. Her office had no windows and was rather small, but it gave her the privacy she needed to do her job. *Both jobs*, she thought with a silent chuckle.

She sat down at her new desk and opened her new laptop. Everything felt different from what she had envisioned her first day as an executive to be, but she didn't feel like a real executive either. This job was about something else, she reminded herself, this job was about finding the way to right some wrongs, some extremely serious wrongs.

A knock on the glass wall disrupted her thoughts. A young man popped his head in.

"Hi, I'm Louie, Louie Bailey, your analyst?" The young man paused.

Alex smiled, acknowledging him with a nod.

"When you're ready for us, we're in conference room 302," he said, gesturing vaguely.

"Just a minute," Alex said. She sat up, grabbed her briefcase and laptop, and followed Louie across the IT floor.

"The conference rooms are numbered. The first digit or digits stand for the floor number, and then most floors have the same layout for conference rooms, so it's quite simple to remember. You can book the conference rooms, just like you'd book any resource, through Outlook."

They were there. Conference room 302 also had glass walls. There didn't seem to be much privacy anywhere in this building, which was going to be quite helpful from one perspective and a potential problem from another.

At the conference table, two men and a woman were already seated. Louie sat next to the woman, leaving Alex to take the seat at the head of the table. She sat with imperceptible hesitation. It was the first time she had ever led a meeting.

"Hello, everyone, I'm Alex Hoffmann, your new director of support and infrastructure," Alex said, smiling encouragingly.

Without delay, the people around the table started introducing themselves.

"Bob Foster, infrastructure manager." Middle-aged, with a nice smile and kind eyes, he leaned across the table and firmly shook her hand.

"Nice to meet you," Alex replied.

"Alan Walden, hardware deployment manager, nice to meet you." A tall man stood to come around the table to shake her hand. He had intense eyes and a look of permanent worry on his face, yet still managed to convey an image of reliability and dependability.

"Nice to meet you too," Alex replied.

"Lisa Murphy, your support manager. It's a pleasure to meet you." This was a young woman with long, sleek, dark hair, and a look of shyness on her face. She didn't have the face for technology; she seemed more the soft, artistic type.

Alex shook her hand with a smile. Lisa's handshake was in contradiction to her soft demeanor, expressing determination and openness.

"And I'm Louie Bailey, senior analyst for infrastructure and support." Louie looked professional in his charcoal suit and gray shirt, yet his build and gait were revealing of some military background of sorts.

"Nice to meet you, Louie, and thank you for showing me to this conference room." Curious, she continued. "Let me ask you, were you in the Army?"

Chuckles were heard around the table.

"Navy SEAL, retired last year," Louie said. "How could you tell?" he asked, with a wide smile, denoting pride in his background.

"Oh, well," Alex responded with a hand gesture, bringing more smiles around the table, and a more relaxed attitude by all the team members.

Their new boss appeared to be all right.

"Let's allow the lady to order first," Steve said, inviting the waiter to break the old etiquette and pay attention to his guest.

Blushing slightly, Alex picked up the menu.

"I'll have the *controfiletto al pepe nero*, medium well, please."

"Umm . . . nice accent!" Steve smiled and continued, "I'll have the *lombatina di vitella alla griglia*, if you please. Oh, and could we have another bottle of this wonderful wine?"

"Yes, sir, I'll bring another bottle of Chianti."

"So, how's everything going for you?" Once the waiter was gone, Steve's voice had come down to a pleasant, intimate whisper.

"Well, I've met almost all the senior executives, met with my team, but I am yet to meet with my boss for more than five minutes. The guy hates me. I never had that happen to me before. But the feeling is mutual, he gives me the creeps."

"It's normal to have feelings of all sorts regarding the people we work with, but you have to remember not to let those feelings cloud your judgment. On the other hand," Steve continued, not allowing Alex to reassure him, "these feelings can be strong indicators of potential problems, or, as Tom would call it, the voice of your gut. Listen to your gut, but find proof before drawing your conclusion." He took a long, appreciative sip of wine. Then, as he put his wine glass down, he reached and touched Alex's hand.

She almost jolted from the unexpected emotion she felt from the contact with his warm hand.

"What I want to know, first and foremost, is how you feel."

"I feel that with every day I spend there, I am descending lower and lower into a snake pit. The head of operations, Walker, is cynical and aggressive from what I've seen, but I haven't spent too much time with him yet. Kramer, the CFO, is tired and preoccupied. It's as if her mind is constantly on something else, while she struggles to pretend she's there with you. Chandler Griffiths, head of sales, is the only one who behaves somewhat along the lines you'd expect; very driven, very energetic, yet not pushy or intimidating. Prescott, the human resources executive, is the fashion leader of the company, showcasing high-end suits, jewelry, and shoes. As a business leader though, she seems to do exactly what's expected of her, nothing more, and nothing less. I think this woman is beyond politically correct, even in her sleep."

"Most HR people are like that; it's ingrained in their natures. Because they usually have to terminate the employees who make mistakes of all kinds, early on they learn the lesson of acceptable, corporate behavior, and they get reminded daily."

"I get that, but here's what I am noticing. All of them, I mean all the employees, not just the leaders, are stressed in an impersonal, business-only type of behavior. They all seem to want to demonstrate just how professional they are, and how well they can behave. This tells me there is an artificially created stressor at play."

"Good call, Alex, do you know what that is?"

"Wait for it," Alex said, in a playful tone of voice, "I've only been there three days."

"You're right." Steve paused, as the waiter set their plates in front of them. "Looks yummy. So let's shift gears. How's your new home?"

Alex's face lit up. "I absolutely love it! You know, this is my first house since. . . since I left my parents' home. It's peaceful and quiet, the neighbors are reasonably far away from me, I don't even see them, and it's great! You should come visit sometime," she said, then stopped abruptly, blushing at the thought of how Steve might interpret the invitation.

"I will," he responded quickly, unperturbed.

Silverware clattering and casual conversation flowing with ease, they started exploring the exquisite taste of Tuscan cuisine at its best, oblivious to anything else but each other.

Two tables away, munching casually on a selection of cheeses from his plate of *festival di formaggi*, a man watched every move they made.

The laptop on her desk was powering up. Alex impatiently waited for it, so she could get a few things checked before ending her day. Her first week at NanoLance had been quite intensive, with back-to-back meetings with executives, department leaders, program and project managers, and other people she had identified as potentially valuable to meet. Using the cover provided by a somewhat formal on-boarding plan, she was able to meet with almost everyone of interest at this early stage. The only team she was yet to meet was the manufacturing team at the Alpine plant. She was carefully delaying that, waiting for the meeting with her boss to take place first, rather than surprise him with her visit at the plant.

A chime advised her that the laptop was ready. She started digging through system folders and registries, looking for any indication of spy programs or keystroke loggers. *Of course*, she thought, *there you are. I was expecting nothing less*. A software-based keystroke logger was installed on her machine, configured to save in a particular place on the hard disk every single keystroke she typed. This was the perfect surveillance tool for the person who wanted to know everything she did in a day.

With more digging, she was able to locate another spyware program, this one configured to capture screenshots of her work at fixed intervals. The third component to the perfect electronic surveillance was the browser log, a small piece of software that would record all the websites she visited and the time spent on each one.

Alex paused, considering her options. She could install a personal firewall. *They'd find that in no time*, she thought, dismissing the idea. She could uninstall all these pieces of spyware, but they'd also figure that one out pretty fast. She could change the registry settings on her laptop, so that the spyware programs would never start, but they would be on to her immediately, as soon as they got no input from these programs.

She closed the laptop, pulled the power cord from the wall plug, and stuffed everything in her laptop carrying case. She knew exactly what she needed to do.

Almost two hours later, she was ringing the doorbell at Tom's house, laptop bag in one hand, bottle of Martini in the other. She smiled, remembering how stressed she had been on her first visit. Now it felt more like coming home.

Tom opened the door, his eyes directly on the laptop bag.

"How are you, sweetie? How was your day?"

Sweetie? Tom had never called her that. She gazed at him in surprise. His eyes remained on the bag.

"Let me take that from you, come right in. Dinner's almost ready." He stepped quietly in the house, Alex following.

"Where's your smart phone?" Tom asked. "You know how we hate being interrupted over dinner. Please turn that thing off."

She reached inside her pocket and gave Tom her NanoLance issued phone. She was starting to understand.

Tom took the phone, put it in the laptop bag, and shoved everything inside a gun safe he kept in the garage, and then closed the door.

Coming back into the living room, followed closely, as usual, by Little Tom, he turned to Alex and said, "Now we can talk. We're having stuffed portabella mushrooms for dinner. Sound good?"

"Yes," Alex replied cheerfully.

"Great, one more mushroom going on the grill." Tom headed for the kitchen, followed by his human and feline companions.

"Tom, how did you know it was the laptop I was coming to see you about?"

"I didn't. I was being cautious, in case there's a bug planted in your equipment somewhere. Why, what's wrong with it?"

"You mean a voice recording bug? I didn't think of *that*," Alex said and frowned, "but I guess it's just as likely. What I found was spyware, and lots of it."

"Spyware?"

"Little programs installed on the computer, with the sole purpose to record everything I do, every website I visit, every email I write. Even if I work in Word or Excel, they'd still be able to capture every bit of what I am doing."

"Oh, I see." Tom looked preoccupied, almost worried. "Is this common practice?"

"For some companies, it can be. Nothing is private anymore, not at work anyway."

"So you don't believe they're on to you?"

"I would tend to say no, but that's a bigger discussion. Please let me finish with email and computer spyware first."

"Sure." Tom headed out of the kitchen with a Martini for her and a glass of wine for himself. He set both glasses on the coffee table. "I'm all ears."

"Back in the early days of email at work, employees had expectations of privacy regarding the use of company email for personal communication. That's long gone. Technically, the emails are being sent and received on company hardware situated on company property, so the entire email content and activity belongs to the employer—no privacy rights whatsoever. As technology progressed, more advanced systems allowed the recording of all email traffic from a particular server, practically copying each email message going out or coming in. This is, for many companies today, the standard. Smaller, or less-circumspect companies employ a more relaxed policy, screening and copying email traffic only if it contains specific keywords, attachments, or by using other criteria to select messages of interest to them. Questions so far?"

"No, keep going, this is very interesting," Tom replied.

"This technology takes care of all email activity an employee conducts on her business computer. How about everything else? Companies that are extremely sensitive about their activities, or extremely suspicious about their employees, engage the use of keystroke loggers. These are software applications that record every keystroke, allowing those who supervise to reconstruct in detail all of the employee's activity on that particular machine, regardless of software or application used. I could be working five minutes on a Word document, then switch to building a spreadsheet, then enter data in the accounting system—they would know it all, step by step."

"I see," Tom frowned. "Is this typical?"

"Not really, not for everyone anyway. With a company like NanoLance, you would expect to have keystroke loggers in place, due to the sensitive nature of their business. I would also assume that they only audit usage randomly or on complaint."

"On complaint?"

"Having someone read through every employee's keystrokes every day would be unfeasible, due to the sheer volume of work. Some employers assign a couple of data security employees to do random audits—pick someone different every day and go through a couple of days' worth of keystrokes. If they don't find anything out of the ordinary, the employee never hears about it and has no reason to suspect he is being audited. That's the random model. Another one is to search for particular keywords in all activity, just like the NSA searches for particular keywords in all communication, keywords such as 'bomb,' 'terrorist,' and others just like these, as part of the counter-terrorism effort. Makes sense. For companies with specific concerns in data security, it works best to install a keyword analyzer on top of the keystroke logger, to reduce the amount of work required to perform audits and surveillance on employees' computers." Alex paused to take a sip of Martini from her sweaty glass.

"What would be such an example?" Tom asked, using her pause as an opportunity to interject.

"Of using keyword analyzers in a corporate environment?"

Tom nodded.

"Oh, quite simple. Let's say your company is looking at patenting this new solution to reduce cost in the manufacturing of plastic bottles. It could mean millions for the company—the competitive edge needed to secure the company's future. In this case, you'd want to know if any employee discusses, writes specifications, or in any other way looks to steal your intellectual property and sell it. This employee would probably take notes, copy documents and data, or even write email messages containing keywords, such as 'manufacturing,' 'cost reduction,' 'process,' 'redesign,' and so on."

"But wouldn't all employees' work be riddled with such keywords? After all, it's their line of business to produce plastic bottles, right?"

"Correct. That's why the keyword analyzer doesn't work automatically or on its own. It just flags particular documents for review, documents that are then reviewed by a human and categorized as legitimate or suspicious. Keyword density also has something to do with it."

"What do you mean by that?"

"Keyword density is a measure of how many of the red-flag keywords are encountered in the same document. To your point, most documents on the majority of employees' computers would contain the words 'plastic,' or 'bottle,' or 'manufacturing,' or 'cost reduction,' because that's what they do. However, a document that contains more than one keyword, or all of them, is by far more likely to reflect suspicious activity. Therefore, keyword density is measured and used as a trigger of red flags, prioritizing suspicious documents for review by size of risk. This is *auditing on complaint*, or following the red flagging of a specific user account."

"I see."

"Finally, there is another category of such spyware—applications that monitor, in detail, Internet browsing. They capture each page visited and how much time was spent on it, even the links that are clicked, which allows the employer to draw conclusions as to employees' interests. This is also something that would be monitored randomly or on complaint. If, for example, the employee is seen by a supervisor as being constantly on the Internet or on Facebook instead of working, the supervisor usually has the authority to request an Internet usage report for that employee."

"What happens next with the employee? What's acceptable in terms of Internet usage at work?"

"That largely depends on company policy. Some companies restrict it to absolutely zero. You went online for five minutes; that is grounds for termination. Others allow unlimited usage during breaks. Others simply look the other way—but these wouldn't install browsing monitoring software. However, fewer companies are open about employees' use of the Internet during business hours."

"This has been informative, I appreciate it. You possess a wealth of knowledge that will benefit us all." Tom stood up and headed for the grill. "Let's see if the portabellas are done." He grabbed a large plate from the table. "How does it all relate to your laptop?"

"Well, I was definitely expecting to find a keystroke logger, considering that I am working for a company such as NanoLance. It makes sense for the business to be cautious, because it works with innovative technologies. The employees do a lot of research and development for the government, so there are lots of valid reasons. What I did not expect to find was a full array of monitoring and surveillance applications—all of them installed on my laptop, including a screenshot capture application. It captures my screen every ten minutes, saves the image, and indexes it against the keystroke logger. It's a very sophisticated monitoring application package."

"I see. So you'd have to be extra careful with the work you're doing on that laptop, including the volume of work itself."

"True, but that's not all. I need to be able to log into the main email server to look around, I need to be able to use my laptop without restrictions while I'm there, so that I can figure out what's going on. Plus, the thought of a voice bug never crossed my mind." Her voice trailed off on a saddened tone.

"Voice and video, perhaps," Tom added. "Let's not forget video."

"So, what do we do? We can't just remove everything and wipe it clean—they'll be on to me in no time."

"True. First, we look at everything—the laptop, the bag, and the phone, to find out if they are bugged already. But even if the equipment is not bugged now, you shouldn't assume it would stay like that forever. They might put one in, without notice or cause, at any given time. So you have to be careful."

"Buy a gun safe for my garage?" Alex chuckled.

"That could work. Or you could just leave it in the garage, somewhere. Or in a closet in your basement. Or, even better, leave the entire thing in your car. It's more natural, fits typical human behavior, and that shouldn't raise any red flags."

"That's what I'll do, great idea."

"I can't think of a good solution for your laptop, though. Any ideas that might work?"

"I thought of something, but it's complicated and somewhat risky."

"OK, let's hear it."

"Clone it. Clone both of them—laptop and phone."

"Clone? How?"

"Buy absolute replicas of both pieces of equipment—same makes, models, and configurations. Install the same applications, with the same user account and registrations, including the spyware."

"Why the spyware?"

"In case someone grabs a hold of the clone, they could see in fifteen seconds that it's not the same machine. But if they see a clone of their own spyware on it, they'd be absolutely convinced it's theirs. This cloned spyware would not transmit anything to anyone, though."

"I think it's brilliant!" Tom clapped his hands. "Why is it risky?"

"I would have to carry both of them and swap, when needed. All offices and conference rooms at that company have glass walls. Someone might see me swap."

"Somehow I'm not that worried about that. If you remember that the official one could potentially have audio and video bugs on it, you should be fine. Just be careful."

"I will." *Or at least I hope I will*, Alex thought. "I am starting to feel paranoid."

"Think of it this way: on a battlefield, in a war zone, paranoia is your best friend, it keeps you alive."

She sighed, letting a faint frown settle on her face.

Tom caught that glimpse of concern, but quietly turned away and started serving dinner.

They sat at the table, plates in front of them filled with steaming portabellas, covered with molten Swiss cheese. Claire joined them, happily sharing her satisfaction with her work results in the rose garden.

"What else is on your mind, Alex?"

"My boss. He is weird. He hates me."

"Are you sure? He has no reason to," Claire chimed in.

"Oh, he said so himself. His contempt for me, and people like me, was almost the only subject for the half hour we spent together so far."

"People like you?" Tom asked, intrigued.

"Yeah. Not too smart, young, aggressive hot shots who come and go. And that's a quote from Sheppard."

"I see. Then I think he's not really that smart himself, is he?" Tom offered, and everyone smiled.

"He might not be, but I am meeting with him tomorrow for an hour to discuss my goals, and I am dreading it." Alex paused, her frown becoming more visible. "Please, keep your fingers crossed."

Vincent Moran flashed a quick smile before changing topics.

"A major mover today, although in the wrong direction, was NanoLance Incorporated. NNLC dropped 8.89 percent on the markets, trading at the closing bell for only $113.89 per share. This stock has constantly declined since the friendly fire incident in Kandahar, on April 20 of this year.

"Despite the strong reputation held by this corporation, and its intense focus on quality, NanoLance struggles to overcome the public perception regarding the safety of its drones. Since NNLC has been around for more than twenty years, and our analysts still give it their vote of confidence, we are expecting a strong comeback soon from this innovative defense contractor. Until then, unfortunately, the sustained drop in stock price that we have experienced in the past few weeks will continue to drive jittery investors to cash out.

"From *Money Markets Review*, this is Vincent Moran, wishing you a fortunate day."

"How much longer do I have to sit and wait for you to honor me with your presence?" Sheppard's unexpected appearance in her doorway startled Alex.

"We were scheduled for 9:00AM, and it's 8:35. I'm not sure how—"

"I said first thing in the morning," Sheppard hissed in an angry, almost grinding tone.

"I'm sorry, sir," Alex offered, "that usually means 9:00AM in typical office environments. My misunderstanding."

"Do you expect to be working 9 to 5 here? Do you think you're a clerk or something?" He paused, rolling his eyes in contempt. "Next thing you'll do is want to get unionized, maybe? Or be paid overtime? You are an executive, Miss Hoffmann, although I *cannot* fathom why. Your duties never cease as an executive in an information technology department. Your day never starts at 9 and never ends at 5."

"Understood." Alex was trotting behind Sheppard, as he was going toward his office, where they were supposed to have their meeting. "What time would you like me to come in then?"

"*Jesus!* I cannot believe this." Sheppard laughed in derision. "If you have to *ask*, then you need to seriously reexamine your attitude, because this is not going to work." He sat at his desk, leaving Alex to stand in silence for a long minute. "Sit down."

Alex sat in the chair he indicated and opened her portfolio, ready to take notes.

"You're the director of infrastructure and support," he said, and then exhaled slowly. "Did you know that?"

"Yes, sir, I do." *What kind of question was that?* Alex braced herself.

"Pay attention to what I am about to say, because I have no interest in saying it twice."

She nodded.

"As director of infrastructure and support, you support all operations, regardless of physical location. That means the corporate offices and the manufacturing plant." He paused.

Alex nodded again.

"All infrastructure must work. Period. At all times. Downtime is not acceptable. Uptime performance of 99.998 percent is of no interest to me. It has to be 100 percent. Understood?"

"Yes, sir."

"I am also expecting you to upgrade the infrastructure, on a continuing basis. The work is never done, and the systems are never down. That should be simple enough even for you to understand."

Alex nodded again.

"Your department has a budget of seventy-three million dollars a year. This includes your overhead, maintenance, and infrastructure costs. By the end of this year, I expect to see that cut by 10 percent." He looked her in the eye.

"I'll see what I can do."

"What?" He spat the word.

"I mean, yes, sir, I'll get it done. I'm sorry."

"I am expecting you to increase the productivity of your team. Do *not* ask me any questions," he stopped her, as she was about to say something. "I'm *not* doing your work for you. You figure it out."

"Understood."

"I expect the productivity improvement in your team to be significant and measurable. That is all."

"What do you consider to be the highest priority?"

"*Everything* is a priority!" Sheppard paced the syllables of his words as if he were pounding at her. He had the amazing ability to yell while whispering, conveying so much hatred, contempt, and venom, it was almost unbearable. "Everything must be done perfectly, or else. Do you think I want to hear excuses? Do you think I will ever accept to hear a server was down because you were prioritizing this, that, or the other?"

Alex took a deep breath. *Remember why you're here*, she thought, giving herself the needed strength to continue.

"The first thing I will do is set goals for my team," she started.

"I don't care what you do, or how you do it. Just get the job done."

"Yes, I get it, but I need last year's performance numbers, so I can put these goals into perspective and challenge my team."

"Previous performance numbers?" He scoffed. "These aren't any of your concern. Previous performance will not be used as an excuse for future lameness. Previous performance, if I can call it *that*, has been achieved under the mediocre leadership of the former director of infrastructure, and he's no longer here, now, is he?"

"I see," Alex said, carefully backing away from the hot topic.

"Before you waste any more of my time with your infinite supply of stupid questions, I will ask you if you know what employment-at-will is. Any idea?"

"Yes, sir, I know what that is."

"Good. *Finally*, we're making some progress. *Please*, do keep that notion in mind before asking any more questions."

She nodded, painfully aware she was blushing under the threat.

"Until you can convince me you know what you're doing and that you can deliver results, we will meet here once a week. First thing in the morning every Friday, and do *not* ask what time that is. Come prepared to show me progress. These meetings are not for your questions, they are for mine. Dismissed," he said, and turned his back to her, looking out the window.

Alex stood and quietly left Sheppard's office, closing the door behind her. She didn't have to take more than two or three steps to realize how badly her knees were shaking. She felt the urge to sit down.

"Glad to see you're still here." Louie's cheerful voice grabbed her attention. "You look like you need a smoke."

"I'm sorry, I don't smoke, or at least I am trying not to," she said.

"Maybe," he said undisturbed, "but you still look like you could use a smoke, so why don't you come with me?"

He led her outside in the back of the building, where numerous benches were scattered on the lawn for the use of the company's smoking personnel. She happily sat down, letting the morning sunshine dissipate her gloomy mood.

"Hey," Louie started, after lighting up. "Don't let him get to you. Every time you do, he wins."

"He is a bit intense, I'll give you that," she said, allowing herself to relax a notch.

"He's more than that. He's one of the few true-blooded, hard-core assholes still living on this planet," Louie said, and they both laughed. "But you learn to live with it. You do the best you can, and you live through another day."

"Speaking of living through another day, what time does he expect us to come in?"

"Oh, before he does, and we do not leave before he does. But we have that figured out down to an art. We've watched his car pull in and out of the parking lot for many days and compiled a behavioral profile, based on the observed times of arrival and departure, by day of week and by season. We have the data available for you," he said, winking. "So far, we haven't been wrong once. We come in fifteen minutes earlier than he does, and, if one of us runs late, another one of us—we draw straws—goes in there with an issue and keeps him busy until the lost sheep makes it to the flock."

"Down to an art indeed," she said, impressed with the creativity of the defense mechanisms put in place by her team.

"Data-based decision making—that *is* the key to operational excellence, right?"

She nodded, smiling wide.

"Our data tells us you have to be in the office on Mondays by 8:15AM," he said, referring to a small piece of paper he removed from his pocket, "and most likely you'd be able to leave by 5:45PM on Monday night."

"Wow, thank you," Alex said.

"Good thing the bastard is so predictable, or we all would have been in a world of trouble."

Alex was grateful to see her desk, after struggling to haul from her car a brand new coffeemaker and her laptop bag, now twice as heavy with two laptops inside. She was confident she would get used to the laptop bag's heavy weight, but the coffeemaker she was carrying made it difficult for her to open doors and make her way inside the building. Nevertheless, it was going to be worth the effort.

The cafeteria downstairs was one elevator trip down and one big open floor across, time consuming and potentially an issue, considering she had other priorities, rather than putting in all that commute for each cup. She only hoped she wasn't breaking any company policy by bringing the coffeemaker into the office, or that no one would catch her if she was. She tucked it in a small closet in her office, and, with a smile of deep, mischievous satisfaction, brewed her first cup. This cup was going to come in handy, as she was preparing to attend the first operational review meeting with the chief operations officer, Benjamin Walker.

The company had a simple, straightforward structure, complemented by an equally simple and effective set of operating mechanisms designed to ensure that performance was managed constantly and efficiently. Each chief executive had monthly business reviews, in which results were analyzed, conclusions were drawn, and priorities were set. During these meetings, their immediate teams would attend, in addition to representatives from the shared support functions, such as human resources and information technology.

This is where Alex came in. She was assigned to support Walker in all his operational and strategy meetings, on top of her daily duties related to infrastructure and support. The thought had been that Walker's division, including, among others, the manufacturing plant, had the highest demand and usage of infrastructure, hence Alex would be the IT representative of choice for this area. This was not new; the director of infrastructure and support had always supported the operations team. Nevertheless, this created a lot of opportunity for Alex, opening the doors for her to have access to the plant and to the operations group overall.

Coffee mug in one hand and portfolio in the other, she made her way to conference room 1704, up on the operations floor. She entered the room, finding yet another group of unknown faces around the table. Walker had not come in yet; she had made it on time.

She started briefly introducing herself, as she walked around the table to take an open seat.

"Hi, I'm Alex Hoffmann, the new director of infrastructure and support," she said, extending her hand to the first of the people sitting around the table.

"John Dunwood, vice president of manufacturing."

"Janet Templeton, director of manufacturing quality. Welcome aboard!"

"Robin Maxwell, human resources."

"Miles Putnam, director of research and development."

"Peter Wilson, director of Six Sigma."

"Nice meeting everyone," Alex said, taking her seat.

Seconds later, Benjamin Walker stepped in, firmly closed the door behind him, and slammed his portfolio and notebook on the table.

"Good morning, everyone," he said, with a hint of a smile. "Have you all met? Good, let's proceed then."

A PowerPoint presentation was displayed, its title page said, "Operations Results—May." The head of manufacturing, John Dunwood, started his presentation without delay.

"May has been a relatively good month," he said, clicking a small remote to advance the slides. "Most results were at or above goal," he continued, as the projected image was showing a spreadsheet filled with performance indicators, numbers, and red-yellow-green indicators. This type of color-enhanced presentation system had numerous advantages, allowing everyone present to see, at a glance, if various areas of measured performance were reaching the goal that was set.

"Mostly greens, as you can see," Dunwood continued, "in critical areas such as manufacturing throughput, inventory cycles, overall budget spending, and most of the people-related indicators." He cleared his throat, and then continued. "A couple of yellows, one in generated waste, missing target by only 0.5 percent, and the other in the research-and-development testing area, missing target by 3.45 percent."

"What does that mean?" Robin asked.

Alex thanked her silently.

"This measure of performance reflects the successful test rate that new equipment scores, while still in an R&D phase. For the newly designed equipment, we want to measure how successful the design is, how stable and reliable it is, and how consistently it performs. We subject prototypes to a series of tests, then we compile, based on the pass/fail test results, this overall score of prototype test performance."

"And why is it underperforming?" Walker asked. "Which prototypes are dragging the results down?"

"Not sure yet, we have to look into this and figure it out. The fail rates are higher than expected on a number of prototypes, including the new RX series drone, all the way to the custom designed, in-dash NanoGuide for next year's BMWs."

"Great," Walker said. "When can we know what's going on in there? Six Sigma, can you help?"

Six Sigma, as Alex had learned from Tom's condensed lectures, was a set of methodologies designed to eliminate defects from a process. Based on the statistical analysis of all performance and characteristics measures of a process or output, Six Sigma had been a presence in many organizations, especially those with stringent quality and performance targets. Some organizations were starting to shy away from Six Sigma as a methodology, due to the large and expensive complications triggered by poorly managed Six Sigma initiatives. That was mostly, if she remembered correctly, because Six Sigma was heavily geared toward cost reduction, rather than growth or strategic business process improvement with no associated cost reduction. A fun fact, Alex remembered, was that Six Sigma professionals were organized in a system of levels, depending on knowledge and skill, with karate-inspired names. They could be Green Belts, Black Belts, or even Master Black Belts. She wondered what color Peter Wilson's Six Sigma belt was.

"We can definitely send some Green Belts to pull data and get some answers. Until now, we have had little exposure to the new designs. Unfortunately, R&D does not involve us at all in the early phases of the work."

"When can I have some answers on this, then?" Walker pressed.

"Not before the end of the month, I am afraid," Dunwood replied, his wrinkled face waiting with concern for Walker's reaction.

"Great, that's just great," Walker lashed out sarcastically, "I can't understand the results of May until it's July! I don't understand how you can run a business like this. I definitely don't want to run my business like this, do you?"

When Walker finished his escalating diatribe, a silence, thick as smoke, fell on the room. No one dared to move, say anything, look him in the eye, or even breathe.

"Let's proceed," he said.

Everyone breathed.

"A few notable reds." Dunwood paused for a brief second to clear his throat again. "One is in the area of retention of high-performing personnel."

"How many did we lose this month?" Walker asked.

"Two. One was a shift supervisor in the drone assembly line, the other one was the US Navy product quality liaison. They were both top performers; we're sorry to see them leave."

How very interesting, Alex thought.

"Good riddance is what I say," Walker said abruptly. "If they were not thrilled to be here, I, for one, don't see any loss. How are we replacing?"

"We've posted ads, internal and external. We should have an idea on replacement within a couple of weeks," Robin said. "I've tasked human resources recruiting to step on it with this one."

"Who's picking up the slack in the interim?"

"The other shift supervisors are rotating through longer shifts, until the replacement comes in and is trained, and the Army product liaison is also handling the Navy contacts for a while."

"Make sure he doesn't screw this up," Walker said. "If you're not comfortable with his handling of the issue, you do this job yourself, personally, so that I don't have any surprises on the client side. Is this understood?"

"Yes, sir," Dunwood answered in a heartbeat.

"Let's continue with the reds."

Dunwood clicked, advancing his presentation one more slide.

"The next notable red is the hours of testing. We didn't achieve our target of total testing hours for May."

"Which tests didn't achieve and why?" Walker asked.

Dunwood clicked again to display a breakdown of testing scores by product.

"The worst one is the RX series drone, with only 82 percent of required testing hours, followed closely by the SX series drone, with 86 percent. Moving down the list we have NanoGuide in-dash mounts series varying between 89 percent and 93 percent, and—"

"Let's keep it simple," Walker interrupted him, with a tone of voice reeking of sarcasm, "did you make goal on the testing time for any product?"

"Um . . . the only ones were the MX series of enhanced drones, and the handheld GPS devices."

"So, let me summarize for you," Walker interjected again, "almost all your products failed the required testing time this month." Walker paused briefly, leaving a deafening silence in the room. "Tell me, please, have you seen your wife and kids during the month of May?"

Confused, Dunwood hesitated before answering. "Um . . . what do you mean?"

"Have you been by your house during the month of May? How often?" Walker rephrased the question in an apparently calm and friendly tone of voice.

"Sure, I go home every night," Dunwood replied hesitantly, not sure where this was going.

"And why would that be?" Walker continued his line of interrogation.

"Excuse me?"

"How dare you go home, how dare any of your incompetent people go home every night, when you're coming in front of me with your testing goals unmet? Testing only requires time, dedication, and willingness to do whatever it takes to achieve results, nothing else. Not only you don't do your job, but you don't even care that you don't!" Walker slammed his fist on the table, startling everyone. "Why didn't you complete testing within the allotted hours?"

"Well, sir, th-th-the t-tests failed in s-some cases," Dunwood started explaining, stammering and slightly trembling under the pressure and the humiliation of this public embarrassment. "W-when a test fails, it takes more time, 'c-cause you have to see what's wrong, t-then f-fix and r-replace and retest, sir."

"So, let's see if I hear you correctly. The tests failed, then you and your less-than-mediocre team ran out of time to retest, then you just threw your arms in the air, said 'oops, sorry, no time left, tough shit,' and just went home to enjoy your pathetic TV dinners, surrounded by your pathetic little families, right?"

Dunwood stood there silently, his chin trembling. There was nothing left to say.

Oh, God, he's going to start crying, Alex thought. *Oh, no.* Her own boss, Sheppard, looked like an angel now, compared to this maniac.

Walker allowed the uncomfortable silence to continue, as he was looking at everyone, to see if their faces displayed the expected approval. Alex was stunned to see that two people were nodding their heads in approval of Walker's tirade: Robin and Peter. From Robin, an HR professional, Alex would have expected anything but approval for this type of behavior. Peter, as a Six Sigma leader, had to work with Walker every day, so Alex gave him the benefit of the doubt, but Robin was a sad disappointment.

"Let's continue, we're not done yet with the reds, are we?" Walker interrupted the silence.

Clicking ahead, Dunwood displayed a new page, showing a complicated chart.

"The last red is for product quality at the end of the assembly line. It missed target by nine percentage points."

"This is the one you measure before shipping to the users?" Walker clarified.

"Yes, sir, this is the final quality test before the product leaves our facility."

"And you have an almost double-digit miss." Walker paused. "Why?"

Dunwood stood silently, not sure if the question was the beginning of yet another diatribe.

"What causes the double-digit miss? What part of the quality check is failing?"

"Overall, the microchips fail, mostly across the board."

"And how do you explain that?" Walker asked.

"Microchips fail at a higher rate than any other components, regardless of manufacturer or chip type; it's the nature of the product. They always have and always will be."

"Then, what's wrong now?"

"We're seeing a higher-than-average failure rate after install. We check these microchips on the test bank before installing; yet at final quality checks, they fail the tests, at an unexpectedly high rate."

"Why? Why are they failing, do you know?" Walker continued, apparently undisturbed by the news.

"We have to analyze the failures and find the root cause, so we don't know yet. This will take some time," Dunwood said, avoiding Walker's gaze by looking at the slide.

"Can you at least venture a guess?" Walker pressed him.

"The only thing that comes to mind is all the cost-cutting initiatives we have executed in the plant in the past two years. We kept pulling cost out of the processes and the products. That can only go so far without compromising the quality of the product."

"So, how are you planning to fix this? We're almost at the end of June, which means the June failure rates will also be in the shit can, right?"

"That is probably correct, sir, but we are working as fast as possible to contain and fix this. We have a rigorous check at the end of the line, to ensure no damaged product makes it out the door, to the client. We are even holding back those items that borderline pass the test. Just to make sure."

"I bet this is costing me a fortune, isn't it? The entire throwaway inventory, all this scrap? How on earth did you make your budget numbers for the month? Now I know why your waste numbers are in the yellow, but how come budget is in the green?"

"Like I said, sir, it's because of the cost cutting and Six Sigma projects at the plant. We took a lot of cost out of every single area, no stone was left unturned."

"And that's the way it's supposed to be. Could be even better if you wouldn't throw all those defective products down the drain, right?"

"I guess so, but something has got to give. Now we're robbing Peter to pay Paul. We've cut costs so deeply, that it has come back to haunt us in the form of defect rates and scrapped product. If we are to fix this issue, we will probably need to add cost back into the product."

"Let me get this straight," Walker said, and then paused to think.

Alex took a long, deep breath. *Here we go again,* she thought, bracing herself.

"You don't have the root cause of the failure," Walker continued, "but you know it's because of the cost-cutting initiatives, and you know that fixing it will cost me more money. Correct?"

"That will probably be the case, yes, sir."

"And how exactly do you know that?"

"I have been the head of manufacturing for almost nine years, and I have never had such low quality rates. I have more than twenty years of experience in manufacturing and assembly process for electronics, and I know what changes were made right about the time the product quality started to drop."

"What changes were those?"

"At the end of last year, when our operating budget was cut by 30 percent, while maintaining the production goal for most items, and increasing it for a few of them. Those are the budget cuts that I am talking about—they touched all areas of the manufacturing process and significantly impacted the workforce. We let a lot of people go."

"And why is this starting to show only now?" Walker probed.

"I think it has to do with the parts inventory levels. Until now, we have used our older parts inventory, the parts produced before the budget cuts. We've started to phase in new parts only since March or so. We manage our inventory first-in, first-out, so we worked through the older inventory first." As he was explaining the circumstances, Dunwood was regaining his confidence. He had data on his side, facts, common sense, and logic. He should end up being fine.

"Tell me, please," Walker asked in that calm, yet threatening, tone of voice he used before he started yelling, "who authorized you to take quality out of the product to cut costs?"

"You can only go so far with cost-driven process redesign and optimization, before you start negatively impacting the product, even if you don't want to. If you recall, sir, I sent you a series of emails about this last November. We even met a couple of times, and I told you back then—"

"And *I* told *you* back then," Walker interrupted, "that you are to cut costs by 30 percent, while maintaining, or increasing, current quality levels. Do you recall that?"

"Yes, I do, sir, but—"

"But what? You come in here now and try to pin this on me?"

"I didn't mean—"

"Didn't mean what? Didn't mean for me to find out just how lame and incompetent you are? I have never, *never* authorized you to jeopardize product quality to achieve your budget goals." Walker had raised his voice to thunderous levels, punctuated by rhythmically slamming his fist on the table.

"But sir, you have to understand that—"

"I don't *have* to understand anything!" Walker pounded. "I don't *have* to understand incompetence, I don't *have* to tolerate incompetence, and I absolutely don't *have* to keep paying for incompetence! If you can't get this job done, I'll find someone else who can! Just say the word!"

"But, sir, if you consider—" Dunwood's chin was trembling again, and so were his hands.

"Are you saying the word? Should I replace you?"

"No, sir."

"Then, are you going to finally start doing your job? Are you going to fix this without burning a hole in my pocket?"

"Yes, sir, I'll try to find some—"

"Don't try! Get it done! You have sixty days. This is your last warning!"

The same two heads were nodding in approval, filling Alex with disgust.

"That's it, I'm done with you." Walker pounded his fist again, for dramatic effect. "Dismissed." He grabbed his portfolio and notebook, and left, slamming the door behind him.

Dunwood sat on the nearest chair; he looked as if he were going to be sick. Somehow, his heavily wrinkled face seemed well-suited for his job, reflecting as much worry, pain, embarrassment, and fear, as a human face could possibly reflect.

Alex noticed the others were slowly leaving the room. She saw Miles Putnam from R&D pull out a pack of cigarettes, and she took the opportunity, following him into the elevator.

"Miles, right?" she asked him.

"Yes, that's right," he answered.

"Going out for a smoke? Mind if I join you?"

"No, not at all, please do."

They stepped out of the elevators and into the nicely trimmed lawn behind the building. He lit up.

"You're not smoking?" he asked in surprise.

"Oh, I just quit a few months ago, but after a meeting like that, I'm sorry I did," Alex replied. "This time I'll settle for a few breaths of passive smoke," she said with a chuckle.

"I know how you feel; it gets pretty intense in there. Must be hard on you, being new and all that. Hope we didn't scare you away."

"No, not yet," she responded, laughing at the thought. "It was tough, though. Is it always this painfully uncomfortable?"

"Pretty much, but you shouldn't be asking such questions. You never know who hears you, and what they do with what they hear. Walker demands absolute loyalty and beyond."

"But you have to admit," she pressed on, "this is pretty extreme. I wonder how come no one tells him anything about it. It doesn't have to be so painful and stressful."

"Look, there's a lot of value in being pushed so hard. There is a lot to learn about your own limits, and what you can achieve under pressure. Just as wartime stimulates innovation and generates a significantly higher number of groundbreaking inventions than peacetime, we push our limits further under pressure than we would ever push them under different, less challenging conditions. Overall, it's good for you. Trust me. You'll learn to appreciate it. Anyway, I don't want to talk about this anymore, and I suggest you don't either," Miles said, turning his back to Alex and walking away.

"I'm telling you, Alex, grilling is a sophisticated art form at this address," a cheerful Richard Ferguson stated, putting his fork and knife down on his empty plate.

"So I have learned," Alex replied, still amazed at the refined combination of tastes presented by the pork tenderloin with mushroom sauce. "Our boss knows his way around the grill, that's for sure."

"How have you been? I haven't seen you since we came back from Minnesota," Richard asked. A rare presence at their team reunions due to his client assignment, Richard had lots to offer in terms of the advice Alex was seeking.

After they finished their dinners, they grabbed their drinks and went into the living room, gathering around the small coffee table. Alex took an armchair, sharing it with Little Tom. The cat allowed her to push him over slightly, just enough to make room for her to sit on the edge of the chair, then stretched his legs and yawned wholeheartedly.

Tom was the last one to join them.

"Thank you for yet another wonderful dinner," Alex said.

"Hear, hear," Steve chimed in, raising his glass.

"You are welcome. It's a pleasure to see all of you gathered around our dinner table. That's why," he said, turning toward Alex, "whenever I get the chance, I invite everyone. Alex brought today's opportunity. She wanted to talk through a couple of issues with me, so why don't we do this now?"

"Sure," Alex said. They were all watching her, listening carefully to what she had to say. "First off," she continued, "I need your help to reach out to Dr. Barnaby and ask him to somehow make sure I don't get fired before I even have a chance to do my job."

"Is it that bad?" Tom had concern in his voice.

"I'm not sure, but there is a distinct possibility that it could happen on a whim. These executives are a bit extreme. And, if I get terminated, it would make it very difficult for us to continue to work this case."

"That is a valid point of view," Tom said. "So, how should we do this?"

"Dr. Barnaby could easily put out a memo saying that all hiring and firing of leadership have to go through him for prior approval, effective immediately,"

Richard offered. "The executives would think that someone screwed up; they would never think Alex is in any way connected to this."

Richard's solution made sense. The rest nodded in approval.

"Solved!" Tom said, rubbing his palms together. "What else is on your mind?"

"I wanted to pick your brains to see how I could be a smoker without really being one. My presence on the smoker's lawn would be beneficial; that's the only place where people open up and chat, but they will be suspicious if I don't smoke. Problem is, I never smoked in my life, and I'd rather not start now."

"There's that e-cig, right?" Steve said. "Have you heard of it?" No one offered a yes, so he continued. "Relatively new on the market, the e-cig has been around for a few years. It's an electronic cigarette, a device that delivers nicotine, without the smoke. It puts out a small puff of harmless water vapor imitating smoke. It even lights up at the end, just like a real cigarette would."

"Then, no one would notice the difference?" Alex wondered.

"I think they would notice. It's like a cigarette, but also quite different. It doesn't consume itself during use; you don't have to throw it away. However, it would help you get accepted as a smoker. You'd tell anyone who asks that you used to smoke, but had to quit smoking the real stuff because of long meetings and days without a break, and you couldn't stand it anymore. Any smoker will relate," Steve said, winking. "All smokers endure hell when they are prevented from smoking, in meetings, during flights, or in airports. They'll understand and accept you."

"I don't see why," Alex said, "Wouldn't you need to get out of the meeting, airport, and so on to smoke the e-cig?"

"No, that's exactly it," Steve clarified. "The e-cig doesn't put out any kind of smoke or smell, so it won't trigger any smoke sensors. It can be safely used indoors."

"How about the nicotine?" Tom asked. "I wouldn't ask Alex to start puffing nicotine either. It would be just as addictive as real smoke, and who knows what other side effects it might have."

"I think we could rig that thing to be nicotine-free," Brian Woods intervened.

"Thank you, Steve, for sharing your in-depth knowledge on smoking and smoking alternatives," Tom said. "I think we have a solution for this challenge. Alex, we could potentially have that set up for you and ready to use in the next couple of days."

"Thank you both," Alex said, "it will be very helpful for me. This particular work culture is strange, and I need people to open up to me."

"Strange, how?" Tom asked.

"Both executives I have spent time with are abusive, insulting, and unbelievably aggressive bastards. Sorry," she said, while a faint blush colored her cheeks, "didn't mean to use that word."

"Why? If they are indeed bastards, then you need to describe them appropriately, right?" Steve said, making everyone laugh, including Alex.

"Yes, they are. Nevertheless, the strangest thing is that no one seems to care about it or do anything about it. They are between numb—which I could potentially understand—and supportive—which I can't."

"Probably these executives have surrounded themselves with enablers, so the interactions you are seeing are unnatural," Steve said.

"Enablers? Could you please explain what you mean by that?" Alex asked. She was not familiar with the concept.

"Enablers are those who will supply the despot what he needs to make things possible for him," Steve said.

"I get that," Alex replied, "I know the definition of the word. What I don't understand is how that plays out in this situation."

"Very simple. Imagine the following conversation, taking place in a meeting. The boss says 'I hate that painting; it's ugly.' Then, enabler number one would say 'It's ugly because it's green, sir.' Enabler number two would say 'It's ugly because it's square, sir.' And so on. Is this what you're seeing?"

"Yes, definitely," Alex said. "But why would anyone do that?"

"Mostly for survival. They know they can't stand up to the despot and actually win the battle, so they build themselves a method of survival, one that would ensure that the despot picks on someone else. It's as simple as that."

"Tell me more about the bastards, Alex," Tom asked. "Do you think they are to blame for what's going on?"

"Yes, I am starting to think so, maybe just in part, if not entirely. Walker, the COO, does not want to listen to anything coming from his head of manufacturing, after he had cut the spending into the ground, forcing them to take cost out of the product. That could well be the cause for the drone failure we've seen—it could be as simple as that."

"Why did he cut spending, do you know?" Tom asked.

"Not sure. I was unaware of any financial difficulties the company might have."

"So was I," Tom confirmed. "I will ask Dr. Barnaby about it first thing tomorrow morning."

"Walker was keen on the cost thing. He kept referring to 'spending my money,' 'burning holes in my pocket,' and so on," Alex added, making quotation mark gestures with her fingers, to underline the phrases she was quoting from Walker.

"I see," Tom said, raising his eyebrows.

"Very interesting," Steve, said. "You know why, don't you?"

"Um . . . not sure," Alex said.

"In his mind, NanoLance is his. Manufacturing is spending *his* money. He is *the* one, or one of those who are behind the unexplained stock price fluctuations. He may be planning to take over the company. We need to carefully watch this man."

"I've set it up so that all email traffic from specific individuals gets cloned as it passes through the email server, and I get a copy of everything that they send or receive," Alex said.

"That must be a gazillion emails hitting your inbox," Brian said, "how do you manage?"

"That's true," Alex smiled, "but first of all, I didn't clone everyone's email account, just a targeted few people. Then, well, that's what evenings are for, right? It's only for a short while. I'm more worried about the budget cuts Sheppard wants me to execute in my area."

"Him too?" Tom asked.

"Yes, I was tasked with identifying and executing a 10 percent budget cut in infrastructure and support."

"Send me a copy of your P&L, and we'll work on it together," Richard offered.

"Thank you, thank you, thank you." Alex's exuberance was contagious.

"What's P&L?" Steve asked.

"Aww . . . you dreamer, wake up, will you? Profit and loss statement, remember? The financial tool of choice to manage departmental or companywide income and expenses," Richard clarified.

"Ah, *that* P&L, yes, I remember," Steve said, and everyone laughed.

"What would you expect from a shrink?" Richard continued, mercilessly.

"Whoa, buddy, stop it right there, before I quiz you on your corporate culture syndromes and related stress-induced psychological and physiological effects in employees," Steve said, making mock-aggressive gestures toward Richard.

"Tell me more," Alex intervened.

"About what?" Steve turned.

"About corporate culture. From what I have seen at NanoLance, the culture is highly dysfunctional. I know I'm there for a limited time, and with the purpose of doing a specific job, but otherwise I would have run away screaming by now. I wonder if the culture might be, even partly, to blame for this mess."

"OK, let's examine the culture a little," Steve said, all serious now and lighting up a cigar. "What is corporate culture? Not just at NanoLance, but in general?"

"It's the way a company does things, right?" Alex ventured.

"Yes, exactly that. The definition in the big book of organizational behavior is three paragraphs long, but, in essence, it's the way a company does things. Let's apply this to practical examples. The anonymous note's author stayed anonymous because of the culture—he or she was afraid of consequences, which means the company does things this way: when presented with a whistleblower, of sorts, the company causes that person harm in one way or another. Well, what's that telling you about the company?"

"I see," Alex said, "but I don't see Dr. Barnaby being at fault at all in this."

"We've already established that," Steve continued, "but he might be too isolated in his ivory tower."

"Ivory tower?" Richard asked.

"Gotcha!" Steve turned and fired an imaginary gun in Richard's direction. "Mr. Wall Street here hasn't heard of this biblical term, depicting the intellectual who lets himself become disconnected from the real world."

"I see," Alex said again, "so he's essentially not seeing what's going on around him, that's what you're saying?"

"Yes, that's exactly right. All he sees when he's walking those hallways are smiling faces. No one has the guts to approach him with anything, and everything that goes wrong in that company stays behind closed doors, where he does not reach."

"How badly do you think the culture can be damaging things?" Alex asked.

"A company's dysfunctional culture can drive the company into the ground in some cases. We've all seen examples in recent years, a few resounding bankruptcies come to mind, famous for how executives refused to hear the truth from their teams."

"That's exactly what I've seen happening here," Alex said. "But what can we do?"

"Culture is generated, influenced, or enforced by a few people. Culture is just a process, so it can be re-engineered, analyzed, taken apart, and put back together again, or simply replaced with a newer, better one. The key to addressing cultural issues at this level is to identify the drivers of the bad culture and remove them. Just like you would do with the proverbial rotten apple."

"Who are these drivers?" Alex asked.

"They are the people driving the bad culture. The abusers, the deaf ears, the insulters, and the tyrants who promote the climate of fear, the corporate bullies, in one word the toxic leaders."

"Toxic leaders?" Alex asked again for more details, grateful for all the information she was getting.

"A toxic leader is not your typical hard-assed boss. Toxic leaders are much more than that. To qualify, they have to inflict harm on the members of their team, or even on the entire organization. They do this harm with the sole purpose of promoting their interests. They would not hesitate to insult, humiliate in public, threaten with consequences or with physical violence, even violate basic human rights. They would purposely undermine and demoralize team members, as they work their way to dismantle all the mechanisms that organizations have in place to ensure their existence does not occur.

"They are clearly sociopaths, displaying no conscience and no remorse, leaving hundreds, sometimes even thousands, of broken hearts and destroyed careers in their wake. All that, while doing their best and using all their charisma to persuade their leaders that they are the best thing that could have happened to business since the invention of electricity, and that they are, first and foremost, irreplaceable. "

"Sociopaths? Really?" Alex pushed back, surprised.

"Remember your first week's readings?" Steve continued, unabated. "Sociopaths are quite numerous, at least 4 percent of the population. They don't all turn homicidal; unfortunately, some of them just turn to business leadership. I've read somewhere that there is a strong correlation between sociopathic traits and business leadership achievement. Sad, isn't it?"

"Yes, very sad," Alex said.

"Back to our 4 percent of sociopaths at large. How many employees does NanoLance have?"

"Almost 950," Alex replied.

"Let's say 1,000. Shrinks aren't that great with numbers, you know," Steve said, smiling. "So, what's 4 percent of 1,000?"

"Forty," Alex replied, eyes wide in surprise.

"Correct. Chances are there are forty sociopaths among the ranks of NanoLance staff. Because of the earlier mentioned correlation, they are more likely to be found among management, than in any other job category within the organization."

"Wow," Alex said, "I never thought of that."

"There might be more, there might be less, this isn't an exact science. But it seems to me you have already identified at least four or five."

"I thought I only had two, Sheppard and Walker. Who are the others?"

"The enablers. I am biased this way, you see. Although this might well be a defense mechanism, I still think that at least a part of them has to agree with the bully's attitude."

"How come? Why do you think that?" Alex asked.

"Give me an example of an enabler you have seen supporting one of the abusers."

"Um . . . Robin Maxwell, from human resources," Alex replied.

"Excellent example. The role of an HR leader is to ensure that abuse does not happen. If she sits in meetings, such as the one you described, and nods her head in approval, she not only enables the aggressor, but also doesn't do her job, and she is well aware of it. Does she show remorse or empathy? Does she seem rattled and upset after the meetings? No? Then that's a good candidate for the count of sociopaths. She has no conscience." Steve ended his demonstration by putting his cigar out.

"But you said it's a defense mechanism," Alex continued to probe, sounding confused.

"It is. But let me ask you this: Would you have enabled this individual by nodding your head in approval, while he stepped all over the fellow from manufacturing?"

"No, definitely not."

"You already told me what you would have done," Steve added, "you said, and I quote, 'I would have run away screaming,' right?"

Alex nodded silently.

"They do have options, these enablers; they could always quit their jobs, if their consciences were present to dictate that. They are not hostages, you know, at least not all of them."

"Some of them are?"

"Yes, those limited in their options by lack of financial stability or by lack of a good background. Maybe they declared bankruptcy in the past couple of years, and no one would hire them as leaders of anything with that showing on their records. Maybe they were caught driving under the influence, and now they have a criminal record. Those are true hostages, and if they have consciences and are forced to work for sociopaths, such as Walker, I pity them."

"So, we do have a plan for tomorrow, right?" Tom asked, standing up. "Let's meet with the client in the morning. I'll set it up and communicate with you."

Storming through the office-building door at The Agency, Alex was hoping she'd find a freshly brewed pot of coffee upstairs. The phone call that woke her at five in the morning was to let her know the client was coming in early. That wasn't entirely bad, despite the few hours of sleep she had managed. If the client meeting didn't last long, she could still hope to make it to the office before 8:30AM or so.

"Good morning, everyone," she said cheerfully, as she entered the conference room. Dr. Barnaby had already arrived. He looked a little bit better than he had at their last encounter.

"Let's proceed." Tom said, "Alex, feel free to get some coffee from over there." He pointed in the direction of the service table next to the wall.

"Thank you," she said gratefully.

"The reason why we asked you here today, Dr. Barnaby, is that we have to establish a strategy to address the stock price issue that you have brought to our attention. As you mentioned in the beginning, there is no data or evidence to substantiate a potential connection between your intentions to sell your stock and the articles or rumors that appear after the announcements are made, thus dragging your stock price down."

"Yes, that's correct, I'm afraid," Dr. Barnaby confirmed.

"In such situations the only possible approach is to stage another such event, in the hope of triggering a similar response. We can hope that this time, because we're expecting it and are ready for it, we would be able to figure out who the aggressor is."

"What would you like me to do?" Dr. Barnaby asked.

"We will work together to set up a communication strategy with your executive team. You would be letting them know that, regardless of what happens, for personal reasons, you will have to sell your stock at the end of the next quarter. Then we watch all of them, and see what happens. So far, the preferred method of aggression was through press leaks and rumors. We'll be prepared to counteract. We'll have the best public relations agency working for us, along with a strong legal team on our side to force retractions, send cease-and-desist letters, or apply whatever forms of pressure within our means to contain this. The PR team can issue statements that reinforce the public's confidence in NanoLance."

"I can't help thinking how risky this is," Dr. Barnaby said, rubbing his forehead in concern.

"It is risky," Tom confirmed, undeterred, "but it's something that would have to happen anyway, if you are ever to sell your stock. If we handle this in a controlled manner, when we're ready for it, we reduce your exposure. And we're ready to intercept communication and action meant to undermine the stock price."

"How confident are you that you will be able to identify who is doing this to me?"

"Almost 100 percent," Tom replied.

"Almost? Not entirely?"

"We do run the small risk that, despite our best efforts in monitoring and surveillance, the person responsible for the attacks will use some already established back channel that we don't know about, or that we wouldn't be able to identify in time. But, nevertheless, it would still be helpful to you to have us control such aftermath, and help restore the stock price in time for you to be able to sell at a good value."

Tom finished arguing the issue and stopped, giving Dr. Barnaby time to decide.

Dr. Barnaby turned his attention toward Alex.

"Have you identified any potential issues? Do you have any preliminary findings?"

Alex looked briefly at Tom for support and approval. He nodded slightly, encouraging her to speak.

"I have seen some measure of dysfunction that could be the early indication that we are on the right track to identify the person or persons who are behind this. From my initial findings, I can say that we're looking at a complex root cause, not just a simple one, as in one person pulling all the strings or pushing all the buttons. I would like, however, to continue my work and come to more definitive answers before I start naming names."

"So, you're thinking it could be a conspiracy of sorts?" Dr. Barnaby pressed on.

"Potentially. I need more time to make sure we identify all parties involved, and uncover all the aspects of this dysfunction."

"You're kind to call it a dysfunction," Dr. Barnaby said. "I'm sure you'll find it's more than just dysfunction."

"For now, I'm keeping an open mind, Dr. Barnaby. Please let me assure you that we are making significant progress, and that we'll be able to prepare a comprehensive report soon."

"Young lady, I have every confidence in you. I know you'll be successful. Since we've talked last time, I have been able to fall asleep at night, now that I know you all are looking into this for me. I haven't been getting much sleep since it started, but you've restored that for me, and you'll restore everything else, I am sure. My entire life and my legacy are in your capable hands, and I thank you."

"I will not let you down, sir, I promise," Alex said, blushing.

"Before we adjourn, we have a question and a request for assistance, if I may," Tom interjected.

"Sure, please go ahead."

"We would need your assistance in making sure that no executives or even senior managers are hired or terminated without your knowledge and preapproval. We need to make sure that Alex will continue to keep her job, for as long as she needs, to finish her investigation, and that no key players are removed from the organization before we are done."

"You got it, consider it done."

"As for the question, Dr. Barnaby, are there financial difficulties that the company is facing right now? Maybe cash-flow issues?"

"No, there aren't any. The company is extremely profitable and has had constant growth in the double digits every year since we started. We are doing just fine. Why do you ask?"

"Some of your executives seem quite focused on cost cutting. Aggressive cost-cutting measures are being put into place," Tom clarified.

"That can't be right. Who's doing that? I haven't tasked any of my executives to reduce costs. We have always been a growth-oriented company. They are all supposed to focus on growth and development, through innovation and research. Can you tell me who's doing this?"

"I'm afraid I can't, not at this time. You will find all these details outlined in our report, but until then we have to ensure that the status quo stays unchallenged and no appearance is different. Even a goal realignment memo clarifying the issue of cost cutting could potentially be hazardous to our plans. These are people who have their antennas out there, assessing carefully every single change, no matter how small."

"I see," Dr. Barnaby conceded, "maybe you're right. It's hard for me to wait, you know."

"I understand, sir, and we promise you the wait won't be long."

"So, what's next?"

"We will work with you to announce the sale of your stock and watch what happens."

"How much longer, Daddy?" An impatient six-year-old boy, dressed in cargo shorts and an angler's T-shirt, was banging his feet against the seat in front of him.

"Shh . . . stop that," his father said, and gently put his hand on the boy's knees, getting him to stop kicking. "We're almost there."

"But why did we take the bus?"

"Well, how many times have you traveled on a tour bus before?"

"Never," the boy answered in a firm voice.

"And how many times have you traveled in Dad's car before?"

"Um . . ." the boy attempted to count from memory, using his fingers as a guide. "Every day," he concluded, giving up on the actual count.

"See? Now you get to experience something new today," the dad continued, arranging his son's baseball cap. "What else are we going to be experiencing today?"

"Fishing?"

"Yes, Teddy, fishing. We're going to rent a boat, a large one, a pontoon, and we're going to take that boat out to sea and catch us some fish."

"Why didn't Mommy come with us?" The boy was no longer smiling.

"You know how mommies are, they sometimes want to spend time lying in the sun, just sitting there, idle, on the beach. And what happens when that happens?"

"We get bored!"

"Exactly, Ted. Because this lovely day can't go to waste, we'll have some serious fun today, son, that's a promise. All those fish will be in serious trouble."

"How are we going to catch them?"

"Well, we don't have fishing rods, but what else do we have?"

"Dynamite?"

The man seated in the row of seats to their left chuckled.

"Dynamite? Why would you think that?"

"'Cause I've seen it on TV. Merlin the cat used to go fishing and couldn't catch any. He got hungry, and he stole dynamite, and he caught many fishes."

"Oh, I see, but Merlin is a cartoon character, and we are real, so we can't do that."

"Then what?"

"We are going bow fishing, Teddy, and that's going to be really fun, 'cause you see the fish from the boat and you shoot it with your bow and arrow, but only if you like it."

"What if I miss?"

"Well, if you miss, you get your arrow back and you try again. Remember how you used to train with Daddy, shooting at the target in the backyard?"

"Yes," Teddy nodded vigorously.

"It's just like that, only this time we train with fish. The better we are, the more fish we're going to get."

"Will they let us bring the fishes on the bus to take home to Mommy?"

"We'll rent a car for the trip home, son, so we can take all the fish with us."

"Bow fishing?" The stranger at their left intervened. "That's a new one for me. Where are you planning to go for that?"

"Near Destin, in the bay, maybe near Crab Island. Fish are everywhere, jumping out of the water. You can see it coming, you have time to take aim and shoot."

"I have to try that sometime. By the way, I'm Stan," the man extended his hand.

"I'm Zack—Zack Cooper, and this is Teddy."

"Very smart kid you have there, Zack, he's a pleasure to be around."

"Look, Daddy, a plane!" The boy's finger was pointing at something over the ocean.

"That's too low to be a plane," Zack said.

"That's not a plane, it's too small," Stan added.

"What is it, Daddy?"

"Looks like one of those military drones," Zack said, squinting to see against the sun.

"Daddy, what's a drone?"

"It's sort of a plane but without a pilot."

"The real question is why is it flying so low?" Stan's question reflected Zack's worry. The other passengers were also commenting on it, speculating about the potential reasons why a drone would be flying in this area.

"There's a military air base not far from here, I bet that's where it's going," one of the other passengers said.

"Yeah, but it's flying way too low and coming straight at us." In an instinctive gesture, Zack put his arm around Teddy's shoulders. The boy fidgeted to get away.

"Oh, my God," someone said in a high pitch, "it is coming straight at us!" The man got off his seat, panicked. "Hey! Hey!" He yelled trying to get the driver's attention. "Hey! Do something, for Christ sake; the goddamn thing is coming for us! Call somebody!"

"Can't be, we're on American soil," someone else said, sounding unconvinced.

"Oh, my God," Zack whispered, eyes fixated on the fast-approaching drone. "This can't be happening." He grabbed Teddy in his arms in a desperate attempt to shield him. "Oh, God, oh, God, please, no," he whispered, amid the escalating screams   of   the   passengers.

A young technician waited for Alex to come in. As she approached her office, the technician came forward and touched Alex on her arm to get her attention.

"Hi," she said shyly, "I wanted to thank you from the bottom of my heart for what you did for me yesterday."

"Ah, it's all right, Melanie, you're welcome," Alex said, "Did it go well?"

"Not sure yet, it might have though, I still have hope for us."

"Good, that's good to hear, I am sure things will work out just fine," Alex said.

"May I see you in my office, Miss Hoffmann?" Sheppard's unexpected request startled her. She turned to follow Sheppard, while the technician disappeared in a hurry.

"What was that all about?" Sheppard asked, sitting down behind his desk. His voice was the usual hissing whisper, only somehow it sounded even more threatening.

"Oh, that? Melanie needed to leave early yesterday to go to a marriage counseling session. She and her spouse have some problems, and she's desperately trying to save her marriage."

"Marriage counseling," he repeated, punctuating every syllable with an almost imperceptible pause. Words dropped like stones. "What is this country's divorce rate, do you know?"

"I am not sure," Alex replied, bracing herself for what was to come.

"It's about 50 percent. Your employee's marriage is nothing else but just that—a marriage. They fail anyway."

Alex was not about to interrupt him and argue in her defense. She hoped this would soon be over and forgotten.

"So, why should we care, exactly? I don't care about anyone's marriage, family, or issues," he continued in the same threatening, yet calm, tone of voice. "I do not *have* to care. What I do care about is that you don't even have the basic leadership skills required for this job."

Oh, boy, she thought, *this is going to get much uglier than I expected.*

"What do you want from your employees? Do you know?"

Not sure if he really expected an answer, Alex hesitated. The silence persisted. "I expect them to work hard, be dedicated, loyal, focused, and creative," Alex replied eventually.

"If you want your employees focused on work, then aren't they better off without a spouse? Huh?"

Shocked, Alex was speechless.

"You aren't very smart, I'm afraid. We have no interest whatsoever to make even the tiniest of efforts to preserve our employees' marriages. It is illegal for us to favor singles for employment or to actively pursue actions to get married employees divorced. But I sure as hell don't want to do anything to keep an employee married. If she were single, she would spend more hours in the office."

Alex swallowed with difficulty. She couldn't believe what she was hearing. The viciousness in Sheppard's voice added to the cruel callousness of his words.

"I am urging you to spend time thinking what you want, and make up your mind about how you're going to do your job. If you're not ready to be the executive I hired you to be, please be reminded there is a door you could be exiting through. Don't hesitate to use that door if you are not ready, with every bone in your body, to give me what I expect." He paused, apparently thinking what to do with her. "You are not very smart, are you? I'm afraid I might have been mistaken about you. This job is probably too much for you to handle. From now on, please run all such decisions by me. You seem to lack every single useful leadership skill, even the basic ones. Dismissed."

Alex stepped out of Sheppard's office without a word. She was heading straight for the smoker's area, but her private cell phone's message warning beeped and stopped her.

The message read *emergency meeting at agency hq—asap.*

Alex quickly entered the conference room at The Agency, after speeding on I-5, and paying no attention to the breathtaking landscape on her left. Between stoplights, she had managed to send Sheppard a quick email advising him that she was feeling sick and had to go home. She could see, in her mind, how satisfied Sheppard would have been at the receipt of that email, thinking he had rattled her to the point of making her sick, or even causing her to quit. *Oh, I'll be back, buddy, don't you worry*, Alex thought, as she was pulling out a chair to sit.

Tom entered the room, with a look of deep concern on his always-composed face.

"What happened?"

"I'm afraid there's been an incident in Florida—involving a drone."

Alex felt the adrenaline hit her gut like a fist.

"How bad?"

"Significantly bad, Alex," Tom said, "I've sent Steve to pick up Dr. Barnaby; they should be here shortly." He prepared the conference room audio-video installation for projection of video from a DVD player, finishing just in time for Dr. Barnaby's arrival.

Alex had trouble recognizing Dr. Barnaby. His hair was in disarray; the top button of his shirt was undone; a loose, crooked tie hung disorderly, and his eyes glazed over. He looked pale, fragile, and twenty years older. A thoughtful Steve sat him at the table and offered him a cup of coffee, murmuring to him in a low, reassuring tone of voice.

"Good morning, sir. We're ready to start," Tom said.

Dr. Barnaby waved his hand in approval. Tom pressed the "play" button on the remote.

The TV started with a breaking news bulletin.

"We interrupt our program today to report a serious incident that happened just an hour ago, in Florida's Okaloosa County, on the highway between Gulf Breeze and Destin." The images on the screen behind the popular news announcer showed many emergency response vehicles, several were trying to extinguish the fire, others were evacuating the wounded, and some were cleaning up what seemed to be the scene of a serious traffic accident.

"A military drone hit a tourist commuter bus carrying thirty-three people onboard, plus the driver," the female reporter continued, while the images were showing the wreckage in detail. "Nineteen passengers from the bus were pronounced dead at the scene. Fourteen more and the driver are en route to area hospitals; some of them were airlifted. We will return with details about their conditions as soon as we have that information."

Alex felt a knot in her throat, which kept her from breathing. She struggled to hold back tears.

"A car traveling behind the bus," the reporter continued, "was too close to avoid an impact with the exploding bus. The car had New Jersey plates. The passenger was pronounced dead at the scene, and the driver was airlifted to the Naval Hospital in Pensacola. More details to follow.

"A witness told us that the drone came from the Gulf of Mexico flying low, and headed straight for the bus. Apparently, the bus driver tried to stop. As he was braking heavily, and the bus was slowing, the drone hit, turning the bus and its passengers into a roaring ball of fire. Stay tuned for details and interviews. We will return shortly. You are watching *News of the Hour* with Stephanie Wainwright."

The TV screen went dark and silent. Alex realized she had been holding her breath. She looked at Dr. Barnaby. Tears were silently falling on his cheeks.

"Dr. Barnaby," Tom called for his attention in a strong, assertive way. "We need your help to understand how these drones operate." Pause, no answer. "We need you, sir, you have to help us," Tom insisted in a somewhat softer voice. "Everyone needs you right now, your wife, your employees, the families of the wounded—"

"I'm here. What do you need to know?" Dr. Barnaby recomposed.

"Can a drone go astray? How can that happen—under what circumstances?"

"There are various degrees of autonomy to these drones, depending on the model. All of them, however, are remotely guided or assisted by an operating team situated at a nearby base. That operating team is probably being questioned right now."

"How do these drones work? Please give us as much detail as you can," Tom continued.

"Drones are more than just robotic, unmanned aircraft. They are complex weapons. They are versatile and highly autonomous; they can be in flight for many hours. They were built to be used 24 hours a day. These unmanned aerial vehicles or UAV come in various sizes, depending on application and purpose, in addition to the missiles or other equipment they need to carry. Some are combat ready, the UCAVs, and can carry up to 16 Hellfire missiles. We're now working on a new model, able to carry up to 20 Hellfires, and some other smaller weapons on top of that.

"Other drones, much smaller, are not intended for weapons deployment. They can be surveillance drones, cruising over a border or another targeted area. These would mainly be equipped with high-resolution cameras and landmark recognition software. Other non-combat drones can be relief drones or communications drones, portable repeaters of wireless signal or range expanders, to deploy above flooded areas or at the scenes of various natural disasters. They are used to enhance communications capabilities in the absence of infrastructure."

Everyone listened carefully, taking notes.

"Do we know which type this drone was?" Tom asked.

"Not sure. By the location, I would have to assume it was a surveillance drone, watching the territorial waters along the Gulf Coast. By the size of the damage, I have to infer that it was at least a partially armed drone. An unarmed UAV would have caused less damage. It would have still caused an explosion, due to the fuel it carries, but less than what I've seen. Oh, God," he said, covering his eyes, remembering the horrific scene he had just viewed on TV.

"Why do you say it might have been partially armed?" Tom asked.

"If this drone would have been fully armed, it would have pulverized the entire area. No survivors, plus a huge gaping hole in the highway. I'll need the details about the drone, model, weapons, and fuel levels, to tell you more."

"How about the crew?" Alex inquired.

"Ah, yes. These drones have a remote crew of operators, usually two. These crews can change midflight. For example, if the drone took off from somewhere in Alabama, the takeoff crew would have been local. If it goes to Miami, then the landing crew would be different from the takeoff crew. Somewhere along the way, the drone changes hands from one crew to the next. These operators are highly trained pilots, in perfect health and physical shape. They are, in fact, fully licensed pilots. The drone transmits video information from its cameras, direct or via satellite link. The operator crews see those images on their screens, and they are able to fly the drone and take subsequent actions, based on the images displayed from the drone's cameras."

"So they are not autonomous?" Tom asked.

"No, the UAVs are unmanned, but not autonomous. They don't do what they want. They have to be guided, controlled into taking any action. Our latest research looks at increasing the degree of autonomy by enhancing their landmark recognition software to include target recognition, by loading target images for them to 'hunt.' This research is due in field testing, maybe before the end of this year. With today's disaster, I don't think we'll be able to proceed with it anymore. It will create a public relations nightmare, the moment people hear that these drones have the 'power' to hunt and kill targets on their own—which they will probably never have. They will always have to be guided by the ground team. Target recognition and auto target lock is meant to speed the process of finding and locking onto a target, thus quickly removing the drone out of the danger zone. It also prevents the drone from crashing, if it hits a thunderstorm or interference area, and it loses connection with the ground operations team. That's all there is to it."

"Dr. Barnaby, what consequences could NanoLance face due to this incident?" Tom asked. "What's to be expected?"

"We are a defense contractor, one of the contractors of record for the manufacturing of these drones for the majority of the branches of the US military. We are not the biggest drone manufacturer in the United States. There are a few other companies supplying a greater number of UAVs than we are. Some drones are also imported from foreign manufacturers with the purpose of studying and comparing performance in field-testing, war games, and simulations. Even NanoLance purchased some foreign drones with the help of the Air Force. They rerouted a few they had ordered for war games to our research facility."

Dr. Barnaby stopped and closed his eyes for a few seconds, recollecting his thoughts. "There will be an investigation into the drone manufacturer of record for the stray drone, and there is a chance we are that manufacturer of record. There is even a greater chance that we supplied components and software for this drone, even if we are not the manufacturer of record. Documents will be subpoenaed; employees will be interrogated, asked to testify. There will be lawsuits, potentially criminal charges, for negligence, at least. There will be civil litigations; a large number of families out there have lost loved ones today."

He paused, rubbing his forehead with his right hand and shielding his eyes for a couple of seconds. "Oh, God . . . There will also be a strong media attack on us, from what I've seen in the past. Some time ago—I can't recall when—there was the case of a weapons manufacturer that shipped defective ammunition to the Iraqi battlefields, causing the ammo to misfire and wound or kill the soldiers who were handling it. In the case of that company, well, what can I say? . . . It was completely destroyed by the scandal. Media pressure was huge, driving the stock price into the ground. Investigators found that the errors had been known and reported internally, then discarded by the management. Part of that management is now serving time at a nearby correctional facility. The rest of them are unemployed; no one will hire them now."

"Let's discuss next steps," Tom cut in, changing the path of the discussion to a more positive direction. "We need to establish what we do next, and in what order."

"It's too late," Dr. Barnaby said, shaking his head in disapproval of any action plan.

"I don't think it's too late, if we think fast on our feet and move quickly."

Dr. Barnaby stood abruptly, causing his chair to be thrown back. His face was showing turmoil and anger.

"Give me one scenario," he bellowed, "one single, damn scenario that ends well. You want action?" He paced the floor with his fists clenched, continuing to raise his voice. "I'll give you action. I'll go straight to my basement, get my handgun out of my safe, and spare my wife the shame and embarrassment to see me brought to my knees and dragged in handcuffs out of our home. That's what I would consider action right now." He spat the words in bursts of deep-set anger, riddled with pain.

Tom exchanged a quick look with Steve, encouraging the professionally trained psychologist to take over the handling of the situation.

"We understand how you feel, sir—"

Before he could continue, Steve was abruptly interrupted by another burst of anguish.

"One scenario! That's all I ask for . . . Is that too much? If you cannot think of a single possibility how this situation will not end in disaster for me, my family, and my company, then why even bother talking about it?"

"I'll give you one scenario," Steve said, changing his approach to a more assertive demeanor. "We crank up the speed, find the responsible people for this mess, and make them pay. You obviously had no idea this was happening. You had suspicions, and you hired us—that's proof of your good intentions right there. Will it fly in the face of any jury, regardless of the number of deaths? Civil lawsuits? Something tells me a strong legal team can negotiate and settle out of court on each and every one of them.

"Maybe the military will pitch in with you, who knows? Do we even know for sure it wasn't their fault? How about the media pressure? We'll get you the best public relations sharks that money can buy, and they'll help you steer through these troubled waters. Stock price? Have you seen the stock market lately? Everyone goes down from time to time, and then they come right back up again. You fix the issue, and then you continue to make better drones. You lose the defense contract? You stick to the consumer market for GPS navigation systems, and you expand to kitchenware, or whatever else your innovative mind will think of next." Steve paused for a few seconds, and then continued, in a much softer, compassionate tone of voice. "That is, of course, if you don't put a bullet through that brilliant brain of yours."

Dr. Barnaby slowed his furious pacing of the room, then came to a stop. He pulled his chair back to the table and sat.

"I'm listening."

Tom went to the whiteboard to take notes.

"We have questions we need answered," Tom started, splitting the whiteboard space in two columns, and titling one side "Questions."

"We need to know the following things," he continued.
- "Who manufactured the stray drone?
- Who deployed it?
- Who was operating it, and from which base?
- What do their records indicate as failure?
- How can we speak with the drone operators?
- Was the drone armed?
- What type of weapons?"

Tom was listing the questions one under the other, arranged neatly in a bulleted list. "Oh, very important," Tom said, and squeezed a few questions at the top of the list:
- "What model was the stray drone?
- What type?
- When was it purchased?
- If it was a NanoLance produced drone, when did it leave manufacturing?
- When was it produced?
- If confirmed, let's try to track it down to the assembly team who built it."

"That's not hard. We give our drones serial numbers that are recorded by the defense clients. We keep detailed records, reflecting these serial numbers, showing all the manufacturing and testing details for each drone," Dr. Barnaby clarified. He was back in problem-solving mode.

"OK. Let's move to actions. We need help in here as soon as possible. We need a strong, legal representation, external counsel. Until we figure out who is doing what at NanoLance, I would recommend against using the internal counsel for this. Steve will set up an emergency appointment with the toughest, meanest son-of-a-bitch lawyer that ever came into existence in this land."

Steve nodded approval, and then disappeared from the room.

Tom listed "lawyer" under the second column, marked "Actions."

"We need strong PR representation. There is an excellent public relations firm here in San Diego. If you recall, a few years ago it handled that huge Salmonella contamination scandal for that deli manufacturer . . . can't recall the name. All I recall is the company came out of it looking squeaky clean, and no one refrained from buying their product. I'll get that covered. Then, we need you to announce the sale of your stock tomorrow, just as we discussed."

"This will make things even worse!" Dr. Barnaby stood again, agitated.

"No, it won't, if you think about it. The conspirators will assume it's because of the drone crash; they'll rub their hands and make a move fast—carelessly fast. We'll be there, watching and waiting."

"But what about the effect that this combined attack will have on the stock price?"

"Their attack will only be a blip on the radar, among the nonstop wave of interviews, comments, opinions, and every other single way the media will dissect this. However, because of this incident, you will have PR and legal on your side to help, and I am confidently estimating the cumulative effect of their efforts to bring the added media-inflicted damage to zero. Now is the time. Tomorrow."

"Tomorrow is Saturday," Alex intervened.

"Right. Then Monday, or as soon as possible," Tom clarified. "But without any further delay."

"I'll do it. What else?"

"Alex," Tom said, turning toward her. "You need to go back in there and crank up the heat. Make your moves faster than we had originally planned. Let's uncover who's behind all this, in time for us to prepare a good handling of the entire situation."

"Understood," Alex said. *No pressure*, she thought.

"One more thing," Tom said, turning his attention back to Dr. Barnaby. "Don't worry about the stock price."

It was Alex's first executive meeting. Only directors and above, assistant vice presidents, vice presidents, and chief officers of all departments were gathering in the large conference room on the top floor. They were quite numerous; Alex had no idea there were so many. She recognized few faces, though, and not a lot of people recognized and greeted her either.

She could see signs of worry and low-voice chatter going on, as her colleagues were filling the room, starting from back to front. They were behaving somewhat like schoolchildren, these executives, none daring to sit in the first two rows of seats. Alex saw the opportunity to situate herself in a manner that would give her great visibility to the reactions and expressions of everyone else. She took the first seat on the right, on the first row of seats. She would be able to sit half-turned toward the back, keep an eye on Dr. Barnaby as he spoke, but also see the reactions of most of the people present.

Dr. Barnaby entered the conference room, bringing the low-key chatter to a halt. He looked composed and dignified, his usual self.

"Good morning, everyone, and thank you for joining me in this meeting on such short notice. I have an announcement to make. At the end of the fourth quarter of this year, when the trading window will be open, I will be liquidating a significant portion of my stock."

Murmurs filled the room.

"I know you have heard this announcement before, and nothing happened. Let me explain a few things. First and foremost, this company has been my life, my passion, and my dream. It is difficult for me to bring to fulfillment the idea of separating myself from it. Therefore, in the recent past, I have tried to do this a couple of times, yet unsuccessfully. This time it's different. For family reasons, I will no longer be able to procrastinate on this task . . . I must retire as soon as I can and dedicate much more time to my family."

Another wave of murmurs came and went.

"In the months to follow, we must work together with the board of directors to ensure a smooth transition of ownership, control, and leadership that will follow at the end of this year. I will be communicating my decision to the board at our quarterly meeting in July. Does anyone have any questions?"

A tense silence, then someone in the back of the room raised his hand.

"Is this decision related to the drone incident in Florida?"

"Not directly," Dr. Barnaby answered calmly. "I have promised my wife I would spend our golden years with her in some peaceful place. My work has taken a tremendous toll on our family life. Now is the time for us to catch up on all the things we wanted to do in this life and never had time for. Why now? Unfortunately, my wife's health is deteriorating . . . I am now pressed for time. However, regarding the drone incident connection I said 'not directly,' because I think the time has come for a younger leader to take over the reins of this company and make sure he or she steers the company clear of all potential problems."

Another hand rose in the back.

"What are your thoughts about the Florida drone incident? How will this affect us?"

"It's hard to say at this time. We don't even know if it was one of our products. Our liaisons are working to get this information. If it is indeed one of ours, we are to expect an inquiry into the causes of this unfortunate incident. Please count on my full commitment and dedication to ensure we get to the bottom of this and figure out everything there is to know about what might have caused this tragedy. We will leave no stone unturned, and no question unanswered."

"Are you concerned at all with how the press will perceive the timing of your exit, vis-à-vis the Florida incident?"

"To some extent it is like a controlled detonation. If my exit will take the heat off the company to even the smallest degree, I would rather have the press think there is a correlation. You, however, know this was not the decision point in this case, as I have planned twice before to sell my shares and retire, but I just couldn't break away."

"How are we addressing the media questions at this time?" This question came from a familiar face—Peter Wilson from Six Sigma, one of Walker's nodding enablers.

"We have secured the services of one of the most powerful public relations agencies in this country, Leesman & Koch."

The mention of this well-known name brought a wave of appreciative whispers from the executive group. Leesman & Koch had earned a solid reputation assisting various politicians to weather corruption or lewdness scandals; handholding movie stars through bail hearings, parole hearings, and rehab trips; and managing the media angle of several presidential election campaigns.

"Leesman & Koch is top dollar, but worth every dime. We are fortunate to have them on our side through this, and they will work to get us trained on how to handle media questions. Expect media training appointments to start appearing on your calendars as of today. Please plan to attend. In the meantime, they have advised me to ask you not to speak with the media at all. Please do not answer any questions, even those that might appear harmless. Defer all media inquiries to our new PR office, the extension is on the Intranet. Please instruct your teams to do the same."

"Going back to your retirement, sir. Who are we allowed to discuss this with?" A young, pale man in the third row asked the question without raising his hand.

"For now, this is executive insider information only. Do not discuss this with your teams and definitely not with the media. If this leaks out before the time has come to file paperwork with the SEC and announce it to the markets in a well-orchestrated media campaign, it could bring this company to its knees. It could destroy us. So please do not discuss this with anyone whatsoever."

Another hand rose from the middle of the crowd.

"Will this change of control bring a restructuring of the company's leadership?"

"There is no way anyone can estimate what changes the new leadership will bring, because we don't even know who the new leaders will be. However, in most change-of-control situations, the new leaders rethink the organizational chart to match their goals. So, yes, the new leadership will, most likely, make changes to the leadership team."

A wave of concerned chatter rose abruptly.

"I wouldn't let this affect your current work," Dr. Barnaby continued, "or scare you away from working at NanoLance. Not all change is bad, you know. For some, it could mean promotions, for others, new challenges and opportunities."

"Then, what are the next steps for us?" Someone seated behind Alex, on the third row, asked in a hesitant voice.

"We will prepare for two important challenges: the aftermath of the Florida incident and the change of control. I will have meetings with you and help you work through both issues. I'm sure we all are quite anxious to put both issues to rest with the best possible outcomes, so you will see, in the next few days, the first steps of an action plan aimed to deliver exactly that. In the meantime, though, the most important thing you need to remember is to keep everything we discussed here today strictly confidential." Dr. Barnaby paused for a minute, waiting for additional questions. None came.

"Thank you all for coming; enjoy the rest of your day."

The attendees rose and began to disperse, Alex trailing behind the crowd. She felt a hand touch her shoulder and turned.

"Please join me for a couple of minutes; there is something I'd like to talk to you about," Benjamin Walker said.

Alex followed Walker into his office, blood rushing to her cheeks, and adrenaline churning her stomach. Had she done something wrong? Had she tipped her hand somehow? Racing thoughts were speeding by, in a desperate effort to anticipate what this conversation might be about. She remembered clearly how easily Walker could inflict psychological pain; she had seen him casually turn the vice president of manufacturing, John Dunwood, into a trembling, disarticulate wreck, in just minutes. She sat where Walker indicated with his finger.

He closed his office door and got right to business.

"Who exactly are you, Miss Hoffmann?"

"Huh?" Surprised, Alex tried to gather her thoughts. What would prompt Walker to ask her that question?

"Yes, you heard me, who are you?" Walker pressed on.

"How do you mean?" Alex asked, slowly but surely regaining her cool. He was just another mean bastard, and she was not going to let him intimidate and bully her as he had Dunwood.

"I've been watching you, since you came here, and there's definitely something off about you."

Oh, God, Alex thought, *I'm blown out of the water. That didn't even take long.*

"I still don't get it," she probed, mimicking surprise. Tom had taught her to stand up to a bully, or if need be, even bully the bully. He had said that most of the times it worked. She hoped this was going to be one of those times.

"You are not affected by anything that affects the rest of us. You're watching us just as much as I'm watching you." Walker stopped, expecting an explanation.

"Who's us? Who do you think I'm watching?" She continued her line of questioning, causing Walker to frown.

"Today, in the executive meeting, you were carefully studying the reactions of everyone present. In my operations meeting, you were undisturbed, just like watching a game on TV."

"And this is wrong why, exactly?" Alex pressed back.

"Even now, you see?" Walker said, his anger rising and his clenched fist finding its way to the desk's innocent surface. "You are not intimidated by me at all. You are . . . unafraid. This is not normal."

"Ah, I see how that can bother you," Alex said, at the risk of being rude, thinking just how wrong he was.

"Unbelievable," Walker responded, riddled with anger. "So, who are you exactly? Why were you studying the reactions of everyone in there today?"

Alex realized she wasn't going to get away without providing explanations. She constructed her explanations carefully, making sure they sounded plausible enough.

"I am new here, as you might have noted. I'm learning about the company's culture, from people's reactions. Some of the things happening around me are more serious than others; how can I tell which ones I should be concerned about, unless I let the reactions of my colleagues guide me?"

"So that's what you're doing? Learning about our culture, huh?" Walker frowned some more, not buying it. "But why aren't you concerned? Everyone in my operations meeting was intimidated, except you. Even now, you're composed and fighting back, instead of fearing for your job."

"Why do you want them to be afraid?" She pushed back, buying herself time to think. "If you knew they were intimidated, that means you are doing this on purpose, and I can't see why. Fear stifles growth and creativity."

"I'm not running a kindergarten here, where all kids have to be happy and tell nice stories about it when they get home. I run a business, a complicated business that needs to make me lots of money. No one gives performance, unless they're pushed. No one gets to come to me and say goals can't be achieved, or the job can't be done. If they do, I get someone else in their place who can do the job. Why the hell am I explaining myself to you, instead of you to me?" Walker resumed his angry outburst, raising his voice to thunderous levels. "You still didn't tell me why you're not intimidated, or compelled to change your relaxed demeanor to a more focused or concerned one. So?"

"First, again, I am new, so I don't have a lot invested in this company. If I were to lose this job today, it wouldn't mean a big emotional loss for me. If you were to fire me now, I wouldn't even list this company on my résumé. Second, I'm financially secure," she said, humorously thinking of The Agency's credit card, the one with the unknown spending limit, hoping this stunt would work.

"Ah, you're rich!" Walker said, clapping his hands. "How unfortunate."

"I wouldn't call myself rich," Alex clarified.

"Then what?"

"Financially secure. If I don't have to work for a while, I can be all right."

"Still unfortunate. I have no use for people who can't be pushed as hard as they need to be pushed to be successful here."

"Well, I don't work for you. I work for Sheppard," Alex said bluntly.

"How wrong you are. You report to Sheppard, but you work for me. What else do you think you were doing in my operations meetings? You are my support person for infrastructure. Without my say-so, you won't even make it past your ninety-day review. Considering how financially secure you are, you probably won't make it anyway."

"Why would you say that?"

"Because I am going to push you, as hard as I can, and being that you're so damn financially secure, you'll walk out of here on your own, before I even get the pleasure of firing you."

"I love a challenge," Alex said, with a crooked smile, "I'll think I'll stay for a while."

"Be careful what you wish for," Walker concluded.

She stepped out of Walker's office, allowing herself to breathe again. She was hoping this explanation had put his mind at ease, at least for a while. *Very perceptive, this son-of-a-bitch Walker. Gotta be super careful around him*, she warned herself, heading toward her own office on the third floor.

"Hey, I was looking all over for you," Louie Bailey, her analyst, said cheerfully. "Where have you been all day?"

"Around," she said casually. "What's going on?"

"I was trying to get you set up on the printers," he said, following her into her office. "You need to log into your laptop, so I can map the printers." He stood there, waiting for her to put in her password.

She looked down at her laptop and cringed. The clone laptop was on her desk, not the official NanoLance one. She quickly balanced her options. Sending Louie for coffee would not work; she had her own coffeemaker hidden in her closet, and he knew about it. What else could she ask him to do, to get him out of her office long enough to get the two laptops switched? She opted for a different approach: stalling.

"I was just heading out again, Louie, but thanks."

"How about your printers?"

"Louie," she said, with humor in her voice, as she was leaving, "are you a good techie?"

"Yes, ma'am!" Louie replied, executing a perfect military salute.

"Then why don't you go ahead and hack into my laptop and get the job done?" she said, laughing out loud.

"Ha, that's a good one," Louie said, exiting her office and laughing as he walked away.

She breathed easy again, heading for the smoker's area. He wasn't going to come anywhere near her laptop. He wasn't going to hack into anything. After all, it was illegal.

Passing through the large, sun-filled atrium on the way to the rear exit, she checked out the long line in front of the coffee shop. She was looking for familiar faces of interest, someone with whom she could discuss the announcement regarding the sale of the stock and the upcoming change in company ownership.

Outside Alex's line of sight, on the other side of the café, through the tinted windows facing the parking lot, a gray sedan became visible, pulling behind Alex's car. The man behind the wheel stepped out and looked briefly around, to see if anyone was paying attention. Satisfied with his observations, he pulled a small camera from his pocket and started taking pictures of Alex's car. Full front. Full right side. Full left side, with some difficulty, because the car parked next to it had parked too close. Full back. Close-up shot of both license plates, back and front. Once the job was done, the man climbed back in his car and drove away.

"A few days have passed since tragedy hit, when a bus, carrying thirty-three passengers plus the driver, and a car with two more unsuspecting victims, were abruptly stopped by a collision with a military drone. Twenty lives were lost on Highway 98 near Gulf Breeze, Florida, last Friday; sixteen more victims are fighting for their lives at nearby hospitals. And yet, despite the staggering dimensions of this tragedy, today there are more questions than answers."

A short pause in Stephanie Wainwright's report, and the camera zoomed out and engulfed the entire scene of the incident. Reminding the viewer more of a war zone, the blocked highway was still covered with dried blood, debris, spilled motor oil, flame-suppressing fluids, along with smoke stains and ash from the fire that had engulfed the vehicles following the collision with the drone.

The camera refocused on Stephanie.

"What we do know is that the drone was coming in for landing at Mackenzie Air Field, just across the highway. The UAV was coming from the south, moving over the Gulf waters, and was supposed to cross the highway at a safe altitude, then descend and land safely at the air base. Mackenzie is an Air Force base; the death drone also belonged to the Air Force. However, the Air Force is yet to provide the public with details into its inquiry. So far, the military has only shared a press statement with the media, expressing its commitment to investigate this incident in detail and examine all causes that led to this tragedy."

Another pause in the voiceover, the camera showing the panoramic view of the air base behind the highway to the north.

"The question the Air Force will need to answer is this: Was it a pilot error? Or did the drone malfunction somehow? For those of you who might be surprised at the questions I have just mentioned, yes, these drones have pilots, but not onboard the actual aircraft.

"The drones were developed to reduce the cost of military aircraft and the associated loss of equipment, when an aircraft is shot down in enemy land. They were designed to preserve the lives and freedom of our pilots, keeping them safe and out of harm's way, during aerial reconnaissance or combat missions. Therefore, these drones are being flown with the assistance of remotely located pilots, who operate the drones just as they operate any traditional aircraft. Many countries in the world have increased the use of drones, instead of traditional crewed aircraft, like the one you see taking off behind me from Mackenzie Air Field."

The roar of a military jet taking off forced Stephanie to stop talking. When the roar of the jet died down, she continued.

"The use of drones, the array of applications for unmanned aircraft has increased exponentially in the past few years. From highly experimental in the 1990s, now we are seeing unmanned aerial vehicles, or UAVs, serving a wide variety of purposes, mostly with military applications, but also some civilian purposes. A cheaper, more expendable, more fuel-efficient alternative to the traditional fighter jet, these drones are equally capable of recon missions and launching missiles on predetermined targets.

"But are they safe enough? Over time, we have seen a couple of drone-related incidents, causing loss of lives. In April, there was a friendly fire incident in Afghanistan, where a Canadian unit reportedly came under attack from a drone wearing American markings. Four Canadian lives were lost; more soldiers were wounded. So far, no official finding was released in this case.

"Another incident took place in a hot zone in the Middle East, but even less information was made public about it. This incident was only reported in the local media, which blamed a drone for the loss of several civilian lives somewhere in Iraq, near the small city of Karbala. The Air Force, which had a presence there at the time, refused to comment on the alleged incident, calling it *unconfirmed*."

A short, dramatic pause, then Stephanie continued.

"This time, disaster hit us right here, at home, where we all should feel safe and protected. The Air Force will not have a choice. It must provide us with official findings about this incident, and, hopefully, stringent safety measures must be imposed, so we can all feel safe again within the boundaries of our homeland. While the vigil in our hearts continues for those struck down here last Friday, we pray for the well-being of those still fighting for their lives.

"Reporting live from the scene of the drone incident near Gulf Breeze, Florida, this is Stephanie Wainwright, with *News of the Hour*."

Alex breathed in the refreshing fumes of steaming coffee coming from her mug, deeply enjoying the wonderful aroma of Brazilian dark roast.

She opened her laptop, the cloned one, to see if any interesting emails had accumulated overnight. The screen came alive immediately, going straight to the login screen, meaning the evening before she had just slammed the lid, instead of shutting it down properly. She put in her password. In front of her bewildered eyes, the screen displayed a message: *printer installation complete*. She verified in a hurry: yes, two printers had been installed on her laptop, one laser and one color inkjet.

Oh, my God, she thought, leaning back against her chair, thinking of possible implications. *First*, she concluded, *Louie is one hell of a hacker*. Her password was long, complex, unpredictable, not a dictionary word, and included numbers, letters, and special characters—an exclamation mark and a number sign. *But had he seen anything?* She checked for signs of anything out of the ordinary, checking folder access time logs, not really sure how else to gauge if he had noticed anything unusual. He could have checked the settings of the keystroke logger; he could have seen that the data was being saved, but not transmitted, unlike the rest of the company-issued computers. He could have noticed her archive of cloned emails from a number of key players in NanoLance's leadership.

She checked the email archive's last date and time of access and breathed with ease; it showed an access time stamp prior to her conversation with Louie, the conversation during which she had so naïvely invited him to hack into her machine. *Let's assume everything is all right, but watch for signs of otherwise*, she concluded, getting ready for her staff meeting.

All her direct reports were waiting in the conference room, ready for the weekly staff meeting. Bob Foster, the infrastructure manager, his kind eyes having a secretive smile hiding in them. Lisa Murphy, apparently a decorative doll, but with the sharp wits of a junior PhD in physics, was blatantly smiling ear to ear. Alan Walden, whose permanent worry had succumbed in favor of a more relaxed expression. And, of course, Louie, whose face was reflecting the playfully innocent look of a nine year old whose bicycle is in the middle of the driveway, while he's telling everyone he didn't leave it there.

"Good morning, everyone," Alex said, and then sat down. She looked again at everyone around the table and decided to grab this bull by its horns.

"By the looks of it," she continued, "you are all aware of Louie's exceptional hacking abilities."

A roar of laughter burst in the room. Louie blushed.

"What were you thinking?" Alex asked, with visible amusement, yet watching carefully for his reactions. "You're not supposed to hack into anything, that's illegal!"

"No, ma'am," Louie said, "not with your consent, it's not."

Another roar of laughter. They had all known about this for a while.

"I see. I guess you're right, I did specifically invite you to hack in, didn't I?"

"Precisely. The way I read your orders, ma'am, was that you did not have the time to input your password, and you delegated the task to me."

"Lovely," Alex said.

"By the way, you have one extremely complicated password," Louie continued, "took me a full fifteen minutes to crack it."

"Oh," she said, with an admiring tone that acknowledged his ability.

"He is the meanest hacker out there, this guy, but don't tell anyone," Lisa offered.

"All right," Alex said, changing direction, "let's talk a bit about what we can expect from the aftermath of the drone incident, and how infrastructure and support needs to prepare. Thoughts, anyone?"

"First of all," Lisa said, "I don't think we were to blame at all. We do one hell of a job here, you know."

"Who do you mean, we?" Alex wanted to know for sure.

"We, infrastructure and support, this team," Lisa replied.

"It's not about putting blame on the department. The company might have a rough patch ahead of it, though, even if the company wasn't to blame. I want us to focus today on our readiness to support the larger organization, as it deals with the aftermath of all this. Regardless of who was the Florida drone's manufacturer, we still need to be ready to assist."

"We can allow access to our data, in a structured manner, with zero or little warning," Bob said. "Our systems are designed to allow quick retrievals of data and activity or service logs, to do exactly that—support potential investigations or performance assessments. We're good on this end."

"On my end, though," Alan said, "we could run into potential problems."

"Why is that?" Alex asked.

"Well, we deploy the hardware associated with the loading, testing, and deployment of the drone landmark acquisition and recognition and the target recognition software."

"And why would that put us in a hot seat?"

"Because, well, corners were cut," Alan said, looking down. "Not by us, of course, but we have knowledge of that being the case."

"What corners were cut?"

"The software testing did not occur on specs. Hardware deployment sees the activity logs and can figure out what testing had been done, and if it's up to par with the spec. You see, for all the software we deploy, we have specifications for the particular hardware that goes with it—this is what my team does. There are also clear specifications as to how software should be developed, tested, deployed, and retested. That's where the corners were cut, in the software deployment team."

"Did you report your findings?" Alex asked.

"Yes, more than once."

"What happened?"

"I was shot down, told to mind my own business."

"Did you report these findings by email?"

"Oh, sure, CYA, right?" Alan smiled sadly.

"CYA? What's that?" Alex looked confused.

"Aww . . . don't tell me you've worked in corporate for so long and you don't know what CYA means?" Louie laughed. "Stands for cover your ass, as in having paperwork to prove you've done your job."

"I see, well, thank you for educating me," Alex said, then turned her attention back to Alan. "Can you please forward me such emails? They would probably come in handy in the near future."

"Will do," Alan said, looking less at ease. "Other than that, we're in good shape. But if there's an official inquiry, and they ask me direct questions, I will have to tell them the truth."

"I would expect nothing else," Alex said, supportively.

"On my end," a now-serious Louie said, opening his portfolio to look at his notes, "there has been, in the past, business analysis done ad-hoc, by request of several executives, reflecting less-than-expected performance results for various areas touching infrastructure. I have also been asked, over time, to run reports for areas that were outside of the scope of infrastructure and support, such as software reliability and testing analysis reports, R&D-related reports, and so on.

"I have to confess I kept my head down on these reports. I ran the data, drew the conclusions, sent them over, and never followed up if the results were bad. Maybe I should have said something to somebody, I guess. My thinking was that if they were running the reports, then they were planning to do something to address the shortcomings, so I didn't feel compelled to do anything about the subpar performance that I found in my reports. Now, well, I don't know anymore."

"All right," Alex said, "I wouldn't worry about it now, what's done is done. Let's be ready to assist in every way possible going forward. Let's keep one another informed at all times. It's better to over-communicate issues going forward, than risk missing key information. Anything else?" Alex asked, preparing to adjourn.

Silence.

"Then, we're good. Have a great rest of the day!"

"Going out for a smoke, boss?" Louie asked, invitingly. She nodded her approval. Lisa tagged along.

Out on the lush lawn, Alex pulled her e-cig from its holder and inhaled the light vapor.

"Not doing the real deal anymore, huh?"

"Nah . . . stains my teeth and stinks up my house, but I can't quit either," she replied laughing.

"Listen," Lisa approached her with timidity, "there's something I wanted to tell you."

"Sure, go ahead."

"There were some people asking questions about you yesterday. Sheppard was with them."

"What people?" Alex felt her heart doubling its rhythm.

"Not sure. They wanted to know if you ever mention anything outside of work, if we ever met with you socially, if we heard you reference anything out of the ordinary, stuff like that."

"There were two men," Louie clarified, "pretending to ask casual questions, but they seemed really interested in you, specifically."

"I see," Alex said. "Does this happen often?"

"It does happen now and then," Louie said, "we are, after all, a defense contractor. We all have security clearances to be able to enter this building. Sometimes there are audits being run, just to prevent potential problems."

"Ah, then I'm sure that's OK, nothing to worry about, but thank you both for letting me know. I really appreciate it," Alex said, putting her e-cig back in her pocket.

"One more thing," Louie whispered, close to her ear, "don't ask people to forward you certain emails. You never know who's watching email traffic, do you? Then you'd both get in trouble . . . If you want to see Alan's CYA emails, ask him to print them. That's what printers are for."

Vincent Moran's voice took a lower, more serious pitch, usually reserved for bad financial news of sizeable impact.

"After the numerous lives lost in Florida last week, as to be expected, NanoLance stock came under serious pressure from investors looking to cut their losses and liquidate their assets while their value is still notable. NanoLance lost today the biggest percentage in its trading history: 17.45 percent lost in a single day of trading. That's a cumulative 26.44 percent loss since the Florida incident last week.

"While markets were closed over the weekend, and not many investors were ready to pull out this past Monday, the volume really picked up this morning, following the *News of the Hour* report on the Florida drone incident. The report was syndicated nationally last night. While findings in the Florida incident are yet to come, all drone manufacturers share in the losses brought by this unfortunate incident, but NNLC, again, leads the parade of high-dollar losers on Wall Street. With shares trading now under the hundred-dollar threshold, for only $83.47 at closing bell today, NanoLance has lost its investors tens of millions of dollars, and most say this decline is not over yet.

"From *Money Markets Review*, this is Vincent Moran, wishing you a fortunate day."

The landscape in Tom's backyard was designed to inspire peace and tranquility. Alex was feeling neither, instead pacing restlessly on the patio, around Tom and his grill.

"Grab a seat," Tom invited her, "it's better in the shade."

"It's all right, can't settle down, don't know why," she replied.

Steve's eyes met Tom's in an inquisitive wordless expression. What was going on with her?

"Tell me about your day," Tom asked.

"Nothing to it, really. The team is great, I love working with them. Every morning I look forward to getting there."

Steve's concern rose, a slight frown shading his face. Tom picked up on it and continued.

"You make me curious, give me some details, what did you do today? How is your boss?"

"My boss is a wicked asshole. By the way, I just learned I have two bosses now. I report to Sheppard, the chief of technology, but, in fact, I work for Walker, the biggest, slimiest snake of them all. Huh! I guess that's my luck!"

Alex was behaving quite out of the ordinary. Her usual attention to detail and focus on the specifics of her complex task were gone, replaced by this restless indifference.

"And your day? Anything worth mentioning?" Tom pushed.

"I had a really amusing staff meeting with my team. They are nice people, you know. One of them hacked into my laptop, but that was because I told him to. I didn't think he'd do it."

"You're not making any sense, Alex, slow down. Who hacked into your laptop?" Tom asked.

"Louie, he's my analyst. He's also an ex-Navy SEAL."

"Interesting," Tom said, "but why did he hack into your computer?"

"'Cause I told him to. Never mind, it's OK. Has no meaning, I checked. But two people were asking questions about me today."

"Who were they?" Tom was getting seriously worried.

"Not sure, could have been a routine check for new hires. I heard it happens every now and then."

"You have to promise me you will be extra careful. At the first sign of real danger, you have to step away. You need to promise you will call me, and then walk away." Tom had left the grill to cook on its own. He was standing in front of Alex, getting her full attention. "Is that understood?"

"Yes, sir." She looked pale. "I'm not so hungry anymore."

"Just a burger," Steve intervened, bringing the salvaged, yet overdone, hamburgers to the table, "it's not going to kill you."

"OK, I'll try to eat something."

Claire had joined them earlier, going unnoticed while everyone was caught in their conversation. They were all seated, thoughtfully chewing their hamburgers. Alex was playing with her food, more than she was eating, extracting the patty from the bun and nibbling at small pieces of it.

"Gotta run," she said abruptly, standing up, "I have a lot of emails to browse and a lot of stuff to do before I go to bed. Thanks for dinner!"

Before they could react she was gone, climbing behind the wheel of her Toyota and driving away.

"OK, what just happened?" Claire asked.

"Wish I could tell you, honey," Tom said, "but the thing is I don't know." They both turned and looked at Steve.

"I don't know either, but something is definitely off. She is obviously preoccupied. Her brain was working in high gear on a different subject than our conversation. And she wouldn't share—that is what scares me. Whatever it might be about, if we know, we can deal with it."

"True," Tom said thoughtfully, "do you think she might be stressed out?"

"Dealing with a secret agenda such as hers in an environment like NanoLance can definitely take its toll. Add the twenty dead and sixteen wounded in Florida as a form of pressure, and it's possible that she might be caving in. She might be ridden with guilt that she's unable to solve the case fast enough. She might be deeply tired and in a state of hyper-vigilance, due to hiding her real identity for so many hours a day. Remember, she has two of everything: two identities, two difficult and challenging jobs, two laptops, two phones. Most of us struggle to properly handle only one of each."

A sad chuckle came from Tom. "How do we help her?"

"We need to watch over her carefully. In a state of hyper-vigilance such as this, the brain and the body get tired and become unable to correctly deal with stressors. She could overreact to otherwise normal stimuli or fail to perceive a threat in due time. And she was definitely not eating much either."

"I was hoping she had what it takes to be successful on her own in this type of work," Tom said, letting his disappointment take over.

"I wouldn't write her off just yet, we actually don't know what's going on, and she hasn't made any mistakes. She's also new at this and dealing with a case way more difficult than my first case was. Back in the day when I started working for you, if I had been hit with the pressure of twenty bodies, I would have probably caved under that strain."

"She's just a kid," Claire pleaded, "a kid you threw to the wolves. You have to take care of her." She reached across the table and squeezed Tom's hand. "Promise me you will."

Alex arrived at the office earlier than usual, to catch up on cloned email review before the place got busy. She felt tired and edgy; she could hardly wait for the small coffee machine to finish brewing.

Two emails caught her eye in the first minute. Both emails came from Walker, the chief operating officer; both were worrisome. About the first one, there was nothing she could do.

From: Benjamin Walker (COO)
To: Angela Prescott (VP HR)
Subject: Request
Sent: Wednesday, June 30, 8:47PM

Angela,

Please run an extensive, in-depth background check on the new director of infrastructure and support. There's more to her than meets the eye, and I hate surprises.

Thanks,
Ben

The second email though made her jump to her feet.

From: Benjamin Walker (COO)
To: Angela Prescott (VP HR); Chandler Griffiths (CSO); Audrey Kramer (CFO); Dustin Sheppard (CTO)
Subject: Strategy Meeting Re: Leadership Change Announcement
When: Thursday, July 1, 10:00AM—11:00AM
Where: Conference Room 501
Sent: Wednesday, June 30, 9:02PM

All,

Let's get together and discuss Barnaby's announcement, and what we need to do to be prepared.

Thank you,
Ben Walker

She stood for a few seconds, staring into the laptop screen, thinking about options. She slammed the laptop shut and headed out. She had two hours to prepare for this meeting.

Alex checked the time nervously. She had only seven minutes left to finish bugging Conference Room 501. Audio was the easiest one to place. With video, she still struggled. Finding the right spot for the tiny camera, installing the receiver at a close enough distance, yet in a secure spot, and doing all that without being seen through the conference room's glass walls—that was the challenge.

The conference room had a small closet with wooden doors made of narrow wooden segments installed under an angle, imitating window blinds. That closet was going to be secure enough to house the receiver. The doors provided the needed privacy; the wooden blinds were at an angle that allowed a person to see from the inside out, not the other way. It was a safe bet for Alex to assume that no one would have any business opening that closet; this was not going to be a conference call or a video conference. Just a conversation among five people.

Her mind was made up, so she opened the closet and looked for a good place to put the wireless video receiver. She reached up and put it on top of the video conferencing equipment.

Just as she was preparing to get out and close the doors, she heard voices. Griffiths and Kramer were early, heading into the conference room. Out of options, she pulled the closet doors shut and went as far back as she could, leaning against the AV equipment rack, hoping no one would hear her breathe.

"I came home last night and my kid tells me she won't go to college, unless she gets an apartment off campus. Can you believe it?" Kramer was half-frustrated, half-amused. "In my day, we were happy to go to college at all, and if I would have dared set terms with my parents like that, I would have been grounded forever."

"Different times, I'm afraid," Chandler said, "I'm amazed at how these things evolve. My boy is fifteen now and overheard me talking to my wife about trading in my Jeep. He came and literally told me that I can't do that, since he'd be turning sixteen in under a year and he'll be taking the Jeep!" They both laughed the sweet laugh of loving parents.

One by one, the rest of the meeting attendees were arriving. Alex could see out through a sliver in the wooden slats. Angela Prescott looked like she came to showcase a fashion show. Her dark gray business suit was impeccable, coordinated with her shoes and blouse in a shiny shade of light blue gray. Sheppard came in dressed in black, as usual, managed a faint smile and a whispered "hello." He sat quietly, not participating in the casual conversations. Walker, last to arrive, closed the door behind him and sat down.

"Thanks for joining me this morning on such short notice. I think we need to figure out what we are going to do to prepare for Barnaby's stock sale and the subsequent change in company leadership. First, I want to ask you if you are planning to purchase any stock. Are we at least going to attempt to gain control of NanoLance?" Walker's scrutinizing eyes went around the table, inviting everyone to respond.

"Before putting all my money into this," Kramer said, "I'd be curious to see where the Florida incident inquiry leads. How confident are we that the result of that inquiry will not destroy the company?"

"I don't think that any of us is able to gauge that at this time." The hissing voice of Dustin Sheppard came to life. "Like with everything else regarding stock speculation, there's an associated risk. If we have the intention to purchase significant amounts of stock, we should be prepared to make a commitment and negotiate pre-emptive, discounted rates with Barnaby. That requires, according to SEC regulations, that we're ready to make that commitment no later than mid-October. We might not be able to foresee if the inquiry will be over by that time or what the outcome will be. It's a risk we have to take."

"Before we get ahead of ourselves," Kramer said, "let's examine if we have the possibility to even think about obtaining control of the company among ourselves. After all, we're talking about a company with a market capitalization of 1.3 billion dollars, and I, personally, don't sit on comparable amounts of cash. I'd suggest we add up what we already have, and figure out if we should even be thinking about this in the first place. I'll do the math," she said, taking her pen and a sheet of paper out of her portfolio.

Walker frowned and fidgeted. No one spoke.

"OK, I'll start," Kramer offered. "I own 3.7 percent, a little over 330,000 shares." She wrote the numbers down.

"I have 2.6 percent; that is 230,000 shares and some change," Griffiths said.

Kramer neatly wrote the numbers.

"I've got 3.2 percent here," Prescott raised her hand, "which is 290,000 shares or about there."

Walker and Sheppard looked at each other, in a standoffish manner.

"Write me down with 5.16 percent," Sheppard whispered, "for 475,000 shares."

"When did you pass the 5 percent mark?" Walker blurted. "I haven't seen you listed."

"Last quarter," Sheppard said, undisturbed.

"Add my 4.5 percent, and let's see where we are," Walker said. "with 400,000 shares and some change."

"OK, let's see," Kramer said, pulling a small calculator out of her portfolio. "So, between the five of us, we own 19.16 percent of the total outstanding shares. If we are to obtain control, we need to acquire almost 31 percent, or nearly 2,800,000 shares. Considering today's trading price per share, that leaves us with a need for a little over $250,000,000. And that's a lot of money."

"Then there's another issue," Prescott said, "what makes us think that Barnaby is going to sell at least that many shares? He could be selling only 25 percent, or less. He definitely doesn't want to sell all his stock, and, for sure, he doesn't need to. Do we know anything about his intentions?"

"He owns 53 percent," Sheppard said, "and I heard him say he'd be looking at selling at least half of that. Close . . . Not sure if it's close enough, though."

"If we're missing a few points we can always go on the stock market and get what we're missing, right?" Walker encouraged everyone.

"Let's talk money," Kramer said, "who's got how much? I could raise 20, maybe 23 million dollars."

Alex watched in bewilderment, breathing silently and careful not to make even the tiniest move. *I had no idea these people were so loaded*, she thought. *Maybe that explains the arrogance.*

"I could potentially come up with 16," Griffiths said, with an apologetic tone. "I don't think I can raise a penny more."

"Maybe 30 here," Sheppard said, "only if I liquidate every investment I have, outside of NanoLance shares."

"Angela?" Walker asked.

"Only 20, maybe 22, with difficulty," Prescott said.

"And I can bring in 42," Walker concluded. "Where does that leave us?"

"That puts us at $133,000,000. That's a little over half of what we need to have."

Silence dropped in the room and lingered for a few seconds.

"As of now," Walker said.

"What do you mean?" Kramer looked straight at him.

"At the current trading price, right? You used today's stock price for your calculations, right?"

"Yes, I did, but what—"

"Well, who's to say that the stock price won't continue to drop? Especially in the aftermath of the current Florida incident, plus the upcoming investigation— that's gotta do something to the stock price, right?"

"Safe to say it will do significant damage," Angela Prescott agreed.

"Yes, but will it be enough?" Walker pressed on. "You see, we need the stock price to drop enough to allow us to gain control, but not much lower than that, so we can restore the company after we've purchased enough stock."

"What are you thinking?" Griffiths asked.

"Nothing much, just saying . . ." Walker backed away.

Damn it to hell, he's so close to tipping his hand, Alex thought. She now believed, without a doubt, that Walker was behind the stock price pressures. She also had suspicions about Sheppard, but his attitude, regardless of how unbearable, was not showing any sign of involvement. As for the rest, Alex couldn't tell if they were in on this or not. Walker could have been working on these plans on his own and just manipulating the others into supporting him.

"What about the media?" Prescott said.

Hello, Alex thought, *bring it on*!

"Well, what about it?" Kramer probed.

"We could work with the media on this; try to control the stock price using the media."

"Bold," Walker said. "How are you planning on driving the stock price down using the media?"

"I did not say that, not now, not ever! Stop putting words in my mouth!" Prescott rose, filled with anger. "You were talking about not letting the stock go too low, and that's what I responded to. How do we stop the stock price from dropping using the media? Publish favorable articles, and so on."

The others nodded their approval. Walker sat there, grim and silent.

"Definitely worth keeping in mind," Kramer said. "Whatever happens, we shouldn't sit idle and let the stock price collapse through the floor. I mean, even if we can't gain control of the company, we should still make sure we're thinking long term on this, especially considering that all of us have already invested significant amounts of cash."

"All right, then we're set." Walker rose, giving the signal for the meeting to adjourn.

Everyone started to make his or her way through the door.

"Can you stay behind for a few minutes? I'd like to speak with you," Walker said, touching Prescott's arm.

"Sure," she replied. Walker waited for the others to exit, and then closed the door. He stood there silently for a few seconds, then, without any warning, turned and grabbed Prescott by her lapels, slamming her against the wall. He grabbed her wrists and held them together above her head with one hand, leaning heavily against her body, and grabbed her chin with his other hand. Prescott gasped.

"Do not ever talk back to me again," he growled near her face, "not ever again! Understood?"

Prescott nodded slightly, opposing no resistance to the attack. She could have tried to fight him and at least get out of that corner and into the plain sight offered by the conference room glass wall. Walker had picked his spot carefully. Next to the door, an entire section of the wall was hidden from the outside hallway.

Walker squeezed her wrists harder, making her close her eyes and give a quiet whimper of pain. He leaned against her body with his massive weight, pressing his thigh against her pelvis with a vicious, lustful thrust.

"You'll get what's coming to you for this, bitch!" He abruptly released her and walked out, slamming the door behind him.

Alex had covered her mouth with her hand, to suppress any sound she could have made. She couldn't believe such things happened in an office environment. She felt frustrated in her inability to intervene and stop the abuse. She felt tempted to get out of her hiding place and help Angela. She thought best to stay put, though. The time would come for all this mess to be exposed and addressed in her final report.

Angela still stood there, leaning against that wall. Slowly, she began to recompose, arranging her clothing, checking her hair to see if everything was in order. In doing so, she turned slightly toward the AV closet, allowing Alex to see the expression on her face. Angela Prescott was smiling, the aroused smile of an anticipating lover.

"Good evening, ladies and gentlemen, I am Stephanie Wainwright, live from the *News of the Hour* studios, here in New York. Our guest for this evening is Major Darrell Montgomery, spokesperson for the United States Air Force. Welcome, major; thank you for joining us tonight."

"Thank you for having me," Montgomery answered.

"I am hoping you can help us shed some light into last week's tragedy in Florida. What a disaster!"

"Indeed. We are deeply saddened by this unfortunate incident. The United States Air Force is taking this matter seriously. We have launched an in-depth investigation into the incident, looking at all possible angles—"

"Tell me about these drones," Stephanie interrupted. "How safe are they? Why are we using them?"

"The Air Force has deployed drones, or unmanned aerial vehicles, for the purpose of increasing the safety of the military personnel, pilots, other crew, and also for the increased safety of ground operations. Even if a UAV should crash, having a smaller mass, there is less damage generated on the ground by the crash. Our pilots are safe, operating the UAVs from safe locations, such as airbases on US land or from our allies' territories. There is significantly less risk to their lives."

"How many drones have crashed since you began their deployments? And when was that? When did the first drone fly?"

"The first drone was primitive and was developed by the British in the 1930s. It was radio controlled."

"Really? I had no idea this concept was so old."

"Yes, that's right. The concept has been around for a while. During World War II, more experimental drones were flown, but, unfortunately, not by us or by our allies. Some specialists think that the Nazis were ahead of us in this technology back then, flying what is commonly known as the V-1, long-range missile, which was a drone carrying a bomb."

"Interesting," Stephanie commented.

"Then, in the 1960s, we started more intensive research here, in the United States, flying thousands of drone flights—mostly target and surveillance. But the drones didn't become what they are today until the mid-1990s."

"So, a long history, I see. How about their safety record? Any notable incidents in the past?"

"None worth mentioning, no. The key point in the favor of utilizing drones is their safety."

"And their low cost, let's not forget," Stephanie added, sarcastically.

"And their cost, definitely. But this low cost is driven by the safety of their operations. No deaths. No pilots captured by the enemy. No wounded."

"So, in the entire history of their operation, has a drone ever been responsible before for loss of human life here, at home?"

"None whatsoever."

"How about abroad? Have drones been responsible for civilian deaths abroad?"

"In recent years, a couple of incidents abroad have claimed drone involvement, with minimal confirmation."

"But, just this April, in Kandahar, a Canadian patrol was attacked by a United States UAV, in what was then reported as a friendly fire incident, isn't that right?"

"Yes, that was what was reported. However, the investigation in this case is still underway."

"So, you're saying it wasn't our drone that killed those Canadians?"

"Quite the opposite, unfortunately. We were able to confirm that it was ours, but these are preliminary results, so I wouldn't call this a confirmed incident, because we are still investigating."

"Well, were all drones in the area accounted for? How about all ordnance? Any Hellfire missiles missing from your inventory?" Stephanie's voice was filling with sarcasm, as she kept asking the logical questions.

"It's not as simple as that," Major Montgomery tried to explain; "it's not an issue of counting the Hellfires."

"Well, seems to me it should be, if someone really wants to get to the bottom of this."

"The investigation into what happened with the Canadian patrol in Kandahar in April is still underway. We're exploring different angles. We are looking at all our drones deployed in the area—their operators, their flight plans—to get a better understanding of what happened. We're examining all circumstances of the incident.

"Two things we know, as of right now, regarding Kandahar. One is that we were able to confirm it was our drone that opened fire on the Canadians. We have their reports indicating that the drone was wearing U.S. markings. We have precisely identified which air base the drone originated from and who was flying it. We have analyzed the site of the attack, and the explosive trace analysis indicates our Hellfire missiles were launched there. However, we have no record of any operations underway in that area.

"The second thing we know about the Kandahar incident is that the investigation is not over. We will not close this investigation until we have all the answers to the questions about this unfortunate incident. We are committed to bring closure to the families of all the Canadians killed or wounded in that incident and to make sure those responsible for the incident will be held accountable. We are also committed to get to the bottom of the Kandahar incident, to ensure that we will take all steps needed to ensure that such incidents will not happen in the future."

"Here's another possibility for you," Stephanie offered. "Could the drone have been hacked?"

"Hacked? What do you mean by that?"

"If I understand this correctly, these drones are operated remotely. Could someone else have taken control of the drone and guided it to attack the Canadian patrol?"

"I don't think that could even be possible. The drone's connection to the remote guiding station is highly encrypted, designed to securely maintain and handover the drone control between ground stations and the UAV's controls. The uplink to the drone is highly secure."

"But wherever there's an encryption, there's also the possibility for that encryption to be, well, decrypted by unauthorized personnel," Stephanie insisted, the sarcasm in her voice picking up.

"We're examining all angles, but this, again, doesn't have an even remotely considerable likelihood of being at the root cause of the incident."

"How about Florida? What's the Air Force planning to do to find out what happened?"

"Regarding Florida, we have a little bit more information. We have determined that the UAV was inbound to Mackenzie Air Field. We have determined it was returning from a routine surveillance mission that was part of a joint operation with the United States Coast Guard, patrolling the territorial waters of the Gulf of Mexico coast. We have determined it was carrying surveillance equipment, not Hellfire missiles, or laser-guided bombs, or any other type of ordnance."

"When will we know what happened?"

"We are hoping that, within a few months, we will have all the answers to the questions regarding last week's tragedy in Florida."

"Thank you for your time and answers, even if they are so disappointingly limited at this time, major. We are hoping to see you back in our studios soon, bringing all the answers we are looking for."

"Thank you, Stephanie, looking forward to it."

Well into the evening, Alex was finally heading home. She had taken advantage of the quiet Friday afternoon before the Independence Day long weekend, to finish some work she needed to turn in the following week. That maniac, Sheppard, was expecting her plan for budget cuts by Tuesday morning. She needed the rest that was promised by this long weekend, although she felt edgy and anxious, thinking how far she still was from completing what she had come here to do.

The parking lot was almost deserted at this late hour. A few scattered cars, here and there, probably belonging to the night-shift security guards and to car-pooling employees. Upstairs, not many lights were on. NanoLance had motion-sensor lighting in the offices and hallways, so as soon as there was no activity for ten minutes or so, the lights went off.

She reached her car, got behind the wheel, and started the engine. Before pulling out of the parking space, a police car pulled in front of her, flashing red and blue lights in a blinding display. It was a Chevy Tahoe, wearing the marks of the San Diego Police Department.

"Oh, crap," she muttered, "I didn't even pull out."

Behind her, a second police car was pulling in. She felt her blood come to a freeze. This was not a routine traffic stop. She put her hands on the wheel and waited.

An officer stepped out of the Chevy Tahoe in front of her, leaving those blinding lights on. He approached her car, flashlight on, and tapped on her window.

"Step out of the car, ma'am." His tone did not allow for any negotiation.

She reached for her bag, but was interrupted by an impatient bang on her window, this time with the tail end of a flashlight.

"Step out of the vehicle, right now! Leave everything there."

A second cop was approaching, this one from the car that was pulled behind her Toyota.

She stepped out, and somehow found the courage to speak.

"What is this about?" She was embarrassed at how faint and trembling her voice sounded. She became aware that she was shaking, feeling weak in the knees.

"Step over here," the first cop continued, ignoring her question.

The second cop opened her car door and flashed a light inside. Seconds later, he emerged holding a small, transparent plastic bag with white powder inside.

The first cop swiftly grabbed her arm, and she felt the coldness of handcuffs on her wrists.

"Alex Hoffmann, you are under arrest for possession of a controlled substance. You have the right to remain silent. Anything you say or do can and will be held against you in the court of law. You have the right to speak to an attorney. If you cannot afford an attorney, one will be appointed for you. Do you understand these rights as they have been read to you?"

This was not happening. Her mind was in a state of shock. *I never had any controlled substance*, she thought. *That means drugs? I have no drugs.*

The cop put the flashlight beam right in her face.

"Do you understand these rights?"

"Y-yes," she stuttered.

"I'll get this towed," the second cop said, pointing at her car.

She felt a firm hand guide her toward the first police car; same firm hand tilted her head to prevent her from hitting it against the doorframe, as she was placed in the back seat of the Tahoe.

The car started to roll, its blinding red and blue lights finally turned off. Alex felt the suffocating knot of fear strangling her, rendering her unable to breathe. She was scared out of her mind, couldn't focus on any rational thought, or come up with any explanation as to what was happening to her. She felt like screaming and sobbing at the same time; she somehow managed to do neither. The panic-driven weakness she was feeling was changing to full-blown shivers, making her teeth clatter. She desperately tried to figure out what to do. *Yes*, she thought, *Tom will help me, I have to call Tom.*

"Excuse me," she pleaded, "can I please make a phone call?"

"Well, pardon me if I don't stop this car right here to offer you my personal cell phone so you can make your goddamn phone call," the cop answered.

That settles it, she thought bitterly.

"I'm sorry, I didn't mean to—"

"Will you shut up, already? Don't wanna hear it! Jesus!"

She fell silent, feeling the coldness of the air chilling her blood. Before she could stop, tears started rolling down her cheeks.

He grabbed the remote, clicked to turn the wall-mount TV off, and slammed the remote on his desk.

"Aww . . . damn it!"

His finger pushed nervously on the intercom.

"Yes, sir?" a soft-spoken female voice answered within seconds.

"Get me Lynch and Nichols in here, on the double!"

"Yes, sir."

General Randal Hamilton II was not a patient man. Patient men rarely climb so high in the Air Force ranks, or in any ranks for that matter. Proud son of a highly decorated, three-star, Air Force general who had brought visionary innovation to air combat during the Vietnam War, Hamilton was incessantly competing with his father, long after his death. The day Hamilton had been awarded his fourth star and promoted to the office of the United Stated Air Force chief of staff was marked as a special day in his heart, one that he would commemorate with annual visits to the Arlington Cemetery. He had paid only two such commemorative visits to his father's place of eternal rest; his appointment to this office was relatively recent.

The intercom buzzed.

"They are here, sir."

"Good, send them in."

General Howard Lynch, vice chief of staff, was the first officer to walk through the open door. Following closely was Brigadier General Seth Nichols, in charge of regional affairs. They both saluted promptly.

"Sit down," Hamilton said. "It's great to have these TVs installed in our offices. Maybe by watching TV, we can find out what's going on in the goddamn Air Force!"

General Hamilton was not in a good mood. Regardless of the given situation's severity, Hamilton had gained the respect of his team by always keeping a cool head under pressure. In fact, the bigger the pressure, the cooler, more analytical and supportive the general would get.

"So I heard on the news today that the media correlates the April incident in Kandahar with the Florida incident last week," he continued. "Are we working this angle?"

"Sir, if I may," Nichols responded, "regional affairs was only looking into the Kandahar incident."

"Where are we with that one? Do we have any findings?"

"Not full findings, sir, we have partials."

Hamilton encouraged Nichols to continue.

"The drone was ours, sir. That's for sure. The Hellfire's signature was also ours. We're looking into the ground station operators and interviewing every single one of them who had anything to do with that drone. Unfortunately, one of the pilots is dead, so that leaves some questions unanswered."

"Dead? How?"

"His Humvee was hit by an IED on the way back from leave—little over a month ago, sir."

"Damn it. We need to keep a tight lid on this until we are ready to close the investigation. With the Florida incident, the media is going to get aggressive, questioning everyone—pilots, their families and friends—everyone they can reach."

"Yes, sir," both Nichols and Lynch responded simultaneously.

"Lynch?"

"Yes, sir."

"I want your team to work with Nichols on this correlation angle. Set up a task force. Bring analysts in, lab techs, everything you need. Is it possible that the same defect or error triggered both incidents? Compare behaviors, analyze the flight paths, all the data transferred to and from the drones in question, and let's figure out what went wrong."

"Yes, sir."

"One more thing. There will be a congressional hearing on this."

"Was it announced?" Lynch asked, turning pale.

"No, not a word yet. However, I don't think we can get away with blowing up a busload of people on American soil without having to attend a congressional hearing. Be prepared, assign the best resources you have to close these investigations as soon as you can, keep a lid on this, and give me rock-solid facts and plans for action. You know," Hamilton said after a brief pause, "Air Force chiefs of staff can be fired too."

"Yes, sir," both men acknowledged, after a brief hesitation.

"Good luck and keep me posted. Dismissed!"

"What do you have?" A man in his thirties, wearing civilian clothes, asked the uniformed cop who was dragging Alex by her left arm through the main doors at the police station.

"Possession. Doesn't seem to be enough of it for intent to sell, but I'll get it weighed and let you know. Looks like meth, not sure yet."

"OK, I'll take it from here." Alex's arm changed hands from the uniformed cop to the plain-clothes cop.

"I am Detective Jordan Holt, narcotics division. What's your name?"

"Alex Hoffmann," she replied, still sobbing.

"Were you read your rights?"

"Yes."

"Wait in here," Holt said, pushing her into what seemed to be an interrogation room. She sat down on one of the two beat-up chairs, facing each other at a worn-out table. Holt uncuffed her and left.

She rubbed her wrists to re-establish blood flow. The initial shock was starting to clear, while she began to comprehend what was going on with her. She had been arrested. She had been found in possession of a controlled substance. This was her new reality. It was time to deal with it.

Holt stepped back through the door, followed by an older man, dressed in a relatively worn-out suit.

"This is my partner, Lieutenant Adrian Reyes," he said, and offered the spare chair to the older man.

"All right," Reyes said in a kinder voice, "what happened?"

All of Alex's knowledge of how police procedure worked was telling her to shut up and ask for a lawyer. Not a word was to be said. Everything she could say, would, indeed, be used against her in a court of law, just as Miranda warned. Nevertheless, all that theory wasn't worth much under pressure, when all she wanted was for someone to believe her.

"I don't know," she started saying. "I honestly don't," she insisted, when she saw the two detectives exchange disappointed, rolling-eye glances. She was going to be the "I don't know" cliché . . . how boring. "I was leaving work, and I got pulled over. I actually was stopped before I started," she threw out in a frenzy, not making much sense.

"Slow down," Reyes said. "Who gave you the meth?"

"That's the thing, I don't know. Really, I don't. I don't know where it came from, I hadn't seen it until the police officer took it out of my car, and I have never touched drugs in my life."

"Have you touched this particular packet?"

"No, not at all," she continued to plead.

"So, you're absolutely sure you haven't touched this bag of drugs?" She nodded energetically. "All right," he continued, "are you using any drugs?"

"No, never," she said.

"Not even smoke a joint now and then? To take the edge off?"

"No, never."

"How about prescription drugs, such as Valium, or Xanax, or Oxycodone?"

"No, I'm not taking anything. You can test me, and you'll see I'm not lying."

"We will," Reyes said, leaving the room.

Minutes later, a technician was fingerprinting her, using dated technology involving an inked roller, to stain the tips of her fingers, and a fingerprint 10-print card. He manipulated her fingers gently, yet impersonally. One of the most traumatic events in her life meant absolutely nothing to this man.

When he was done, she was escorted to a small lab at the back of the station for the drug test. This area was up-to-date in technology, as the young lab technician immediately explained.

"The urine drug test is almost instantaneous and gives us information about trace amounts of many recreational substances in your system. Sign here, please," he said, offering her a release form where she signed in confirmation that she was aware of how the drug test process was being handled. "As the urine is collected in this small plastic jar, these side strips, covered with chemical reactives, will turn color if your urine contains the residue of the specific drugs they indicate. For example, if this particular stripe colors green, you're positive for heroin. These five strips at the end are measuring the physical characteristics of the urine, indicating if you attempt to tamper with the test, by taking a diuretic, to dilute the drug concentration in your urine. Ready?"

She nodded. This was going to be easy. She would pee in the cup, the test would come back negative, and then they would apologize and release her. By tomorrow morning, all this would be just a bad memory.

"You have to take your jacket off and leave the restroom door open. We have to make sure you're not tampering with the test. Please don't flush before handing me the urine."

Silently, she went in, wiped the soiled toilet seat with some toilet paper, and sat on it. Urinating came easily, after so much stress. She handed the cup to the lab technician, and washed her hands.

"We have to wait for a minute or so," the tech said, rolling the filled cup on its side, so that urine would come in contact with all the reactive strips. He peeled off a piece of adhesive from the side of the cup and picked up the phone.

"We're done here. She's positive for meth."

Alex felt a kick to her stomach.

"No, no, that can't be true! I swear to you I have never touched any drugs, please test me again," she pleaded, sobbing hard.

Detective Holt came through the door.

"You almost had us fooled, you know."

"You *have* to believe me, please, I am not taking any drugs! Test me again, do a lie detector test, do whatever, but please believe me!"

"Chemistry never lies, missy, this is it. You have methamphetamine in your system. Regardless of how it got there, right now it doesn't make you look good at all. Let's go."

"Where are you taking me?"

"We're going to book you, do some paperwork, and prepare your arraignment."

Holt led her to the same interview room she had occupied before. Another young technician came to take her clothing in a paper bag, offering her a jumpsuit instead. The jumpsuit stank of chemical cleaners, and was stiff and rough to the touch. Initially repelled by the smell, Alex realized that the smell of disinfecting chemicals was, in fact, a guarantee that these suits were cleaned before being handed over from one prisoner to the next.

Prisoner! The word resonated in her brain. She decided to finally apply the wisdom she had deliberately ignored until now. She knocked on the mirrored window. Holt opened the door.

"I'd like to have a lawyer present, please, and I'd like to make my phone call now."

Holt disappeared, and soon reappeared with a cordless phone. She looked at the time—almost 10:00PM. She dialed Tom's home number.

"Hello?" His warm voice brought back tears to her eyes.

"Tom? Hi, it's me, Alex."

"Hi, what's up?" He sounded a bit worried.

"I don't know how to say this . . . I was arrested for drug possession tonight, I'm at San Diego Police, West," she said, between uncontrollable sobs.

"Arrested?" Tom repeated in disbelief.

"I never took any drugs . . . but they tested me and found me positive for meth."

"Oh," Tom said, in a visibly colder voice.

"Please help me get out of here," Alex pleaded, her eyes flooded in tears.

"Oh, Alex, drugs were never part of the deal, you know. I'm afraid you're on your own. When it comes to drugs, well, for me they're a game changer. Once you've taken that path, well, there's no real turning back."

"No, you've got to believe me, I never took any drugs!"

"Alex, please, calm down. If you're indeed innocent, this situation will resolve on its own. If that's the case, get back in touch with me later, so we can resume our work together. I'm sorry, but that's all I can do," Tom said, then hung up.

She crouched on the floor, hugging her knees, and sobbing hard. She was all alone again, and the nightmare was there to stay.

The aroma of fresh baked donuts and hot coffee made Detective Holt stop typing.

"Finally," he said, thankfully reaching for the treats handed to him by his partner.

"You're welcome," Reyes said, taking a mouthful out of a glazed Krispy Kreme. "What are you entertaining yourself with?"

"Just paperwork on the Hoffmann broad. I want to have her booked before the shift is over. It's quiet around here for a Fourth of July weekend."

"Not so fast, hot shot," Reyes said, leaning against Holt's desk. "So, your mind is made up, she should be arraigned?"

"Why not? She had drugs in her car, drugs in her system. What more would you like to have before you call a case perfect?"

"How long have you been a detective? Five minutes?" Reyes scoffed.

"Huh? That's not fair, you know—almost six months. What am I missing?"

"Well, the obvious. You're not detecting anything. You're not doing the job of a detective; you're being an overly zealous and over-empowered secretary, eager to fill out forms—"

"Screw you," Holt said, punching Reyes in the shoulder.

"—and book a dubious collar, who'll step out of court whistling free, in less than five minutes."

Holt looked up, intrigued.

"So, you think she'll walk? Why?"

"Well, first of all, because you're not doing your job," Reyes said, then laughed some more, "and second, because her lawyer will do his."

"I give up. So teach me, oh, wise one," Holt said, mimicking the respectful bow given by a martial-arts trainee to his master.

"Hmm . . . I'm still considering not to, for the pleasure of seeing your butt kicked by the captain. The problem is my own butt would also get kicked in the process, and I'm particularly fond of my butt. I don't want any of his boot prints on it. It will ruin my reputation, as my butt's been kick-free for years, you know."

Reyes paused, taking a sip of steaming coffee.

"OK, so what do you have? You have a bag full of meth found in a car, and trace meth found in a urine test. That's all you've got. Out of context, it might look good," Reyes emphasized.

He loved to teach. He had always been partnered with young detectives, because of his passion for developing skills in others.

"In context—not so much," he continued. "What's your context?"

"The broad lied to us when she said she wasn't using," Holt ventured the argument he thought was the key point in this case.

"First of all, calling her a "broad" is uncalled for and clouds your judgment. Considering the cases you normally handle and the company you usually keep, I can see why you would call all women broads." Reyes stopped to receive the second fist to his right shoulder. "This lady is no broad in the sense you mean it. She's a highly paid professional," Reyes said, going through Alex's purse, extracting a business card. "This woman is a director with NanoLance, no less. What do you know about NanoLance?"

"They're a large defense contractor, right?"

"Right. Pay attention now. What does it mean for our case that NanoLance is a defense contractor?"

"I-I don't know," Holt admitted, reluctantly.

"Stringent security checks, random drug tests, and at least 'confidential' or 'secret' clearance for employees. For a director-level employee, I'd think 'top secret' clearance is more likely."

"So, practically, what does that mean?"

"You are more of an idiot than I had assumed," Reyes said, his smile softening the harshness of his words. "That means the employees are scrutinized periodically, and they know it. She would never willingly touch drugs."

Silence, as Holt processed the information. "OK, I guess you're right," he conceded.

"Let's look at the lab reports next." Reyes took the case file and browsed through it. "Someone has to, you know," he said laughing, as he was taking yet another stab at Holt's unsatisfactory work. "Her clothing—high end. Her suit is labeled "Calvin Klein." I looked it up online; it's one of the current models, sells for more than $700. Her blouse is pure silk—has this French brand name I can't even pronounce, but it must be worth a couple of bucks. Her shoes are," he struggled to read, "Salvatore Ferragamo. Did my job, sorry, did *your* job and looked these up on the Internet too, they go for $400 a pair."

"So, she must be selling a lot of drugs then, or making a lot of money at work."

"If you make a lot of money at work, would you risk it all to deal drugs? Why?"

Silence again. Holt started to feel the blood of embarrassment climb to his cheeks. He tilted his head down to hide it.

"Is this your typical user or dealer profile? She's a successfully employed executive, in a job requiring high security clearance, no less." Reyes waited for Holt to say something, but he didn't. There was nothing to say. "If you're not yet experienced enough to examine profiles, let's look at evidence." He flipped through the lab report. "Her clothes had zero trace of meth, or any other drug for that matter. I'd think she isn't using or dealing too much in these clothes, is she?"

Holt nodded his silent approval.

"Fingerprints report," Reyes continued to the next page of the lab report. "Not only does our lady have a whistle-clean record, not even a parking ticket, but her fingerprints were nowhere on that bag of meth. Someone else's were, though. They found a partial that doesn't match any of hers. What does that tell you?"

"She never touched the bag of drugs," Holt accepted.

"That means she wasn't lying when she was saying that. How about her meth use? What have you noticed?"

"The lab test came back positive; she had a trace of meth in her urine."

"The operative word here is 'trace.' In fact, the trace was so fine that the lab decided to do a hair-strand analysis to determine the history of drug use." Reyes pushed the lab report in front of Holt. "There is none. This lady isn't a user. It was all in the file, for you to read and consider."

"Oh. OK, but then how do you explain all this incriminating evidence? There were drugs in her car. She had drugs in her system."

"Oh, yes, because whoever is framing her is doing a thorough job. Very thorough for you, anyway—you almost sent her to prison. Not thorough enough for me. I need to see context, to understand the motive for the crime. If there is no motive, I get suspicious, and I have a lot of questions I need answered before sending someone to jail."

The small office grew silent again.

After a few minutes, Holt looked at Reyes and asked. "Lieutenant, do you think I have what it takes to do this job?"

"I think you do. These were rookie mistakes, nothing more. Remember not to jump to conclusions, always get the full context, get all your questions answered, and better let a guilty person go free than an innocent one do time."

Alex sat on the cold floor of the detention cell, crouched in the far corner. There was a bed in her cell, but she could not bring herself to come near it. Occasional tears would still run down her cheeks, but she had lost the strength to continue sobbing. Memories of all kinds ran through her mind, like snapshots from movies. Her mother saying, "You will leave here with nothing, and I expect the clothes you are wearing to be returned . . . Oh, and don't ever come back." She rarely thought about her mother anymore, but she would have loved to be able to call her now.

Tom's voice saying, "You need to learn to trust." She had trusted him, and he'd let her down. Dr. Barnaby's desperation-filled voice, shouting, "I'll go straight to my basement, get my handgun out of my safe, and spare my wife the shame and embarrassment to see me brought to my knees and dragged in handcuffs out of our home." She had a new understanding of his anguish, seeing things through her own imprisonment experience. She was going to let him down. She was not going to be able to do anything for him, or for all those people—the dead and the wounded on Highway 98 in Florida. The enduring employees at NanoLance, going through day after day of abuse. Who knows how many more lives would be lost, out there in remote places, in foreign lands?

A loud, clattering noise brought her back to reality. Detective Holt was jingling some keys on a ring.

"You're free to go," he said, "we're dropping all charges."

She stood, unsure of her legs, afraid this was her imagination playing tricks on her brain. She stepped through the open cell door and into the main hallway.

"Are you OK to drive?" Holt asked.

She nodded.

"Your car is right across the street in our impound lot. I'll get an officer to release it to you, and you're free to go."

Forty-five minutes later, she entered her home. She kicked off her shoes and took off her clothes, leaving them on the floor where they dropped. She went straight to the kitchen and poured Martini Vermouth into a tall glass, over a handful of ice cubes, until the glass almost spilled over. She took that with her into the shower. Crouched in the tub, hot water running down over her, she took sip after sip of Vermouth and cried until her tears ran dry.

Alex didn't ring the front doorbell when she arrived at Tom's house. Instead, she went around the house and into the backyard, where everyone should have been gathered by now. Everyone was, including the two most elusive of her colleagues, the aristocratic Brian Woods and the perfectly dressed Richard Ferguson.

The crowd was engaged in the typical Independence Day barbecue, gathered around the grill and the beer-filled cooler. Alex took the twelve pack of beer she was carrying straight to the cooler and grabbed a cold one for herself.

"Hey, hey," Tom cheered her arrival, "welcome! We weren't sure you'd be able to join us after all."

"Hello, Alex," Brian greeted her with a quick handshake, "great to see you."

"Hey there," Richard said and gave her a quick hug, careful not to drop Little Tom from his arms.

"Lovely to see you," Claire said, offering a smile and a warm hug. "We were worried about you."

From across the lawn, Steve just waved at her, his distance making her sad for an instant.

"Yes, it's great to see you all and to be here." She turned to Tom. "Most of all, I wanted to thank you for coming through for me and for getting me out of that hell hole."

There was a moment of silence in the group, while everyone was looking briefly at everyone else.

"Alex, well," Tom hesitated, "it wasn't me. Or any of us."

"What?" Alex blurted, voice filled with anger. "So, then, what happened?"

"Not sure. We never got to pull any strings. We were checking the facts—"

"Checking the facts?" Her anger was rising, getting the best of her. The traumatic experience of her arrest was still fresh, and so was the painful memory of Tom hanging up on her, leaving her all alone to deal with the mess she was in—because of him, because of this job. "Listen to me, and listen good," she heard herself say, "you told me during my first week with you to learn to trust. You had no business teaching me that. *You* need to learn to trust. You know what kind of job you're giving me to do. You preach to me about how dangerous this can get. You play the nice guy, giving me all kinds of advice on how to stay safe, yet at the first sign of trouble, you don't trust me. Instead, you abandon me. I trusted *you*. And you let me down. You abandoned me. You left me in jail to rot in hell.

"I don't know how I can work for you in this situation. I will finish this client, because it was me, personally, who looked Dr. Barnaby in the eye and promised to help him, but then I'll be on my way. Until you can learn to trust. Because, you see, if you don't trust me, then you don't have my back, and I can't do a job like this on my own." She stopped her rhythm of angry, pain-ridden short phrases, and took a few gulps of cold beer. It felt great to have all that off her chest.

A heavy silence took ownership of the backyard, with the exception of birds and crickets chirping.

"Tom, you better get this young lady another beer," Claire interrupted the silence, "and pray that she forgives you, or you won't be able to forgive yourself."

"Hear, hear," Steve said, from a distance, raising his bottle in a toast.

Tom reached toward the cooler and grabbed another beer. He opened it and offered it to Alex.

"I'm sorry I didn't trust you. I hope, in time, you'll be able to forgive me and rely on me again. If it were anything else, I wouldn't have doubted you for a second. When it comes to drugs, I . . . I just lose my judgment. I am truly sorry."

"But, we were looking into the facts about what happened to you," Brian chimed in, "and we've figured it out."

"What?" Alex turned to him, filled with curiosity. "You know, I was positive on the drug test, but I have never touched any drugs in my life."

"That you know of," Brian said.

"What? What are you talking about?"

"We found methamphetamine in your coffee filter and more meth in the coffee jar next to it. Someone in your office is rigging your coffeemaker."

"Oh, my God! Who the hell would do that to me? Am I already addicted?"

"I don't think so," Steve approached, "you've taken small quantities for too little time. If you were starting to feel edgy or restless, that should go away in a day or two."

"Just this past week, when you were here, you were acting a bit strange—on the edge," Claire said, "and you wouldn't eat your burger. We blamed it on the work-related stress that I'm sure you're experiencing, but it seems some chemicals might have been contributing to that after all."

"Oh, crap," Alex said, "I hope I'm not hooked. Only yesterday, I had coffee from that machine. When I get back to the office on Tuesday, I will take the damn machine outside and set it on fire."

Brian chuckled.

"No, you can't do that," Tom said. "You'll have to pretend that you're unaware of the source of the drug. You'll have to prepare coffee and drink it every day, just like you usually do. Well, don't really drink it; pour it in down a drain somewhere, where no one sees you. The person who tried to frame you will be watching."

"How come I didn't see it? How come I didn't notice any white powder in my coffee?"

"It's easy to miss, especially in the dark closet where you have your coffeemaker stashed," Brian said. "And it wasn't that much."

"And what's going to happen when I get back to the office? Whoever set me up will see me waltz right in there . . . then what?"

"Maybe we could use that moment of surprise to find out a few things," Richard said, approaching the group.

"How do you think we can pull this off?" Tom asked.

"What if we start Tuesday with an executive meeting and videotape it. Then we have Alex enter, say, ten minutes after it starts. Maybe we can catch a glimpse of surprise on the face of the person who orchestrated all this. For such an elaborate plan, there must be a connection to someone on the executive team, I can guarantee that. No smaller rank would've had the reason, or the guts, to devise such a bold and complicated plan."

"She's got to enter from the front of the room," Steve added. "To ensure that everyone sees her at the same time. We have to use a conference room with the door in the front of the room. Most rooms have the doors behind the seats."

"That makes sense, but it will pose issues," Alex said, "there's no such conference room that I know about."

"I'll call Dr. Barnaby, and we'll figure out a way," Tom concluded. "It's good we have all day on Monday to set this up."

"That's what long weekends are for," Brian said, and everyone laughed.

"We've got something else for you," Tom added, "the analysis on the written note just came back."

"Sure took a long time," Alex frowned.

"Thank you kindly, ma'am," Richard bowed in her direction. "I only had to compare it with more than 950 different handwritten applications for employment or benefits, and all that was done in the dead of the night."

"Oh, I'm sorry . . ." Alex blushed. "I didn't mean to be . . . inconsiderate."

"It's OK," Richard said. "It did take a long time; that's true. Initially, we concluded the author of the handwritten note is most likely a woman. That's what the expert in graphology said. From that point, we moved to compare the note with handwriting samples taken from benefits enrollment forms and applications for employment. We wanted to be confident in our findings, so we compared the handwriting with the entire NanoLance employee population, not just the women. The author is Janet Templeton, director of manufacturing quality at the Alpine plant. This confirms the theory that the note's author rarely has the opportunity to meet Dr. Barnaby."

"I think I met her . . . But we can't just question her," Alex said.

"No, we can't," Richard confirmed. "However, we can create an opportunity for her to open up and have an unsuspecting dialogue with you."

"How?" Alex wondered.

"Her Facebook page has helped us a lot," Richard continued. "We found that she is looking at buying a Rottweiler puppy, female, and that the dog has got to be perfect. She is single, our Janet, lives alone, and she just lost her Rottweiler, named Alma, of twelve years. She is heartbroken."

"How are we going to use all this information?" Alex continued to ask questions, still unclear on the strategy.

"Simple. We're going to help her find the puppy dog of her dreams, the best Rottweiler there is to find. That's where you two are going to meet, at the breeder's house."

"You have already found a breeder with Rottweiler pups?" Alex asked in disbelief.

"Yes, the stage is prepped. We were lucky on the breeder thing, simply lucky. We didn't have to travel to buy an entire litter of puppies to set this up. No . . . We were just unbelievably lucky. There's a Rottweiler breeder with six-week-old puppies who lives a few miles away from the plant. The breeder is going to get some free advertising through the NanoLance intranet. Flyers have been already posted at the Alpine plant café. Bait is set."

Who's in Control of Our Skies? The Flying Robots Saga Continues
By Neil Bocci, editor-in-chief

Some of us might still remember when the first drones started flying in our skies; voices of concern rose and were silenced. No, we were not heading for a Terminator world ruled by heartless, ungraceful chunks of metal. No, we were not giving up any of our rights and liberties if the skies were to be patrolled by drones. No, the drones would not invade our privacy; they weren't meant to be spies in the skies. Finally, yes, these drones are perfectly safe and at all times under the control of a human being.

But are they? Both safe and under control? The recent slew of events raises this legitimate concern.

The April incident in Kandahar, Afghanistan, responsible for the loss of four lives, is still being investigated. The US military still owes our Canadian allies an answer, to bring closure to them and much-needed changes in the manner that drones are operated. Three-and-a-half months later, we still have no definitive answers to any of our questions.

Last month's incident in Florida, with twenty dead and sixteen wounded, has broken the pattern of remote, unseen combat mishaps, by bringing disaster to our homeland. No word as of yet about the cause of this mishap from the US Air Force. In this case, the Air Force admits ownership of the rogue drone but has not yet released any findings, or shed any light, into what could have caused the tragedy on Highway 98.

Just last night, again on foreign land, again in Afghanistan, in the isolated, little town of Panjab, forty-two civilians came under a drone attack. Only six of them survived, seriously injured. This time, the mystery is even harder to solve; the survivors' reports did not identify the drone by its markings. No one has identified to which branch of the military the drone belonged. Naturally, no combatant force wishes to take responsibility for this meaningless, devastating act against non-combatant civilians, including men, women, and children. There will probably be a long time before we have any release of information in this case.

There have been enough reports of drones causing serious trouble to prompt some questions. Are we really in control of our equipment? Are these drones reliable enough? Are they as safe as advertised?

One by one, we'll attempt to answer these questions, with the limited knowledge of a news crew.

Control. The Florida incident is related to a drone out of control, or described as such by the numerous eyewitnesses present at the scene. We have explored the scenarios that would cause a drone to be out of control. There aren't many. Human operators, using a joystick and guiding imagery captured by the cameras installed on board, remotely control the drones. The scenario, in which an Air Force pilot, deliberately or in error, slammed the drone into a bus full of tourists, makes no sense. The pilot who was at the controls of the death drone in Florida was not available for comment. Our guess is he won't be available for a while, at least until the Air Force finalizes and releases the findings in this sensitive investigation.

So, what else could have caused the crash? Some kind of malfunction, in either the drone itself, the comlink between drone and operator, or the remote control station. These are the three possible areas to investigate and find potential technical issues that could have been at fault for the incident.

If we're considering technical malfunctions or defects, let's examine the manufacturers' records of quality. There are only a few drone manufacturers. California-based NanoLance has a significant percentage of the defense contracting for the flying doom machines. Having a remarkable quality and reliability record spanning decades, as of late NanoLance disappoints in the more visible areas of consumer goods, such as handheld and in-dash GPS devices.

Consumer reviews, posted on many different venues, are indicating failures in recent models of handhelds, from hardware and software perspectives. While the reported hardware errors were not able to shed much light, due to consumers simply reporting the devices as "broken," the software angle gives a little more insight, such as loss of satellite reception and the inability to re-establish a link; frozen screens, the devices need a restart to be able to resume operations; intermittent defects of all kinds, causing the devices to get stuck in search mode, or not guide properly.

Hmmm . . . not guide properly? Why does this particular defect ring a bell of interest? Speculating here . . . These drones are guided using, among others, the GPS technology developed by NanoLance. The same technology that has been reported to malfunction. Could there be a connection? History will reveal it, not a moment too soon.

Reliability. This is a matter to be fully established after the Air Force releases its findings into the Florida incident, and the first of the Afghanistan incidents, in Kandahar. The key question that needs to be answered is if these were because of pilot error or. technical malfunction. Normally we think of reliability as the capability of a particular device to be physically dependable, somehow assuming this is mainly from a technical perspective. That is not entirely correct. Both the drone and the operator have to be reliable, so that the system comprised of the physical drone, the pilot flying it, and the communications link between them, is reliable in its totality. Furthermore, this drone–comlink–pilot system has to be reliable 100 percent of the time. Ninety-nine percent reliability will not be good enough. Ninety-nine percent reliability is what could have caused the Florida incident.

Safety. Operational safety stems from reliability, with a touch of safety-driven procedures and controls. With our limited knowledge of such procedures and controls, we can't even begin to speculate on how safe they are. However, so far, the safety record of the UAVs doesn't impress anyone. Hopefully, the findings into these incidents will reveal opportunities for added safety features into the operation of robotic aircraft, here, in our own airspace, or anywhere else.

One thing remains certain: as of right now, drones are both unsafe and unreliable, claiming lives of innocent civilians, here, at home, and in combat zones, overseas.

The sun was still high enough to cause a bothersome glare on Alex's cloned laptop screen. She moved around the table a bit, to get rid of the glare and distinguish the needed detail she wanted from the images on the screen. Recalling Tuesday morning, when she had deliberately entered an executive meeting ten minutes late, with the sole purpose of surprising the person who was out to get her, still churned her stomach. She remembered the effort she had to make to walk in there with full confidence and her chin up, knowing that at least one of those present wanted her seriously harmed, enough to drug her and set her up to be arrested and thrown in jail.

She carefully watched the video, insisting on reviewing the minutes just before her entrance, to get familiar with the faces present and their overall demeanors. Unfortunately, from what she could see, neither Sheppard nor Walker had been in the room. Dr. Barnaby had to think of a reason to have the meeting in the company's recreation center gym, the only space large enough that could be fitted with seats facing the entrance. The gym was, on occasions, used for company-wide meetings, although it could barely hold 200 people, not even close to the almost 1,000 on NanoLance's payroll. Those present were quite fidgety, Alex noted. They were restless and concerned, as one would expect from the leaders of a company faced with investigations into the safety of its product, and potential involvement in incidents that had led to numerous deaths.

There it was, the precise moment she had entered the room. The camera, installed on the projector mount, close to the ceiling, only captured her from an angle that was above and behind as she made her way from the door to a seat in the front row. She could pinpoint with precision the moment she had entered the room, as she scrutinized the familiar faces for reactions.

The CFO, Audrey Kramer, just as tired as usual, looked up when Alex entered, then frowned. The frown on her face lingered for a good ten seconds, then faded away. That was too long time for it to have been an accidental or coincidental frown. Could it have been triggered by the rudeness of her being late? It was a possibility. In the case of Kramer's reactions, the results were inconclusive for now. Alex would have to observe Kramer on an ordinary day and figure out if lateness bothered her enough to cause such a reaction.

Angela Prescott's reaction was more troublesome. She had put her hand to her mouth, to disguise her surprise. Alex had not expected the HR fashionista to be involved in this mess. At best, Alex would have considered her the silent and oblivious, yet intimate, partner of Benjamin Walker, looking the other way and ignoring Walker's abusive leadership style, due to the nature of their personal relationship. But no, there it was, genuine surprise at the precise moment Alex had stepped through that door.

Rewinding the video a few seconds, Alex increased the zoom and centered the image on Prescott's face. Not only did her hand jump to cover her mouth, but also her mouth had opened in surprise, just before her hand covered it, her eyes widened and her eyebrows raised. She then composed herself before two seconds had passed but remained fidgety and uneasy for the remainder of the meeting. In her case, the conclusions were clear. *Bitch,* Alex thought, *you wanted me nailed. Well, we'll have to see about that!*

Chandler Griffiths was undisturbed by her entrance, showing no reaction at all. With Walker and Sheppard absent from the meeting, this concluded her analysis of the video. Opening her email and connecting through the Starbucks WiFi, she wrote an email to Tom.

Good evening,
Finished video analysis, Prescott is the only one showing a definite reaction. Walker and Sheppard were absent, Kramer inconclusive.
Could we please speed up the extensive background checks into the three remaining on the favorites list?
Thank you.

She hit the send button. The screen refreshed, showing a new email in her inbox.

Hey,
Templeton is five minutes out.
Good luck!

A cell phone, her personal device, chimed from her left pocket. The same message had been texted to her, making sure she got it on time.

This was the signal she had been waiting for at the local Starbucks, sipping from a glazed Frappucino. This particular Starbucks had a favorable location relative to the home of Mrs. Kingsley, AKC registered breeder of Rottweiler dogs. As the message had indicated, Janet Templeton, director of manufacturing quality at NanoLance's Alpine plant, and the author of the anonymous note sent to Dr. Barnaby, was on her way to Mrs. Kingsley's house, heading there to select her next Rottweiler puppy.

Pulling into Mrs. Kingsley's driveway ten minutes later, Alex made sure she was blocking the exit for Janet Templeton's car.

She rang the doorbell and heard a concert of barks and yelps. The breeder owned both parents—proud, imposing Rottweilers, acting protective of their young. After greetings and introductions, she sat down near a small table, across from Janet, ignoring her. She picked up a puppy and allowed herself two minutes of blissful enjoyment of Rottie kisses. Then she remembered what she had come there to do.

"Don't I know you from somewhere?" Alex probed.

"Not sure, maybe; you do look familiar," Janet responded, studying the little Rottie curled up on her lap.

"Do you live around here?"

"Nah . . . in Alpine."

"Oh, near our plant," Alex said.

"Which plant are you talking about?"

"The NanoLance plant. I work for them."

"So do I," Janet said, smiling. "I work at the plant, but I haven't seen you there."

"Nope, I work at corporate."

"Operations?"

"IT, in infrastructure. I'm Alex Hoffmann, director of infrastructure," Alex said.

"Janet Templeton, quality assurance."

They shook hands, both careful not to drop or otherwise disturb the puppies they were handling.

"Too bad they're only six weeks old; I wish I could take her home today," Janet said.

"Yep, same here. But two more weeks will give me enough time to puppy-proof the house, clean it up, and make it really nice for the little one."

"Have you thought of a name?"

"Yes, well, I'm somewhat undecided between Skye and Alma."

"Oh . . . Alma is nice; my last dog's name was Alma. She just died."

"I'm so very sorry," Alex said, "it is, indeed, a nice name. Was Alma a Rottweiler too?"

"Yes. My heart is set on this breed."

The connection had been made and rapport was building fast. They continued small talk on the topic of dogs, and then advised Mrs. Kingsley of their intended choices and pickup dates. They wrote checks with deposits to hold their pups. They discussed behaviors, personality testing, rearing, feeding, training, and everything else there was to discuss between two people passionate about dogs.

"Wanna grab a cup of coffee?" Alex asked, as they were ready to leave the breeder's home.

"Would love to," Janet said.

"Would you prefer something stronger than coffee, maybe?" Alex winked.

"Oh, no, unfortunately, I can't touch any alcohol for another twenty days; I'm on an antibiotic regimen after gum surgery."

"Ugh, that sounds painful," Alex said. "Then we'll stick to coffee. I know a Starbucks around here; I stopped there on my way in."

Minutes later, iced coffee treats in front of them, their casual conversation resumed.

"I think I know where I've seen you before," Alex said, moving on to business, "weren't you in a Walker meeting a couple of weeks back?"

"Ah, yes, you're right, we did meet," Janet said, her face lighting up. "Sorry, I'm really bad with faces. It's amazing how things out of context can affect my memory."

"No need to apologize, I couldn't remember you either, so we're even," Alex said with a warm, sympathetic laugh.

"I guess. Those meetings are hard to endure, and I try to suppress any memory after they end," Janet said, starting to open up.

"Are they usually like that? I thought it was just my beginner's luck."

"No, not at all. You go in there not knowing if you're going to get your head bit off, and for no reason that makes any sense. It's really stressful, and it's a continuing pattern of stress. You'll see. Tomorrow we have another meeting, and it's going to be just as bad, if not worse. I'm ashamed to say, but after a couple of years of doing this, the only thing I can hope for before these meetings is that he doesn't pick on me for the ritual sacrifice."

"What's his problem? What's wrong with him?"

"He's an idiot with unrealistic demands, that's what he is. He doesn't understand our processes, nor does he want to. He just wants more, more, more, and nothing is ever good enough. I know every leader needs to challenge his organization, but keeping goals achievable is part of the game. A big part of the game. If the goals aren't achievable and people are afraid, that's when problems start. Errors are made and covered up, not fixed. People cut corners, fudge numbers, and make desperate decisions that do not serve any greater good, just buy them some time to figure out an alternate solution."

"Alternate solution?" Alex asked.

"Another job, I mean," Janet explained with a faint smile.

"Are you looking?"

"You're not going to tell on me, are you?"

"Oh, no, absolutely not. You can count on me," Alex reassured her.

"Yes, I'm looking, and so is everyone else from Walker's team. It takes a while though, 'cause we're depressed, exhausted, and in a constant state of crisis. Fires burning everywhere, little consistency, and no consideration for his people."

"How do you mean, fires burning?"

"Figuratively speaking. Emergencies of all kinds, some real, but most of them are imaginary."

"I think I get it," Alex said.

"Today, everyone focuses on cost reduction. Tomorrow, he wants staff reductions. The next day, he wants a new product model to be ready for testing in 90 days. And so on. For example, he wants cost taken out of the product year after year. Every year we have to think how to make these products cheaper by anywhere between 5–10 percent, all barfed up numbers with no foundation in reality.

"Plus these products are not TV sets made in China, for the wide consumer market. Few of our products are consumer products. The military products are under contracts, and there is no need for cost pressures, other than stupid, destructive greed. This hurts me in particular, 'cause I am in charge of quality. How can we deliver an improving quality, if the product is disappearing in front of our eyes due to cost reduction challenges?"

"You're right," Alex said, "you can't."

"And he's a sadistic bastard too, if you haven't noticed yet. He gets his kicks from making people suffer. The moment he sees someone on the verge of breaking down, I swear to you, he's pre-orgasmic or something . . . just watch him tomorrow. We've all noticed that about him, but, regardless, he's a skilled torturer. When you're in his line of fire you *will* hurt, and you *will* give him pleasure by hurting, and you *will* hate yourself for it."

"Wow," Alex said in a soft voice.

"You should see how he does performance appraisals. After each performance appraisal, the bottom 10–20 percent of all teams will be fired without cause and without the reason of poor performance. Even if you reached your goals and made your numbers, you could still be fired. This is a stupid method to manage performance—stupid and dangerous too. No one cares about the company or the product anymore. No one does what's right anymore. Everyone hopes that someone else is on that list of terminations, when next February comes. This method destroys teams, and overall human values. It degenerates, as a method, everything that was at the core of our success as a company.

"He didn't invent this method. Someone else did. Walker is just happily applying it, 'cause it creates pain, uncertainty, and suffering in his people, and he loves that. He calls it a competitive, high-performing environment, 'cause everyone is willing to harm everyone else and do anything to survive. He wants all of us to become just like him."

"HR doesn't do anything about this?"

"Hah," she laughed wryly, "you don't know much, 'cause you're new. There is no human resources department on our side here. You should keep in mind they're not to be trusted."

"Thanks for the heads up," Alex said.

"He's also a liar, our COO Benjamin Walker. I've seen him lie, then fire people to cover it up. The former VP of manufacturing, the one before Dunwood, used to tell him in every operations meeting that cost pressures were too high, and that they impact negatively the quality and reliability of the product, in addition to the employee morale and engagement. Every meeting he said that to Walker, and Walker replied he doesn't want to hear it, 'cause it's nothing but a lame excuse for poor performance.

"Then, one day, Walker comes by the plant to visit, and some assembly workers reach out to him and tell him exactly the same thing. That they're disappointed by the fact that the company is cost-driven, rather than quality-driven like it used to be, and that they feel disengaged and disrespected. Walker listened, and then expressed complete surprise, stating he had never been told about such concerns. What was the VP to do? Call him a liar in front of everyone? The former VP held his mouth shut, and minutes later, Walker turned on him and fired him right there, on the spot, for keeping the situation from him. Many of us knew that the former VP was telling Walker about the situation every week. It served as a warning to all of us . . . we are to silence our disgruntled employees or be fired."

"Wow, it's unbelievable," Alex said.

"I hope you won't repeat a word of our conversation to anyone," Janet insisted again. "It's important that you don't."

"I won't, don't worry. And I appreciate you speaking with me; it will help me navigate the waters at corporate. It's hard, you know. You come on as a new hire, filled with hopes and aspirations, and within days, the honeymoon is over and you wake up to such a reality. By the way, my boss is competing with your boss for the 'Asshole of the Year' title."

"Who do you report to?" Janet asked.

"Sheppard. Dustin Sheppard, CTO."

"Sorry to hear that," Janet said, with a sad smile, "indeed another bastard. Not easy with him either. I heard he's filled with so much hatred and contempt for people that it makes you sick to the stomach."

"That's correct. He is . . . vicious. That's the only word that comes to mind."

"Well, we better turn in and get some rest. Tomorrow morning we'll be offered our weekly serving of public humiliation."

Before starting the computer, the man looked around for a third time, just to make sure. No one was there yet; it was too early in the day. He started the self-guidance configuration application, and then flipped through the various screens. The graphical user interface was designed to allow humans to control all the parameters for the self-guided drone flight. A flight plan included landmarks, targets, and coordinates of interest for both combat and recon missions, and well-defined safety collars.

A safety collar was a restriction imposed by the system to prevent the drones from launching missiles on their own, without prior target confirmation from a human operator. The drone would find the target, based on geo-coordinates, or a combination between preloaded imagery and a set perimeter. If a target was identified while the drone was flying above the set perimeter, the drone could even lock the missile targeting system on the identified target, but not launch the missile until the human operator manually confirmed each and every launch.

The man flipped through screen views until he reached the screen labeled **Target Imagery.** He read through the configuration and review options available on the screen. **Load, Review, Restrict, Prioritize, Remove.** He spent a little bit of time reviewing the existing target imagery. Most everyone from the FBI's Ten Most Wanted Fugitives list was preloaded. Osama Bin Laden, although confirmed dead, was included on the list, together with his adjutants. In addition, there were known vehicles of terrorists and strategic landmarks and military equipment belonging to hostile forces of countries currently at war with the United States.

"Uh-huh," he muttered, content with what he was seeing.

He removed a USB flash drive from his pocket and connected it to the computer. Then he clicked the **Load New Images** option on the **Target Imagery** configuration screen.

One by one, the images stored on the drive were opened, allowing the man to confirm the load of each one.

A front view of a silver Toyota 4Runner, showing the car license plate.

A detailed view of the California license plate.

A head shot of an attractive young woman.

A rear view of the same silver Toyota, showing the rear license plate.

A full body image of the same woman, approaching the parked silver Toyota in NanoLance's parking lot.

All selected images loaded correctly, and the confirmation screen disappeared, leaving the user to move on to configuration.

Satisfied, the man clicked on the **Distribution** screen tab. Under **Distribution,** he had three options: **General (all flight plans), Single (create new flight plan), and Test (field test and simulator).** Without any hesitation, he clicked **General (all flight plans).** His choice ensured that the target imagery he had loaded would become a part of every active drone's target search.

Then he moved on to the **Restrict** screen. This was the collar management screen. Again three options, reflecting three different levels of security: **Do Not Target, Do Not Lock on Target, Do Not Launch.** These options clearly specified which actions were not to be taken without ground control input. The default setting was for all three options to be checked. Ideally, the drones would not be allowed to get a lock, release a missile, or even set a target without a human's confirmation. The man unchecked all three boxes, removing all restrictions requiring human input. The self-guided software now allowed any drone to target, lock, and launch missiles at will, on any of the targets reflected in the images he had just loaded.

The next screen was **Prioritize.** He checked the box labeled **Very High,** this being the highest level of priority available.

The man reviewed all his settings in a hurry, looking over his shoulder every minute or so. It was getting late, but he was almost done. He clicked on **Save and Exit.** The system prompted him for the access username and password required to save any changes in the self-guiding software. He took a piece of paper out of his pocket, and started inputting the data in the required fields.

Username: DSheppard

Clearance: Top Secret / L1

Password: EJgF236jhg@k34g5

When he finished entering the sixteen-character password, he clicked **Confirm.** The screen returned an acceptance message and an option button labeled **Distribute.** He clicked it, watched a status bar for a few seconds, and then saw the message he was waiting for: **Field Distribution Complete.** Satisfied, he removed his flash drive, turned off the PC, and left hurriedly.

With a sigh of relief, Alex walked through the conference room door. She had made it on time. The usual players were already gathered around the table. Janet was there, but Alex decided not to acknowledge her specifically, or divulge the fact that they'd met in private. She greeted the entire group with a brisk "good morning," then took her seat.

John Dunwood, VP of manufacturing, looked even paler, older, and more wrinkled than he did at the last meeting. He was biting his fingernails. Alex wondered what supreme effort of will, or what desperate situation could make a man come through that door again, after enduring what he had endured. What could be the reason he was still here?

Robin Maxwell, from HR, was fresh and relaxed, as only an uncaring professional can be in a dysfunctional corporation. Alex could barely refrain from grunting at her. She still remembered Robin enabling Walker in his continued abuse. *Ugh* . . .

Miles Putnam, director of R&D, the guy who told Alex that pushing people the way Walker did generates innovation and drives performance, looked a bit worried, sifting through his pile of paperwork and reports. From the peek into the meeting's agenda, R&D results were on the table for discussion, so he was going to be in the hot seat.

Finally, Peter Wilson from Six Sigma was looking down, avoiding eye contact with everyone. At the last operations meeting, he had been tasked to look into the reasons behind the failure rates of the new designs. He could also end up in the hot seat, despite all his previous enabling. Alex almost smiled.

Walker slammed the door behind him, startling everyone.

"Good morning, I guess," he said. "What do you have for me today? Six Sigma, Mr. Wilson, have you finished the root cause analysis on R&D's new model failures?"

"We have some preliminary findings," Peter said, shuffling his papers. "We've looked at failure rates for all models currently in a design phase and compared these failure rates with the models already in production. A few of the in-design models have higher-than-average defect rates. The RX5, the reconnaissance drone, has a defect rate of 5.65 percent. This is the worst. Then the CX12, the UCAV, failed at a rate of 5.12 percent, also extremely high."

"Remind me, please, what is the target rate for the quality of in-design drones?" Walker asked.

"They shouldn't be failing in more than 1 percent of cases, cumulative, regardless of point of testing. Lab testing and field-testing results are compounded to create this failure rate. Combined, it should not exceed 1 percent," Peter clarified.

"That is fantastic," Walker responded, in his sarcasm-filled voice. "We're only missing the target by some 500–600 percent! Any insights about what's causing these high failure rates?"

"From what my team could assess, electronic components fail at an accelerated rate. Microchips failure rates are quite high, even after installation. However, we have also encountered software failures. The CX12 and CX15 combat drones and the RX series are all self-guided prototypes."

"What's failing on the software side?" Walker asked. "I thought we had the software piece figured out. If I recall correctly, we've already been shipping self-guided drones to the clients, right?"

"That is correct, sir," Peter resumed his explanation. "We've been shipping self-guiding enabled drones to the clients for almost eight months now, for their testing phase. The drones are still to be flown with remote guidance, rather than self-guided. But the Army, Navy, Coast Guard, and Marines, all wanted the opportunity to test the self-guidance module and prepare procedures for the next phase of deployment. They're not supposed to deploy them into active operations as self-guided—not yet—at least not until we've cleared them, and they have finalized all testing on their end."

"When's that supposed to happen?" Walker asked. "When can we clear them for self-guided operations?"

"Not for months, sir, not at these failure rates."

"We're shipping drones with defective software to our clients for testing. These high failure rates must be costing me a fortune. Hmmm . . ." Walker rubbed his chin angrily. "Someone *will* pay for all this waste. Let me reassure you, someone *will* pay." He wasn't yelling. His voice had that bone-chilling calm that preceded his anger-filled incursions into the land of psychological abuse. "What's failing on the self-guiding software?"

"The drones we tested have failed in orientation, navigation, and target acquisition," Peter answered. "They get lost somehow. They're supposed to navigate themselves via GPS and establish their patrol perimeter or attack, coordinated by either the landmark or target imaging that is preloaded in their systems, or by pre-entered geo-coordinates. In the case of coordinates, the drone's performance is satisfactory; defect rate is well under the 1 percent limit. In the case of landmark and target-image recognition, they fail quite significantly. They exceed their patrol area and have to be manually overridden and brought home. They fail to recognize a target and they just miss it. In a couple of cases, there were issues with correctly recognizing ground captured imagery; the drone in question opened fire on a civilian landmark, one that should have been ignored."

"Can someone please refresh my memory on how this works?" Robin asked.

"Yes," Peter answered, "quite simple. We load the drone's memory with two sets of images. One set is landmarks, items that are easy to recognize and should be used for guidance only. The drone should patrol, for example, from the Statue of Liberty, all the way to the Empire State Building and back. While flying, the drone captures ground imagery with its cameras and runs image recognition software, enabling it to recognize the landmark for what it is. The moment it recognizes Lady Liberty, it's supposed to execute a turn and head the other way, scanning the ground for the next landmark in its programming. So, quite logically, if a drone fails to recognize a landmark, it will not correctly execute the patrol or the attack plan. On combat drones, the situation can be even trickier if the drones fail to recognize correctly the imagery that was picked while traveling. It can generate a drone run into enemy territory without any targets being taken out. It can trigger attacks on different targets than intended."

Silence fell around the table, while the Kandahar friendly fire incident was on everyone's mind. No one spoke a word about it.

"But the active drones, the ones currently in service, are not cleared to run on self-guided, right?" Walker wanted confirmation.

"No, sir, no drones currently deployed are cleared to run with self-guidance. This is in the research-and-testing phase only. So far, we have only been evaluating these drones on our testing fields. However, there are also situations in which a hardware error will combine with a software error. We lost a prototype drone like that, on the testing field, just a few days ago." Peter finished explaining, and sat quietly, awaiting instructions.

"Then, how are you fixing this mess?" Walker asked. "I am not talking to just Mr. Wilson, you know. This is everyone's mess. For all I know, it could have to do with crappy parts being installed on the drones, crappy parts and crappy assembly work, provided to us all by the experienced and knowledgeable plant leader, Mr. Dunwood. Do you also have some lame excuses for this, Mr. Dunwood?"

"I will have to investigate and see—"

"You didn't investigate yet? You had no idea this was happening?" Walker slammed his fist down with every phrase, leaning over the table in an attempt to get closer to John. "A couple of weeks ago you came in here with embarrassing performance results for the month of May, and you assured me that you were going to finally step up and do your job for a change. Now you're telling me you didn't even investigate the quality performance of the related parts and assembly processes? Explain to me again, Mr. Dunwood, why the hell should I continue to keep you around here?"

"This type of investigation takes time," John ventured an answer, in a trembling voice. "If you want good results, then it doesn't happen overnight."

"You should be the one to want good results, before I do!"

"That's what I meant—"

"Mr. Putnam, how does R&D feel about all this?" Walker shifted his attack unexpectedly toward Miles

"We're extremely concerned with the failure rates, and we're working around the clock to identify any concept failures that might be hiding behind these defect rates." Miles was on top of his game, giving Walker exactly what he wanted to hear. "We are working to isolate the modules, hardware and software, that are related to these defects, and redesign the modules in question, using new concepts and new components. We should be able to give you results within a month."

"How about you, Miss Templeton, are you sure your quality measurements are correct?" Walker shifted his line of fire again.

"I'm quite sure," responded Janet. "The quality assurance methodology is standardized, well documented, and followed religiously on every testing point. I vouch for the accuracy of our numbers. The fact of the matter remains that there's something wrong with some of our models, and we just need to identify and fix the problems. My team is ready to assist with all testing, at any time of day you should need us."

"OK," Walker said, turning toward another victim. "Mr. Wilson, what are you going to give me?"

Peter replied, "We started a number of projects geared toward identifying the root causes of failure in certain modules. So far, we have identified a substandard component in the guidance module. This module is common to many models. We've also identified a somewhat minor software issue that would require an investment in developer hours to fully evaluate and fix."

"Investment?" Walker's voice was calm again. "What's your return on this proposed investment?"

"I thought," Peter said hesitantly, "that these are strategic projects, requiring no return on investment. There is no ROI, or none calculated yet," he corrected himself, as soon as he saw the glimmer of anger in Walker's eyes. "We can estimate the ROI, if we consider the cost of all the defects we would eliminate."

"Well, do that," Walker said, "and give me the financial benefit of this investment. Once the projects are complete and the solutions implemented, I'll take that estimation out of the plant's operating budget."

"This will add some more time to the length of the project," Peter said. "I thought we were focusing these efforts on net quality, without necessarily going after a dollar amount."

"Mr. Wilson," Walker said, in his dreadfully calm voice, "how much money did you and your team make me this past month?"

"Sir, we were involved with this quality assessment, as per your request," Peter offered an explanation.

Alex became painfully aware she was holding her breath. *Here we go . . .*

"Involved with a quality assessment, as per my request," Walker repeated in a cadence. "How wonderful. Didn't I make it abundantly clear that you, and any of your Six Sigma belts, are supposed to generate, every year, enough net financial benefit to cover at least three times your fully loaded salary expense?"

"Yes, you did." Peter was looking down at the papers in front of him.

"So? Where are we with that?"

"At our current run rate for the year, we'd fall a little bit short, but we still have almost half the year left to recover. We've also been engaged in these strategic projects that don't necessarily yield much ROI."

"What's keeping you from making me money out of the strategic projects? Just because we're fixing an issue doesn't mean we shouldn't be looking to cut some costs while we're at it, right?"

"Yes, but—"

"No buts, Mr. Wilson, get me my money. That's what you signed up for when you took this job. If you can't find me my money, I'll take it out of your paycheck. It's too fat as it is."

"Sir, it might happen that the solutions we propose to some of these issues could potentially require us to put money back into the product. Our numbers indicate that, in some cases, the cost cutting might have been the root cause."

"Really? Didn't I say as clearly as possible that you were supposed to cut costs without bringing down quality?"

Robin was nodding her enabling approval again.

"Yes, sir," Peter mumbled.

"Then put back the cost you absolutely have to, fix the errors you've made, and find the money elsewhere. Find some people we can fire . . . I can't possibly believe we need all these people around here. Have you seen the cafeteria lately? This morning I had to wait almost five minutes to get my coffee. Our payroll is way too fat."

"Well, sir," Peter ventured, "we also grew quite significantly as a business. Our revenue increased by almost 20 percent over the previous year. We do need more people if we're growing so fast."

"I don't care about any growth. I *don't!*" Walker slammed his fist some more. "Do you know why I pay people like you more than they're worth?" No one dared to respond. "Because I need you to figure out ways in which you can get me the money I want. Growth rate is no excuse for hiring hordes of incompetents to crowd the parking lots and coffee lines. Find me some money, or I will take it out of your paychecks."

"If I might intervene," Alex heard herself say. She couldn't tolerate the abuse any longer.

"No, you may not!" Walker slammed her, without hesitation.

Janet gave her a comforting glance.

"We'll meet again in two weeks," Walker said. "Better have it figured out by then. Defect rates under control and cost savings as planned. Is that understood?"

Everyone nodded slightly.

"Dismissed!"

They started gathering their things to leave the room, while Walker did not move from his chair.

"Miss Hoffmann, please stay behind," he said, giving Alex the chills. She should have seen this coming.

Peter was the last to leave the conference room, gently closing the door behind him.

"Yes, sir?" Alex said.

"Never, *ever* interrupt me again," Walker said, in his roaring voice, filled with anger and contempt. "The only opinions you are authorized to express in this room should be in direct alignment and support of our goals, such as quality improvement and cost cutting. Do not speak, unless spoken to. As a support function, you are here to take notes of what I want to have done, by when. Your opinions aren't welcome, not now, not ever. This is not a democracy, where everyone gets to vote and feel important. This is a business. Is that understood?"

She nodded silently.

"Dismissed."

She rose and left the room, trying to walk straight and keep her knees from shaking. *Goddamn, sick son of a bitch! You do get off on humiliating people!*

Alex was trying on outfits in front of the mirror . . . seemed like déjà vu, only this time she found herself aiming for more seductive attire. She didn't know why and refused to think about it or rationalize any of it. Ever since Steve's invitation for dinner, she had been restlessly anticipating the date. What was it? Steve was just a colleague of hers, a mentor and a friend, nothing more. This was not a date. This was going to be more of a business meeting. He probably wanted an update on the status of her investigation, and to check up on her, to see if she was all right. Maybe. Whatever. She could still look sexy for it, right? *Sexy, but not desperate*, she tempered herself cynically, as she chose her attire with care.

Probably everyone else at that mysterious restaurant would wear short skirts, so she opted for a black Jones New York Platinum Collection pair of pants, which accented her slim waist, and a shimmering white, silk blouse, which showed just enough cleavage to be intriguing. She picked up a leather Gucci travel wallet, instead of her usual briefcase. She was ready. She sat in front of the TV, waiting for the doorbell to ring and reminiscing of high school dates, filled with the anxiety of anticipation.

The doorbell finally rang, startling Alex from her reverie. Steve, looking better than ever, stood in the doorway.

"Ready?"

"Yes."

He opened the car door for her, in a gesture of gallantry rarely seen these days.

"Nice ride you have here," Alex couldn't refrain from commenting. "I haven't seen a six series in this color."

"Well, I've customized it a little," he said proudly.

"How little?"

"Not much, really. I've increased its horsepower, which led to the need to enhance the suspension and drive control. Then I had this special order matte charcoal paint done and a few other minor things."

"Ah, *that* little," she said, and they both laughed.

Alex noted the luxurious feel of the leather interior and the overall feeling of comfort and class.

"Oh, and it has the same customized air conditioning system that you have," he added with a wink.

"Just a little customization, huh?" She smiled appreciatively. The 650i was definitely a head turner. "Where are you taking me?"

"We're going to explore one of southern California's finest dining places, called the Garden of Sins."

"Sounds intriguing, where is it?"

"A few minutes away. Well, more like thirty or so."

"Ah, *that* few," she laughed again. "You have a natural gift for understating."

It felt good to be able to relax and chat casually with someone who knew who she really was. No secret agendas, no concern for saying the wrong thing, tipping her hand, or getting caught. No concern for her safety either, while traveling with this careful and thoughtful man and enjoying the ride in his luxurious car.

The restaurant, set up nicely in the backyard of a sizeable home, was divided by intriguing landscape arrangements, lit discreetly by lanterns suspended in mature trees. Half-buried light projectors delivered well-positioned beams of ambiance light to emphasize particular aspects of the landscaping. Alex noticed there was no sign to indicate the restaurant's name.

"It's more like a private club," Steve clarified. "You have to know it's there and be a member. Membership is free, yet exclusive."

"How's membership granted?"

"Referral and approval only. I was lucky to be accepted; the owner and I went to school together. This is the house he grew up in. His parents died when he was still in college, and he starting throwing these parties to pay for school, to support himself, and to try to keep the house. Nothing outrageous, just good food and good atmosphere. Before a couple of years had gone by, he was highly successful. Now he's netting a few million a year from this."

"I bet the food is great, if that's the case. Good, 'cause I'm starving."

They sat at a remote table, in a distant corner of the garden, lit discreetly by a lantern hanging from a huge California oak. She opened the menu and smiled.

"Now I see why it's called the Garden of Sins. 'Wicked Coffee-Cured Steak, Immoral Lobster Tail, Indecent Midwestern Filet,' wow . . . They are all sinful, I'll give you that. Really creative, this high school buddy of yours," Alex said, smiling. "What do you recommend?"

"The Shameless Crab is amazing, and all the steaks are quite off the charts. I actually can't think of one item that I don't enjoy."

"I'll take the Wicked Steak. I am curious about this coffee-cured thing." She closed the menu and set it aside, for the waiter to pick up.

"You should hold on to that menu, you might want dessert."

"Usually they take the menu away."

"True, yet strange and counterintuitive for the restaurant owner who wants to sell more. My friend knows that rule. Therefore, this is one of the few dining places where they do not yank the menu out of your hands while you're still at the table."

"Makes sense," Alex agreed.

The waiter noted their preferences. Steve ordered the Maliciously Peppered Filet, for himself, and French wine to go with their steaks.

"So, how are you?" Steve asked, as soon as the waiter was gone. He soon returned with aperitifs, giving Alex time to think about her answer. She needed Steve's advice on a lot of things.

"Well, I don't really know sometimes," she said, blushing slightly. "This was supposed to be an easy enough question, an ice breaker, right?"

He nodded, his eyes focused on her delicate features.

"Well, it's not so easy for me, I'm afraid," she continued. "Sometimes I feel that I'm close to finishing this assignment. I think I know who the bad guys are. Then I stop and think: what do I really know? I know that some of these leaders are abusive, mean, selfish, greedy, and acting as such. I know that some of their demands are ridiculous, and that these demands might have caused failures in some processes. However, I still think I'm missing something. Do I know precisely who spiked my coffee and set me up? No, I don't. Do I know precisely who all the players are in the stock-price game? No, I don't know that either. There has been some mention of using media articles to control the price of the stock, but I have no hard evidence that someone is actually doing it."

"I see," Steve said, carefully listening. "How do you feel about all this?"

"You're being a shrink with me," Alex said, with a sad smile.

Steve shrugged. "Can't help it, it's who I am."

"Never mind, I need it. I feel frustrated and scared. I'm frustrated, because I can't seem to get to the bottom of this. I can't seem to make enough undisputable progress to take these guys down and make things better. These are dangerous people, you know, and I'm right there in the middle of the snake pit, afraid for myself, afraid that I won't be able to figure them out, and afraid that my hesitation, or maybe my lack of experience doing this kind of work, could cause delays in our ability to stop this chain of drone-related events. And that means more people could die, because I'm not fast enough, or smart enough, or bold enough."

"Oh, but you are fast enough to bring blame on yourself, aren't you?"

Steve surprised her with his question.

"What do you mean?"

"Let's think of serial killers, for example. After they kill their first victim, and she is found, the cops working that case should be, in your opinion, directly responsible for all the subsequent killings, until the serial killer is caught. Right?"

"Well, to some extent—"

"No, that's not correct. Not unless they do a sloppy job, lose evidence, not show up for work, or whatever else they could do other than their absolute best to get the killer caught. Are you with me on this?"

"Yes, but I don't see how it correlates to my situation," Alex pushed back.

"Wait for it. Are you doing your absolute best to get this job done?"

"Yes, I am," she smiled, starting to see the encouragement he was giving her.

"Then you should be fine, and you shouldn't be blaming yourself for any potential future drone-related deaths that could happen until you catch your killers."

"OK, I get it."

"Self-blame, check!" Steve said humorously, marking an imaginary task list. "Let's move to self-doubt now, shall we? What's on your mind?"

"I don't know that I'll be able to figure all this out, to the last one of the questions we have. Who did what and why? I've been right there among them for a month now and I don't seem to know any more than I did the first week. I have more suspicions about some individuals, but nothing concrete. What am I missing? I can't stop thinking that someone faster, more experienced than me, would do a better job at this."

"Do you want to throw in your towel? You know, you would have every right to, especially after last weekend," Steve asked, referring to the traumatic event of her arrest.

"That was scary and disappointing. I felt alone, frightened, and abandoned. I hated feeling like that. Then I felt relieved and grateful when they released me, only to feel cheated hours later, when Tom said he had not raised a finger to help me. None of you did."

"I can understand that, and you're justified in feeling all that." Steve paused for a minute, letting Alex appreciate he was not challenging her at all. "You know, Tom lost someone a couple of years back. One of us."

"I didn't know that. Who? And how?"

"He was a promising and talented computer expert, just like you—ambitious, bold, and smart. He was deployed to work with a client, and then he caved under the pressure and turned to drugs. Never said a word to any of us. We all noticed he was a little edgy, but we blamed it on the stress of his double job. When asked, he also blamed it on the stress of his work. A month later, he was hooked badly on amphetamines, crystal meth, and any other form of performance-enhancing drug he could lay his hands on. Then he made a mistake on the client side, and jumped off the roof. Tom was devastated, he felt personally responsible. We all did."

They sat silent for a while.

"I'm still not going to forgive Tom that easily for last week, you know," Alex said, in a softer voice. "He should have trusted me. He should have given me the benefit of the doubt."

"Yes, he should have. Brian got the coffee filter analyzed, and the rest of your office and home, looking for clues."

"He was in my home? Oh, my God!" She thought of her habit to leave her clothing scattered on the floor, just where it happened to fall, and blushed.

"He didn't mention anything worth worrying about. When he found the meth traces in your coffee filter, Tom realized just how wrong he'd been. But, by then, they had already released you."

"Not forgiven yet," Alex repeated.

"I'm not asking you to forgive him. Just allow him to make it up to you."

"That, we shall see," Alex said, smiling.

"Ah, the steaks are here," Steve said, rubbing his hands together.

They started eating their succulent meals.

"You know," Steve said, "the best way to gauge the quality of the food is by observing how silently people eat. Good food allows for no conversation."

"True. So, why are you talking?"

"I gotta apologize for not speaking with you while we have our dinner together, right?"

"Wrong. Please let me enjoy this steak without having to talk my way through it." They both laughed. It felt so good, just being herself with him.

With dinner out of the way, Steve resumed the original course of conversation.

"We haven't dealt with self-doubt yet, you know. What else is bothering you?" Steve asked, refilling her glass with wine.

"These guys, I can't figure out their limits. How far would they go? Initially I thought they would only go so far, but then I ended up in jail and figured out we were in a different kind of game. I'm afraid I'm not that good at reading people. I don't know, even from the victims, if some of them wouldn't do something stupid, just because of the pressure."

"The victims?"

"Some of these leaders are victims of others. They are constantly pushed and humiliated, mocked, insulted, set up to fail, and threatened. Some of them might cave. I can't even figure out why some of them don't just get the hell out of there. Why do they let themselves be subjected to such abuse? You see, I feel like I lack the basic understanding of human nature, to figure out even this much."

"OK, let's figure it out together," Steve said calmly. "Life is mostly easy when you're young, free, and single. If you have a wife, potentially sick, and a bunch of kids to feed, you don't own your life anymore. Chances are you barely make ends meet, and you can't afford the dignity of walking away from abuse, holding your head up. Nope, if you're that man, you endure. Sometimes it happens that you can't endure anymore, and can't leave either. Then you snap. You do something stupid, break the law, get a gun, and shoot someone. We've all seen it in the news. It even has a name, it's called going postal."

"In reference to the incident where a postal worker shot his manager?"

"Yes, only there wasn't just one incident, there were many more." Steve paused to take a sip of wine. He raised his fingers discreetly, pointing at the empty bottle. The waiter returned promptly with a new bottle.

"It could also happen that, due to prolonged exposure to abuse and the impossibility to leave, some victims, as you call them, end up developing Stockholm syndrome. You'll recognize these victims by the fact that they will endorse the abuse, find excuses for it, even defend the abuser."

"I think I have seen one of those," Alex said, thinking of Miles Putnam.

"You have to keep in mind that, most likely, the majority of these employees are, in fact, hostages. Do you remember we discussed this?"

"Yes. How far can a hostage go? After all, it's just a job—"

"It's not just a job, it's survival. It's having food and shelter for tomorrow, for yourself and your family. It's so much more than just a job. They can go really far if they're pushed."

"Let me ask you something else then."

He nodded, encouragingly.

"How far would you take this? Would you settle to figure out the majority of the problem, and the most likely wrongdoers, so Dr. Barnaby can fire them and fix the issue? Or would you continue digging until you have proof enough to hold some of them responsible in court?"

"Personally, I would hate to let the villains go with a nice severance package instead of a prison sentence. Setting you up last week was a crime, you know. Do you know who did it?"

"I have an educated guess, that's all I have," she sighed.

"Then that's not enough, or, at least, it wouldn't be for me."

She agreed, tapping gently on her glass to signal it was empty. She felt a bit lightheaded, but relaxed.

"I wasn't even able to visit the plant, you know, during all this time. I am sure that I'll understand more once I see the plant. It took the client's intervention to make it happen, but I am finally going there next week."

"Dr. Barnaby stepped in?"

"Yes, he put out a memo stating that all executive new hires should tour the plant and fully understand the business. Nicely done; I finally get to see what's going on out there."

"How are we doing on self-doubt, then?" Steve asked.

"Check!" Alex laughed. "Let's order dessert." She opened the menu. "Oh, this is what I want, Depraved Ice Cream!"

"Are you sure?" Steve asked. "It's loaded with alcohol."

"Bring it on," she laughed, slurring a bit.

The ice cream was an unbelievable treat. Vanilla ice cream covered in chocolate syrup, swimming in the finest Courvoisier cognac. The cognac, poured over the ice cream right before it was served, caused some of the ice cream to melt, creating an unbelievable palate delight.

Steve had ordered an Unchaste Tiramisu, exquisite, yet no alcohol included.

"It's a shame you're not trying this," Alex said, pointing at her ice cream.

"Someone has to drive, you know. What's left on our list?"

She suddenly became sad. Steve noticed and refocused.

"Fear. I am so goddamn afraid and can't seem to grow out of it. Someone yells at me, my knees are shaking. Since last weekend, my heart stops every time I see a police car. I hear sirens at night, I can't fall asleep. I don't feel safe in my own home anymore. It's pathetic . . . I know I'm supposed to be this fearless, bold, secret agent of sorts, but by the time I get out of that building, I am wiped out. Everything scares me . . . what if someone figures out I have a clone laptop? What if the fact that I see other peoples' email messages surfaces? And I'm not afraid just for me or my safety . . . I'm afraid of letting everyone down—Dr. Barnaby, Tom, you . . ."

A few moments of silence passed. Tears started flooding her eyes.

"You know, fear is an inherited mechanism of defense, ancestrally built to steer us away from trouble. You *should* be scared of being caught with two laptops. That prevents you from being careless, hence keeping you from being caught. Fear is the means through which your body helps you deal with all this. The issue is what we do about our fear, how we handle it, and how we use our fear to make us better at what we do."

"I get it." Tears were running down her cheeks, but she didn't mind.

"The questions I have for you are these: What do you want to do? Do you want to pull out?"

"Absolutely not," she said, sounding determined. "I have to do this, no matter how scared I am. I'll be all right . . . I just wish I could feel safe again, just for a few hours, so I can rest. I need to rest."

Steve hesitated for a split second, studying her, and then stood up.

"I think I can make that happen. Let's go."

"Where?"

"My place. We need to change cars."

Vincent Moran turned to the last page in his portfolio.

"And finally tonight, a significantly bad week for NanoLance, whose decline continues at an accelerated pace amid the swarm of drone scandals. While details are still owed to the public by the US military authorities, fewer investors are confident that these details will clear NanoLance's battered reputation and restore its once impressive fame and fortune. NNLC gave 3.18 percent more in cumulative losses this past week, closing the day today at $80.82 per share. Those investors still hanging on to their NanoLance shares are betting their money on the unlikely turnaround of the company as being the only way they could recover the significant losses they have incurred in the past month.

"From *Money Markets Review Late Edition*, this is Vincent Moran, wishing you a fortunate day."

She hated to admit it, but she was mostly out of it, falling asleep just seconds after each sentence that Steve said. She could barely remember anything from the drive, since they left the restaurant. They drove by Steve's place; she wasn't sure how long that took or where Steve lived. She had slept the whole way. He carried her from one car to the other. She wasn't that drunk . . . She was just immensely tired. She needed to explain that.

"You know, I'm not that drunk," she said, half asleep.

"Uh-huh," Steve said, pulling out of his driveway. "That's what they all say."

"Ugh . . . Not fair . . . I'll prove it to you. I'm still alert. Why did we change cars?"

"I don't know, you tell me," Steve chuckled.

"Now you want me to observe stuff, right?"

"Right. It's a long drive, and we need a topic for conversation."

"How long?"

"An hour and a half."

"Understated?"

"Nope."

"Where are we going? You never told me."

"Up in the mountains. I have a cabin there. It's the safest place on Earth."

"Oh." She desperately tried to wake up so she could process the information. No good. Her brain simply refused to operate.

"Did you drug me?"

"What? No," he laughed. "You must have me confused with the coworkers from your other job."

"I've never been so tired," she said, slurring her speech and yawning.

"It's because you finally feel safe after a long period of non-stop stress. Your body is claiming its toll. You've been running on adrenaline for a while, depriving your body of the deep sleep and relaxation it needs to rest properly and recharge. Here, in the car with me, you know there's nothing much that can happen to you, so you're finally stepping out of your constant state of hypervigilance."

"So, you know I am not that drunk, right? That's all I care about right now. The rest you can explain to me again tomorrow, 'cause I won't remember much."

"Yes, I know you're not that drunk."

Alex could hear the smile in his voice, despite the darkness that surrounded them. Interstate 8 was quiet at that time of night, as they headed toward the mountains. She continued to battle her sleepiness.

"Why did we change cars?"

"What can you tell me about the car we're in?"

"It's an SUV?"

"Yes, more suited for a ride to my cabin on unpaved roads than the BMW, wouldn't you agree?"

"Yes," she sighed, closing her eyes and falling asleep instantly.

"Hey, we're driving by the plant," he said, a few minutes later.

"Huh?" She tried to keep her eyes open.

"Yep, we're driving through Alpine." He briefly looked her way. Her eyes were closed. "Ah, go back to sleep."

She had no idea when they got there. At some point, she felt the road had become somewhat bumpy, but this car was just as comfortable as the other one. She remembered thinking that they should be getting close, once they left the highway. Then she fell right back to sleep.

Somewhere between her blurry dreams, they arrived at the cabin. Steve carried her inside, where a dim light was on and an immense black dog was waiting in the doorway. The cabin was chilly. Steve took her to a sofa in front of a fireplace and laid her down. Minutes later, a nice little fire was casting shadows on the walls. The dog was lying at her feet. After a while longer, she woke up to see she was cuddled with that enormous dog, on the extended sectional couch, covered with a blanket that dissipated a strong cedar scent.

Steve was sitting on the floor next to her, stirring the logs in the fireplace.

"I'm sorry," she said softly, touching his shoulder, "I was not a good date for you tonight."

"It's all right, kiddo, there will be plenty more opportunities for that."

"You promise?"

"Promise. Now go back to sleep."

When she woke, it was daylight, the sun was already high. Sensing her move, the dog stretched his paws and licked his nose. She rose and noticed she was wearing Steve's pajamas. She blushed. *Oh, well* . . . She noticed a note, pinned to the fireplace mantle.

Good morning, or maybe afternoon?

Sorry I had to leave—some of us still have to work, you know.

The cabin is all yours to enjoy. It's remote and secure; you need not worry about any humans bothering you. As for bears, they could happen by, but if you don't leave any food outside, they won't show.

By the way, the dog's name is Teddy. He looked just like a bear cub when he was little. He still does. He'll take good care of you, he promised.

There's a hammock in the back, along with a grill. There's plenty of food in the fridge.

I'll be back as soon as I can. Until then, enjoy your stay and get plenty of rest.

The note wasn't signed.

The day passed quickly, between naps, meals, and brief walks around the cabin. The landscape was breathtaking. The cabin overlooked one of the few wooded gorges of the southern California mountains. She had no idea where exactly on the map the cabin would be. From the back, you could see all the way into the valley. Down there, far away, a road was barely visible. She could not distinguish the cars on it. The front of the cabin was facing a thickly wooded patch, and the road leading to the cabin was nothing more than a forest path. She listened hard and could only hear the forest sounds: birds chirping, leaves rustled by the wind. The sounds of serenity.

Teddy nudged her, waking her from her daydreaming. He was a huge Terra Nova, from what Alex could tell, in great shape and obviously hungry by now. It was dusk already. She went inside and prepared food for her and Teddy. They both sat in the dimming daylight, eating and watching a spectacular view through the window.

Suddenly she became aware of Teddy's low growl. Hackles raised, he started walking toward the cabin door. She looked out the window, trying to see clearly in the darker dusk. A silhouette moved near the tree line. Alex gasped, seeing a man carrying a shotgun. Teddy's growl grew louder. She crouched, reaching for her cell phone. There was no coverage here, so high up in the mountains. She looked around for something she could use as a weapon. There wasn't much. The man was approaching the door, and she could see him better under the porch light. He was huge.

The man grabbed the screen door handle and opened it. He knocked on the doorframe.

"Hey, there, miss?"

Teddy's attitude suddenly changed, recognizing a familiar voice. The hairs on his back settled, and his tail started waving.

"Miss? Are you in there?"

Alex rose from behind the couch.

"Yes. Who are you?"

"I'm your neighbor to the south, miss, just came by to see if everything was OK with you. Steve asked me to. Oh, and I also feed the dog when Steve can't make it up here."

"Oh, I see. Thank you for checking in on me. I've already fed Teddy. You nearly scared me to death," she laughed.

"Didn't mean to do such thing, miss, I apologize. I'll be on my way now."

"Uh . . . excuse me?" She did not know the man's name.

"Yes," he turned.

"Did Steve say when he was coming back?"

"Later tonight, that's what he said."

She waited, curled up on the couch, in front of a newly started fire. When she woke, the sun was high again, and Steve was holding a cup of steaming coffee in front of her nose.

"Good morning, sunshine, how are you feeling today?"

"Aww . . . you said you'd come last night." She voiced her disappointment before she could restrain herself. She had made plans for their evening together.

"Oh, but I did, and you were fast asleep," he smiled. "Here's some coffee, and I promise you there's no meth in it. Come on, you're going to need it."

"Huh?" Alex took a sip. The coffee was excellent.

"You have a plane to catch. You're going to Florida. Dr. Barnaby managed to arrange for you to interview the Florida drone operators. We're leaving in an hour."

Waiting for her flight to board was going to be a while. The incoming flight was late, and the gate was already crowded by loud, impatient travelers. She found a remote corner and sat on the floor. Connecting her laptop, she checked on the emails she didn't review while at Steve's cabin.

There was only one message that caught her interest, but it was troubling.

From: Benjamin Walker (COO)
To: Angela Prescott (VP HR)
Subject: Reminder
Sent: Friday, July 9, 10:23PM

Angela,

My biggest technology problem has not been solved yet. How much longer do I have to wait? You need to make this happen immediately.

Thanks,
Ben

His biggest technology problem? What could that be? Alex felt a chill down her spine. Was that email about her? Had she become Walker's biggest technology problem, which had to be dealt with immediately?

Whoa, she thought, trying to curb her paranoia, *there's no reason to think that.* The technology problem on Walker's mind could be anything. On the other hand, he was emailing HR about it, so the technology problem was, most likely, an employee, not a printer, or a paper-jammed copier. But was he emailing an HR leader? Or a lover? Did he want the employee fired? Or hurt?

She got so engulfed in her thoughts that she nearly missed the final boarding call for her flight. She grabbed her things in a hurry and, as she was boarding the undersized, crammed aircraft, she decided it was safe to assume Walker's email was indeed about a person. Her.

"Good morning, ladies and gentlemen."

The young anchor seemed sure of himself and joyous for that early hour of the morning. "We're kicking off this new work week with an examination of a GPS system from NanoLance, the Guide. This GPS model has been around for a few years, yet constantly evolving, redesigned, and enhanced. For many, it has proven to be a great device. Yet, as of late, more consumer complaints end up in our mailbox. Therefore, we decided to give the NanoLance Guide a test drive, to see for ourselves."

The TV screen was showing the anchor handling the GPS device and using it to get guidance on a hiking trail.

"We've hiked around with the little Guide in our hands for quite a few miles before it started acting up. When it did, it simply lost satellite connection and wouldn't restore it. However, the NanoLance Guide was quick to re-establish satellite connection after a full power restart, as in removing and reinserting its battery pack.

"Then, just a couple of miles later, the LCD screen went completely dark. The voice guidance worked, but the screen stopped showing any information or map detail. This time, a restart didn't do the trick. A good shake did, the type you'd see given in the movies to dying flashlights. Finally, we tested a second handheld unit, but that worked properly for the duration of our test run."

The image changed to show the anchor back at his studio desk.

"Somewhere between design flaws and manufacturing flaws lies the explanation for NanoLance Guide's decreasing quality standard. Just a couple of years ago, this particular device scored five stars on consumer satisfaction, best in class for reliability in the last year's Las Vegas Consumer Electronics Show, and overall best performance as indicated by our consumers. Today we can only award it 4.1 stars, a significant loss of prestige for this proud manufacturer. With the hope that this product will soon regain the superstar status it lost, we are rooting for the NanoLance Guide to make a comeback."

A ticker appeared at the bottom of the screen, displaying an email address.

"Remember, for any product or service quality concerns, our email address is shown below. From *Ted's Consumer Central*, I am Harry Hosteen, always on your side."

Alex had expected higher security measures at Mackenzie Air Field. Just stating her name at the front entrance seemed to have been enough. She was led into a small meeting room, whose dirty windows were facing Highway 98, the place where the disaster had struck a couple of weeks before.

The door opened, allowing two young men to step through.

"Lieutenant Donald Cohen, ma'am," the first one said.

"Lieutenant Barry Jennings, ma'am, a pleasure to meet you."

"Alex Hoffmann, director of infrastructure with NanoLance."

They were so young, so unbelievably young. She studied their faces in amazement. When did they even have time to complete flight training?

"Thank you for taking the time to speak with me today," she opened the conversation. "As you might guess, NanoLance would like to get some more details about the incident that happened here," she said, pointing at the window facing Highway 98. "I'd like to understand from you what happened that day and what your perception was about the cause of the incident. I would also like to know more about how these drones are operated on your end."

"Well, it's simple to operate them, ma'am," Cohen said. "We see on our screen the images captured by the drone's cameras. We have a joystick panel, about this big," he continued, indicating a shape and size with his hands, "and we control the drone's flight from there. All we need to see to be able to control the UAV's flight appears on the control panel's screens. We make it take off, fly, change altitude, attitude, and direction, operate onboard cameras—the sensor array— and launch weapons."

"Tell me a little about the weapons launch, how does that happen?"

"Part of the imagery we receive is an infrared view. We pick up heat signatures from people and equipment, such as motor vehicles, missile launch sites, mostly anything that heats to operate. If we're guiding a combat drone, it will transmit this imagery and we decide which targets we're gonna hit."

"So the drone doesn't fire on its own?"

They both chuckled lightly, looking at each other for a split second.

"No, ma'am, it's always a human operator who decides when the weapons are launched."

"Then tell me please, what do you think went wrong that day?"

Neither responded for a few seconds, looking at each other.

"The thing is, ma'am, we don't know," Cohen said. I was bringing the drone in for landing, after a mission with the Coast Guard over the Gulf of Mexico waters. The drone needed course adjustment; it had the wrong vector for the approach.

Alex blinked when she heard the word "wrong."

"Oh, nothing was *wrong* at that point, ma'am," Cohen clarified. "The vector was wrong for the approach—the runway is at this angle, and the drone is approaching at this angle," he said, making wide gestures with his arms. "Happens on every landing. All pilots have to correct approach vectors, so they are perfectly aligned with the runway."

"I see. OK, let's continue."

"The drone's vector was 30, our runway is 350, so that required me to change course by making the drone turn. Again, nothing out of the ordinary."

"30? 350?" Alex asked.

"Degrees. Heading. It's the angle between the drone's direction of movement and magnetic north. Or the runway's angle with magnetic north. The drone needed to change its heading from the 30, coming from the gulf, to 350, and align with the runway for final approach."

"Got it, thank you."

"So, I was starting to turn," Cohen continued. "Nothing was out of the ordinary at that point. But then the drone, despite my control, stopped turning and resumed flying straight. I remember saying, 'What the hell?'"

"He did, I remember him saying it too, 'cause that's how I knew something was wrong, and I turned to see what was happening," Jennings added.

"Then," Cohen continued, "I started trying to see if movement in the joystick correlated with any change in the UAV's direction. I was testing the joystick's responsiveness, and I wasn't getting any for a while. For a few seconds, the joystick completely failed to control the drone."

"Then what happened?" Alex asked.

"The weirdest thing. As I was playing with the joystick to see if I could get any response from the drone, well, I suddenly got it. A response, that is. The drone resumed obeying the joystick control, and I had to compensate in a hurry to bring it to the needed heading."

"Why the urgency?"

"When the drone resumed its connection with the joystick, I was in the middle of testing the joystick by pushing it to the extremes of all possible motions, so I was abruptly transmitting extreme course changes. If I hadn't instantly corrected the course after I noticed it had become responsive again, I would've crashed the UAV in the Gulf, within seconds. In retrospect, I wish I had."

"That means you were able to restore the drone's responsiveness to the ground controls?"

"For a few seconds, yes," Cohen answered.

"That's where it gets weird," Jennings said.

"After a few seconds of responsiveness, in which I was, again, applying the course corrections to bring the drone in for final approach, the UAV lost it again and resumed a zero bank angle flight."

"Zero bank angle?"

"It's when an aircraft is not turning, the wings are level, it's not tilted, just flies straight," Jennings explained.

"You're saying the drone lost connection with ground control a second time?" Alex asked. This was getting interesting.

"Yes, that's what I mean," Cohen continued. "For a few seconds, it was responsive; then again, it wasn't anymore. Then it was responsive again, and then we lost it one more time. It was coming in and out of connection with ground control or something like that. At that point, Jennings was running for help, trying to find our commanding officer, and I was desperately trying to get the drone under control. By the time anyone came, and after a series of under control—out of control—episodes, we saw on the screens that it was heading for the mainland, under the wrong heading, and flying too low. The drone was, at that time, completely unresponsive to any of the ground controls. Seconds later, it was all over," Cohen said, dropping his voice to a whisper.

"You see, ma'am," Jennings said, "we took apart the control panel in the room, trying to figure out what went wrong. The technicians said that the ground control panel was working correctly, and that something went wrong either with the drone's navigation controls or with the comlink between ground control and the UAV. Both of us are beating ourselves up over what happened. Did we screw anything up? I seriously doubt it. We weren't even playing with self-guidance that day."

Cohen gave Jennings an angry flash of his eyes, for just a fraction of a second, then resumed looking straight down.

"Do you normally play with the self-guidance feature?"

"This UAV came equipped with self-guidance software, but it's for testing purposes only. It wasn't cleared for deployment, as you well know. It is, if you will, like a trial version, reduced in functionality and designed to help us, the drone pilots, to figure out if it does what it should do, and what other functionality we'd like to have built in. It's more of a research tool. We sometimes play with it, but not that day, and never in populated areas."

"You're positive this drone was not self-guiding?" Alex asked.

"Yes, I am," Jennings answered.

"Yes, we are," Cohen answered, at the same time. "You have to physically turn on self-guidance to make it work. No one flipped that switch that day. Like Jennings said, the self-guidance feature is under development, it's not complete yet, and shouldn't be used outside of a test environment."

"But you said something about playing with it?"

"I'm sorry, ma'am," Jennings said, trying to fix it. "That was a slip of the tongue, more than anything else. We rarely test the self-guidance, and, when we do, the drones are out at sea, or over desert areas with no target in sight."

"All right, I get it. Tell me about ordnance. What was that UAV armed with when it hit the bus?"

"Nothing, ma'am," Cohen said. "It was a surveillance drone, not a combat one. The surveillance UAVs are equipped with video cameras and all kinds of imaging and monitoring technology. This particular one was helping the Coast Guard patrol our territorial waters."

"The explosion would have been far worse, if any type of missile had been involved," Jennings confirmed.

"Then what caused such a big explosion if the drone was unarmed?"

"Fuel, ma'am," Cohen said. "The UAV's tanks were more than half full."

This time, Alex was late for her own staff meeting. She hated when people had to wait for her. She considered lateness a rude gesture. When she finally stepped through the conference room door, her team had been waiting for a while and was engaged in the casual chatter that occurs in such cases.

"Good morning, everyone, sorry I'm late," Alex said. She had no hesitation apologizing to her direct reports for being late, or for any mistake she made. The theory saying that apologizing is a sign of weakness didn't go well with her nature.

"Welcome back," Louie said, "I hope you're feeling better."

"Y-yes, I am," she replied, almost taken by surprise. In the whirlwind of the previous day's events, she had nearly forgotten she called in sick on Monday morning, claiming a bad case of food poisoning.

"Back where I'm from, especially on a Monday, food poisoning means something else," Louie said, to the amusement of the rest.

"Like what?" Alex asked.

"Like a serious hangover." Laughter erupted around the table.

"I promise you I was not hung over," Alex said, unable to contain a smile. "OK, back on track here. This week we're going to work with R&D in assessing the self-guiding software. There are complaints about the software, specifically about its unreliable performance. In last week's operations meeting with Walker, Peter Wilson mentioned software failures in all models. Who can take a look at that and let me know what's going on?"

Alan's face changed expressions from his usual degree of worry to a deeply concerned frown.

"This isn't the first time this has happened, you know," he said. "We've seen it before, last year, when we deployed the first version. There were so many bugs to fix that we didn't even try. We pulled back and went straight to the drawing board, designed what we have today. Today's version didn't go through formal QA, or a bug-fix period of testing and redeployment. There's plenty of work to do there."

"I'll work with you on that," Louie offered.

"Hey, I'll take all the help I can get," Alan said gratefully.

"I could help too," Bob said. "Everything else I have can wait or be delegated."

"Heard you're going to the plant today," Lisa said, with her usual charming smile.

"You are?" Bob asked.

"Yes, I am leaving right after this meeting."

"It's an interesting tour; you'll love it," Lisa continued. "I wish I could get out there more often. You learn more about the product from a visit to the plant than you learn from a month of theoretical dissertations."

"Well, if you're going there today," Bob said, "maybe you can help me with something."

"Shoot."

"I have this small, bomb-dismantling robot that needs to be tested. It needs to get there. You would save me a trip."

"Sure, no problem, I'll take it. Is it big and heavy?"

"No, just a few pounds, kinda looks like a toy. The Air Force wants to assess the feasibility of having these robots dropped from low flying UAVs. Folks at the plant are going to fit the little bugger with a parachute of sorts and start dropping it for testing. I'll walk you to your car, so you won't break a fingernail."

"Ah," Alex gave an amused sigh of pretend irritation. "OK, let's go."

"I'll tag along," Louie said, "got a question for you."

The robot wasn't large. It had a mechanical arm with a gripping claw, extending toward its front, much like an excavator. This robot's claw had a complicated design, involving multiple degrees of freedom, which allowed it to reach various locations and under different angles, to grab, detonate, or project a detonating laser beam from a safe distance.

"Where do you want this?" Bob asked.

She opened the rear car door on the passenger side.

"Put it down on the floor, between the seats. It won't budge from there. If we put it in the trunk, it will bounce around the whole way."

"Wanted to ask you," Louie said, "in the analysis of the self-guidance software, anything specific we should be looking for? Did Wilson mention anything in particular?"

"If I recall exactly, he said they fail in orientation, navigation, and targeting."

"Targeting? Or target acquisition?" Louie asked. "Targeting is in a different software module than target acquisition."

"Acquisition, yes, you're right. He said the drones get lost, exceed their patrol perimeter, and fail to pick up targets based on preloaded imagery. Fact is, I'd like to be able to have some kind of response for the operations team before the next meeting, which is in a week or so."

"All right, we'll all get on it then, full priority."

"Where should I put this?" Bob asked, holding a small device in his hand.

"What's this?" Alex asked.

"It's the remote for the bomb-dismantling robot."

"It works with a remote?" Alex asked.

"Oh, yeah," Bob said, thrilled at the opportunity to demonstrate. "You open it like this. It opens like one of those full keyboard cell phones. On this screen, you'll see what it sees with its cameras. You can select front view, side-left, side-right, rear, and above," he continued, demonstrating the robot's views. The views were showing incredibly detailed images of the interior of her car.

"Someone needs to vacuum under her seats," Louie said cheerfully.

"Ah, shut up," Alex fired right back at him.

"Here," Bob continued, unabated, "you have the arm controls. A small joystick, embedded in the remote, would snap up and become operational when in place. See?"

She nodded with interest.

"This is how you control the arm," Bob was demonstrating all the possible movements of the arm. "Combining the joystick with these four controls, you can get it to move sideways but also on the vertical axis, like this, or grip its claw, like this. You can lock the grip, like this," he continued, showing more combinations of controls.

"Ah, this is fun," Alex said. "I know I'm never gonna need to know this, but this is really fun. I could play with it for an hour or two."

"And this is how you move the unit itself, not just the arm." Bob said, taking the robot from the car and setting it down on the asphalt, showing her how it would turn, advance, reverse, and spin in place. "If the surface is good and allows it, this robot can do fifteen miles per hour."

"Quite versatile," Louie said.

"Oh, yeah, it is, and it's not from the disposable generation anymore, you know," Bob said. He was passionate about all things to do with robots and artificial intelligence in general. His kind eyes filled with sparks as he walked his audience through feature after feature.

"How do you mean, disposable?" Alex asked. "These things must cost a fortune."

"Yes, they do," Bob continued, "that's precisely why now they're equipped to detonate a bomb from a safe distance, by activating this laser, here," he pointed first at the robot's laser source, and then at the laser activation command button on the remote. "Before they had lasers the robots ended up destroyed while detonating bombs they couldn't dismantle, because of their close proximity. They had to detonate the bomb mechanically, which required the little guys to be right there, near the bomb, and get blown to bits in the process. If dismantling fails and the remote operator decides detonation is the best course of action, this laser technology allows the operator to detonate remotely."

"OK, you guys, thanks for the crash course in bomb-dismantling robot operations, but I gotta go. I am going to be seriously late for my plant visit. I'll take that," Alex said, reaching for the remote. She took it, flipped it closed, and put it in her inside jacket pocket. Minutes later, she was speeding toward the NanoLance plant.

Somewhere in the dense traffic, a few cars behind her, a gray Ford sedan was catching up.

"Another challenging week for NanoLance Incorporated has started with an unfavorable consumer review report, issued yesterday by our colleagues from *Ted's Consumer Central.* The findings are putting NanoLance's global quality under a big question mark, signaling notable drops in product quality in the consumer branch of the business. These findings have generated yet another knee-jerk reaction from shareholders, who have dumped relatively high volumes of shares at declining prices. NNLC gave 6.24 percent on NASDAQ today, bringing the stock price at an unprecedented $75.78 per share. Probably the decline will continue, if the negative media attention doesn't fade and the company's reputation is not restored.

"From *Money Markets Morning Review*, this is Vincent Moran, wishing you a fortunate day."

"Umm . . . late, as usual," Alex grunted, looking at the time while she was parking in one of the plant's visitor parking spots. She should have been there by 11:30AM, no later.

In the lobby, John Dunwood, vice president of manufacturing, was waiting for her, casually chatting with the receptionist.

"I'm so sorry I'm late," Alex said, as soon as she stepped through the door.

"No problem, I just arrived," Dunwood replied, shaking her hand. "We are scheduled for a quick introduction about plant operations, then the tour, per se, and then we'll have a picnic."

"A picnic? Here?" She was surprised. This was not the usual business lunch invitation.

"Yes, exactly. You haven't seen the plant until you've seen our testing airfield and our drones flying. What better place to have lunch? Don't worry," he continued, looking at her stilettos, "we have pavement and picnic tables. We eat out there a lot."

He led her to his office, a modestly decorated, functional room.

"It's rare that we have an IT leader visit. This almost never happens. Or happened, I should say. I've seen the memo that Dr. Barnaby put out regarding the plant tours for all newly hired leaders, and I think it's a great idea. Even if it takes a little bit of time from our days, the value in having all new leaders exposed to the products, both military and civilian, is priceless. Coffee? Water?"

"No, thank you, I'm good."

"Let's proceed, then. The plant is organized into three main sections. There's one section dedicated to building and assembling the electronic components that we install in all products, such as circuit boards, command modules, and so on. That's a static-free, dust-free environment, and we have two options to visit it. We can either see it through the glass walls, or, if you'd like to see more detail, we'll have to dress you up in anti-static work wear."

"Through the glass walls would do it, I think," Alex said.

"A second section of the plant manufactures the bodies of all the UAVs. Few components that participate in the full assembly of a UAV are built elsewhere. We're vertically integrated almost to perfection, and this helps greatly with quality control." He frowned. "I am sure you remember quality hasn't been our greatest achievement lately."

Alex nodded, sympathetically.

"Most drone bodies are made of composite materials. There's no foundry here," he clarified with a smile. "There are numerous advantages to composites. They're lightweight, non-corrosive, high-strength, re-enforceable, and flexible. Therefore, all UAV body components are shaped here, on site, from carefully designed formulations of composite materials and reinforcing fibers. We buy the wheels and tires from a parts vendor, you know. But mostly everything else is built here."

Dunwood spoke with great pride about the plant's capabilities. Watching him while he was speaking about all the components built at the plant, Alex thought of a different reason why Dunwood would still be around, continuing to endure Walker's repeated abuse. Maybe he wasn't a hostage in his job, after all. Maybe he just loved what he did with such passion, he couldn't think of living without it.

"The third section of the plant," he continued, "is also the most exciting to see. It's the drone assembly line. Many visitors are surprised that we even have an assembly line for drones. After all, how many are we making? The answer is quite a few. And we're constantly growing our output numbers. Unmanned flight is the future of combat aviation, with great potential to encompass significant pieces of the air-cargo market and numerous other civilian applications. Removing life support and the crew's physical space requirements from a plane, plus the cost of the actual flight crew is a significant cost advantage.

"This translates into a full-blown assembly line, capable of delivering a few hundred units per year. This is the section we're going to be visiting last, to give you all the time you'd like to look around and ask questions. Your clearance level is high enough for your badge to access all doors in the plant, except the static-free areas, for which you need a special clearance. Please feel free to move around as you wish."

"Wow, thank you," Alex said. For some reason she hadn't thought that the plant would be so complex and large.

"And, of course, there's R&D. Our research department makes us proud. They are forward thinking and creative. They come up with ideas, which have secured, over time, this company's leading role on the market. For example, R&D is playing with the idea of designing guidance-and-control software that could be deployed in a matrix, on multiple identical drones, to test—"

"Swarm behaviors?" Alex couldn't refrain from interrupting him. "Sorry, please continue."

"Yes, precisely. We're looking to see if we could embed swarm intelligence into combat strategies. All right, let's go. Let's start with the first section, the module-and-component assembly."

They walked along a path marked by two yellow lines, delimiting the pedestrian safe zone. Dunwood was a tall man and walked fast. Alex could barely keep up on her high heels.

"Would you like some loaner boots for today? I am sure we can find a pair your size," Dunwood said, encouragingly.

"Yes, I would like some boots," she admitted, smiling.

Minutes later, she was able to trot happily, keeping up with Dunwood's wide steps without any problems.

They reached a glass wall extending over tens of yards, against the far left wall of the plant. Behind the glass walls, neatly dressed technicians wearing hairnets, lab coats, and anti-static bracelets, were seated at assembly tables covered in rubber mats. They were assembling or inspecting electronic circuits. Farther in the back, robotic assemblers were soldering components of circuit boards, feeding the technicians finished modules for them to inspect, then wrap in static-free packaging and set in output trays. Complex testing stations were operated with the same efficiency on some of the rubber-coated tables. The larger modules reaching these tables were set on testing stations, and panels with colored LED displays lit up, indicating the quality status of various circuits.

Alex became aware of the extended period of time she had spent looking through the windows at each type of operation. Dunwood stood right beside her, ready to answer questions.

"This is so fascinating, I lost track of time, I'm sorry."

"No problem, that's what we're here to do—show you the entire plant, top to bottom. It's a lot to absorb, so take your time."

"I think we can proceed," Alex said.

"Let's go to body-parts manufacturing then, and if you want to come back here after you've finished the tour, that's not going to be a problem."

"Thank you," Alex said, resuming her brisk walk beside Dunwood.

They entered a noisy, smelly area, where large machinery was producing body parts for the UAVs. Some parts she could easily recognize: wings, main body covers—top and bottom—and landing gear panel doors.

"These," Dunwood said, making a wide gesture toward a line of bulky machines, all equipped with computer monitors, "are compression-molding presses. These machines fabricate almost all parts in a UAV's body structure, including brackets and other similar smaller components. They can be compression, injection, and transfer presses. These over here," he pointed to a different set of machines, "are high precision vacuformers. They use a technology based on vacuum and high temperature to mold parts that have tolerances under ten microns. And these are micro-molding machines, which manufacture the smaller components we use, such as screws, nuts, bolts; all these are produced using extremely high pressures."

One of the micro-molding machines was spitting out oval-shaped components with an amazing speed.

"They are incredibly fast and accurate," Dunwood said, seeing what had attracted her attention. "We rarely use these fulltime, although every single one of them can mold multiple designs."

She approached a couple of machines as close as she dared. They were fascinating in their speed, precision, and automation. The manufacturing workflows were neatly organized and logically designed, and the entire plant astounded her with its highly optimized, efficient, smoothly running processes.

"Now let's proceed to assembly," Dunwood said, leading the way to the largest section of the plant. "In assembly, we have multiple lines. The GPS handheld and in-dash lines are here," he said, pointing to a rather small assembly line, operated in a corner by technicians wearing white lab coats. "The products are small, so they don't take a lot of space. We've adapted a system, invented for picking and packing in warehouses fulfilling large numbers of items, called 'pick-a-light' or 'pick-to-light,' for our assembly needs.

"Pick-a-light signals the human operator, by having lights go on and off on the shelving behind him, to indicate which items, and how many, need to be picked and packaged in the box that is traveling on the conveyor belt in front of him. We have adapted it to our assembly lines to integrate all stages of assembly into one line. On our assembly lines, there is no pre-assembly, assembly, QA, packing, and shipping. The entire flow covers all stages of the assembly, and the assembly workers are guided through the process by lights and LCD panels installed next to them, advising what the next part to install is and the next step to perform."

"Wow," Alex said, impressed. The line moved swiftly, workers picking parts off the shelves without hesitation, guided by lights that would come on and go off in harmony with their moves. "But they don't scan bar codes, so how does the system know when the part was picked off the shelf, and if it was the right one?"

"We have installed weight-sensitive panels on the shelves. If, for example, a component weighing precisely 12.7 grams should be picked next, the system watches for that particular change in shelf items weight. If it records a change by more or by less, the line comes to a stop."

"I understand, from what you are showing me, that quality is quite easy to control and achieve at high standards with this system in place, right?"

A frown clouded his wrinkled face.

"From an assembly perspective, yes. We can't go wrong in picking parts and modules. We could still make assembly errors, such as faulty soldering of modules and so on. However, most quality errors are coming from lower quality parts, such as chips and circuit boards. My money is on the circuit boards, because we thoroughly test the chips before installation."

"What would it take to increase the quality of the circuit boards?" Alex treaded carefully, knowing she was entering an area of high sensitivity for Dunwood.

"Money. Lots of it. We took so much cost out of the product, I am surprised it's not worse. You can only go so far, you know." His face was expressing sadness and a touch of anger.

"Who invented this system?" Alex changed direction.

"What system?"

"The pick-a-light for assembly. By the way, what's it called?"

"Oh . . . I don't know that it has a name."

"Who invented it? That's pretty darn brilliant."

"I did," Dunwood replied modestly. "I adapted pick-a-light for the assembly lines, it works now on most of them. The weighing is so precise that the line will stop even if we miss a label of only 12 milligrams."

"You should give it a name, you know. After all, it's your baby," Alex said, smiling.

"Maybe I will, we'll see. Over here, we have the RX5 assembly line. All the assembly is done by technicians, no assembly robots here. Technically, we use the same system to manage parts and control the quality of the assembly. The RX series are recon drones; they have no combat capabilities. They carry enhanced imaging equipment, not ordnance. On our right side, you can see the longest assembly line of all, dedicated to the CX series drones. The CXs are combat UAVs, or UCAVs, designed to carry significant amounts of ordnance depending on size, range, and payload. They also carry sensitive detection-and-imaging equipment, including visible spectrum and infrared cameras, and a satellite comlink."

Dunwood walked along the assembly line, from finish toward the start. He passed the finalized drones, in various stages of final assembly, until he reached a drone that was still missing the upper housing on its body.

"The reason why the UAV's body has this hump here, resembling the shape of the cockpit in some piloted aircraft, is because it's holding a satellite dish, specially designed to operate in flight. This here," he continued, sneaking his hand deep inside the open drone, "is the navigation system. It guides the drone just like your GPS guides you. This other one is the targeting module. It searches for targets, and when a drone locks on a target, this module lights green, signaling the weapons module the target lock, so it can launch the missiles. Nevertheless, it first asks for ground control's permission to launch. This here, this little black box, is the drone's brain. It communicates with ground control and interprets the communications received into mechanical actions, such as gear down, for example. It also confirms to the drone when to launch a missile. The rest is avionics, fuel tanks, hardpoint controls, and landing gear controls.

Dunwood looked briefly at his watch and frowned.

"May I please ask you to give me thirty minutes before going to lunch? I forgot a conference call that I have in about four minutes."

"Ah, sure, don't worry about it; I'll get out of your way."

"Feel free to look around, don't touch anything, though. Do you remember where my office was?"

"I-I think so," Alex responded, hesitantly.

"If not, you can ask anyone. Can you meet me there in half an hour?"

"Sure, will do. Thank you for the tour, it was amazing!"

"It's not over yet," Dunwood said, leaving in his agile step.

Left alone, Alex wondered what she could do best with the thirty minutes of freedom she had gained. She started toward the start of the assembly line for the CX model, and then she backtracked. *No, instead let's talk to some people.*

She made her way to the cafeteria, the one place guaranteed to have human traffic any time of day. She had almost reached the cafeteria door, when she ran into Janet Templeton. Despite all the time they had spent together discussing Rottweiler puppies, Janet didn't seem to recognize her. Alex smiled and prepared to greet Janet. Seeing her approach, Janet looked down, then suddenly turned right and disappeared behind a door marked Authorized Personnel Only. Alex was sure Janet had recognized her, yet refused to be seen talking with her. *What the hell is going on here?*

She grabbed a can of Coke from the vending machine and took it outside to the designated smoking area. She took out her e-cig and slowly walked around, hoping to spark a conversation with someone. There were a couple of people, smoking quietly, nervously, not interacting with her or with each other.

She approached one of them. "Hi."

"Hi," the man responded, lacking any interest in her or the conversation. He was pale, with eyes deep set in their sockets, giving him an appearance of sickness and famine. Maybe smoking wasn't the best thing for this guy.

"How's today treating you?" Alex asked.

"Just like any day, I guess," he answered, showing just as little enthusiasm as before.

"I'm Alex Hoffmann, visiting from corporate," she said, extending her hand to greet him.

"Hank Baker." He briefly grasped her hand, and then eagerly let it go. His hand was cold and sweaty, unusual in the 102-degree heat. "Corporate, huh?"

"Yes, I'm here to visit the plant. I'm fairly new, I just started mid-June. This place is amazing!"

"Yeah? Well, try working here for a while, then we'll talk amazing," he said grumpily.

"Why? What's wrong? Like I said, I am new, so I don't know much about anything."

"What's wrong? I'll tell you what's wrong. We, the workers, mean absolutely nothing to you corporate brass. Every time our boss goes to corporate, he comes back with more cuts, more changes, more cost reductions, or whatever the hell they want to call it when they suck the life out of us and this plant and put people in the street for no reason. That's what's wrong."

"I see. Well, has anyone tried to do anything about it?"

"Do you think I want to see a pink slip with my name on it? Do you think any of us wants that? We tried, and that's exactly what happened . . . Firing people, that's what corporate knows how to do. And it happens a lot. Since you're new and all, I hope you won't get me fired over our little chat, here—"

"Oh, no, don't worry about it," Alex said, reassuringly.

"Not this week, anyway," he said bitterly, throwing away his cigarette butt, and walking away without saying good-bye. Just before entering the building, he spat on the grass with a gesture that expressed the deepest contempt, rather than the need to get rid of a foreign particle in his mouth.

The other smoker had been watching silently, from a close-enough distance to be aware of what was discussed. Alex turned to him and smiled. The man started walking away, taking one more drag off his cigarette.

"Oh, no," he said, making rejection gestures with his hand, "I have nothing to talk to you about. How do I know you're not some fancy-dressed corporate rat sent here to spy on us? Hank's got three kids; I have two. Leave me alone, I have nothing to say to you," he said firmly, and went inside, slamming the door behind him.

OK, that was interesting, Alex thought. She looked at her watch and decided to head toward Dunwood's office. The thirty minutes he had requested were almost gone.

Dunwood was wrapping up his conference call. He waved her to come in and sit.

"Now, for the fun part," he said, after hanging up the phone, "we're going to take an electric cart and head out to the testing field. Let's see what we have going today," he said, flipping through his calendar. "In about twenty minutes, we have a couple of Hellfire missile launches scheduled, an air-to-ground attack on fixed and mobile targets. This will be fun to watch, but we'll need protective gear for our eyes and ears." He opened a cabinet and took out two hardhats, two sets of noise protection earmuffs, and two pairs of clear, protective plastic eye shields. "We're going to circle by the cafeteria on our way, to pick up a couple of sandwiches."

They headed out deep into the fields, behind the plant. Adjacent to the plant's main building, a few storage hangars housed the finished drones. A strip of asphalt road led from the plant to the field, running by each hangar. This was the taxiway for the UAVs, allowing them to commute between their allotted storage space, to the landing strip, and to the testing field. Dunwood maneuvered the cart with speed and precision, and as soon as they passed a small ridge, the landing strip became visible. It was fully equipped with complete landing lights and a windsock. The landing strip was long and wide, much longer than needed for UAV use.

"Does anyone else use this strip?" Alex asked.

"Yes, visiting military often land here, rather than go to John Wayne Airport and drive back here. It depends on the aircraft size—if we can accommodate, we will. It saves everyone a lot of time. ATC is there," he said, pointing at a small tower overseeing the strip.

"What's ATC?" Alex asked.

"Air Traffic Control. The control tower," Dunwood clarified. "We only staff it when we expect visitors. Drones don't need ATC, because they have the ground operators to supervise everything during testing. Here we are."

He stopped the cart next to a row of picnic tables, set in line along a fence. There were posted warnings every thirty feet or so, advising potential passersby that they are trespassing if they enter this testing area and testing takes place using live ammunition. Unlike other No Trespassing signs, which might indicate the legal consequences of trespassing, this one didn't mention any negative outcome of committing the trespassing crime. Just mentioning the live ammo was enough to scare anyone away.

They unwrapped their lunches, carefully prepared by the cafeteria. Double-sized sandwiches, cookies, and soft drinks. Before they were finished, the hum of a UAV engine drew their attention.

"This one is preparing for takeoff. It came out of the hangar there," he said, pointing at the only hangar that had a door open, "and it's moving toward the runway. It will take off momentarily. Time to put on the gear," he said, handing her the hardhat, glasses, and earmuffs. "According to the testing schedule," Dunwood added, consulting briefly a printed schedule, "the drone will self-guide today, acquire the fixed land target represented by that concrete bunker there," he said, pointing at a distant structure, barely visible, "and blow it up. We are outside the drone's perimeter, but we're close enough to see all the action."

With all that gear on, her head seemed twice as big. The hard hat came all the way down to her eyebrows; it must have been a couple of sizes too large. The protective glasses were also too large, covering half her face. She squinted, trying to distinguish the target, holding her hand up to shade her eyes.

Dunwood went to the cart and came back with binoculars. "Here, this will help."

Through binoculars, the bunker was visible in detail. Nothing more than a prefab concrete cube, set on the ground, marked with lettering in white paint.

"What's the lettering for? What does it mean?" Alex asked.

"It doesn't mean anything, per se; it's an identifier," Dunwood said. "Drones acquire targets in multiple ways. One way is to preload images of the target object or site into the self-guiding software, and then send the drone searching for targets. In this case, the target image has to be distinctive enough to allow the drone to differentiate clearly between the intended target and other buildings that are not to be harmed, such as those." Dunwood pointed toward a set of bunkers, to the left of the target bunker. These bunkers had different lettering on them, but it was a similar font, color, and letter size.

"Why are there doors to these bunkers?"

"They are reinforced doors, able to withstand the blast just as well as the concrete walls do. We set measurement equipment in there, devices that capture and analyze the force of the impact when the missile strikes, so we can perfect our approach techniques. The same type of structure is being used to design anti-missile defense systems."

The drone was roaring above their heads. It was large, carrying multiple Hellfire missiles. It circled the area for a few seconds, identified the ground target with unbelievable precision and released the missile without any delay. The missile took out the bunker in a deafening explosion, throwing debris and dust high in the sky. By the time the dust cleared, the drone had already left the area, scouting farther away for new targets to hit.

"Wow," Alex said, numbed by the shock of the explosion. Even from this safe distance, she felt the shockwave in her chest and stomach. "It didn't take much, did it?"

"Nope, they are incredible weapons, taking significantly less time and hesitation than any human-operated aircraft."

"Well, weren't these human-operated from the ground?" Alex asked.

"Not this one. This drone is in testing for self-guidance and targeting. It's the software that's been causing us a bit of trouble lately, if you remember our last meeting."

"Yes, I do remember, and my team is also looking into the software on our end. I thought that regardless of human or self-guidance, no drone could possibly release a missile without human intervention. And this happened so fast, no human could have had the time to validate the target and approve the launch."

"Good observation," Dunwood said, "but this is a forward-thinking research-and-development environment, and we test and break boundaries every single day. No drone in service today can launch a missile without human intervention; that is correct. There are safeguards put in place to ensure exactly that. Maybe in the near future, we'll be able to achieve automatic, precise, yet safe missile launches. Today, we're not there yet, but we are developing technologies for that future. Who knows what tomorrow will bring?"

Still processing the vast amount of information she had gained while touring the NanoLance plant in Alpine, Alex was slowly going about her normal evening rituals. These rituals encompassed checking the cloned emails, her own work email, logging in remotely to check on her work systems and servers.

She took the clone laptop in the quiet, now almost dark, backyard and powered it up. It took a few minutes to download from the network the numerous emails she needed to check, but among the first one that caught her eye was yet another intriguing email from Walker to Prescott.

From: Benjamin Walker (COO)
To: Angela Prescott (VP HR)
Subject: Request
Sent: Tuesday, July 13, 3:17PM

Angela,
I would love to watch the news, or read something or other in a newspaper, but there's nothing out there of any interest for me to watch or read, now, is there?
I wonder why that is . . .
Thanks,
Ben

The weirdest thing about Walker, she thought. He was obviously involved with Angela. Alex had almost believed they had a romantic involvement, but what she had witnessed in that conference room was anything but romance. Nevertheless, they were involved somehow outside work. Still, he sent her such emails on the work email account. Was that a proof that nothing was wrong about that email? Or that Walker was just becoming careless? Was that email a solicitation of media pressure of sorts? Or quite the opposite? Asking Angela to work her magic and get favorable media coverage for them? *They definitely need it*, she thought, remembering how low the stock was trading these days. However, if this was a positive call for action, why be so cryptic about it? Something was definitely off about that email.

She took her private cell phone out of her pocket. Before calling anyone, she looked at the time and grunted. 10:12PM. Too late to make calls, but Steve would understand. She found herself cheering up at the thought of hearing his voice.

Two short rings, then voicemail. *Damn it!* She still wanted to get someone's opinion about this, and fast. In seconds, she printed a copy of the email, grabbed her wallet, and left.

She quietly approached the house, engine idling, and low beams off. She didn't even pull into the driveway, afraid she'd wake them up. She took the printed email, scribbled on the back "What do you think?" and walked toward the front door. She was crouching to slide the paper under the door, when nearby she heard a cat purr. She turned left and looked for the source of the sound.

"Good evening," Tom said.

She gasped. "You scared me to death," she said, standing.

"I scared you? I was sitting here, on my lawn, drinking my tea, petting my cat, when you came around behaving like a burglar. You scared *me*!"

Alex laughed. "OK, I guess we're even, then."

"What brings you here in the dead of the night?"

"This," Alex said, handing him the paper.

"It's too dark to read, what's in it?"

"Hold on, I've got a flashlight." Alex went to the car and returned with a small light. "I need your first impression of the message, not through my conveyed version of it. Here you go."

Tom read the email message in the flashlight's dim beam.

"I see," he said, "interesting."

"What do you think?" Alex asked. "Is this foul play? It reeks of foul play to me, but why would he take this risk and send this by email, rather than tell her?"

"He is getting high on the fumes of power," Tom said. "People like him cannot conceive that they could be less than perfect, or that someone could not be awed by their power and charisma. They are the sociopathic narcissists, those who combine the total absence of conscience with absolute conviction they are God's greatest gift to humankind. It's an intoxicating combination, likely to lead him to make mistakes."

"So, do you think my gut was right to make me drive all the way here?"

"Definitely. This is not a benign email message. This email demands action and is riddled with poisonous sarcasm, the type of sarcasm someone like that would reserve for those who have deeply disappointed him. This email is manipulative and punitive, and at the same time, demands immediate action."

"What should we expect?"

"I would expect a seriously negative media exposure incident. Whether a TV newscast, a press article, or who knows what other media vehicle they might choose, this exposure will probably take place within two days," Tom said, hitting the page with a finger. The noise made Little Tom open his eyes for a minute or so, while silence fell in the dark garden.

"What should I do?" Alex asked, in a whisper.

"I think the time has come to cut Dr. Barnaby's losses. We need to move in for the kill. We need to close this case in the next forty-eight hours." Tom's hand was stroking Little Tom's back, causing his legs to stretch with every motion. His purrs were louder than their voices.

"Are we ready? Do we have enough?"

"Well, get what more you can in the next couple of days, then that's it. Be more visible in your inquiries, start making some noise. Ask uncomfortable questions, scare them a bit."

"Won't that get me in trouble?" Alex asked.

"Not if you're careful. Plus, we'll have your back."

She looked in his eyes, with a flicker of doubt.

"This time I really mean it," Tom said. "You know, I'm also smart enough to be able to learn from my own mistakes." He smiled sadly. He had beaten himself up numerous times about the error in judgment that caused him to abandon Alex in jail. He was determined to never let it happen again. Not ever. Alex read that determination in his eyes, although he didn't speak a word.

"But what's the benefit of making noise and raising potential questions?" Alex asked. She was missing Tom's strategy, could not grasp his thinking.

"Well, for some of these executives, we have enough incriminating evidence to recommend termination of employment and maybe even involve the authorities. The final call belongs to the client, because such court cases can tarnish the company name and public image. That's an aspect we need to manage carefully. As we move on to address the ones we can, those who know they did something wrong will start fearing exposure and will disappear on their own. Or they will make an incredibly stupid mistake."

"We're betting on scaring them off?" Alex asked. "It doesn't seem like a foolproof method to pull all the bad ones out of this mix."

"You're thinking like an honest person again," Tom smiled. "What if you were one of these crooks? What if you saw all, or most of, your partners in crime eliminated from the company, and you'd never be able to hear from them again? Wouldn't that scare you just a little bit?"

"More than just a little bit, I get it. You're right, this might work out just fine," Alex said. "Then we should be done and wrapped up in two days. I'll need your help figuring out my exit strategy, so we don't raise suspicions and cause the client any issues. I only wish I could find out which one of these bastards set me up."

Louie liked testing software—testing the limits of software, understanding how a particular piece of software can interact with other pieces of software—leading to new results for him to discover.

He had started playing with the self-guidance software a while ago, forgetting about time, dinner, and his favorite TV show. He had validated several modules of the software, exploring the configuration settings, and the simulated functioning. So far, there was nothing out of the ordinary. He took another sip of cold coffee from his giant travel mug, and then moved on to the next module—target acquisition.

Based on image recognition, target acquisition was a simple module. If the drone captured an image that matched a preexisting, preloaded image from its library of targets, the drone would acquire the target and ask ground control for permission to fire. Curious to see who had most recently made Homeland Security's shit list, he started browsing through the images. A number of well-known terrorist figures paraded in sequence, some he recognized, some he didn't, but they all looked equally dangerous.

As he was quickly browsing through a relatively vast collection of images, comprising residences, hiding places, vehicles, helicopters, and wives of wanted terrorists and enemy leaders, his eye caught an image of the front view of a Toyota 4Runner with California plates.

"What the hell?" All his weariness disappeared in a second. He clicked the mouse again, and the next image displayed. It was a close-up head shot of Alex Hoffmann, his boss.

He froze for a minute, thinking. No other target images involved any targets on American soil. Foreign soil only, in countries unfriendly to the United States, faces of known terrorists. He paced the room for a few times, nervously examining options. Who would want Hoffmann killed?

He tried to access the image upload details. The images of Alex and her car had been uploaded on July 8, at 6:57AM, by Dustin Sheppard.

"Uh-oh . . . That's strange, he's never here that early," he muttered. "Well, maybe he would be, if he was planning to do this . . ."

He felt a chill down his spine. The self-guiding software's library of images and general settings were common to all drones in operation. He suddenly realized that this image was on every drone, distributed by the central system. He tried to remove Alex's image. The screen prompted him to enter a username and password. Hesitating a split second, as he knew he was about to leave a trail of his actions, he entered his credentials, but the system rejected them. *Insufficient authority level. Authority level needed: L1.*

He started thinking who could help with this. There were only a few L1s in the company. Only Barnaby was above them, as L0, but grapevine had it that Barnaby was semi-retired already, not caring about much of the business anymore. HR? Definitely not. Cops? He thought of what his top secret clearance level meant, and how unlikely would it be to find a cop with a high enough security clearance to be allowed to see the software and its imagery. The Feds? Too slow to get them to listen.

A split second of hesitation, then he cracked his fingers and started his attempt to break the security codes of the self-guidance system.

Her throbbing headache wasn't going anywhere.

Alex had struggled with the insufferable pain almost all day long, despite the need to be extra alert and perceptive in her activities. She had one day left before closing this case, and she still had a lot more questions than answers. Wednesday had yielded little gain from that perspective, bringing zero new data. Maybe that had triggered her headache, the frustration of not being able to nail all the sons of bitches involved in this mess. But the thought of leaving this assignment with a half-done job caused her stomach to churn. *Not acceptable*, she thought.

She grabbed a jacket and her wallet and stormed through the front door. She needed a fistful of painkillers to do away with the obnoxious migraine and restore her critical judgment.

She opened the rear door of her car to throw the jacket on the back seat and saw the bomb-dismantling robot sitting there, forgotten on the rubber mat between the seats.

"Oh, crap," she muttered. "Forgot all about you," she said, slamming the door. Now she had to drive by the plant again and drop off the robot—probably tomorrow.

The drugstore was just a mile away.

She came out of the drugstore within minutes, grasping a bottle of Double Strength Motrin. Walking toward her car, she became aware of another set of footstep noises behind her. As she turned to see whom it was, a stranger grabbed her arm in a painful grip.

"Hey, there, pretty face, what are you doing out so late? Looking for me?"

She tried to free her arm, but the man's grip just grew tighter and more painful. She whimpered, trying to set herself free. The man was leading her away from her car, toward the back of the building, where a residential construction site was deserted at that late hour and almost completely dark. With half-built houses cloaked in darkness, it resembled a ghost town.

She turned to look at his face. Eyes of steel on a bony face, partly covered by long hair, huge Adam's apple, pulsating with his heartbeat. Somehow this face seemed familiar, but Alex couldn't place him at all.

"I can give you what you need," she started negotiating, hoping he would settle for some cash and let her be.

"Oh, I know you can, and you will," he said, continuing to drag her toward the unfinished houses. "I'm not going anywhere until I get everything I want." He tightened his grip even more, and shoved her over a small ditch at the edge of the construction site.

She gasped. "I can scream, you know." She could try, but chances were no one would hear her in this deserted construction site. She remembered clearly how the night pharmacist had a TV on, watching the game reruns at high volume.

"Go right ahead, scream, knock yourself out." The man was unperturbed.

"What do you want from me? I have money, lots of money," she said, thinking hard.

"I don't need your money, although I might clean out your cash after we're done. We're just going to have some serious fun together," he said, in a coarse voice filled with lust," before I finish you off."

Finish me off? Alex thought desperately. *Oh, God . . .* She kicked her shoes off and lunged in a desperate attempt to make a run for it. He didn't loosen the grip on her arm, and grasped her hair with his other hand, bringing her down to her knees.

"Nowhere to go, bitch."

Alex started whimpering and sobbing, unable to control herself. *I need to think*, she kept repeating to herself, but she was unable to stop crying. *Oh, God, please don't let this happen!*

The man dragged her into one of the houses, shoving her on the floor.

"Have you ever been fucked by a real man? Real hard? You'll die screaming tonight, I promise you that." He unzipped his pants and undid his belt, removing it completely. He used it to tie her hands above her head and secured them against a two-by-four structure that was going to become someone's kitchen wall.

She whimpered, feeling the cold belt cut into her flesh.

"I have lots of money, more than you'd think. You can get plenty of women, and better looking than me, for the kind of money I could give you," she pleaded, trying to get him interested in anything else.

"You think you're so smart, trying to talk your way out of everything, huh? This should be a lesson for not minding your own business. Too bad you won't live long enough to apply what you learn here tonight."

He ripped off her blouse and bra, with little effort. She gasped.

He grabbed her throat and started suffocating her. "Why aren't you crying anymore, huh? That turned me on," he said, gripping her throat and squeezing tighter.

She choked, started coughing and blacking out.

"Oh, no, not yet," the man said, releasing his grip. "I told you it's gonna be fun. We got all night. And we haven't even started yet." He started pulling at her pants. She desperately kicked and screamed, hoping someone would hear her and come to rescue her.

"'S'cuse me," a slurred, coarse voice came from the dark.

The man turned to face the intruder. Alex breathed with more ease, as hope filled her heart.

"D'ya need help with that broad?"

What? Oh, no . . .

"Get lost before I knock your lights out," her attacker said, visibly annoyed.

The man approached them, and as the dim light shone on his body, Alex's heart sunk even further. He was one of those street bums, covered in layers of shredded clothing and stinking of crud and booze. His hair was a tangled mess of filth—yellowed gray hairs and street debris.

"Don't ya' kick *me* out, this where I live. Y'all are in my house." He slurred something incredible, and he could barely stand up. "Here's wha' I'm thinkin'. I'll help you fuck her, and then you help me fuck her, so we both have a piece of that fine ass. What'd ya' say, huh? Got ourselves a little deal, huh?"

Oh God . . . No! Alex thought desperately. There was no way out.

"Don't need your help, you stupid moron. Fuck off!" Her attacker was standing now, ready to punch the bum in the face.

The bum grabbed the man by his shirt, in a pleading gesture. "D'ya know how many years since I've seen me a fine piece of ass like that? D'ya know? Huh? 'Cause *I* don't even know it, eh?" His stench was unbearable, turning Alex's stomach. She wriggled some more, trying to set herself free.

"Please, man," the bum continued, "You'll have at her first, how many times you like, I can wait . . . and watch," he said, with an aroused chuckle that made Alex whimper again.

The attacker grabbed the bum and slammed him against a partial wall. "You shit for brains moron, you got two seconds to disappear, or I *will* kill you. You can count on that."

"Ah, ah, you see, that's rude," the bum said, in a disapproving, yet unperturbed tone, fueled by alcohol-induced courage. "You come into my house, and you wanna throw *me* out? I take offense at that, man . . . There's more of us here, ya' know, all I gotta do is whistle. You just a mean, selfish mothe'fucker, who won't share the goodies with his host."

The bum approached again, grabbed the man once more and continued his plea. "C'mon, how hard can it be to let me have a piece? I can go first if you don't mind waitin', then give y'all the privacy you need. I'm thinking, maybe you wanna do stuff to this fine lookin' broad ya' don't wanna let me watch . . . still rude, but . . ."

The bum stopped his begging, as he tried to control his gagging, leaning his dirty forehead on the other's shoulder. He was about to throw up on the other man's chest. The man stepped back, made a disgusted gesture with his hand, zipped up his pants and abruptly walked away with a brisk pace.

"The hell with it," Alex heard him muttering as he departed, "some other time."

"I have money," she started pleading with the bum, hoping it would go better this time. "I have lots of cash with me; you can buy yourself plenty of booze."

"Where's the green stuff you're so kindly offering?"

Think, think!

"At my car, right there," she pointed with her head, although her wallet was in her back pocket. "You can come with me, and I'll give you all I've got."

"I guess that'll work . . . let's go." The bum freed her. She covered herself up as best as she could with her torn blouse and headed for the car in a hurry, not caring about the construction site debris hurting her bare feet.

Seconds later, they were at her car. She opened the door and sat behind the wheel. From here, she knew she could easily push that lowlife away and make a run for it. He was barely standing, too drunk to pose a real challenge. She put her key in the ignition, as discreetly as she could. The man didn't react. She slammed the door shut and reversed as fast as she could, leaving the man in a cloud of dust. He stood there, immobile, just watching her leave.

She sped home running every stoplight, barely able to see the road through the blur of her tears. Once in the safety of her home the adrenaline vanished and shock took over. She headed straight to the shower, her shaking hands struggling to turn on the faucet. The warm jets of water helped her somewhat, but the shock lingered on.

Minutes later, curled up on her sofa, clasping an ice-cold glass of Martini Vermouth, she struggled to slow her heart rate and stop her tears. Flickering memories started to play with her weary brain.

"I don't need your money."

"Before I finish you off."

"A lesson for not minding your own business."

Her tears stopped falling. This had not been a random attack. "You bastards," she said out loud, breaking the midnight silence of her quiet home. "I don't know when and how, but I will get you for this!"

"Recent developments have placed NanoLance, the San Diego-based corporation and well-known defense contractor, into the media spotlight. A series of incidents, resulting in significant loss of lives here and abroad in combat zones, incidents involving NanoLance manufactured drones, have led the markets to shy away from the company's stock and the public to ask some pointed questions regarding the operational safety of these drones.

"Until recently, the quality of NanoLance's products, for military use and for the consumer market, was enjoying an undisputed reputation for best in class, endless reliability, and unparalleled operational safety. Well, not anymore. Through the voices of a heartbroken public, still mourning the twenty lives lost in Florida last month, concern is being expressed toward the company's ability to regain control over the safety of its products.

"Some voices say that Dr. Barnaby, founder and majority shareholder of NanoLance, is now too old to be able to exercise the needed control over his company. NanoLance needs to take immediate and decisive action to prevent further losses of lives at the mercy of dangerous products.

"Unspecified sources have leaked news of a potential transfer of control, scheduled to take place at the end of this year, when, sources say, Dr. Barnaby will sell the majority of his shares and retire. The same unidentified sources are talking about a potential congressional hearing, scheduled to investigate the defense contractor status of NanoLance and any wrongdoing related to the Florida drone incident.

"However, the US Air Force has not yet released its full report about the Kandahar incident in April, and the Florida incident in June. While a spokesperson with the military was quick to confirm the fact that NanoLance had manufactured both drones, no other findings were released to the public in these two cases. In a third case, the Afghanistan incident last week, no confirmation has been issued about the allegation that a UAV was behind the thirty-six dead and six injured. Therefore, we have no confirmation of a link to NanoLance in this case. Yet.

"NanoLance stock, traded on NASDAQ since 1998 under the symbol NNLC, closed yesterday at $73.28 per share, a 50 percent drop since it started its decline in April of this year.

"Here, from our news studio, we are monitoring the situation and will come back with details as they unfold. You are watching *News of the Hour* with Stephanie Wainwright."

Tom's hand was squeezing the TV remote, holding his breath, waiting for the massacre to be over.

"You are watching *News of the Hour* with Stephanie Wainwright."

Finally, her irritating face disappeared from the TV screen. Nothing else was left to say to further harm NanoLance. For the first time since he had taken this case, Tom was having doubts that he and his team were going to be able to bring the case to a successful conclusion and restore this company's reputation.

The phone's loud ringing brought him back to reality. The LCD display read "Barnaby cell." He picked it up without delay.

"Dr. Barnaby," he said, sounding surer of himself than he felt.

"Have you seen it?" Dr. Barnaby's voice was trembling, breaking up.

"Yes, I have. It is a worrisome—"

"Isn't it enough? How much more time do you need to find out who's doing this to me?"

"We have some information, but not all we need. We're only asking for twenty-four hours more, that's it," Tom pleaded, holding his head down. He wished he could have something more encouraging to say to his client, something to help him regain the confidence he had lost. There was nothing more to say. Results were needed badly, plus a miracle.

"Twenty-four hours could be all that this company has left. What do you think the markets are going to do today? We need to issue a statement today, not tomorrow. A statement naming names, not just dancing around the facts, like we have done lately."

"Dr. Barnaby, I promise you'll have significant findings by this time tomorrow. Please come by my office in the morning, so we can discuss the next steps and containment actions."

"You are my last hope on this Earth; you know that, don't you?" Barnaby said, in a quiet, defeated voice. "Please don't let me down."

"I won't. We won't, I promise," Tom said, grasping at straws of hope that he would be able to keep his word.

The first email Alex saw when she opened her work laptop was from Angela Prescott, addressing the entire staff. She had to read it twice.

From: Angela Prescott (VP HR)
To: All Staff (HQ, MFG)
Subject: Announcement
Sent: Thursday, July 15, 7:42AM

We are deeply saddened to announce the untimely death of Janet Templeton, director of manufacturing quality at our Alpine plant. As she was driving home late last night, Janet was killed instantly when her car smashed into a guardrail. Early findings indicate that she might have been intoxicated, contributing to her inability to steer and maintain the car on the road while approaching a tight curve.

Janet leaves behind an aging, ill mother. We will deeply miss Janet, who was a valued contributor to the organization, and a good friend to many of us. Please keep Janet's family in your thoughts.

Visitation and funeral details will follow.

The leadership team has opened an account to help raise funds, to assist her family deal with this tragedy. Please contact HR for details about making a donation.

Thank you
Angela Prescott,
Vice President, Human Resources
NanoLance Inc.

At first, Alex could not comprehend the fact that Janet was gone. Then, she struggled processing the poor taste of a companywide death announcement naming the victim a drunk driver. Afterward, she felt a wave of sadness come over her. Janet was young and full of life—wanted a beautiful Rottweiler puppy—was afraid—was afraid to be seen talking with Alex. Why?

Alex tried focusing on other emails, but a rebel thought, a faint memory, stuck somewhere at the edge of her brain, kept bugging her. After a while, the fog lifted and she remembered.

"Oh, no, unfortunately I can't touch any alcohol for another twenty days; I'm on an antibiotic regimen after gum surgery."

Janet had told her she couldn't drink! When was that? More than a week ago? She struggled to remember, and then realized she had received a text message on her private phone that day, advising her that Janet was approaching the breeder's home. She pulled the message and looked at the date: July 7. No way she could have been a drunk driver last night. *I gotta go back to the plant*, she decided, grabbing her stuff.

On her way out of the building, she ran into Bob Foster, the infrastructure manager who had trusted her to deliver his precious bomb-dismantling robot to the plant.

"Hey, boss, in a hurry?"

"Yeah, and I'll take your robot to the plant today, right now, I won't forget this time," she said, heading for the elevator.

Bob took out his cell phone and speed-dialed a number.

"She's going in," he said, then flipped the phone shut.

In the downstairs lobby, she ran into Sheppard.

"Leaving us so soon?" he hissed.

"Personal emergency, but I'll be back before lunch, I hope," she said and stormed out the main door, against the solid inflow of employees coming to work.

Sheppard took out his cell and dialed a number.

"She's on her way," he said, and put the cell in his pocket.

On her way to the plant, she remembered to stop by her house and grab the robot's remote from her other jacket. She had no idea why she wanted to go to the plant. It was just a hunch. Her gut was telling her that the plant held the answer to Janet's death and hopefully to a lot more.

Alex approached the plant on foot, after parking her car in the middle of the crowded lot, avoiding the first row of visitor spots. She had decided to enter the facility by the side door, reserved for the smokers going in and out for their breaks. Dunwood had mentioned that her card would open almost all doors in the facility, with the exception of the static-free lab. It did.

She didn't have a specific plan in mind; she hoped she could find a lead in the areas touched by Janet, some clue about what caused her death, an idea of who might have killed her. Alex was 100 percent positive that Janet's death had been no accident, although she couldn't think how something like that could have been pulled off. Tampering with her car? That would have worked, for sure. No doubt, her killer had access to technology of all kinds, which could easily be rigged to cause a car to become unresponsive after, for instance, reaching the speed of 60 miles per hour.

She spent a few minutes puffing at her e-cig, next to the few smokers scattered on the lawn, mostly plant workers. No one acknowledged her, or responded to her tentative greetings and smiles. No one was going to talk to her; that was clear. She put her e-cig in her pocket and went inside.

Her first stop was Janet's office. There was a framed picture of an older Rottweiler on her desk. She took the picture in her hand. Alma had been a beautiful dog. The office seemed quiet enough, no one passing through the hallway for several minutes in a row. Encouraged by the silence around her, Alex started going through Janet's files. The unlocked filing cabinet was packed with suspended folders, neatly arranged by category, with separating tabs. The majority of the folders held results of quality testing, by date, by product, by types of failure, and if specific testing had been done for particular failure modes.

One label caught her eye. *Ad Hoc Self-Guidance.* This folder contained the results of a series of on-demand tests completed for the self-guidance software, assessing drones on the testing field. The folder had a cover page, neatly summarizing the less-than-stellar results. The software had failed in more than 23 percent of test cases, that percentage breaking down somewhat evenly between target identification accuracy and navigational issues. Nothing new, just confirmation of what Alex had already heard in meetings.

Alex flipped through more folders; none of them held any significant information, just confirmed the facts she already had. The self-guidance software was unreliable for many reasons. The newly designed drones were failing at a much higher rate than older models. The quality standards suffered due to numerous cost-cutting programs. Alex found a chart mapping the quality rate over time, spanning a period of two years. It was declining, but not on a linear path. It came down in steps, and Janet had correlated those steps with significant events in the history of the plant.

The budget cuts at the beginning of the previous year had caused the quality to drop 2.3 percent within 60 days. A reduction in workforce that had taken place more than a year earlier was correlated with another 3.5 percent loss in quality score. Obviously, Janet was documenting her point of view, which would have been expected, considering she was being held accountable for the overall quality of the product. Alex was convinced that Janet had been vocal about these findings, not willing to be blamed for declining quality rates she didn't ultimately control. Being vocal hadn't helped her much. Alex folded the chart and put it in her pocket.

There was nothing else left to do in Janet's office. Alex sneaked out, unseen, and proceeded to the testing end of the CX series assembly line. Janet touched that area on a daily basis. The long assembly line passed through two different quality-testing points. One was the final inspection point, at the end of the assembly line, where a quality technician carefully inspected each drone. He then proceeded to escort the drone, on its own wheels, to a small taxiway that connected to the storage hangars. Once on that taxiway, the technician would then fire up the drone and test the engine on a test bank. If everything scored in the green, the quality technician would proceed to do a short test flight, having the UAV take off, zigzag above the testing field, acquire a target, simulate a missile launch, then return for landing, and move into the finished product storage hangar. At this stage, the quality technician tested the drone's functionality, as per set parameters, and the comlink with ground control.

The other testing point on the assembly line took place a little earlier in the process, while the drone's housing wasn't fully assembled. As soon as the drones had all their components installed, before attaching the upper half of the body, they were connected to an electronic test bank, which would power up all components inside the UAV. This allowed active testing of all the installed parts, with the drone safely on the ground. From Janet's notes, this particular testing point had caused repeated concerns, revealing high failure rates for a variety of modules and circuit boards. This is where Alex wanted to look around, challenged by the fact that these modules failed the tests after being installed although they had passed the pre-installation test. Faulty installation? For sure, Janet would have thought of that, so it must have been something else.

Parked on the low, rubber, conveyor belt, some twenty feet apart from one another, four drones were standing on their landing gears, missing their upper body covers. They were connected to the testing station by colored wires with labels and connectors at the ends. The conveyor belt wasn't moving, allowing the connected drones to finish the automated testing phase on a simulated operational status. The drones were fully powered, their sensor array cameras moving in search of landmarks and targets. Everything was functional for these drones while being tested, except for the engine.

There wasn't any technician in sight. No wonder, after all the staff cuts. Alex walked along the testing belt, looking at the multicolored LED panes reflecting the various states of tests being run: blinking yellow for test in progress, solid green for test completed and passed, solid red for test completed and failed. She came closer to one of the drones, curious to see how the test wires were connected to the modules. There were connectors on each module, so it was easy to connect or disconnect a module from the test bank.

She suddenly became aware that the drone next to her had its cameras trained on her, moving with her as she moved along the conveyor belt. Intrigued, she took a few steps forward, sideways, and back, to see if the cameras stayed on her. They did. Since she was the only moving object in the drone's visual range, she didn't think much about it. Not until the targeting module gave a faint beep and turned its status LED green. She recalled the information she received while visiting the plant with Dunwood.

"And when a drone locks on a target, this module lights green."

This drone had locked on her? She felt a chill down her spine, but tried to calm herself down. This must be a clear example of poor quality target acquisition performance. She approached the drone, looking around to see if anyone was approaching. She reached inside it and tried to remove its targeting module. She released the module brackets and gently pulled the module. It wouldn't budge. She pulled just a little bit harder and the module broke in little pieces, crumbling like a piece of cheese. The testing bank next to her turned a few LEDs solid red and beeped. She grabbed a fistful of module fragments and stuck them in her pocket. Then she moved away from there, hoping no one had seen her.

Outside in the parking lot, she took out her cell phone and called Tom.

"It's me. I need a technician, someone who can assess circuit boards and electronic modules in the field, and do it fast. I need him to look at a module as soon as possible. Uh-huh . . . OK, then, please let me know where he's coming from, and I'll meet him halfway. Great, I'll wait."

Although checking the time every minute didn't help the technician get there any faster, Alex still couldn't help it. On her last day on this job, she was wasting a whole lot of time on a hunch, waiting for the tech to show up.

Preoccupied with her worries, she resumed her work, checking emails on the cloned laptop. Nothing much was happening, not by email, anyway.

"Excuse me?" The man seemed to have appeared from nowhere. "I am Josh Barnes from the lab. Mr. Isaac sent me; he said you needed my help?"

"Oh, yes, please sit down," Alex offered. "I need your help with this," she said, unfolding a napkin on the table and setting the pieces of broken circuit board on it. "I need any information you can give me, anything at all."

"How did it break?" Josh picked up a piece and studied it up close.

"I tried to pull it out of its mount. I released the brackets on both sides, and pulled gently. Not hard. I work in IT, so I know how to manipulate circuit boards."

"Show me how hard you pulled," Josh said, holding one of the bigger fragments with two fingers. "Pull at this piece, just like you pulled at the entire thing when you tried to remove it."

Alex grabbed the other end of the fragment and pulled. The fragment gave again, breaking into smaller pieces.

"Oh," Josh said, examining a fragment with a magnifying glass he took out of his toolkit. "That's interesting . . ."

"What?" Alex asked, feeling anxious.

"Well, from what I can tell, the entire circuit board is substandard. The thickness of the board itself should be significantly higher. For these complex modules, the manufacturer usually uses a reinforced board, so it can't become so brittle. This one almost crumbles in your hand. What's this supposed to do?"

"Did Tom have you sign an NDA? A nondisclosure agreement?"

"Yes, and he mentioned that you'd ask," he said.

"OK, then, these are circuit boards installed on UAVs."

"On drones? No way!"

"Yes, I'm afraid so."

"Something must be wrong with them," he said, scratching his head. "Electronic modules installed on equipment in motion is subjected to vibrations of all kinds. Therefore, they have exact standards of execution that are in place specifically to ensure that these boards don't crack, due to the shocks and vibrations they absorb."

"I think I follow," she said hesitantly.

"You see? Here," he said, pointing at the edge of the broken board fragment, "on the crack line, you can see there's not much coating applied. When a board is designed to work in a vibrating environment, it has to be coated with a special film, designed to increase elasticity of the board itself and to reduce the risk of coming apart or becoming loose from the original soldering. No such coating has been applied in this case. For the larger installed components on the boards, I was expecting to see vibration mounts, tiny little silicon or gel pads, to ensure that vibration doesn't harm the sensitive components. Takeoffs and landings pose a lot of mechanical stress on components, that's why circuit boards for aviation have special standards, designed to address this level of mechanical stress."

"I see," Alex said.

"You said you worked in IT? Well, I'm sure you can relate, then, if I can trigger your memory with this example. How are laptop components different from desktop components?"

"Ah, yes," Alex said, following his point.

"The laptop components are designed to work during motion, vibration, or even shock, as in dropping your laptop," he continued. "They have vibration mounts; the boards are coated to ensure they won't crack and parts become loose. Some components or subassemblies are even encased completely in gels or resins, to confer them the durability needed to withstand repeated shocks. This, however," he said, picking another fragment and studying it up close, "has none of that, or almost none. There are traces of anti-shock gel around this processor, right here, but nowhere else. This circuit board didn't spend enough time in the coating chamber. Are these boards even working properly?"

"Well, I'm not sure. Outside of breaking when trying to remove it, how else would this defect manifest itself?"

"Intermittent defects, that's what comes to mind. Before it breaks, it cracks. Let's say this board has a crack in it, from vibrations, a tiny little crack, barely visible, what we would call a hairline crack. When the cracked board is under stress, some of the circuit lines drawn on it would be interrupted, and the current would stop flowing through them. That would cause the board to malfunction, or completely shut down the system. After a while, when the board wasn't under stress anymore, these circuit lines would be restored, and the circuit board would resume proper operations."

"How would it malfunction?" Alex asked.

"It's impossible to predict. It varies from circuit board to circuit board and from crack to crack. It would also vary by the intensity of the stress applied and the duration of the disruption."

"So, for instance, could it cause a drone to be in and out of comlink with ground control, apparently with no reason?" Alex asked, thinking of the Florida incident. "Or, one minute it would obey ground control commands, then the next it would fly wherever?"

"Absolutely. It could have any type of intermittent defect you can think of. It could have entire modules shut down or function out of spec. The usual outcome for this type of defect is unpredictable, random, and on-and-off defects."

"Could it cause the drone to fire on targets on its own?" This time she was thinking of the Kandahar friendly fire incident.

"Absolutely not," Josh said. "Defects like these, driven by substandard components, can rarely cause a piece of equipment to start doing something it's not supposed to. Even if that happened, it would be minor, like turn on lights or something like that. Targeting vehicles or people and launching missiles on these targets, that's an entirely different story. It requires a complex set of instructions, which need to be driven by something or someone to make it happen." The tech obviously had put two and two together and was well aware of the Kandahar incident. Media coverage on the Kandahar friendly fire had been intensive; there was no surprise he was able to connect the dots on his own.

"What would then?" Alex asked. "What would cause a drone to suddenly decide to open fire on a number of allied targets?"

"Was it determined with precision that the drone acted independently?"

"Well, not sure yet, but if it was human error, that's on someone else's agenda to figure out. I am only interested in the case in which it was the drone to blame. What would make a drone go rogue?"

"Anomalous behavior like that has to be founded on technical abilities already built into the equipment. The drone had to have had the capabilities to fly itself independently, search for targets, lock on targets, and launch a missile. Then repeat all these steps, until all targets are wiped out. You can't expect this set of complex computations to occur, if the drone wasn't designed to do them in the first place."

"So you're inclined to think it was pilot error? The ground control crew somehow mistook the Canadian convoy for an enemy target?"

"I think that is the most likely explanation. Any other possible explanation would require a module, probably bigger than any other module installed on these drones, and a software component to teach the drone to do things on its own."

"The self-guidance module," Alex thought out loud.

"There is a self-guidance module?" Josh's interest was sparked again, and his eyes focused on Alex.

"Yes, there is. It's not fully functional yet. It's currently being tested, and I'm not even sure the Kandahar drone had it installed."

"That narrows it down. If the Kandahar drone had it installed, then I'd look into whether it was working or not. There should be system logs in the module's memory, and such software should also generate activity logs. If, on the other hand, this software and module were not installed on the drone, it only leaves the ground crew to be at fault for this."

Note to self, Alex thought, *we need to find out if the Kandahar drone had the self-guidance software active. We need to access the activity logs.*

"Josh, this was really helpful, and I appreciate it," Alex said, starting to collect the circuit-board pieces from the table. "There's one more thing I noticed when I was visiting the plant. One of the drones, ground powered for testing, scanned the area, and locked target on me. What type of malfunction could make that happen? Could the faulty boards be to blame for such an incident?"

"I seriously doubt it. I'm not familiar with the architecture of the target acquisition module, but thinking logically, the drone must see you as a target to be locking onto you. Either the drone is doing an incredibly poor job at recognizing targets to begin with, or there's some other error contributing to this, although I can't think of any other scenario. As an afterthought, if the drones do such a crappy job telling real targets from plant visitors, maybe that explains the Kandahar incident."

"Maybe. But what I'm hearing you say is that, either way, the drone had to have had the self-guidance module installed and operative to be able to do that, right? And no ground control authorizing the launches?"

"Absolutely. This drone, the one that locked on you, does it have the self-guidance module installed?"

"I'm not sure . . . How would I find out?"

"Huh?" The technician seemed confused by her question.

"That is, if I cannot really ask anyone," Alex clarified.

"Oh, I get it," Josh said, the new understanding of the situation making him frown. "Do you have access to the drone?"

"Yes, I think so."

"Well, I cannot be sure, because I haven't seen this particular drone and its insides, but you'd look for a larger module, I would think an encased one, with connectivity compatible with a computer—serial port, USB, Bluetooth. If you're lucky, the module is clearly labeled."

"I'd seriously doubt that."

"Yeah, me too. The module should have the answers you're looking for, both for the capabilities to generate the Kandahar incident on its own and for targeting you. If you find the module, see if you can access it. Sometimes, these modules come with an individual configuration screen and controls. How else would you be able to configure it, to tell it what to do?"

"Remotely, I would think, more than by doing it directly from under the hood. You should be able to change instructions and configuration while the drone is in flight, right?"

"Yeah, I guess that's right. But I still think it's worth looking for it, at least figure out if this is what's going on with that targeting system locking on you."

She sat up. "Thank you so much."

"You're welcome. And good luck with all this," Josh said, watching her leave.

Louie had been working steady for more than thirty hours, running on stale coffee, cafeteria donuts, and adrenaline. An entire night of efforts had finally made him successful in cracking the codes needed to delete the images of Alex and her car from the drone system library of images. He had to do this offline though, to prevent the appearance of what he humorously called *the black, unmarked cars arriving in the middle of the night.* Even if he was doing this from inside the NanoLance building, he had attempted, repeatedly, to break the codes of the drone control system. This type of attack triggered the hard-coded security systems that the company had in place, running on each computer. No doubt about that. As he had removed the network connectivity before he started his work, this computer was yet to communicate the attack to the network and trigger the widespread alarm.

Of course, there was little he could do without connecting it back to the network. So far, he was only able to achieve the deletion of Alex's images from the library. It had only taken him fifteen hours to crack that encryption. Unacceptable. Nevertheless, this wasn't over yet. He had to connect the computer to the network and save the changes to the mainframe. And that would trigger the security alarms ... He would have three, maybe four minutes until someone walked through the door to get him.

He took a sharp, deep breath, and inserted the network cable into its wall plug. The network was quickly acquired, and the computer displayed a connected status message. He clicked on the "save" button to make sure the deletion of images would be permanent and reflected on the main self-guidance server.

The screen returned an error message; not what Louie had hoped for.

Unknown Error: Code 054578. If this error persists, please contact your system administrator.

"Shit! Oh, no, no, no, no," Louie said, slamming a desperate fist against the desk. He re-entered the command to save and got the same error message. And again. Not many options were left. He pulled the computer's power cord out of the wall plug, grabbed his jacket and coffee mug, and stormed out the door. Maybe there was another way to fix this.

The drive back from Santa Ana put Alex at the plant right about the end of the shift. She walked in, unnoticed, while most employees were getting ready to wrap up their day. She waited until most of them were gone, at the 4:30PM end-of-day rush hour.

She approached the CX series assembly line, in the powered testing area, where four drones were connected to automated testing panels. She couldn't tell whether they were the same four as earlier or different ones. She was relieved to see that the drones were still powered up, testing panels flashing various colored LEDs. Their cameras were whirring and rotating while acquiring images of their surroundings.

She went to the first drone in the series of four, right about where she had stood earlier in the day, when the drone had locked its targeting system on her. This one's sensor array cameras whirred and buzzed for a few seconds. She moved around, and the main camera, trained on her, followed her every move. Then the targeting module, visible in the hoodless drone, locked on, beeped once, and a green LED lit up.

Alex was certain of one thing: this drone's targeting module recognized her as a target, and it locked on her immediately, preparing for an attack. If this would have happened anywhere else other than a testing environment, and the drone would have been flying above, carrying live ammo and not requiring human validation for each launch, she would have been dead.

"Hmm . . ." she muttered, considering the situations that would make this scenario even remotely plausible. She moved on to the next drone, down the conveyor belt, to see if this manifestation was an isolated occurrence, tied exclusively to a single particular drone. UAV number two trained its cameras on her, and within seconds, a beep and a green light confirmed this was not an isolated occurrence.

She repeated the almost dance-like approach to the third drone, which, without any delay, also locked on her. "Strange," she said to herself in a soft voice, "and creepy. Way creepy . . ." She approached, getting closer to the drone, and leaned over it to reach its modules, trying to see if any of the modules made a good candidate for a self-guidance module. There was a large, gray box installed amid the drone's modules, almost as large as the satellite dish installed next to it. She checked the gray box for connectivity, just as Josh had suggested, and found the self-guidance module. She leaned in a bit more, to figure out how she could remove the module without breaking it in the process.

"And what exactly are you doing here?" A woman's voice, coming from behind her, startled Alex. She jumped away from the drone, turning to see whom that voice belonged to. Recognizing the face, she couldn't contain her surprise. What the hell was Audrey Kramer doing there? Alex never thought she'd run into the CFO so far away from the traditional playing ground of all accounting and finance professionals—the corporate office.

"I am touring the plant," she said, innocently. "I was invited to visit, explore, and learn about the company's product."

"That was two days ago," Kramer said. "Try again." Her eyes were cold as ice.

Oh, shit, she's on to me, Alex thought. "I had no idea I was not allowed to come back. I was actually told that I am welcome here anytime. If I was wrong, please accept my apologies," Alex said in a heartbeat, hoping that would work.

"You're a piece of work, you know that, right? Always snooping around where you don't belong. Come on, you and I are going for a walk," Kramer said, in a voice that did not allow further debate.

"Um, actually, I have to run now," Alex said, "can we do this some other time, maybe tomorrow morning?"

Kramer pulled a gun from her pocket and removed its safety. She didn't speak one word.

"Guess not," Alex said, in a faint voice, turning pale. *I am so screwed,* she thought. *No way can I fight her, not while she's got a goddamn gun.* "OK, I'm coming, if you insist."

"Smart lady, you figured it out," Kramer snarled. "We'll take your car. Move it!"

Alex started walking toward the side exit, the nearest one to her car, painfully aware of the gun barrel pressed against her ribs. They didn't run into anyone on the way; probably most employees were on their way home already.

Numerous questions whirled in her mind. Why Kramer? What was her motivation? Pulling a gun? Really? And how did Kramer know she was here, at the plant? She would have expected Walker, or even Sheppard, but she didn't see Kramer doing this, not in a million years. The absent-minded, always-tired Kramer, with her benign, non-threatening, almost deferential attitude during meetings.

"I am sorry I upset you so much by being here," Alex said, "I could leave immediately and never come back."

"Oh, you won't be coming back, don't worry," Kramer said, coldly, "I'll make sure of that."

"But why?" Alex said, suddenly changing strategies and starting to sob. "Why pull a gun on me? What have I ever done to you? I am so scared!" She was getting into the skin of the character she was trying to impersonate, to get Kramer to open up. The crying, scared, fragile girl she was playing was totally incompatible with someone digging through the insides of a drone on an assembly line. Nevertheless, she was hoping she'd get Kramer to feel overconfident and make a mistake. *If this works*, Alex thought, *I am going straight to Hollywood from here.*

"What have you done to me?" Kramer repeated. "Are you serious? You conniving, sniveling little bitch!"

Alex sobbed a bit louder, as if hurt by Kramer's comment. "But why? What have I done?"

"You nose around into a lot of things above your pay grade, instead of doing your job, keeping that infrastructure department running, and minding your own goddamn business. But no, you have to look into stuff that doesn't concern you, and then prowl for more. I have millions of dollars buried in this project," Kramer said, punctuating the words with a thrust of her gun in Alex's back. "Millions! And I don't have any other millions left, in case you screw all this up for me. Move," Kramer said, pushing Alex through the side door of the plant.

They were outside. Alex's car was quite far out in the parking lot. A couple of minutes of walk time, not more.

"Where's your car?" Kramer asked.

"There," Alex said, pointing in the direction of her 4Runner. "What millions? I don't understand," she continued, in a submissive, almost whimpering voice. The unlikely strategy was working; Kramer was starting to talk.

"When Barnaby retires and sells his shares, where do you think that will leave me? Huh?" Kramer's voice was filled with anger. "At the mercy of some venture capitalist or another, poking and probing into everything I have done in my career. Then they'd fire me just to get someone younger and cheaper in my place. Can't let that happen, I just can't—not to me, not to any of us. We're all in the same jam, you know," Kramer said, looking tired again.

"Who?" Alex dared to interrupt. "I still don't get it—"

"Walker, Prescott, Sheppard . . . all of us. Only Griffiths doesn't give a shit. That asshole was born rich; he doesn't care about anything. He can afford not to care."

"I still can't understand how I upset you," Alex said, maintaining the same non-aggressive attitude toward Kramer.

"You're a stupid, ignorant troublemaker, who thinks she knows it all. You ask all the wrong questions, stir up trouble, and draw attention. This attitude makes more people ask questions. For years, I've been preparing for this . . . I've increased our expenses and kept the stock price under control, so when the fossil finally retires we can buy him out."

"Increased expenses? But everyone in the company is cutting costs like crazy," Alex said, not having to simulate confusion. What was Kramer talking about?

"See? See how you just can't help asking the wrong questions? You're such an idiot," Kramer said. "We're cutting costs, so that when we take over, we'll show an immediate increase in profitability. This will cause the market to react and increase the value of our stock. On paper though, for right now, we can't show too profitable, because that would raise the price of the stock before we get to buy it, and we won't be able to gain control of the company. We actually need the stock price to be quite low, to force that idiot Barnaby to sell more of it, to ensure we have enough liquidity to buy it all. We need the money to buy the stock . . . what did you think? That if I were rich, I would put up with any of this crap?"

Alex knew about some of this takeover strategy from the meeting she had eavesdropped on while hidden in the equipment closet. She tried to remember the details of that meeting. Kramer had not appeared to be leading the takeover conspiracy. At the time of that meeting, Alex had not even been able to fully and undoubtedly ascertain if there was, indeed, a conspiracy going on, or just an innocent plan to invest in the company's future. Now the pieces of the puzzle were falling into place, answering most of her questions.

"But here comes Miss Smartass," Kramer continued, "and you start looking into budget cuts for infrastructure and support. Did you look into the stuff that's normally being done, such as cut staffing, training, benefits, perks, and bonuses? No, 'cause you had to do things differently than everyone else, didn't you?" Kramer's voice was filling with anger again. "Unlock the car," she said.

Alex took out her car keys and unlocked the doors.

"Get in here," Kramer said, pointing the gun at the passenger side door, "and get behind the wheel."

Alex complied, keeping her eyes on the gun. She put the key in the ignition and started the engine. Kramer climbed in the passenger seat.

"Where are you taking me?" Alex asked.

"Out to the testing field," Kramer said.

Alex suddenly remembered the drone that locked target on her. All Kramer had to do was launch a drone. She felt a blood-freezing chill, despite the intense heat in the car. She put the vehicle in gear, and then her eyes fell on the temperature reading on the dashboard. It was 129 degrees; the car had sat in the blazing sun for a couple of hours. Then she remembered.

"Can I turn on the AC?" she asked, not willing to startle Kramer with her hand movement.

"What do you think? Jesus, you are such a moron," Kramer said with contempt.

Alex turned the AC dial to the max, held down the fan button for two long seconds, and then hit the air recycling option. Brian Woods had thought of it all, installing the emergency paging and recording system in her car. Now she had a glimmer of hope.

"Why are we going to the testing field?" Alex asked, hoping that someone at The Agency would listen.

"You'll see," Kramer said, then fell silent. "Turn here," she said.

"You know, I was tasked to cut the spending; it wasn't my idea," Alex said, trying to rekindle the conversation.

"Yes, you were. All department heads were. All of them did the same old budget-cutting dance, except you. You had to challenge every systems and software vendor, especially those offshore. You had to audit every contract we had in place, for hundreds of thousands of dollars per month worth of development costs, or outsourced R&D, or off-shored software development. You didn't think of terminating a single employee or cutting a single bonus, but you damned well thought of doubting the judgment and investigating the decisions of all the leaders who signed off on those expenses.

"In the ten days since you were hired, you found a less-expensive vendor for outsourced R&D—not somewhat more inexpensive, but 89 percent, no less! And you had to advertise your big achievement in cost cutting, making us all look like a bunch of clueless idiots with too much money on our hands! Do you know how hard I worked to get these contracts in place, to keep the goddamn stock price under control? Do you know what I am risking if I get caught? Twenty years in prison, because of you, an ambitious little *nothing*!" Kramer was livid again.

This was not going well, especially considering how far into the testing field they were heading. Alex changed strategies again, hoping to buy some time.

"Why don't you cut me in? I'd be happy to start minding my own business, for even a little bit of the dough," Alex said. "After all, I had no idea I was doing any harm. It was not intentional," she continued in her apologetic tone. "We could become partners, you know, instead of having to hold a gun to my head."

"It's too late now," Kramer said. "You've asked too many questions and spoken to too many people. Now they're asking questions. You've created quite a movement. If you go away in a little accident, they'll know to forever keep their peace. I need to make an example out of you. You deserve what's coming to you, but don't worry, you won't even know what hit you. Pull over there," she said, pointing at one of the concrete bunkers with white letters on it. "Get out of the car," she said, pushing Alex with the gun barrel against her shoulder.

Alex realized her legs had turned to rubber. Her courage seemed to have left her. This was it, and no rescuers were in sight. *They're too far away*, she thought, *they won't make it on time*. Irvine to Alpine was an almost two-hour drive. She didn't have two hours.

"Move it," Kramer yelled. She leaned down, stacking a couple of rocks on top of each other, and setting a small object on the top rock.

"What's that?" Alex asked, in a trembling voice.

"Laser spot. It will paint a laser mark on the side of the concrete bunker you'll be occupying. All drones respond with fire on painted targets."

"Why not set the drone to go for this bunker, by giving it the bunker code? I learned that that's why they have letters on them," Alex said, desperately trying to buy some time.

"You're being a smartass again," Kramer said. "It would require me to log into the drone management system, and that would leave a trace of my access. But you already knew that, and that's what you're trying to achieve, aren't you?" She scoffed. "Unbelievable! I don't know what's more infuriating about you, the fact that you're such an arrogant bitch, or the fact that you think all of us are idiots."

Alex felt a wave of hopelessness hit her. Kramer's laser pointer projected a clearly visible spot on the side of the bunker, in glimmering red. There was no way a drone would miss that.

"I'm not an idiot," Kramer continued, grabbing Alex and pushing her toward the bunker door. "I'll leave you to contemplate your miserable, worthless existence, while I walk out of here and get into town, in a crowded restaurant that will provide the alibi I need. A drone is set to take off at precisely 6:30PM in a test flight, in preparation for the self-guidance software launch. The drone operator will be expecting the UAV to acquire targets on its own, and other laser spots are already in place, everywhere in the field. He won't even react to the drone's attack on this bunker. Meanwhile, I'll be enjoying my dinner, miles away from here."

"People will know I'm missing; they'll come looking for me," Alex said.

"Not much will be left of either you or your car. Have you ever witnessed a Hellfire missile hit a target? Not even a whiff will be left of you. You'll be listed as a missing person, maybe some random sex offender will be nailed for your disappearance. Who cares? But the idiots asking questions at the office will draw the right conclusions, and think twice before asking the tiniest question again." Kramer shoved Alex into the bunker. "Enjoy the rest of your life; you have about fifty minutes left of it. I suggest you spend this time reflecting on how you brought this all on yourself," Kramer said with a wicked smile, and slammed shut the heavy door, leaving darkness to take over the bunker.

Alex heard Kramer lock the door, using the reinforced deadbolts that made the door just as impenetrable as the walls. She paced the bunker floor. It was a ten-by-ten foot structure, completely empty—no windows. Faint light leaked through tiny vents, situated at the junction between the walls and the ceiling. She looked at her watch. It was 5:38PM. She took out her cell phone, with a glimmer of hope. No signal. No bars. She texted Tom's cell for help, just in case the signal gain a little strength and would allow a text message to make it through.

She went to the door and pushed, throwing her body weight against it. It wouldn't budge. She crouched in a corner of the bunker, memories of her night in prison vividly coming back. That night she had hoped for help to come, and it never did. Would this time be different? She felt chilly, despite the afternoon heat that persisted in the bunker. She put her hands deep in her pockets to warm them. In her right pocket, she felt an unfamiliar object. She took it out and felt it—not realizing what it was at first. It was the bomb-dismantling robot's remote control.

The glimmer of hope started to shine again. She opened the remote and activated the robot's camera. She could see inside her car. She started operating the remote, trying to get familiarized with the robot's capabilities. She made it extend the claw and look out the car window. She rotated the camera, to get a 360-degree view of the surroundings. No Kramer anywhere. *Good*, she thought optimistically, *maybe there's a way out of this mess.*

Alex settled on the floor more comfortably, crossing her legs. She took the robot's claw lower and tried to unlock the car door from the inside. It was a tricky move, requiring a firm grip, a pull-out movement against the handle, and a push-out movement to open the door, all synchronized. Her first attempt failed, the robot claw losing the grip on the car handle before it could pull it out. Her second attempt also failed; better grip on the handle, wrong movement altogether. The third attempt didn't work either. Alex was biting her lips, concentrating hard to get the door opened.

"Shit, this is hard," she muttered. "Common gestures we do every day and take for granted." She tried again, this time splitting the complex maneuver into multiple components. Grab the handle with the claw. Good. Lock grip. Done. Pull out the handle to unlock the car door. Complicated. There was a dilemma here. If she wanted the robot's arm to push open the car door, it would have to first release the door handle, which would lock the car door again. Unless . . . Unless she could pull the handle with the claw, and push the door with the entire arm, by flexing it.

"Yes," she yelled, the moment she saw the car door open. "You are *the* robot!"

The car door was wide open. Now she had to safely get the robot on the ground. Careful not to tip the robot upside down, or damage it in the process, she made it tightly grab the door handle, lock the grip, and then she moved the robot forward on its tracks. It made it over the edge of the car door with ease, pulling itself against the handlebar, and barely making it out from between the car seats. Hesitating a bit, it dropped to the ground, undamaged.

"Yes, great!" Alex stood up, ready to proceed to the next phase. She moved the robot's camera around, looking for the laser spot. There it was, just a few feet away. She pushed the controls and moved the robot closer. Then she grabbed the laser spot with its claw and crushed it to pieces. She stepped the robot back a foot, rotating its camera to look for any other signs of a laser beam—none in sight. Now it was time to set herself free.

She rotated the robot's camera to bring the bunker into view, and then "drove" the robot to the bunker door. Extending its arm fully and tilting it, she was able to see the door lock. A massive handle that would have to be moved sideways to get the door unlocked. That wasn't the worst part, though. The handle seemed to be really high. Alex frowned. Would the robot arm be able to extend that far?

She set the robot in the closest, most direct position against the door, and extended the claw arm straight up, full length. The camera didn't capture anything but a dark gray door background—no door handle in sight. She pulled and tilted the claw backward, to get an upward view. The door handle appeared to be at least six inches higher than the robot claw could extend.

Tears of frustration burned her eyes. She looked at the time; it was 6:24PM. In six minutes, a drone looking for a target would be cruising above. While the laser spot was gone, there was no telling whether the drone operator would not suddenly decide to whack this bunker, as opposed to any other available bunkers. Why not this one?

Anything is possible, she thought. She resumed working with the robot, not hoping for much, just to keep herself busy until the drone came. She tried to make the robot climb the door, at least partially. The robot's track length was at least 15 inches, so if it started climbing the door, maybe that would get it close enough to the handle to be able to grab it.

A loud noise disrupted her concentrated efforts. Someone was unlocking the bunker. She froze. The door opened wide, letting the sun in and blinding her for a second.

"There you are. Come on, let's go!"

Alex recognized the familiar voice. Louie grabbed her arm and pulled her up on her feet.

"You? What are you doing here?" Alex asked.

"You're welcome," Louie answered.

A drone was buzzing in the distance, barely visible.

"You need to trust me on this. I'll explain later," Louie said, taking off his jacket and putting it on her head. "Look down, so you see where you're stepping, but keep this on your head until I tell you it's OK to take it off, all right?"

"Uh-huh," she agreed, without knowing why.

He continued to guide her at an accelerated pace, almost running, holding her shoulders in a tight, supportive grip.

"Where are we going? Aren't we taking the car?"

"Too late for that," Louie responded, leading her in the opposite direction from where both their cars were. The drone was seconds away.

"Why is it coming for us?"

"Long story, but I promise I'll share," he said, running faster now.

She could barely keep up with his pace, but he wasn't letting her slow them down. The jacket she was wearing on her head was disorienting and causing her to be a little dizzy.

They reached a small ridge in the terrain and Louie crouched behind that ridge, dragging her down with him. She landed hard on her knees and cried in pain.

"Sorry," Louie said. "You can peek at the bunker now, but keep that jacket on your head."

The drone was heading for the bunker, flying at a moderate speed and a low altitude. It launched a missile, which whooshed loudly for a few seconds, before hitting its target. It was a direct hit on Alex's car, a deafening explosion that resounded in her stomach and chest, making her feel like she'd been pummeled by a huge fist. The explosion threw balls of fire in the air, engulfed in black clouds of smoke.

"They're not very precise, these drones," Alex said bitterly.

"Quite the opposite," Louie said. "Your car was the intended target, not the bunker. I knew that, you obviously didn't. I'll explain in a little while. The problem we have now is that, despite the fact that I knew your car was going to be targeted, I parked mine right next to it. Very smart . . ." he said sarcastically, "so, now we're pedestrians."

"How did you know I was here?"

"Bob called me, the minute you stepped out of the office."

Alex looked at him, surprised.

"I knew you were in some kind of trouble, and that coming anywhere near flying drones would probably not be good for your health. Let's go," he said, suddenly worried. He pulled her to her feet and started walking toward the plant building, barely visible on the horizon line. A faint, choppy noise, approaching overhead from a distance, made their attention go toward the northwest.

"What's that?" Alex asked. "Another drone?"

"Nope. Choppers," Louie said, squinting to distinguish markings. "Unmarked, heavily armed, two of them."

They stopped, not knowing whether to run from them or to them. There was no place to hide anyway. The helicopters landed just a hundred feet away from them, in a cloud of thick dust that darkened the sun.

A man jumped from the first chopper.

"Alex?" Steve's voice was loud enough to be heard over the roar of the chopper engines.

Alex threw the jacket off her head and ran to him. In seconds, she was in his arms, holding back tears.

"It's OK," he said, hugging her and kissing her hair, "it's over, we're here."

"Are you Tom?" Louie said, approaching Tom, as he was jumping from the second helicopter.

"Yes, I am." They shook hands. "Louie, I presume?"

"Yes, sir," Louie answered, smiling.

Alex pulled herself back to reality.

"And how exactly do you two know each other?"

"Well, minutes before we received your distress call," Tom explained, "I received an email, saying that if the name of Alex Hoffmann meant anything to me, I should know that you were in serious trouble, probably somewhere at the plant. The email also said that pictures of you and your car had been loaded into the drone targeting system."

"Pictures of my car? And of me?" Alex asked in disbelief.

"Yes," Louie answered. "That's why I put the jacket over you, hiding you from the drone when it was flying out there. That's why I had Bob keep an eye on you."

"How did you get Tom's email address?" Alex asked.

"Remember when I installed your printers?"

Alex groaned. "I knew it . . ."

"You had his email address configured on a separate email account, that was not company installed. That got my attention, I looked around some more, and I realized that the computer itself was not company issue either, although it looked just like one. Then I wrote his email down, just in case." Louie had the same childish, innocent smile he was wearing whenever he would admit to doing something not exactly by the book.

"You are one mean hacker, you know that?" Alex said, smiling back at him. "And who are these guys?" she asked, pointing at the armed men surrounding them.

"They're feds," Tom said. "We don't exactly have armed helicopters of our own at The Agency," he said, smiling. "I needed their help, to get here fast, and to be able to shoot down a few of these drones, if needed."

"The getting here fast part didn't exactly work," Alex said. "It's almost seven!"

"True, but at least we came this time," Tom said, and winked. "Let's get going. We need to decide how to wrap up this mess. Plus, Dr. Barnaby is coming tomorrow at 9:00AM for the final report, which is yet to be written. We've got work to do."

To: Dr. Anthony Barnaby, President and CEO, NanoLance Inc.
From: Alex Hoffmann and Team, The Agency.
Re: Findings and Recommendations—Final Report, Case #516

Dr. Barnaby:

In response to your request to investigate certain issues occurring at NanoLance, as formulated in our meeting that took place on May 3 of this year, we are hereby filing our findings and recommendations.

The four primary issues brought to our attention on May 3 were as follows:

1. An anonymous note, received by you at the company Christmas party last year, containing the following message: *Please stop this insanity or more people will die.*

2. Unexplained stock price fluctuations, synchronized with your announced intentions to sell your stock.

3. Low employee engagement scores, with little additional feedback.

4. Potentially related drone incident taking place overseas, in Kandahar, Afghanistan, leading to loss of lives in a friendly fire incident.

Section A—Findings

The Agency approached this case by deploying Alex Hoffmann, on site, as a newly hired director of infrastructure and support. I am presenting below the leadership profiles of all the members of NanoLance's senior leadership team. Their roles in the issues listed above are complex and interlaced.

► Benjamin Walker, Chief Operating Officer

Walker is the typical toxic leader, an aggressive and abusive bully, displaying sadistic behavior on numerous occasions. He thrives on publicly humiliating employees, demoralizing and intimidating them into obedience. He pushes them into taking fear-driven actions that are against their better judgments or against any common business sense. However, he doesn't hesitate to hold them accountable for his actions, when the results are bad.

It is my finding that Walker, by applying unnecessary pressures on the employees, pressures that deserve to be called psychological torture, has led to overall decreases in product quality. Walker has repeatedly requested his teams to drive down costs by significant percentages. This request, unaligned with the overall company priorities and unjustified by the company's financial health, was a self-serving goal that will be explained later. While all companies should be cost conscious and should maintain good controls to ensure that costs are contained, Walker has set the cost-cutting goals at unachievable levels, driving product quality down and stifling innovation.

► Dustin Sheppard, Chief Technology Officer

Sheppard has a hatred for the human race that can't be compared to anything I have ever seen. His deep contempt for people is revealed through every word he speaks and every action he takes. Just this trait should disqualify Sheppard from managing in any people-leading roles.

He is not open to any feedback from his employees and doesn't set clear goals, preferring to maintain a generalized state of anxiety in the employees. His team members are second-guessing themselves in a constant attempt to figure out what he really wants so they can offer it to him. Besides being totally non-constructive, his dictatorial and discourteous attitude prevents people from seeking his support. Therefore, as a leader, Sheppard is highly dysfunctional.

► Angela Prescott, Vice President, Human Resources

Prescott is a charismatic figure, mostly displaying political correctness. In her role as an HR leader, she should have brought to the attention of the CEO all issues concerning the well-being of the organization and its employees, such as Walker's continued abuse. She has not fulfilled this role, preferring a defensive stance in which she simply "plays along." This defensive stance could be motivated by the personal, intimate relationship she has with Walker. Nevertheless, Prescott failed in her role. More details will follow on Prescott's involvement in this complex case.

► Chandler Griffiths, Chief Sales Officer

Griffiths is a highly professional and effective leader and raised no concerns during this investigation. He is respected by his employees and is supportive of his team.

▸ Audrey Kramer, Chief Financial Officer

In the case of Kramer, we will summarize the findings and recommendations a little later in this report. The main issue concerning Kramer doesn't involve her leadership abilities.

Going back to the list of issues brought to our attention, here are our findings:

1. The anonymous note

We have identified the author of the note as Janet Templeton, director of manufacturing quality. During my conversation with her, she had expressed concerns regarding the loss in product quality. It was her finding that these losses in quality were being driven by cost-cutting initiatives that were both unrealistic and unachievable.

Unfortunately, Janet was killed in a car crash, under suspicious circumstances. A contact at the San Diego Police Department has been notified and the case will remain open into the investigation about her death.

I have attached a chart that Janet created that examines quality rates over a period of time. The chart identifies events that triggered, in her well-documented opinion, these quality rates to decline. The correlation is obvious, linking cost pressures with declining product quality.

It is my belief that, due to the strong correlation between the two, reversing the current trend will be easily achievable in a timely manner.

The Agency team couldn't identify with any precision which deaths Janet was referring to in her note. Since she wrote the note in December, it could not have been related to the Kandahar incident in April. Last year, few drone-related casualties were reported, no friendly fire incidents, and no incidents took place on US soil either.

The only potential death we could presumably link to Janet's note is the death of Sebastian Williams, former director of operational effectiveness at the Alpine plant. Williams died of a heart attack in October of last year. He was one of the most vocal opponents of the cost-driven actions and employee reductions at the plant. His cardiologist has confirmed for us that Williams had been complaining of stress-related chest pains and blood pressure, and that he had indicated the work environment as being the source of his elevated stress.

2. The unexplained stock price fluctuations.

We have uncovered the fact that four of the five senior leaders at NanoLance were planning to gain control over the company by acquiring the stock that you would be selling in preparation for your retirement. These leaders are Walker, Sheppard, Prescott, and Kramer.

There is nothing wrong with this intention by itself. However, to allow them to obtain control of more than 50 percent of the outstanding shares, the four needed to come up with a considerable amount of cash, which they don't currently possess. The following actions were taken to address their shortage of cash:

- Significant padding of specific, hard-to-trace expenses. Kramer was the orchestrator of this action, setting up overpaid contracts with offshore providers, for services that are hard to quantify and trace, such as outsourced research and development, software architecture, design and development, application testing, etc. This strategy maintained the company's profit margins at relatively low levels, thus keeping the stock price under control. This strategy also led to the accumulation of significant amounts of cash, in various offshore accounts, with the intention to provide the group with the liquidity needed to purchase the stock. Kramer is on tape admitting to this entire scheme, while holding me at gunpoint and setting me up to be killed by a drone, on the Alpine test field, on July 15. The FBI has stepped in to ensure the accounts are frozen and the funds are seized and returned.

- Deliberate leaks to the press, placing the company under unfavorable light, with the intention of driving down the stock price. Walker put pressure on Prescott to "get him something worth reading in the press." While this in itself is inconclusive, we have Prescott's cell phone records, showing she twice dialed a *News of the Hour* direct phone number. These calls took place on days before major releases of reports that were highly damaging to the company's reputation and stock price.

These two separate, yet concerted, sets of actions were carefully timed to maximize the damage. They are responsible for the stock price losing almost 50 percent of its value. The size of the financial loss due to the oversized expenses is yet to be determined, as it would require your permission and guidance on how to investigate, report, and correct this issue. Recovering the offshore cash deposits could potentially pose additional challenges.

3. Low employee engagement scores.

Considering the depth of the damage uncovered with respect to the other issues, it is my strong belief that by replacing the ineffective or corrupt leaders, and by properly communicating the change and its reasons to the broader organization, the employee engagement will be restored. A key point in regaining employee trust would be to recognize the process failures and to set strategies to correct these failures, while giving assurances regarding the future. Clear, honest communication is essential.

4. Potentially related drone incident in Kandahar.

The drone that opened fire on a Canadian patrol in Kandahar last April was a NanoLance drone. However, findings indicate that there is no company liability in this case. The preliminary investigation into the incident has determined that the drone operators were at fault. A US Air Force liaison was able to secure some details about the events of that day. Allegedly, the two operators of the Kandahar drone were aware that the drone had the self-guidance module installed for testing purposes. They were flying the drone over a lengthy distance, from one base to another.

During this commute, no actions were required on their part, other than keeping the drone on course, speed, and altitude. They decided, on their own, to switch on the self-guidance software for a while, without any authorization, and go outside for a smoke. Being unaccustomed with operating the self-guidance module of the drone, they failed to put the safety measures in place, specifically those designed to keep the drone from launching missiles at unconfirmed targets, or to open fire on its own. Therefore, it can be concluded that NanoLance had no responsibility in the Kandahar incident.

However, the subsequent incident that took place in Florida can be blamed on intermittent defects preventing the drone from being under the control of its operators. During this separate investigation, we have learned that these operators also would engage in short, self-guided flights with their drones, lacking proper authorization. However, this was not the case on the day of the Florida incident. The Florida drone came in and out of control with the ground operators, despite their desperate attempts to control it, causing its flight path to be unpredictable, and the consequences to be dire.

This reported behavior is consistent with the lower-grade circuit boards found at the plant. Lower quality circuit boards can lead to intermittent defects, and this drone appeared to have been equipped with a faulty circuit board affecting its navigation and / or communications module(s). The US Air Force is yet to release complete official findings in this case.

Section B—Recommendations

1. Staffing

I would highly recommend the immediate termination of the following personnel:

- Benjamin Walker, COO

   o   Future investigations will be conducted by the authorities regarding Walker's involvement into criminal activities. An indictment is highly likely, in case he is found responsible for instigating Prescott into leaking damaging information to the press. He is also under investigation for a series of SEC violations.

   o   His replacement could well be John Dunwood, vice president of manufacturing. Dunwood is a well-respected and dedicated man with great operational experience, a passion for his work, and consideration for his employees. His moral compass is unaffected by his tenure as a direct report of Walker's. He has my full endorsement for the role of COO.

- Dustin Sheppard, CTO

   o   Further investigations will also be conducted in his case, probing into his involvement into padding technology expenses. Regardless of outcome, his employment should be terminated immediately.

- Angela Prescott, VP, HR

   o   Prescott's contribution to the media leaks will probably not attract any legal consequence, due to the media scandal that would ensue. Therefore, we would highly recommend you avoid pursuing the media leaks angle.

   o   However, following my arrest for drug possession on July 2, after being framed by someone in the office, our team deployed a drug-sniffing dog to identify who planted the drugs in my coffeemaker and my car. The sniffing dog led us straight to her office, where we found a stash of drugs with precisely the same formulation as the packet found in my car. That matter is now in the hands of the San Diego Police Department. They have promised to discreetly handle this matter and are waiting for our approval to take her into custody.

   o   During the course of the police investigation, we are expecting Prescott to name Walker as a partner and instigator, which will probably lead to additional charges against Walker.

- Audrey Kramer, CFO

   o   Kramer will be arrested shortly for a variety of charges, spanning from multiple accounts of fraud and SEC violations, including a charge for attempted murder, in regard to the incidents that took place in the test field on July 15.

o   There is a strong possibility that Kramer contacted a professional to intimidate and/or kill me. This individual is in police custody; however, he has not yet confirmed anyone's involvement, but the investigation continues. We have no reasons to believe this attack was random; therefore, we are expecting at least one of the conspirators to be named in this case.

- Peter Wilson, director of Six Sigma.

o   Peter Wilson has demonstrated support for Walker's practices on numerous occasions. He should be made aware that in his role he needs to do what's right, at any cost, rather than taking the easy way out.

- Robin Maxwell, HR Manager

o   Maxwell has failed in her role of HR manager by repeatedly enabling Walker during his abusive outbursts in operational meetings. She should not be kept on staff.

2. Damage Control

Restoring product quality, safety, and reliability is an immediate priority and can be executed with some investment into the operational cost structure.

There will be financial losses associated with the quality issues containment, losses driven by the destruction of all substandard components, and by the recall of all the drones that have had substandard components installed.

A recall is mandatory in this case, yet quite easy to execute. The execution of the recall could be shared with the media and used to restore the public's confidence in the company's quality and reliability standards.

A potential recall might be warranted for the GPS devices. Due to the lack of hazard associated with those potential failures, I would recommend an "as needed" recall, replacing all reported defective products with a new product, ensuring that consumers will be satisfied with the company's approach to handling the defects and spreading out, over time, the associated costs.

Finally, I recommend adding a higher security control mechanism around the self-guiding software, ensuring that only properly authorized personnel can access and control it.

3. Public Relations

The firm of Leesman & Koch has been retained to assist in this case. It is ready to proceed with the communication strategy and press releases meant to ensure that the shareholder confidence is restored as soon as possible.

Further exposure could be a possibility; however, taking immediate recall action should contain the risk and make it a non-issue.

Regarding the incidents still awaiting public disclosure of findings, the Florida incident could generate the biggest damage. Leesman & Koch will work with the company's retained counsel to ensure proactive management of the damage and reparation to the families of those killed or injured in the incident.

4. Final Notes

Note #1: Mr. Louie Bailey, Senior Analyst in Infrastructure and Support, has accepted an offer of employment from The Agency. He will be starting with us on August 1st. His role in solving this case was a significant one, and he has demonstrated the rare combination of skills and personality traits needed to be successful in our line of work. We apologize for headhunting this employee away from NanoLance.

Note 2: An anti-slip coating should be applied to the main lobby floor at NanoLance Corporate Headquarters. It's very slippery, hence unsafe.

Conclusion

Restoring NanoLance to its previous state will not be an easy task, but it's not impossible.

Please count on our continued support with implementing the suggested recommendations or with any further needs you might have for our services.

Best personal regards,

Alex Hoffmann, Executive

Dr. Barnaby was reading the report, in a palpable silence no one dared to interrupt. Around the table, the full Agency staff was present, Claire and Richard included. Handing a client the final investigation report was an emotionally charged event; they all knew that, while Alex was just learning.

Dr. Barnaby finished reading and quietly placed the report on the table. Then he removed his glasses and rubbed his forehead for a while, not saying one word. When he looked up again, he seemed defeated.

"How could I have been so oblivious to all this, although it was happening right under my nose? Maybe I am too old for this," he concluded bitterly.

"Let's not forget that you are not to blame for any of it," Tom said. "These were deceiving, conniving people, who worked hard to make sure you didn't have a clue."

"But it's my company," Barnaby said, his frustration building. "I should have known."

"And because it's your company, if I may suggest," Steve intervened, "we should all be focusing on fixing things right now. Blaming yourself will never yield any benefit."

"I guess you're right . . . I just struggle accepting that this entire conspiracy could build to this level without showing any sign. I should have seen something; I should have noticed something was out of order."

"But you did," Tom said, "and when you did, you came to us."

"Um . . . right," he said hesitantly, resuming the rubbing of his forehead and staring at the report. The team respected his choice for a few minutes of silence, while he weighed his options.

"All right," he said, snapping out of it, in what they had learned to be his usual instant recovery. "We have a lot of work to do today. Miss Hoffmann?"

"Sir?"

"Would you be so kind and help me deal away with these bastards? I want them out of my company today."

"Absolutely," Alex said. She had never terminated anyone, but she was not about to complain. She just hoped she would be able to handle it correctly.

"Good. I'll have my legal counsel draw up the papers while we drive over there. Mr. Isaac?"

"Shoot," Tom said, ready to take notes.

"While we're handling the terminations and communicating with the authorities, would you please work with your team and Leesman & Koch to issue a recall and a communication to the press announcing the changes in leadership?"

"Will do," Tom said. "Anything else?"

"Yes. I will need your team to work with me for a little while longer, to define a strategy that will bring the stock price back up where it belongs. I can't retire now . . . I can't leave my company when it needs me the most. We need to communicate that to the press."

Conference room 102 was ideal for what they had to do. No glass walls and a secondary side entrance that led directly to the parking lot. Ideal for visitors who did not hold the security clearance to be allowed to visit any part of the building.

"Who do you want to start with?" Dr. Barnaby asked.

"I'd say we start with Kramer, then Prescott, then Walker, so we won't keep our friends waiting," Alex replied, trying to smile.

Two familiar faces were seated at the table; seeing them triggered bad memories for Alex, despite their polite smiles. Lieutenant Reyes and Detective Holt were ready to take custody of Kramer and Prescott, as soon as they stepped through the door. Barnaby's legal counsel was also present.

Dr. Barnaby picked up the phone and called his assistant.

"Moira, would you please bring Audrey Kramer to conference room 102?"

"Yes, sir. On my way."

Minutes later, a confident Kramer stepped through the door. Her confidence vanished in a split second, on seeing Alex in the room, her face turning a sick, wrinkled, grayish pale.

"Take a seat," Alex offered. Kramer complied. Alex pushed a stack of papers in front of her.

"Ms. Kramer, you are hereby terminated, for many reasons I don't think I need to spend time reiterating, do I?"

A defeated Kramer looked at her feet. "No, I understand," she whispered.

"I am glad you do. Please be reminded you have signed a non-disclosure agreement and this termination does not waive that NDA. Any questions?"

"No," Kramer said faintly.

"Then we're done here," Alex said, after briefly seeking approval from Barnaby.

Lieutenant Reyes stood up.

"Audrey Kramer, you are under arrest for the attempted murder of Alex Hoffmann, multiple counts of fraud, insider trading violations, and other charges. Anything you say can and will be used . . ."

The words faded away as Reyes escorted Kramer out the side door.

Barnaby picked up the phone again.

"Moira? Could you please bring Angela Prescott to conference room 102?"

Prescott entered the room with a self-confidence that did not dissipate.

"What is this about?"

"Ms. Prescott," Alex said, "we are terminating your employment, effective immediately. You have failed in your role in a multitude of ways, including the failure to stop and report the numerous dysfunctions in senior leadership. Do you have any questions?"

"We? Who's we? You're nobody! You can't terminate me! This is ridiculous," she said, standing up. "I will not take this bullshit!"

"No problem, ma'am," Holt intervened, "I will clarify it for you. Angela Prescott, you are under arrest for framing Alex Hoffmann for drug possession, for poisoning Alex Hoffmann, for possession of a controlled substance with intent to distribute, and for multiple counts of fraud. You have the right to remain . . ."

His voice also faded, while a feisty Prescott seriously, yet unsuccessfully, opposed arrest.

"Ready to continue?" Dr. Barnaby said.

"Wouldn't miss it for the world," Alex smiled. It made her feel good to see the bastards pay for what they'd done.

Walker entered the room next, letting worry show in his eyes for a glimpse, then stiffening his back in an aggressive demeanor.

"I'm listening," he said, pulling out a chair.

"Mr. Walker, I am terminating your employment, effective immediately. I will have a security officer accompany you to your office to get your personal belongings. The officer will then escort you to your vehicle. You will leave the premises and not come back. I strongly suggest that you do not engage in any libel or slander of the company's name, products, practices, or employees. Should you decide to do so, we reserve the right to seek compensation to the extent the law allows, and file an official complaint with the district attorney's office for repeated abuse of employees and for making threats about their safety. The officer will escort you home and secure your passport, as you will need to remain available for the ensuing SEC investigation. Questions?"

"This company would have been nothing without me, you hear?" He started his usual high-volume, threatening tirade. "Nothing!" He slammed his fist on the table. "You don't know what you're doing, or who you're playing with!"

"Mr. Walker, do I need to call the police?"

It was as if a bucket of ice water was poured on his head.

"No," he said quietly and left the room, accompanied by a security officer.

"The nasty ones are over," Dr. Barnaby said. "Let's get this over with."

Dustin Sheppard came in next. He sat down, assessing the situation in his usual, calm demeanor.

"Yes?" he whispered his question.

"Mr. Sheppard, we are terminating your employment, effective immediately," Alex said. He interrupted her, before she could continue her well-rehearsed speech.

"Why?"

"You have a deep contempt for people. You shouldn't be around people, you hate them too much, and you show it. Plus you are ineffective as a leader."

"Bitch . . ." Sheppard spat through curled lips. "I knew you were trouble from the day I first saw you."

"Happy to hear that," Alex said coldly.

The final name on the list was Robin Maxwell. She came in the room, visibly scared to see the faces around the table.

"Robin, we are letting you go, effective immediately," Alex said.

"But why?"

"As a human resources professional, you shouldn't enable the abusive behavior of any leader, no matter how senior they are. You should report abuse whenever you see it, and make sure it doesn't happen again."

"I don't understand," she whimpered, "what have I done wrong?"

"You forgot the human part of human resources. You need to care about people to do this work, and you obviously don't. You're, simply put, not qualified for the job," Alex concluded.

The neatly landscaped backyard was the setting for a celebration. Tall glasses were ready to be filled, waiting in an orderly fashion on a silver tray. A bottle of champagne, tied with a huge red ribbon, was dripping condensed water on the sparkling white tablecloth. The crowd, the entire Agency staff, was standing around Dr. Barnaby, chatting lively.

"I think it's time to pop this cork," Tom said. "Steve, please do the honors."

"My pleasure," Steve said, unwrapping the bottle. A loud pop marked the opening of the vintage Krug Brut champagne, accompanied by cheers from everyone.

Dr. Barnaby raised his glass.

"To all of you, wonderfully courageous, incredibly resourceful, and obstinately dedicated people, the best friends I have ever had! You saved my company. You have given my life back to me. I am forever in your debt," he said, saluting them with a head gesture, "and I thank you!"

Glasses were raised, to meet his, and clinked cheerfully on contact with one another.

"For you, Miss Hoffmann, a small token of my appreciation," Dr. Barnaby said, handing Alex an envelope.

"Thank you very much," she said, blushing. She opened the envelope, and took out an invitation. "Wow," she said, "thank you!"

"What is it?" Tom asked.

"It's an invitation for two to spend a month at the new Club Maxine, on Twilight Cay, in the VIP suite. Thank you, Dr. Barnaby, this is amazing!"

"But there's a catch," Dr. Barnaby said. "There will be no VIP suite on Twilight Cay for at least two more years. It hasn't been built yet. I can't leave my company now, so my real estate development plans have been put on hold for a while. Nevertheless, Club Maxine *will* be built, you have my word. And it will have the privilege of having you as its first guest, if you'll accept my humble invitation," Dr. Barnaby concluded.

"I will be happy to," Alex said.

"So, what happens next?" Brian interjected, switching the conversation gears.

"Now, the only way is up," Dr. Barnaby said. "There is a lot of work to be done. Restoring the public's faith in the quality of our products will take coordinated efforts among manufacturing and quality, on one side, and public relations, on the other side. I am confident I have the right people in place to assist me with that. I have Brian to thank for accepting the challenge to lead the company with me, as an interim executive until we can fully replace the former executive team." Dr. Barnaby raised the glass toward Brian, in a thank-you gesture. Brian nodded his head in acknowledgment and support.

"There will probably be a congressional hearing about this," Dr. Barnaby continued. "There usually is. However, I am confident that we will be able to maintain our status as a defense contractor, once we present our complete findings and action plan. There is a lot of lost ground to make up, but it's not impossible. The UAV recall has top priority and will be finalized within a month. Until then, not a single drone is cleared for takeoff."

Dr. Barnaby paused, gathering his thoughts, letting sadness cloud his eyes.

"There isn't anything anyone could do to erase what happened, to restore the lives lost. Those unfortunate events will be a part of NanoLance's history. But I feel we owe it to everyone, our clients, and our employees, to be successful again and to redeem ourselves."

"Hear, hear," Tom said, raising his glass.

The clinking of champagne glasses and lively chatter resumed, as some headed for the food platters, and others stayed in a circle around Dr. Barnaby, talking casually.

Alex felt a hand touch her shoulder.

"Would you like to head out, somewhere a bit more quiet?" Steve asked, whispering in her ear.

She felt a rush and couldn't speak. She nodded.

"All right, let's go," Steve said, leading her toward the driveway. He waved in Tom's direction, and then turned his attention back to Alex. "I was thinking of another bottle of champagne, served chilled, in a quaint little cabin, up in the mountains?"

She nodded again, and then found the strength to whisper, "I'd love that."

Steve opened the car door for her.

"Hey, guys?" Tom said, standing at the edge of the driveway with a glass in his hand.

"Yes?" Steve replied.

"Don't stay up too late. New client meeting, 9:00AM tomorrow morning. You both need to be there."

~~~ The End ~~~

Did *Executive* keep you on the edge of your seat as you raced through the pages, gasping at every twist? Find out what happens next for Alex Hoffmann and her team, in the next unmissable Leslie Wolfe thriller.

Read on for an excerpt from

DEVIL'S MOVE

Alex Hoffmann Series Book Two

~~~~~~~~

THANK YOU!

A big, heartfelt thank you for choosing to read my book. If you enjoyed it, please take a moment to leave me a four or five star review; I would be very grateful. It doesn't need to be more than a couple of words, and it makes a huge difference. This is your shortcut: http://bit.ly/ExecutiveReview

Did you enjoy Alex Hoffmann and her team? Your thoughts and feedback are very valuable to me. Please contact me directly through one of the channels listed below. Email works best: LW@WolfeNovels.com.

See *Executive*'s video trailer here: http://bit.ly/ExecutiveVideo

CONNECT WITH ME

Email: LW@WolfeNovels.com
Facebook: https://www.facebook.com/wolfenovels
Follow Leslie on Amazon: http://bit.ly/WolfeAuthor
Follow Leslie on BookBub: http://bit.ly/wolfebb
Website: www.LeslieWolfe.com
Visit Leslie's Amazon store: http://bit.ly/WolfeAll

...Chapter 1: Ready to Play
...Thursday, May 21, 7:58PM Local Time (UTC+1:00 hours)
...Restaurant La Cordonnerie
...Paris, France

The loud ringtone shattered the cozy atmosphere of the exclusive restaurant and caused a few diners to frown and throw disapproving glances.

Oblivious and rude, the phone's owner took the call in a loud, raspy Russian. "Da?"

"Vitya? It's Misha. We're in play," the caller said and then hung up.

The Russian continued his dinner. A spark of excitement in his eyes and a faint flicker of a smile at the corner of his mouth were the only visible effects of the call. He loved playing God.

Waiting. Waiting is the absolute worst part of having to deal with hospitals. Robert Wilton nodded to himself absently, letting his weary mind wander. He had waited for almost two hours, counting every minute right outside the conference room whose opaque doors read "Transplant Committee" in black, bold lettering. The impersonal label on the door and the way it stood out against the white, impenetrable glass held a menacing look. It felt surreal to know that some complete strangers had such decisive power over the destiny of a family.

Robert tried to picture the faces of the committee members. Would they be favorable? Would they say yes? What does a transplant committee do, anyway? His mind wandered again, recalling the articles he had read in preparation for this day. They meet, they review the details of each patient, and they decide if that patient makes it to the waiting list and with what priority. They decide who gets a heart and who doesn't. They decide who lives and who dies. A shudder disrupted Robert's thoughts, and he stifled a sob. *She can't die...she's all I have. Please, God...*

"Mr. Wilton?" A man's hand gently touched his shoulder. The man had a sympathetic smile and sadness in his green eyes, brought forward by the pale teal of his scrubs.

Oh, no... "Yes," Robert managed to articulate.

"The transplant committee has finished its session, and I'm afraid the news is not so good. Your wife does not qualify for a transplant."

"No! This can't be. I'm sure this is a mistake..." Robert's voice was gaining momentum. "This must be a mistake, because you don't know her. She's wonderful...she's all I've got! Please...?" Robert grabbed the man's sleeve, pleading with him, his breathing shattered by uncontrollable sobs.

"Sir, I understand this must be very hard for you to hear, and I can assure you this decision was not taken lightly by our committee. Your wife is almost at the age limit, which is sixty-five, and, unfortunately, our rules are very clear about transplant candidates with a history of substance or alcohol abuse. I am very sorry."

Hope flickered in Robert's mind. "What are you talking about? She's not an addict! You got it all wrong...there must be some mistake. Please tell the committee they can give her a heart, because she's not an addict. You have all your facts wrong. Please."

"Sir, I am afraid our information is accurate," the man continued in the same professional, sympathetic, almost whispered tone of voice. "She might not be an addict, but she has a DUI on her record in the past ten years, and that's an instant disqualifier." The man stopped for a minute, letting Robert process the information. Pallor took over Robert's tired, tear-stained face as he grasped the finality of the transplant committee's decision. "I wish there were more we could do. I am very sorry." The man paused again for a few seconds. "Is there anyone we can call for you?"

Robert stood with difficulty, barely aware his muscles were crying with pain from the tension he had been accumulating on that waiting room chair. *I need air*, he thought, heading with unsteady steps toward a door at the end of a very long corridor. His mind had registered the sunshine coming through that door whenever someone had walked through it. *How do people walk these corridors? How do people leave here and tell their families it's over?* Robert's mind was wandering again. *If these walls could talk, they would scream.*

He sat down on a bench right outside the building in the warm sunshine offered by a mild December. He didn't feel able to walk any farther. *This isn't happening...This can't happen...Please, God!* Holding his head in his hands and rocking back and forth, he finally let the uncontrollable sobs out, gasping for air.

"Mr. Wilton?" a man interrupted.

"Go away...there's nothing you can do for me," Robert said, not even looking up to see who was standing there.

"That's not true, Mr. Wilton. There might be something I can do for you," the man said, taking a seat on the bench.

Robert looked at the stranger. He wasn't dressed like a hospital employee, and he was definitely not the man from the committee. He absently registered minor details about this man: pricey suit jacket worn on top of a black turtleneck, expensive watch, a faint scent of high-end cologne. Light, short-trimmed, thinning brown hair; high forehead; intelligent eyes; but cold as ice. Wrinkled face. Very wrinkled.

"My name is Warren Helms," the stranger continued, "and I have only one question for you." He paused, waiting for Robert to shake his hand. Hesitantly, Robert shook the man's hand. "What would you do to save your wife's life?" Helms asked.

"Anything," Robert answered without thinking, "anything at all. Just ask. I have some money. I could raise more." Hope flooded his heart.

"Oh, it's not that complicated; it's not about money, Mr. Wilton. It's much easier than that." Helms paused, looking at Robert with inquisitive eyes. Robert was hanging on every word. He was ready. "We'll just need a small favor from you, at the right time."

"What kind of favor?" Robert asked, concern seeping into his voice.

"Nothing you wouldn't normally do, nothing out of the ordinary." Helms stopped for a second and then continued, while starting to get up. "But if you're uncomfortable, just say so and I will be on my way—"

"No," Robert almost yelled, grabbing the man's arm. "No, I'll do it, whatever it is. I'll do it."

"All right, then we have a deal. Now go home to Melanie and tell her you both are going to Vermont, where she'll be getting a new heart. I will call you with the details. Start packing today. The surgery will happen sooner than you think."

~~~End Preview~~~

Like *Devil's Move*?

Buy it now!

ABOUT THE AUTHOR

Leslie Wolfe is a bestselling author whose novels break the mold of traditional thrillers. She creates unforgettable, brilliant, strong women heroes who deliver fast-paced, satisfying suspense, backed up by extensive background research in technology and psychology.

Leslie released the first novel, *Executive,* in October 2011. Since then, she has written many more, continuing to break down barriers of traditional thrillers. Her style of fast-paced suspense, backed up by extensive background research in technology and psychology, has made Leslie one of the most read authors in the genre and she has created an array of unforgettable, brilliant and strong women heroes along the way.

Reminiscent of the television drama *Criminal Minds*, her series of books featuring the fierce and relentless FBI Agent **Tess Winnett** would be of great interest to readers of James Patterson, Melinda Leigh, and David Baldacci crime thrillers. Fans of Kendra Elliot and Robert Dugoni suspenseful mysteries would love the **Las Vegas Crime** series, featuring the tension-filled relationship between Baxter and Holt. Finally, her **Alex Hoffmann** series of political and espionage action adventure will enthrall readers of Tom Clancy, Brad Thor, and Lee Child.

Leslie has received much acclaim for her work, including inquiries from Hollywood, and her books offer something that is different and tangible, with readers becoming invested in not only the main characters and plot but also with the ruthless minds of the killers she creates.

A complete list of Leslie's titles is available at LeslieWolfe.com/books.

Leslie enjoys engaging with readers every day and would love to hear from you. Become an insider: gain early access to previews of Leslie's new novels.

- Email: LW@WolfeNovels.com
- Facebook: https://www.facebook.com/wolfenovels
- Follow Leslie on Amazon: http://bit.ly/WolfeAuthor
- Follow Leslie on BookBub: http://bit.ly/wolfebb
- Website: www.LeslieWolfe.com
- Visit Leslie's Amazon store: http://bit.ly/WolfeAll

Made in the USA
Las Vegas, NV
14 July 2023

74736794R00173